Sweet Everlasting

Patricia Gaffney

Thorndike Press • Waterville, Maine

Published in 2001 by arrangement with NAL Signet, a division of Penguin Putnam Inc.

Thorndike Press Large Print Americana Series.

The tree indicium is a trademark of Thorndike Press.

The text of this Large Print edition is unabridged. Other aspects of the book may vary from the original edition.

Set in 16 pt. Plantin by Rick Gundberg.

Printed in the United States on permanent paper.

Library of Congress Cataloging-in-Publication Data

Gaffney, Patricia.
    Sweet everlasting /c Patricia Gaffney.
       p.   cm.
    ISBN 0-7862-3319-2 (lg. print : hc : alk. paper)
    ISBN 0-7862-3318-4 (lg. print : sc : alk. paper)
    1. Physicians — Fiction. 2. Pennsylvania — Fiction.
    3. Large type books. I. Title.
    PS3557.A296 S94 2001
    813′.54—dc21   2001027863

Sweet Everlasting

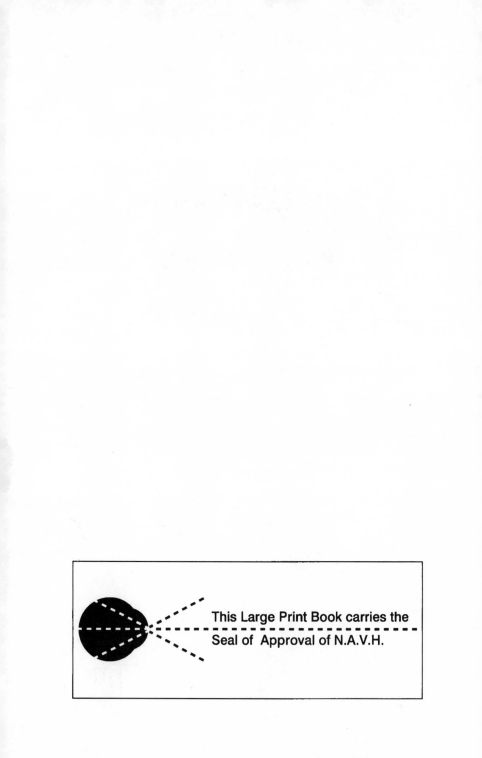

This Large Print Book carries the
Seal of Approval of N.A.V.H.

This book is for
Nora Roberts and Mary Kay McComas,
without whom, etc., etc.
Thanks to you, this writing life
is hell only half the time.

1

"Say, Doc, what the hell is this?"

"That's guaiacol carbonate, Hoyle."

"Yeah, but this is *pills*. I can't swallow no pills."

"Grind them up in a little cod-liver oil, they'll slide down like sardines. One in the morning, and then one —"

"No, but this ain't the right thing — Doc Stoneman always gives me Graves' Tonic for my rheumatism."

Tyler Wilkes reached up to rub the kink out of the muscle in his right shoulder. "Graves' Tonic," he repeated in the slow, thoughtful tone he used when pretending to consider one of his predecessor's lunatic prescriptions. Doc Stoneman had also carried morphia granules in his pocket and had given them out for anything from diarrhea to diabetes. "Well, there's nothing wrong with Graves' Tonic," Tyler conceded gravely. Except that it was about ninety percent alcohol. "But try these for a couple of weeks, why don't you, Hoyle, and see how they suit you."

"I dunno, Doc." Hoyle Taber scratched his

chin stubble while he peered down at the little package of tablets in his palm. "Don't seem right, swallowin' a pill. Like it ain't what God intended, know what I mean?"

The doctor's bad leg began to throb. He slid a pile of advertising circulars aside and propped his thigh on the edge of his desk. "How's that, Hoyle?" he asked mildly. By concentrating hard, he kept his eyes off the clock over the door to his waiting room.

"Well, it don't *come* like that, does it? In nature, I mean. All squashed into this little white dot, stuff I can't see, can't even pronounce. How do I know what's really in here?" Warming to it, he hunkered down with his hands on his knees, fixing the doctor with an intense look. "Same with an atom. Know what an atom is?" Tyler opened his mouth, but not in time. "No, and nobody else does either! That's the *trouble*, there's too much a man's supposed to take on *faith*."

Tyler folded his arms and nodded a few times, as if deep in thought. "I see what you're saying. Makes sense, Hoyle, no question about it. I feel the same way about soap."

Hoyle straightened up. "Soap?"

"Who really knows what's in one of those little yellow cakes?"

"Yeah, but —"

"Could be anything. Or take a salt lick. I

ask you, is that how God intended salt to look?"

Hoyle, who owned the livery stable, looked vacant, then confounded. "Okay, but a *salt lick*, now —"

"Or take Mrs. Stambaugh's blueberry cobbler over at Pennicle's."

"Huh?"

"I've never made a blueberry cobbler, have you? She *says* it's berries and flour and sugar and what-not, but how do we know? It's a lot to ask a man to take on faith."

Hoyle finally got it. He sucked in all his breath and blew it out in a violent whoosh. "Hoo-waw," he said, chuckling and snapping his elastic suspenders against his chest. "Hoo-waw, Doc, you're somethin'."

Tyler got up and thumped him on the back. "You try these subversive little pills for about ten days, Hoyle. If they don't help, come back and we'll try something else."

Hoyle stuffed the pills in his pocket, still grinning. "I'll do 'er, and we'll just see. Yessir, we'll just see."

He went to the coatrack beside the door and took down his old corduroy jacket. While he pulled it on, he leaned over to peer at something tacked to the wall. From experience, Tyler knew it wasn't his diplomas — Harvard College, 1893; Johns Hopkins Medical School, 1896 — that had Hoyle's rapt attention. It was the photograph under them of himself, Tyler Arbuthnot Wilkes, M.D., on horseback in the jaunty uniform of a Rough Rider, only a pace or two behind Lieutenant Colonel Teddy Roosevelt himself. Ty had been reluctant at first to hang the photograph, but now he was glad he'd overcome his reservations, because the picture had done more to instill blind faith in his doctoring skills among the folks of Wayne's Crossing, Pennsylvania, than anything else he'd done in the four months since he'd come here.

"Mm mmm," said Hoyle in apparent awe, jamming on his leather cap and tugging the earflaps over his cheeks. "My, my, my." But he was the town wag, and awe didn't set right with Hoyle for long. "I gotta tell you, Doc" — he couldn't resist on his way out — "you looked a whole lot better down there in Cuba."

"Well, thanks, Hoyle. Thanks a lot."

"Don't mention it. Say, if these pills are so damn good, maybe you oughta try some yourself. No offense, but you ain't exactly a walking advertisement for good health. Haw!"

Tyler's weary smile was as good-natured as he could make it. When the door closed behind Hoyle, he went to the sink to wash his hands, and a glance in the mirror confirmed — no surprise — the old buzzard's appraisal. By now he'd recovered from the worst of the yellow fever he'd contracted in Havana, but the aftereffects still plagued him. He hadn't gained all his weight back, and he still suffered headaches and sudden, debilitating attacks of neuralgia. Thank God he was over the jaundice, though, and most of the depression, and the Mauser bullet in his thigh only pained him at the end of his longest days.

But Hoyle was right, he didn't look like a well man. Luckily he was a hero, or as close to one as Wayne's Crossing was likely to get. Otherwise he might not have any patients at all.

He still had one in the waiting room, the last of the endless, exhausting day. She stood up when she saw him, setting aside her ancient magazine — part of Dr. Stoneman's office legacy — and smiled a coy welcome. Spring Mueller, the lawyer's blue-eyed daughter, looked suspiciously healthy. She had last week too, Tyler recalled, and that mysterious ringing in her ears had cleared right up as soon as he'd said yes to a dinner invitation at her father's house. He sighed, aware that besides being the town's new hero, he was also its most eligible bachelor. Spring wasn't the only unmarried lady who had found cause to visit him with ingenious, non-specific complaints. But he had to admit she was the prettiest. And the most determined.

"Why, hello, Tyler," she greeted him, with the slight lisp she affected for reasons he couldn't fathom.

"Spring," he returned pleasantly. It wasn't worth getting into another argument over what he should call her. "Miss Mueller" would have suited him better, but it always brought on one of her coquettish lectures, and he was too tired today for the rigors of flirtation. He widened the door and stood back to let her pass. "How are you —"

A sudden crash made them both jolt. Spring whirled around with a little cry of shock. The door to the street hit the inside wall and swung back, butting in the chest the man who burst into the waiting room on a blast of icy air. *Boy,* Tyler amended on second look, although he was over six feet tall, thin and hatchet-faced, his chin sprouting the beard stubble of an adolescent. Dirty yellow hair shot out on all sides of his head like straw from a haycock. When he spotted Tyler, he shouted, "Hey, Doc, come on, quick, come on!"

Spring Mueller recoiled. "Broom," she cried, "what on earth —"

"Come on!" the boy insisted, red-faced,

bony limbs twitching as if electrified by violent, uncoordinated jerks. "Hurry, come on, quick!" He started backing out the door.

Tyler rushed out after him.

A girl was standing in the frozen, rutted road behind a mule-drawn wagon. In the fading light he saw that she was tall and angular, with a woolen shawl around her shoulders that looked too thin for the raw February afternoon. She appeared distraught, alternately wringing her hands and hugging herself to keep warm. When she saw Tyler she took a few steps toward him, stopped, and darted back to the wagon. He spied something small huddled under a blanket on the floor of the wagon bed and hurried closer, thinking it was a child.

But when he pulled the covering away, he started back in consternation. "What the hell —!" Under the blanket lay a dog.

"Shadow's hurt," babbled the boy named Broom, spraying saliva in a wide, foot-long arc. "Fix it, come on!"

Tyler dropped the blanket back over the scruffy black mongrel and dusted his hands. "I'm a doctor, I don't fix dogs," he snapped, exasperated — then amused, hearing the sound of wounded pride in his voice. Was anything more fragile than the dignity of a new doctor?

The girl made a grab for his arm when he started to turn away. She let go immediately, but the pleading in her eyes stopped him. "I'm sorry," he said more kindly, "I'm not a veterinarian. I can't help you."

"But Shadow's *sick!* Help, Doc, come on!" The boy jerked and hitched, arms and legs jumping as if yanked by strings. Acute chorea with possible retardation, Tyler diagnosed mentally. So far the girl hadn't opened her mouth, and he wondered if she was slow-witted, too.

Holding his gaze, she put her hand on the panting dog's side, pointed to her own ribs, then back to the dog's. "Broken ribs?" he asked reluctantly. She nodded and sent him another entreating look. "Look, I'm sorry, but there's nothing I can do. I'm a *doctor*." The excuse was beginning to sound feeble even to him. Without warning, her eyes flooded with tears. She twisted away to hide her face — too late — and buried her fingers in the dog's shaggy coat.

Hell!

"I've got a patient," he said gruffly. "Bring the animal inside, and I'll look at it when I have time." Without waiting for an answer, he stalked back into his office.

Spring Mueller's complaint today was dizzy spells. He listened to her sparse history, looked into her eyes and ears, and told her not to lace her corsets so tight. That brought on a flood of eyelash-batting and fraudulent blushes. "Oh, Doctor," she giggled, "what a silly goose you must think I am."

He denied it with suave mendacity.

"What was the matter with Broom?" she asked, buttoning her coat slowly, not ready to be dismissed yet.

He told her about the girl and the dog in the wagon.

"Oh," Spring said, laughing, "that's Carrie. She's dumb."

He managed, just barely, to keep his smile in place, and said evenly, "Not very bright?"

"No, dumb — you know, mute. She can't talk. Broom's always hanging around her. He's crazy, always has been. People call him Fireman because of the way he spits when he talks. Aren't they a pair?" She laughed again, indulgently.

Tyler thought of the girl's silent beseeching, and the boy's agitated loyalty to her. "Quite a pair," he agreed quietly.

Spring strolled to the waiting room door and opened it. She looked back over one shoulder, demurely flirtatious. "I'm having a little poetry reading at my house on Friday evening, Dr. Wilkes. Just a few people, you know, the cognoscenti of Wayne's Crossing," she simpered, enjoying the word at the same time she pretended to mock it. "Everyone's going to bring their favorite poem to recite, and I thought —"

"Doc, Shadow's *sick!* Come on, look at Shadow, okay?"

Spring spun around, startled. Through the waiting room door, Tyler saw Carrie and Broom and the dog, all huddled on the floor beside the coal stove. A strange sight, he supposed, and Spring was visibly offended by it. She turned a look on him that said she was delicately appalled, and shoved her dainty hands into her fur muff.

"Thank you for the invitation," he said, moving her toward the outer door with a light hand on her elbow. "I'll let you know in a day or two, may I? Be careful going home, now, I think it's starting to snow."

"Yes, all right," she faltered, thrown off her stride. "Well. Good-bye." Ty opened the door for her, and she sailed out with her nose in the air.

The girl was sitting on the floor cross-legged, cradling the dog's head in her lap. Tyler squatted down beside her, changing a grunt of pain into a hum of doctorly speculation just in time. "Is your name Carrie?" he asked. She nodded.

"I'm Broom!"

"Hello, Broom. I'm Dr. Wilkes." He reached out a hand to scratch the dog's ears, murmuring, "Good dog, Shadow's a good dog." The long nose was dry and hot with fever; the bright eyes rolled toward him in a feeble panic. A quick touch told him its ribs were broken. "Hold his head," he told the girl, and bent down to press his ear to the side of the dog's chest. Its lungs were filling with fluid. "What happened to him?"

Carrie ducked her head.

"Did Artemis do it?" Broom asked her. She wouldn't look up. "Artemis done it," he said positively.

"Who's Artemis?"

"Carrie's pa."

She glanced up then, but Tyler couldn't read the expression in her eyes. Unusual eyes, troubled, the color of the sky before a violent storm. She'd thrown off her shawl, revealing reddish-blond hair tied back in an artless, disheveled knot. Her clothes were poor and patched, painfully neat, country-plain. But she was pretty, and her long, fine-boned face looked intelligent.

"Where do you live, Carrie?" he asked. Her cloudy eyes darkened; an awkward moment passed, and then she put her fingertips to her lips. She was about to explain her handicap to him — somehow — and he wondered with a

17

stab of regret what had made him ask her the question, any question, when he'd known she couldn't answer.

But Broom spoke up for her. "Lives on Dreamy. Carrie and her pa, they live up on Dreamy."

"Do you? It's beautiful there." He smiled, hoping she would smile back, but she only nodded in agreement. He laid his hand on Shadow's grizzled muzzle. Even though his touch was light, the dog let out a weak, fearful snarl. "I'll keep him overnight if you like," he decided. "He won't suffer. I'll make sure of it."

"Her," Broom corrected. "Shadow's a girl dog."

The distress in Carrie's face lifted at once; she put her fingers on Tyler's wrist, just for a second, and her mouth curved in a wisp of a smile. Her silent gratitude moved him. He and Broom clambered to their feet at the same moment, constrained by the same refinement of feeling, when she bent her head to Shadow's and put her lips on the old dog's temple in a soft kiss. Then she rose, too, in a long, fluid movement at odds with her graceless clothes, blinking back tears.

He told her to come back the next day, and she nodded and thanked him again with her eyes. He stood in the doorway as she walked

18

out to the road and climbed up on the seat of the wagon, settling her worn skirts around her. "Bye, Doc!" called Broom. Carrie waved, a wan, forlorn twitch of the hand that matched her good-bye smile. She gave the mule a light slap of the reins, and they started off, Broom trotting alongside.

Tyler watched them to the corner at Broad Street until they turned east and disappeared. The low twilight sky looked mean and menacing; the wind blew a gust of sleet in his face. How far up High Dreamer Mountain did the girl have to go? Dreamy, the locals called it; he could see its pine-dark silhouette off to his left, hazy with distance and the milky swirl of snow. He shivered and went back inside, where it was warm.

2

It smelled like a big snow coming. You could tell by the sky sometimes, but this late in the day you could only tell by the smell. Carrie took a deep breath of damp air, feeling the prickly frozen pinch in her nostrils. The juncos and tree sparrows had been singing all afternoon, and that was another sure sign a storm was coming. How did they always know? She'd had enough of snow, enough of winter, but the sparrows' music had lifted her heart a little today in spite of everything — for a bird singing on a dark day was a special blessing, and God parceled those out in February pretty sparingly.

"Shadow'll get well, Carrie. That new doc, he'll fix her up, so don't worry, okay?"

She nodded, pulling on the reins to slow the mule down so that Broom wouldn't have to walk so fast to keep up. She put her ice-cold hands between her knees, wishing she'd brought her mittens. But she'd left home too fast this afternoon to think about anything except Shadow.

"He's nice, ain't he? And a good doc, too.

Ain't he, Carrie? Did you see how he touched Shadow? So soft and everything? Remember, Carrie?"

She nodded again, remembering it fine. She remembered how tired Dr. Wilkes had looked, as if he didn't get enough rest. Or food, either — he didn't have enough flesh on his bones for the size of man he was. But mostly she remembered what kind eyes he had once he'd gotten over being angry because she'd brought him a dog. "I'm a doctor, I don't fix dogs," he'd scolded, mad as anything. But Shadow was lying beside the warm coal stove in his waiting room, and Carrie bet he was tending to her at this very minute.

Broom's left arm flew up and flapped in the air awhile before it dropped back down to his side. Like somebody hoisting a flag and then deciding against it, thought Carrie. "Spring!" he burst out all of a sudden, spittle flying. "She don't like me, Carrie, I can tell! You think she likes me? Did you see that fur thing she had? She put her hands in to keep 'em warm, in that little fur thing. Shadow's nice and warm right now and the doc's fixing her. I like the doc, don't you?"

"Carrie! Hoo-ooo, Carrie Wiggins!"

She turned around on the seat, and waved when she saw Eppy Odell coming out of the

21

yard goods store. Eppy was her best friend —
her only friend, to tell the truth, except for
Broom and Dr. Stoneman. Hauling on
Petey's reins, she stopped and waited for
Eppy to hurry along the sidewalk till she
caught up to the wagon.

"Hello, Broom," said Eppy. She looked
plump and pretty in her brown winter coat,
like a little mama rabbit.

"Hi, Miz Odell." Broom backed away, shy
as a turtle, not able to look her in the eye.

Eppy gave a little shake of the head to
Carrie, which she knew meant, *That boy, I'll
swear.* "What brings you into town so late,
Carrie?" she asked.

She started to fumble in her pocket for her
notebook and pencil, but Broom found his
courage and spoke up for her. "Her dog got
hurt, and she took it to the doc's house, and
now he's curing it."

"What's that? You took your *dog* to see Dr.
Wilkes?"

Carrie spread her hands. *I had to,* she
wished she could say. *She was hurt so bad, I
couldn't help her myself.*

"For goodness sake." Eppy looked like she
wanted to laugh, but Carrie thought the expression on her own face must've told her not
to. "You mean the dog's there now?"

"Yeah, the doc's curing her," Broom answered, shuffling his feet, one wild wrist flying.

"Well, I declare."

Carrie put her hand on her stomach and raised her eyebrows, asking Eppy how the new baby was.

"Oh, fine, we're fine. I saw Dr. Wilkes myself yesterday, as a matter of fact, and he says October. I told him it better be a boy this time, or Frank'll leave me for sure."

Eppy laughed, and Carrie smiled, enjoying the sound. Eppy had the best laugh of anyone she knew. And of course she wouldn't really mind another girl — her fifth — and Frank Odell wouldn't leave her in a hundred years. Mr. Odell owned the town newspaper, the *Clarion*; except for Dr. Stoneman, Carrie thought he was probably the smartest man in Wayne's Crossing.

"Carrie, there's a covered-dish dinner this Saturday in the church basement, and Frank and I want you to go with us."

She nodded thank you and shook her head no.

Eppy clucked her tongue. "That's just what I told Frank you'd say. Why not?"

She shrugged, smiled, shook her head again.

"Well, it's too cold to stand here arguing with you. Where's your coat, anyway? You get on home, it'll be pitch-dark before you get there as it is. Have you got a lantern? Go on, and Broom, it's time you got home, too. I'll talk to you again, Carrie, about Saturday," she warned, waved good-bye, and bustled off toward Truitt Avenue.

Carrie slapped Petey into motion and moved on, thinking how grown up and bossy Eppy was to be only twenty-six years old. Most of the time she acted more like Carrie's mother than her friend, and she guessed that suited both of them fine.

"Is Miz Odell gonna have another baby, Carrie?" Broom wanted to know, jogging along beside her again. "Let's you and me have one, okay? We could keep it at my house so Artemis couldn't get it. Want to? Let's, Carrie, let's get one of our own. You could take care of it, and I could . . ." He stopped talking to think, which was rare, and Carrie couldn't decide if she felt like laughing or crying. Because neither one of them was ever going to get a baby.

All at once Broom stopped in his tracks, and she looked up Cumberland Street to see what he was staring at. Three men were walking toward them, swaggering and laughing, bumping up against each other like overgrown puppies. Even though it was almost dark, she could tell the one in the middle was

Eugene Starkey just by the way he moved. She didn't know anyone else who walked like that, as if he owned the whole town, or maybe the whole world. "Uh oh," said Broom. "Uh oh, uh oh, uh oh." He was talking to himself; he didn't even know she was there anymore. *Run away,* she wanted to tell him, *run away before they see you.*

"Hey, Fireman!"

Too late. The two young men on either side of Eugene broke into jerky runs, mimicking Broom, and before he could flee they had him surrounded, with the wagon at his back.

"Hey, Fireman," Lee Burney taunted him, "you put out any big ones lately?"

Henry Sheffler twitched his arms and waved his hands in Broom's face, hooting with laughter.

Carrie had seen it so often, suffered something like it herself more times than she could count. She bit her lips, helpless, wanting to shout. Finally she banged her flat hand against the side of the wagon, over and over, until the boys left off tormenting Broom and looked up at her.

"Hi, Carrie," they said in singsong voices, nudging each other.

Eugene came up behind them. "Evening, Miss Carrie." He tipped his woolen cap and grinned at her.

Out of the corner of her eye, she saw Broom backing away; at the first chance, he whirled around and ran as fast as he could down Broad Street.

"What do you say?" prompted Eugene. "How's Miss Carrie Wiggins today? You're looking mighty pretty. Can I go home with you?" They all guffawed.

Carrie slapped Petey's reins, but Eugene reached out and took hold of his harness, stopping him. "What're you doing in town to-day?" he persisted, coming toward her, patting Petey's rump on the way. "Come on, write me one of your little notes."

She frowned at him and shook her head, mad, pointing at the mule. *Let me go, Eugene.*

"Henry, you and Lee go on ahead, I'll catch up," he instructed without taking his eyes off her. That started them to snickering and teasing, but he ignored them. "Go on, I'll see you at the Duck in a minute. Go on, now." The "Duck" was the Blue Duck Tavern, where Eugene always went after work. The boys joshed him for a little longer but then they obeyed, as she'd known they would. Eugene was their leader: they always did whatever he said.

When they'd gone off, he moved in closer and laid hold of her right shoe with his hand. "Boys didn't mean nothing with ol' Broom,

26

Carrie. Honest. Come on, they didn't hurt him, did they?"

She pinched her lips together, disapproving. He looked as if he couldn't decide whether to keep being nice to her or get mad and say something nasty. She just waited, for it always came to that between them eventually, one way or the other.

"Aw, come on, gimme a smile." He gave her worn old shoe a little shake.

Shame on you, she told him with her eyes; but he kept on grinning, trying to charm her. She knew there were lots of girls — Teenie Yingling, for one — who thought he was handsome, and she supposed he was in a way. He was tall and strong and brawny, with thick brown hair he parted in the middle and a wiry mustache he put wax on sometimes. When he wasn't working at the Wayne Tool and Die, he wore fancy clothes that he went all the way to Chambersburg to buy. Eppy said he was "well turned out," which meant, as far as Carrie could tell, that he spent a lot of time in front of the mirror.

"Guess what, Carrie, I got promoted today. You're looking at the new turning department assistant foreman." He stuck one hand through his belt and puffed out his chest. "I'm making more money right now than my daddy made farming all his life, and I'm only twenty years old."

She smiled and nodded; but she must not have looked impressed enough, because he finally got the belligerent look on his face that she was much more used to. "What's *your* old man make?" he demanded, surly. "When he's not falling down drunk, that is. I heard they don't even let him near the saw anymore at Bone's Mill, because they're afraid he'll cut himself in half, or somebody else. That is one worthless son of a bitch, Carrie, you can't deny it."

No, she couldn't deny it; but she wasn't going to agree with him, either. She pulled her shawl tighter and gave the reins an impatient shake.

"Whoa, now, not so fast." He reached for the lead leather again and held it. Stared at it for a few seconds, fingering it, scowling and tongue-tied. Carrie couldn't have been more surprised when he blurted out, "Will you go with me to the Wolf's Club social on Saturday night?" And when his face got dark and mottled-looking, as though he might be blushing, she couldn't believe her eyes. "You could meet me there, or I could come up the mountain and get you, whichever you want. Starts at seven. So, will you go with me?"

She looked down at her hands, then back

up at Eugene. Slowly and gently, she shook her head.

"Why not?"

She shrugged, then pulled her notebook out of her pocket. Her fingers were stiff with cold, and it took awhile to write, *I just can't. Thank you for asking.*

He folded the paper up after he'd read it and stuffed it in his coat pocket. She thought he'd turn ugly now, but he said almost kindly, "Nobody'd make fun of you, Carrie. You'd be with me, and I'd take care of you. Come on, you'd have a good time."

She shook her head again; it was out of the question. *But thank you,* she tried to say with her smile.

"Okay, don't." He dropped the leather and stepped back. "I don't give a damn, it doesn't mean shit to me." He slapped Petey's rump hard, and the wagon jerked forward. The reins slipped off Carrie's lap, and she had to make a fast grab for them before they could slide over the footboard. "Go on home to your daddy," he called after her. She twisted around in the seat, but he was striding away, big arms swinging, and he wouldn't look back. Why, why was it always like this between them? He could never stay nice for long — so why didn't he just leave her alone? She blew out a frosty, discontented sigh, and turned the mule toward the mountain.

"It's beautiful there," Dr. Wilkes had said. She'd known he was a good man before that, but if he thought Dreamy was beautiful, that meant he was also smart. People who lived in town or on farms in the valley liked to make fun of those who lived on High Dreamer, calling them backward and stupid and no-account. There were pockets of shiftlessness and ignorance on the mountain, no doubt about that, but if she had a choice she wouldn't pick anywhere else to live. It was the prettiest place in the world, and except for Artemis's bad times it was always peaceful. Nobody bothered her because, if you didn't count the Haights, nobody lived nearby. Best of all, she had her wildlings to take care of, which meant she was never lonesome. Well . . . sometimes, but it never lasted long, for there was always work to be done; she didn't have *time* to be lonely.

She was only halfway home when it grew too dark to see the road. She didn't bother lighting the lantern, though, because Petey could see in the dark, even if she couldn't. He was old but he was surefooted, and he knew there were oats waiting for him at home.

Still, if she hadn't been late, she'd have lit the lantern anyway so she could see the woods filling up with snow. It was just a dusting now;

the leathery brown oak leaves' edges would be crinkling out of the thin white covering, and everything would be quiet except for the soft whisper of snowflakes hitting the bare tree limbs. There was a mist over everything, and the trees would look like ghosts gliding by. She loved the way her insides felt when she was alone in the woods on the mountain — breathless and sharp, but calm and peaceful, too. It sounded peculiar, but sometimes she felt that same way in the Wayne's Crossing Lending Library, just thinking about all the books around her, free for the taking. But the snowy woods were even better because there she was alone, and when she was alone she was safe.

She knew when Petey passed the narrow, bumpy turning to the Haights' house, even though the snow and the mist were too thick now to see through. She couldn't see the pale yellow firelight in the front window of her own house until she drove all the way into the yard. The silent yard — no Shadow to bark with lazy, stiff-legged joy because she was back. She unhitched Petey and fed him his oats in the dark, then gave his indifferent nose a kiss and closed the rickety lean-to door.

She approached the cabin warily. When she smelled wood smoke, she relaxed a trifle. If Artemis had a fire going, at least he wasn't

31

blind drunk anymore. But if he was still mean drunk, she'd sleep in the shed with Petey tonight no matter how bitter cold it got.

As soon as she opened the door, she knew from the smell, sour-sweet and stale, that he wasn't drunk anymore. He'd come to the next stage, the sick, surly, silent stage, when you were safe from his violence but not his temper, and you'd better keep your distance.

He sat hunched in front of the fireplace, his shotgun on his lap, oil can and cleaning rags beside him on the settle. "Where've you been?" He didn't even turn around to snarl the question. "I had to heat up my own supper."

Carrie shook snow from her shawl and hung it on the hook by the door. She was freezing; she wanted to go close to the fire and thaw her stinging hands. Instead she picked up the slate from the table and wrote on it with chalk, "Town." He looked around. She held the slate up so he could read it, but didn't go any nearer.

"What for?"

She looked at him, careful to keep anger or accusation out of her face. Even sick, his brutish body frightened her, the arms too long and the legs too short. He had hair everywhere except for the top of his head, and sometimes she thought he resembled an animal more than a man. She rubbed out "Town" and wrote "Shadow."

He looked at the word and then back at her. His black eyes burned with some vacant kind of fire, but they didn't give anything away. *Are you sorry at all?* she longed to ask. *Do you even remember what you did?* He turned away without saying a word, and went back to cleaning his gun.

Broom had told Dr. Wilkes this afternoon that Artemis was her pa. She wished now she'd corrected him. He wasn't her father, he was her stepfather, no blood kin at all. And she was getting scared of him again because his drinking was worse. In the four and a half years since they'd moved to the mountain, he'd always made sure that he got drunk away from the house — in town at the Duck, or on a friend's front porch, or all by himself in the woods. Until today. Today he'd come home from the mill early with a half-empty jar of whiskey, and instead of falling into bed and sleeping it off like he usually did, he'd kept on drinking. After a while he'd gotten up and stumbled toward the door, to go outside and use the privy. Shadow was deaf and she didn't hear him, so she didn't get out of his way in time. He tripped over her and almost fell. And then, in a rage, he kicked her all the way across the room.

He leaned his gun against the wall. The butt striking the floor made a sharp thud, and Carrie jumped. Nervous tonight. She sat at the table eating cold potato soup while Artemis took down his Bible and began to read. She washed her bowl and spoon and put them away, then swept the floor and tidied up around the cabin. It was quiet without Shadow. Snow fluttering past the window in the lamplight made her feel shivery — cold and scared inside, not joyful.

The minute the mantel clock struck nine, Artemis snapped his Bible shut, went into his room, and closed the door. Without a word, of course. Every great once in a while, she felt so lonesome she almost wished he would talk to her. But he hardly ever did, except to complain about something she hadn't done. Right now he was kneeling on his frayed rug in his underwear, saying his prayers. In ten minutes, he'd get in bed and immediately start to snore.

She went to the cupboard and took down a small bag of hazelnuts, and another of raisins and dried apples. Next she sliced three pieces of bread and spread butter on them half an inch thick. Throwing her wet shawl over her head, she opened the door without a sound and slipped outside.

The air smelled fresh and piney, and the

only sound was the high, icy fall of snowflakes on dry leaves. Under the big spruce tree she cleared a place in the snow, which was more than an inch deep now and coming down fast, and spread out her food. It was too cold to wait, but in a minute she knew the gray fox would come, so graceful with his flowing bushy tail and his pointed nose. Then the two skunks she'd decided were married, who were coming every night now as winter dragged on and they got closer and closer to starvation. Last would come the forlorn old possum who lived under the woodshed, blundering and clumsy, surely the stupidest animal God ever made. She loved him dearly, and feared for him all the time, because he was just too dumb to survive.

Back inside the cabin, she blew out the lamp and put on her flannel nightgown in the dark, leaving on her woolen stockings because of the cold. She pulled back the sheet that curtained the padded bench she slept on from the main room and, with cold-stiff fingers, carefully lit a candle. By its flickering light, she fed crumbs to the motherless family of white-footed mice she was keeping in a box on a shelf over the bed. They reminded her of a child's toys with their long whiskers and big, veiny ears, so delicate you could almost see through them. If Artemis knew they were here, he'd kill them. How much longer, she wondered, yawning, before she could open up her hospital this year? That's what she called her secret place in the woods where she doctored the animals she found on Dreamy who were wounded, sick, or orphaned. April at least, she reckoned; otherwise the cold would kill them. She could hardly wait, and not only because her wildlings needed her. The hospital was *her* refuge too, a place where she could go and Artemis couldn't follow, and she could be as free as any creature on the mountain.

She blew out the candle and got in bed, thinking of Shadow. Was she in pain right now? Carrie didn't want to start crying again; she thought of other things — happy times, when Shadow was young and they'd gone everywhere together. Mama had found her under the steps of the house they'd been living in in Raleigh. Someone had just thrown her away, half-grown and starving. She'd followed Mama everywhere at first — so naturally they'd named her Shadow. Right from the start she wasn't like other dogs; she was gentle and sweet, and she never bothered any of Carrie's animal patients, never even chased a bird. Now that she was old, she slept on the floor in the cabin until Artemis went to bed; then she slept at Carrie's feet on the bench.

She was her best friend, even more than Eppy or Doc Stoneman, because she was always there, and she didn't care if Carrie could talk or not.

Carrie dried her eyes on the pillow and turned onto her side. *Please God, help the new doctor make Shadow well,* she prayed. If anybody could, he could. "She won't suffer, I'll make sure of it," he'd promised, and Carrie knew what that meant. She fell asleep thinking about Dr. Wilkes's kind blue eyes and his strong, gentle hands.

3

. . . assure you I've no wish to nag you incessantly, Tyler; if I weren't so proud of you, if I didn't know so well the greatness of which you're capable, I would save my time and write of other things — this wretched Philadelphia winter, Abbey's coming-out ball, the importunities of dreadful Colonel Simonton, who declares he loves me but is really much more interested in the Morrell Shipping fortune. But I'm your mother, a fact neither of us can escape — although I'm certain you would frequently like to — and therefore it's my duty to advise you with all the care, intelligence, and foresight I can summon.

In my own mind, I feel I've been patient with you. Naturally I was disappointed when you chose to study medicine, and doubly so when you insisted on that radical, unknown school in Baltimore instead of Harvard, your father's and your grandfather's alma mater. But I said little, even though I could not help but feel misled (I won't say *deceived*) because for at least twenty years I had assumed, along with everyone else, that you would step into your father's shoes and take over the family's business. But I forbore; I endured my disappointment in virtual silence. (You're smiling, I know, thinking what a large world "virtual" can encompass. Smile away; I still say I forbore.)

Again I bit back disappointment, and this time even reproach, when you shunned the medical partnership I flatter myself I was helpful in arranging. It's been three years now. I can't help pointing out that if you'd joined Feller & Mayne, you would be an established fixture by now in one of the most prestigious practices in the city. But you chose not to follow that road.

You've tried to explain it to me. Perhaps I'm obtuse, but your next folly continues to baffle me, and in all candor I expect it always will. You joined the army — not as an officer, not even as a doctor, but as a private! A *trooper!!* And all for that *opera bouffe* of a war in Cuba which has accomplished nothing as far as I can see except to further the political ambitions of that dangerous oppor-

39

tunist, Mr. Roosevelt.

As incomprehensible as that decision was to me, though, it seems positively Jamesian in logic and practicality compared to your latest one. I understand that you were ill last fall, that your mental state was black and moody. Nevertheless, what you've done now is *tragic* in my mind, Tyler, because you're throwing away such a precious opportunity. You've come home a hero; the world, or at any rate Philadelphia, lies at your feet. You know of my hopes for you in the political realm — once I thought you shared them. It saddens me to think of you wasting away in that backwoods hamlet, of which no one in my acquaintance has even *heard* . . .

Dr. Wilkes threw his mother's letter down on the kitchen table and groaned, automatically beginning to massage an ache in his leg. A note in a different hand at the bottom of the last page caught his eye, and his pained expression immediately cleared.

"She's at it again, I see," he read. "Poor Ty, don't pay her any mind. And count your blessings — you're safe in your 'backwoods hamlet,' but here I am at home, getting an improving lecture every day! I love you and I

40

miss you, and I'll write you a real letter soon, I promise! Love and kisses, Abbey."

Chuckling, Tyler got up to pour himself a cup of coffee. His mother dominated his sister as much as she tried to dominate him, but for some reason Abbey had never chafed under Carolivia's authoritarianism the way he had. She'd kept her sense of humor, rarely confronted their mother head-on, and consequently managed to get her own way and a tranquil house much more often than he had when he'd been her age — twenty. For him the solution had been to defy his mother at every opportunity. He'd known no other way to stay whole — the alternative would have been to let her swallow him up like a minnow. Or so it had seemed to him then, in his rash youth; now that he was a man, he hoped he'd stopped making major life decisions by calculating the opposite of what his mother wanted him to do.

He hoped — but sometimes he wondered. He couldn't deny that enlisting in the First United States Volunteer Cavalry as a private had appealed to him *in part* because he'd known it would drive his mother wild. But that hadn't been the only reason. Like everyone else, he'd gotten caught up in the jingoistic ardor of the moment, and it had been easy to see himself as a dashing hero, off to save the

41

Cuban peasants and drive the Spanish out of *our* hemisphere once and for all. In the Rough Riders he'd been one of Roosevelt's "gentleman rankers," Ivy League enlistees in Brooks Brothers uniforms, recruited to give the regiment the proper "tone." No one had earned his commission without merit, though, and the Yale and Princeton Knickerbockers had ridden and fought side by side with leathery, foulmouthed cowboys and Indian scouts. It had been a glorious little war: short, decisive, and satisfying — to anyone who hadn't fought in it. The last thing young, healthy, idealistic Tyler Wilkes had expected from it was a crippling wound and a long, devastating illness in its aftermath.

Setting up a medical practice in Wayne's Crossing the following year hadn't been an act of defiance at all, regardless of what his mother believed. He'd been too enervated for defiance; he'd moved here out of inertia, not resolve. Ill and depressed, he'd come across an advertisement in the back of a medical journal for a retiring M.D.'s practice in a "small but prosperous town in sylvan setting." After an amazingly brief exchange of letters with Benjamin M. Stoneman, M.D., he'd bought the practice, sight unseen, for the sum of $1000. Now that he'd seen it, a thousand dollars seemed low; he had more patients than he could handle, and the home and office were small but perfectly adequate to his needs. But what he knew now was that Dr. Benjamin Stoneman had sold out cheap because he didn't expect to retire: he expected to die.

Would Stoneman pay a call this evening? When the old doctor wasn't suffering from insomnia, he was plagued with drenching night sweats, both symptomatic of his consumption, and the two conditions were sufficiently aggravating to keep him prowling around most nights until midnight or later. He probably wouldn't come tonight, though; the snow was wet and heavy, deepening by the hour, and Stoneman's tubercular chest "tightened up" on him in damp weather. Usually Tyler looked forward to his visits, even though they had little in common, professionally speaking, beyond the rudimentary fact that they were both M.D.'s. Stoneman was of the old school; he hadn't studied, he'd *read* medicine forty years ago, and in Ty's opinion his ideas hadn't changed much since then. He didn't own a microscope, hadn't kept up with any of the astounding advances in epidemiology or bacteriology of the last decade, and he still argued over the validity of what he actually called the "germ theory."

In his student days, when he was younger

and more arrogant, Tyler might have felt contempt for an old has-been like Stoneman; but experience had taught him the valuable lesson that he didn't know half as much as he thought he did, and that tolerance was probably a higher virtue than knowledge anyway. Patient after patient in his new practice had a story to tell about "the old doc's" utterly selfless dedication. Doc Stoneman never refused a call, day or night, for anybody except drunks with headaches. Doc Stoneman sat for hours with the dying, the suffering, the bereaved. Sure, Doc Stoneman was a drunk, but as soon as he got to your house you started to feel better, just because you knew he cared. He lived in two rooms over the hardware store now, drinking and coughing, claiming he was writing his memoirs. For a man who had spent the last forty years taking care of people, he got depressingly few visitors. He was lonely. Tyler was "the young doc," admired and esteemed and courted; but sometimes on long winter nights, Tyler got lonely, too.

But it was getting late; in all likelihood Stoneman wouldn't pay him a call this evening. With luck, no one would pound on the door with an emergency. Tyler had casebook work to catch up on, but his brain felt cottony tonight and it would be hard to concentrate

— another lingering effect of the yellow fever. God, he was sick of being sick. The only good thing about it was that it made him more sympathetic to his patients, because before his illness he'd always taken his physical strength and mental acuity for granted. He took nothing for granted now, and like a careful surveyor he monitored every inch of progress he made on the long, excruciatingly slow road to recovery.

He put his empty cup in the sink with his dinner dishes; sometimes he washed up after himself, but tonight he felt like leaving things for his housekeeper. He would read the paper, he decided, and turn in early. He had his finger on the kitchen light switch when a knock came at the back porch door. His porch light had burned out; he squinted through the black glass, but all he could discern was the tall, dark, bundled-up form of a man. He hoped it was Stoneman, not Crystal Blubaugh's husband sent to tell him the baby was coming early.

"Why don't you sweep these steps? A man could kill himself trying to get up to your damn door."

"Good evening to you, too." Ty stepped back and Stoneman tramped in, stomping his snowy boots on Mrs. Quick's just-waxed linoleum floor. Unasked, he shrugged out of his greatcoat and hung it up on the hook next to the door. Tyler noted without surprise the old-fashioned Prince Albert coat, striped trousers, stiff collar and tie that Stoneman wore in all weathers. He didn't doubt that the old fool had done surgical operations in the outfit, disdaining sterile garb as foolish homages to the "germ theory."

One useful feature of the Prince Albert coat was its deep inner pocket, from which Stoneman extracted his familiar pint bottle of gin. "You wouldn't have a glass and some bitters around, would you, Doctor?" he inquired, as he always did, with the formal but facetious air he affected when he was drinking.

"I might." Tyler got the required items, as well as another tepid cup of coffee for himself, and followed Stoneman into the sitting room. Stoneman automatically took the big overstuffed chair with the foot rest, leaving Tyler the narrow spindle back with the uneven front leg. Ty doubted if either of them would ever really come around to thinking of this apartment as his, not Stoneman's, no matter how long the "new doc" might happen to occupy it.

"Not squinting into your machine tonight, I see." Stoneman took a sip of his drink, grimaced, and relaxed back into the chair cushions, stretching his matchstick legs out toward the stove.

He looked bad tonight. Tyler had found an ancient photograph at the back of a bureau drawer, forgotten in Stoneman's move four months ago; he found it almost impossible to match the burly, robust image of the man in the picture with the stoop-shouldered, sunken-cheeked, cadaverous individual sitting beside him. But Stoneman still had a full head of white hair, about which he was touchingly vain; he combed it back from an elegant center part, and kept it neat and shiny at all times with macassar oil.

"No, no machine tonight," Ty admitted. "I was too tired." His "machine" was what Stoneman insisted on calling his microscope.

"Tired, eh?" He cackled, pulling out his battered old pipe. His disease had finally forced him to give up smoking tobacco, but he still sucked on his pipe stem. "I guess this little old practice wasn't the rest cure you had in mind, was it, Dr. Wilkes? I guess country doctoring's a bit more than looking at bugs through a magnifying glass, eh?"

Tyler folded his arms, crossed his ankles, and slid down on his spine, resigning himself to smiling through another harangue on the superiority of the *practicing* M.D. to the kind who boondoggled his time away in laboratories and clinics, staring through lenses at "bugs" — what Tyler had done, to Stoneman's way of thinking, for the two years between his medical residency and his army enlistment. Why did he put up with this? Stoneman was right about one thing, though: being the only doctor — Schmidt the quack homeopath didn't count — in a town of two thousand souls had turned out to be no rest cure. He'd never admit it, but he'd come to Wayne's Crossing partly in the naive belief that he could doctor roughly halftime, and spend the other half doing what he liked best: studying the etiology of diseases. But he'd had about four complete days off since he'd gotten here, and now writing and research were confined to the odd free evening, or late at night when he was barely able to keep his eyes open.

"A suffering patient wants *action*," Stoneman droned on, jabbing at the air with his cold pipe. "He says, 'Doc, it hurts right here,' and he wants *attention* paid to that one little spot. He doesn't want you to order blood tests, he doesn't want to piss into a bottle so you can —" He stopped short. "What the hell is that?"

"What?"

"*That.* When did you get a dog?" He got up with a grunt and bent over a blanket-wrapped Shadow on the floor behind the coal stove.

48

With a gnarled hand, he drew the covers back and peered down intently. "I recognize this dog," he said slowly. "It's Carrie's, isn't it? Carrie Wiggins'?" Tyler nodded. "What's it doing here?"

"She brought it to me this afternoon, she and a fellow named Broom."

"Broom, eh? St. Vitus' Dance — agreed?"

"That's what I thought," Ty smiled, and Stoneman smiled back. They got immoderate enjoyment when they concurred in a diagnosis.

"What's wrong with Carrie's dog?"

"Broken ribs. Complications."

"What are you doing for it?"

"Keeping it comfortable. Morphine sulfate and sedatives."

Stoneman hummed his approval, then gave Shadow a gentle pat and resumed his seat.

"So you know Carrie — Wiggins, did you say?" Tyler asked.

"Carrie Wiggins, sure, sure." His gaunt, craggy face softened. "She's a sweet child, gentle as a foal. Too good for this world, I sometimes think. I worry about her."

Tyler eyed him in surprise. Gruff tolerance was the softest sentiment he'd ever known Stoneman to express when speaking of a patient, or of anybody else for that matter. "Why do you worry about her?"

49

"Because of Artemis, mostly — that's her stepfather."

"Stepfather? Broom said he's the one who broke the dog's ribs."

Stoneman scowled. "What wouldn't surprise me, he's such a sorry S.O.B."

"What does he do for a living?"

"Not much. He used to have a fairly good job at the mill, but his drinking got too bad and now they only let him sweep up. Sometimes he takes odd jobs, picking stones or spreading lime in farmers' fields. When he's sober, he's a pious old bastard, quoting the Bible at you like he was St. Paul. But when he's drunk, he's a holy terror."

Tyler rubbed his top lip with his fingertips. "Does he mistreat the girl? Abuse her?"

"I don't think so. I asked her that myself, and she said no."

Relieved, he got up to stir the coals in the stove. Behind him, he heard Stoneman pour more gin into his glass. "That stuff will kill you as fast as those germs in your chest you don't believe in," he observed mildly.

The old doctor took a deep swallow and smacked his lips with exaggerated relish. "You're the one who says alcohol kills germs. Can't have it both ways, Dr. Wilkes. If it works on the outside, it must work on the inside, too."

"That's rubbish and you know it."

"Why? If alcohol's a germicide against bacteria, then it —" He broke off with a sudden choking wheeze and grabbed for his handkerchief.

Pained, Tyler listened to the phthisical coughing until it finally subsided. Stoneman sank back in his chair, gray-faced and exhausted. "Is the hemoptysis worse?" he asked in a neutral voice. Stoneman shook his head. But Ty noticed he put his handkerchief back in his pocket fast — to hide the blood?

"How did Carrie lose her voice?" he asked after a minute.

"I expect she was born that way. Congenital."

"Any history of scarlet fever or diphtheria?"

Stoneman looked down. "Well now, I never asked her that."

"Have you ever examined her?"

"No. Tried to once, but she wouldn't let me touch her."

"Why not?"

"Because that's what she's like. That's just how she is. I've known her for about four years, and I'd say she's as fond of me as just about anybody else around here. But she keeps to herself. Not that she's cold, mind you — there's a family up on Dreamy, the Haights, that probably wouldn't survive with-

51

out her. The father is so worthless and no-account, they'd starve to death if Carrie didn't sneak food and firewood and who knows what else to them whenever Artemis's back is turned."

He hesitated. Slanting Tyler a gauging look, he reached into his copious inside coat pocket and took out a leather purse. From it he withdrew a yellowed piece of paper and unfolded it. He held it at arm's length, squinting at it farsightedly, then gave up and handed it to Tyler. "Carrie left that in my mailbox the day after my daughter died."

Tyler hid his surprise. He knew that Stoneman's only daughter had died of a cancer of the breast two years ago. He'd heard it from others, though; until tonight Stoneman had never mentioned his family, or indeed, anything at all about his personal life.

Ty spread the paper out on his knee. The big, looping pencil scrawl had spread and faded, but he could still make out the words.

Dear Dr. Stoneman,

I've been crying all day for Sophie, even though I know it doesn't make any sense. I guess it's you I'm really crying for, because I know Sophie's in heaven right now and she is smiling down on us, you especially, and wishing you wouldn't grieve so. Once you told me that dying is harder on the living who are left behind. I believe it's true, for when my father passed, and then my mother, I wept for days and days, and yet I know in my heart they went to heaven too. What I mean to say is, do not grieve so hard, please, for Sophie was good and kind, like you, and she is happy now and waiting for you. I hope you like this seed cake I made you. Please don't work so hard now as if nothing had happened, even if it helps you to forget, because you're not so young anymore and you need your rest. I'll come and see you soon if you like.

Your devoted friend,
Carrie Wiggins

Tyler handed the letter back. Stoneman took it without comment, averting his face — but not before Ty saw the shine of moisture in his eyes. The sight amazed him. *Stoneman,* the most cynical old bird he'd ever known, a vigorous atheist, contemptuous of anything approaching sentimentality — turning teary-eyed over a girl's simple expression of sympathy. Or perhaps it was only the poignant memory of his daughter's loss. Whatever it was, Tyler had to admit that something child-like and tenderhearted in the note had affected him, too. He cleared his throat. "But she's a loner, you say?"

"It's more that she's timid," Stoneman said gruffly, pouring more gin. "Or afraid, more like — not without pretty good cause, either. This is a decent town, but it's small and it's got its share of small-mindedness. There's some around here who don't take to anybody who's different."

A gust of wind blew an angry handful of sleet against the window; an answering puff of smoke belched from the vent in the coal stove door. Ty shivered, even though the room was warm.

"Do you know about Carrie's wildlings?" Stoneman resumed, sitting forward, elbows on his bony knees. "That's what she calls all the sick animals she takes care of up there on the mountain. Starving orphans, birds with broken wings, gun-shot deer." He sent Ty another look, as if daring him to laugh. "Sometimes she's like a wild creature herself. She's got a way of gathering herself in and withdrawing, shutting down physically when she feels cornered. An instinct, you know, a defense against danger. I've seen it," he declared almost belligerently, although Tyler hadn't challenged him by so much as a look. "And I'm telling you, it's enough to break your heart."

The two men lapsed into silence. A few minutes later they roused themselves to argue about whether neurotic females outnumbered neurasthenic males, and a little later, about the best way to distinguish typhoid fever from appendicitis before the patient hemorrhaged and died. But their hearts weren't in disagreeing with each other tonight. Before the clock struck eleven Stoneman stood up, drunk but dignified, and took his leave.

Tyler put the kitchen light out and got ready for bed. Barefooted, shivering in his nightshirt, he went back into the sitting room to check one more time on Shadow and try to get a last dose of potassium bromide down her throat. The silence warned him, for he knew exactly how death sounded. He lifted the blanket. The black nose was dull and dry, the eyes vacant, lips drawn back in a pitifully harmless snarl. Carrie's dog had given up the fight.

4

Tyler's shovel hit a rock. Hard. The steely impact jolted up the length of his leg and exploded in the vicinity of the bullet lodged two inches above his kneecap, vibrating pain throughout his body like a struck gong vibrates sound. He stood still, breath gone, waiting for the pain to fade. It did, but the tinny ringing in his ears persisted. He knew too well what that could precede. Gingerly, he stepped up from the rectangular grave he'd just decided was deep enough. Across the yard, a flash of blue caught his eye in the second before the next pain, the real pain, struck.

Then the shovel slipped from his fingers, and he dropped to his knees. He kept the ground from coming up and hitting him in the face by pressing it back with both palms and gritting his teeth. The unlocalized agony along his nerve endings continued at its own leisurely pace, in the rising and falling pattern he knew by heart; but even at its blistering worst, he was aware that the pain wasn't as severe this time as it had once been.

Through the ringing in his ears he heard the fast crunch of snow, and a moment later two arms came around his shoulders. He turned his head. Carrie Wiggins was kneeling beside him, holding tight, anxious-eyed, and trying to read his face. Already the attack was receding — they were shorter in duration than they used to be, too. A minute passed; "I'm all right," he managed to say with a measure of truth at its conclusion. But she held on and didn't let go, not until he took his hands away from the frozen ground and sat back on his heels. When he looked at her again she was staring at him, and in her dark gray eyes he saw grave concern mixed with what looked like guilt. She gestured toward the grave and gave a quick, remorseful shake of the head, and he guessed what she was thinking.

He took deep, steadying gulps of the icy air. "No, it wasn't the exertion," he got out, wiping perspiration from his forehead. Not only that, anyway. "Once in a while I have spells, attacks of neuralgia. It's a residual effect of a disease I contracted a year and a half ago. It's nothing now, much better than it used to be." She didn't look reassured. "I'm all right, honestly." He really was; he stood up to prove it. She reached for his arm to help, and only let go of it, warily, once he was on his feet. He knew how paper-white he could turn during

57

these episodes, and spoke once more to set her at ease. "There, I'm fine, you see? Thanks for your help." For a few more seconds she continued to eye him carefully. Then, apparently deciding he was telling the truth, she stepped away.

He'd wrapped her dog in an old army blanket; the still, dark bundle lay a few feet away from the hole he'd dug in the hard earth. He watched her walk toward it, sorrow in every line of her slow, long-legged step, and sink to her knees beside it. For a few minutes he kept his distance. She had on a coat today, not the thin shawl; it was a man's coat, dark blue wool, the too-long sleeves rolled back at the cuffs. Beneath it were the blue dimity skirts of the same dress she'd worn yesterday. Today he could see a series of faint lines at the hem; if he counted them, he would know exactly how many times the dress had been let down. Her ankles might be trim, even delicate, but it was hard to tell because of her mannish leather shoes and thick stockings. She had on a dented felt hat with a rather chewed-looking brim; it might have been black once, but now it was rusty green with age. For all that, she didn't really look drab; in fact, he thought she looked almost elegant in her inelegant clothes.

Finally he went to her, bent and put a hand

on her shoulder. "I didn't think you'd be able to make it down the mountain today, because of the snow. So — I thought it best to bury Shadow here. Is it all right?" She nodded without looking up. "Are you sure? If you'd rather take her back with you —" She shook her head, glancing up briefly. She was crying.

He crouched down beside her. "I promise you, Carrie, she didn't suffer. She just went to sleep. There was no pain at all." She tried to send him a grateful look through the tears. "Would you like to see her?" She put her hand on her throat, as if it ached; he thought she would refuse, but a moment later she took a shuddery breath and nodded.

He pulled the army blanket back from Shadow's grizzled old head, thankful that the dog's death-snarl had relaxed and her eyes were closed, not glazed and staring. He got to his feet and walked a little distance away. Dusk was closing in; the clouds were a livid purple in the western sky, gunmetal in the east. Delicate lilac shadows darkened the rolling, glittering snow-cover of his yard, shading to lavender under the yew hedges. In the distance he could hear the jingling song of a sparrow, high and light, like tinkling icicles in the twilight. When he turned back, Carrie was climbing to her feet and blotting her face with an oversized red handkerchief.

They buried the dog together. When he'd thrown the last spadeful of dirt, he saw her look around his barren yard, as if searching for something that might serve for flowers, something alive, a token of remembrance to honor her friend. But there was nothing. Her eyes clouded. She knelt in the dirt and put both flat palms on top of the grave in farewell, a last caress. He wanted to comfort her, as he would try to comfort any grief-stricken survivor of a lost patient. The fact that she mourned for a scruffy mongrel dog made no difference. Grief took many forms, he knew now, its objects innumerable and unaccountable. Only a fool disparaged another person's heartache, and it didn't matter if the mourned were a man, an animal, or an insect.

At length Carrie stood up and looked at him across the grave. Dry-eyed, she tried to smile, but her quivering lips gave her away. "Come inside," he invited, realizing she was shivering. She hesitated. "Where's your wagon?"

She shook her head, frowning.

"You walked?"

A matter-of-fact nod.

"Come inside," he repeated, stern this time. "You're freezing — come in and get warm. Come on." He started walking toward the house, watching her over his shoulder.

Stoneman's words came back to him: *Sometimes she's like a wild creature herself.* She looked alert, wary, every sense tuned to the possibility of danger. Tyler stored the shovel in the shed under his porch steps, walked back, and put a foot on the first stair, moving loosely, casually — the way he'd learned to move when trying to calm a growling, distrustful dog on guard at a patient's front door. "Come on," he said once more, mildly. "I'll make us a pot of tea. You can help me."

That worked. She paused for two more seconds, then followed him across the yard and up the stairs to his kitchen.

He hung up his coat, a black, ankle-length wool duster that kept his legs warm on long trips in his rented buggy, and turned to Carrie to take hers. She backed up a step, smiling, giving a mock shiver to indicate she was still too cold to relinquish it. But he suspected the real reason was because she wanted its extra insulating layer of protection between herself and him. She slid her hat off, indifferently ruffling her hair where the hat had flattened it. He thought again that she had pretty hair despite the haphazard style; and yet she seemed unaware of it, or indeed, of any other aspect of her own femininity.

He put the kettle on the stove and got down cups and saucers. "Would you like to sit down?" he asked over his shoulder. When she hesitated again, weighing God knew what nameless fears, he folded his arms and leaned back against the sink, telling her with his posture that if she sat she would be safe, because he meant to stand.

She sat.

"How long a trip is it up the mountain to your house?" he wondered conversationally.

She pointed to her legs and held up one finger.

"An hour by foot," he guessed. "But faster with the mule?" That made her smile, and give a little rueful shake of the head. "No?" He laughed, and her smile broadened. She had a generous mouth, sensitive and self-conscious, with lips that curved up daintily at the corners. Her nose was on the long side, and sharp, almost pointed at the tip; it gave her a sober aspect in keeping with the serious gray eyes but not the wide, sensuous mouth, which seemed to Ty to hint, in an artless way, at any number of possibilities. Because of her coloring, he wondered if there was Irish in her ancestry. What sort of name was Wiggins? But no — that was her stepfather's name, not hers. She flushed and looked down at her hands, and he realized he was staring.

The kettle began to steam. "I can do it," he told her when she started to get up to help.

She lapsed back into her chair, and he could feel her eyes on him as he poured water into the teapot and milk into the pitcher, loaded a tray with everything, and carried it over to the table. He took the chair opposite her. Before he could do it, she reached for the teapot and poured out a cup for him. "Two," he said, answering her silent question about sugar, and "Yes, a lot," to the one about milk.

She poured her own next. Her long-fingered, rather bony hands were strong and work-rough, but also subtle and expressive. How old was she, seventeen? He assumed she was not well-educated; obviously she was poor. Still, with the exception of his mother, he didn't think he'd ever seen a woman pour tea with a more unself-conscious grace.

He sipped his tea, leaning back in his chair. The silence between them wasn't uncomfortable, at least not to him. He broke it anyway, in case it was to her. "There's a mule at the livery stable Hoyle Taber likes to rent out to me every chance he gets. Poison is his name. You've probably seen him around — he's only got one ear, and something's eaten about half his tail off." Carrie smiled and shook her head. "I ask you, Miss Wiggins, how is a young doctor to maintain his dignity behind an animal like that?" That made her grin, showing even white teeth.

"That mule of yours, now, I'll bet he knows the way home by himself." She nodded. "Well, certainly. Even the dumbest animal knows how to get home, especially the closer he gets to his dinner. Not Poison, though. The other night I fell asleep in the buggy, coming back from a call. I woke up just about frozen to death, standing still in the middle of Broad Street at two o'clock in the morning. That wooden-headed jackass was fast asleep with his *lips* on the ground. I swear I could hear him snoring."

Her silent laughter tickled him; he laughed with her. She'd gone so far as to unbutton her coat; she looked as relaxed as he'd yet seen her. Smoothly, gently, he asked, "How long have you been unable to speak?"

The smile in her shadowy gray eyes evaporated. She made a vague, airy gesture with one hand and looked away.

He waited, letting the stillness become awkward. When it was clear she wasn't going to enlarge on that answer, he said, "How long?" again, quietly.

This time she shrugged, and held both palms up in the air.

"For as long as you can remember?"

Another shrug.

"How old are you?"

She held up ten fingers, then eight.

He masked his surprise; except for the adult wariness in her eyes, she looked younger. "Could you speak when you were a little girl?" She looked at him then, carefully, narrowly, as if gauging exactly how far she might be able to trust him.

Not very far. She put her hand to her forehead and gave a futile little wave. *I can't remember.*

He didn't believe her.

She pushed her chair back and started to stand. To forestall her, he said, "I'd like to examine your throat sometime, Carrie."

The chair scraped the floor. She was on her feet, smiling tensely and shaking her head. Tyler stood, too, but made no move toward her. "No? All right, never mind, then." She began to button her coat, never taking her eyes from him. "It wouldn't hurt, though. All I'd do is look. Think about it. Maybe someday." He stayed where he was and kept his voice light and casual, and after a moment some of the strain went out of her shoulders.

She took something from her pocket and laid it on the table. He stared blankly down at a dollar bill. "What's that for?" But then he guessed. "For Shadow? Thank you, I don't want it." Vigorous nods; she pushed the bill closer. "No, really, it's not necessary." She frowned. He took the bill and held it out to her. "Take it back, Carrie, I don't want it. I'm sorry I couldn't do more for her." She took the money reluctantly, eyes troubled, and put it back in her pocket.

A second later her face cleared and she reached into another pocket, withdrawing a small, bumpy-looking parcel wrapped in brown paper.

"What's this?"

With a tentative smile, she laid it on the table. Before he could touch it, she turned and hurried over to the door, pulling her ungainly hat on as she reached for the knob.

"Wait —" But she was already outside, starting down the steps. "Good night!" he called in the doorway, watching her retreating back. She didn't wave, and the cold black night enveloped her quickly. He stopped himself from calling out "Good night" a second time; she couldn't answer, and he didn't think he wanted to hear this forlorn silence again in the wake of his words.

He shut the door on the cold, imagining her long, solitary walk home in the dark. She would cry again for her dog, he was sure. She hadn't finished her tea. He wished he'd thought to give her something to eat.

The paper-wrapped bundle lay on the table. He reached for it — just as a sharp knock sounded behind him and the door squeaked open again.

"Evening, Dr. Wilkes," his housekeeper greeted him, already unwinding the bulky woolen scarf she'd wound around her neck about seven times.

"Mrs. Quick, how are you this evening?"

"About the same, not that perky. I think I got the dropsy in my shoulder."

"Your shoulder? Well, I doubt —"

"Aches like the dickens. I can make your supper all right, but I'm not sure I can run the carpet sweeper or scrub this floor tonight."

"That's all right, just —"

"By the way." She'd taken off her boots and hung up her coat, sweater, scarf, hat, and mittens, and she was facing him foursquare with her hands on her wide, white-aproned hips. She fixed him with her wrinkled-prune look, as he thought of it, and he knew he was in for one of her disagreeable diatribes about something or other. He'd inherited Mrs. Quick from Stoneman, who hadn't minded her because "she's sourer than I am, and that's saying something." She had a million aches and pains, more advice than an almanac, and never a good word to say about anybody.

"I couldn't help noticing that Wiggins girl coming down your steps just now," she said aggressively, thrusting out the foremost of her several chins. "Maybe it ain't my place, but this is a good Christian town, and some might say it don't look right, you having a young girl up here alone with you in your house."

Tyler blinked in surprise and annoyance, and a minute particle of guilt. He couldn't think of a thing to say. Except, "Thank you, Mrs. Quick, for your candor and concern. I'll certainly consider your advice."

She nodded, gloomily satisfied. As she began to clear the tea things from the table, he thought of something else to say: *Nobody in this good Christian town would know I had a "young girl" up here unless you told them, you potato-faced busybody.* Instead of saying it, he snatched up Carrie's parcel from the kitchen table and escaped into the sitting room.

The problem, he thought as he stoked the coal stove and then dropped heavily into his chair, was that the old toad was probably right. Wayne's Crossing was no more narrow-minded than most country towns its size, but he knew there were plenty of people here who would view his innocent entertainment of Carrie Wiggins this afternoon as compromising. *Compromising.* What a laugh. They'd disapprove of her drinking tea with him in his kitchen, but they wouldn't think twice if she lay buck naked on his examining table downstairs, with nobody in the room but him. Private doctors in Philadelphia had women assistants present when they examined naked ladies, but there were no such amenities in Wayne's Crossing. Nobody gave it a thought.

Sighing, he opened Carrie's package — and smiled, his irritation vanishing, when he found under the paper, carefully wrapped in a square of green velour, a tiny bouquet of dried flowers. He set it on his knee and opened the note she'd fastened to the velour. The large, looping letters — generous, not childish, he decided — were already familiar to him.

Dear Dr. Wilkes,
    I knew you weren't a vet, but Shadow was so sick I couldn't think what else to do. I'm sure you are a very good doctor. Thank you for taking care of my dog.
                        Very truly yours,
                        Carrie Wiggins

P.S. The white flowers are sweet everlasting, the pink ones are wintergreen, and the violet are wild hyacinth. If you rub the white ones in your fingers, they smell like perfume.

He leaned back in his chair, listening to the popping sounds the coal stove made, the intermittent bustling of Mrs. Quick in the kitchen. The weightless bouquet rested on his knee; he found himself repeating the names of the flowers in his mind. Wintergreen, wild hyacinth, and sweet everlasting. He caught a tiny white petal between his thumb and forefinger, and gently massaged it. Subtly, just barely, a sweet, woodsy fragrance teased his nostrils, so faint he thought he might be imagining it. "Perfume," she called it. His smile faded. He felt a pang of regret, that came and went as swiftly as his sudden, unnerving apprehension of the meagerness of Carrie Wiggins's life.

Later, long after Mrs. Quick had gone home, Tyler went outside. Barelegged and shivering under his nightshirt and overcoat, he placed the little bouquet on Carrie's dog's grave.

5

It was the last day of March, a half-and-half day in a changeable month of an untrustworthy season. The wind blustered in fits and starts, driving clouds across a bright sun and chilling the unfrozen earth at inconstant intervals. Upwards of two hundred people alternately shivered and basked in the capricious breeze, spread out across Bob Stoops's cornfield on blankets, stools, and chairs lugged from home, waiting for the show to start again. If the Holy and Evangelical Ministry had come to town one week later, Reverend Ewing would've had to stage it somewhere else, because Bob Stoops was set to start spring plowing next Saturday. As it was, the bumpy ground was just right for sitting on — not too hard, not too cold, and not spongy yet from the spring rains.

Reverend Ewing's revival meeting was an all-day affair. This morning there had been preaching and baptizing; this afternoon there would be more preaching and then healing, and finally the Big Saving. It was the reverend's third or fourth visit to Wayne's Crossing, an annual event at least as social as it was religious, and each year, everybody agreed, it got bigger and better. This year it was being held out in the open, because for the first time the crowd was too big for a tent to contain it.

Dr. Wilkes had seen handbills posted around town for weeks, blaring the news that the Holy and Evangelical Ministry was coming; he hadn't paid them any mind, and had no intention of attending — fundamentalist religious revivals hadn't figured much in his Anglican, upper-class Philadelphia upbringing. But Bob Stoops's field abutted the dirt track he was traveling on his way back to town after a sick call on Mrs. Butts, the sheriff's wife, over toward Five Corners. The spectacle of two hundred townsfolk gathered around a wooden platform in the middle of a cornfield was too interesting to pass by. Especially when Dr. Stoneman spied Ty's rented buggy from a distance and started waving at him to make him stop. He found a space for his horse and buggy among all the other conveyances tied up to Stoops's rusty fence and walked toward Stoneman — who was striding out to meet him, weaving carelessly through the scattered chairs and blankets of his neighbors.

"Doctor!" Stoneman greeted him — a little too enthusiastically, Tyler thought; his elderly friend must have brought along his hip flask. "This is wonderful! Never been to one of these shows, have you? No, I thought not, not quite your thing. My boy, you're in for a treat. Come over here, the view's better. You haven't got a patient waiting for you someplace, have you? Good, excellent. Believe me, you don't want to miss a minute of this."

Tyler allowed himself to be pulled along, smiling and nodding to the townspeople he knew. Even the ones he didn't know smiled back, no doubt because of something comfortable and changeless in the sight of the old and the new doc getting along well together. Stoneman led him to a choice spot in the center of things, a rusting corn reaper against which they could lean their backs, about forty feet from Reverend Ewing's makeshift stage. A trio of husky farm boys was already there, but Stoneman shooed them away — "Make room for a sick old man and his doctor!" — and in short order they had the corn reaper to themselves.

"Where've you been?" Stoneman demanded. He still took a proprietary interest in his replacement's daily schedule.

Tyler told him about Mrs. Butts's ischiorectal abscess. "She was a wreck when I got there, completely miserable, swore she was ready to kill herself. All I did was drain it. She

73

felt so much better, she thought I saved her life."

"I trust you didn't dispute her opinion."

"Certainly not."

"That's the ticket! Look grave and modest, and take all the credit you can get."

"Absolutely."

"It all balances out anyway — as many times as they'll praise you for doing nothing, they'll curse you for the failures you can't help. So never correct anybody's conviction that you're a genius, that's my advice."

Both men stared off into the woods beyond the field, nodding sagely.

"Well, look here, if it isn't a fullness of physicians. A plethora of practitioners. A brace of bonesetters!"

Stoneman groaned and said, "Hello, Frank," in pretended dismay, not bothering to turn around. "What brings you out into the so-called real world? Shouldn't you be sitting in your darkened office, wearing a visor and writing featherbrained editorials for the amusement of your, quote, readers, unquote?"

"A surfeit of surgeons. A congestion of consultants. A — What brings me out here? I'm *covering* this event, as we journalists say." Frank Odell, owner, publisher, and editor of the Wayne's Crossing *Clarion*, shifted his youngest daughter from his right arm to his left. "Coming, Eppy!" he called over his shoulder, anticipating his wife's summons. "Hi, Dr. Wilkes, how're you doing? I take it you're here in hopes that the reverend can give you a few pointers in the healing arts?"

Ty grinned and shook hands. "That's right. It had to be divine intervention that kept Stoneman from killing *all* his patients, so I figure it behooves me to come and see what this faith healing's all about."

"Balls," enunciated Stoneman. He reached into his pocket for his flask, remembered where he was, and jerked his hand out empty, scowling.

Frank laughed and jiggled his little girl up and down. Father and daughter had identical pug noses and carrot-orange hair. "Are you coming to the game on Thursday evening, Ty?"

"I hope I can make it — if I've got no emergencies that night, I'll be there."

"Good! We could use some new blood in our hoary old poker game. Right, Doc?"

Stoneman hunched his shoulders. "Depends on whose blood."

"Frank!"

"Coming, Eppy."

"I see your wife's pregnant again," Stoneman noted sourly. "Maybe you ought to get the young doc here to explain how that works, Frank. There's a *causal relationship*, as we physicians say, which you don't seem to have grasped."

"Thanks, Doc, I'll keep that in mind. Good to see you both." He started backing away. "It's always nice to see a surplus of sawbones. A morass of medics. A —"

"Frank!" called Eppy.

The editor saluted them, spun around, and walked off to join his family.

Stoneman made a rusty noise in his throat that might have been a chuckle. "I hope you appreciate the singular honor that's been bestowed upon you, Dr. Wilkes," he rumbled.

"What honor is that, Doc?"

"That poker game's been going on for twenty-five years. Except for me and Jim Durkee, the original six players are all dead. Frank Odell's been in it for ten years, Peter Mueller and Hoyle Taber for about fifteen. And every one of us has lived in this town for longer than you've been alive."

"Well, now, I didn't realize that. I'm glad you told me," Ty said, without a smile. There were aspects of his new life that dissatisfied him, and voids in it he'd overlooked at first that he'd lately begun to find intolerable. But about one thing he couldn't complain: the town's wholehearted and all but instantaneous acceptance of him. He'd never tried to endear himself to people by pretending to be just like them, and most of Wayne's Crossing could probably tell that Tyler Arbuthnot Wilkes's social background accustomed him more to tennis matches and cotillions than outdoor revivals and barn dances. And yet in a matter of months he'd been made to feel welcome and appreciated. Stoneman was joking about the poker game, but the truth was, he *did* feel honored.

"Oh, excellent, it's starting." Stoneman gloated, rubbing his hands together.

"Why do you like this so much?" Tyler asked, laughing at him.

"Why? You can ask *why?* Look around! How often do you get to see this many people in one place making complete asses of themselves?"

"That's a little cynical, isn't it?"

"Cynical? You're saying you believe this charlatan's going to *heal* people?"

Tyler rubbed his chin, pretending to consider. "I'd have to say I don't absolutely rule it out."

Stoneman spat in disgust.

"No, listen," Ty insisted, "yesterday an old lady with a uterine myoma came to see me. She'd never seen a stethoscope in her life. I listened to her heart, and when I was through she thanked me and said she felt much better. She thought I was finished — she thought I'd *cured* her. She started to pay me!"

"I could tell you a hundred stories just like that," Stoneman scoffed.

"There you are. That just proves my point."

"Nonsense. Your old lady *felt* better, but she's still got her tumor." He turned his back on him before Ty could say more. "Shut up and watch this. I'm telling you, Doc, it's the best show in town."

The Evangelical Ministry's afternoon programme began with hymn singing, led by Reverend Ewing himself and enlivened by his wife Roxanne's enthusiastic harmonica playing. "There's a son, too," Stoneman informed Tyler gleefully. "Young Todd — see him over there? Passes the collection basket and helps the infirm up on the stage to get healed. It's a family affair."

When the singing ended, Reverend Ewing swung immediately into a loud and fervid sermon on the power of faith to heal anyone who had Jesus in his heart. No podium for him; he was of the moving school of preachers, a strider, a strutter, a ceaseless walker back and forth across his wooden platform. His voice was a little thin, a little too high for really effective exhorting, but he compensated for it with big dramatic arm gestures, and by inducing the audience to repeat his deepest profundities — "humdingers," Stoneman called them — back to him over and over.

"You've got to tie the boat of your soul up in the Lord's harbor," he advised, striding and gesturing, punching the air with his fists. "Tie up your soul in His *harbor. Tie* up your *soul* in the Lord's *harbor!*" A dutiful echo went up from the crowd. "Oh, hallelujah!" the reverend rejoiced, and they repeated that, too. "Unto you that fear my name shall the Sun of righteousness arise, with healing in his wings. With *healing* in his wings, I say: *Healing* in his *wings!*"

He recounted the story of Lazarus with many colorful additions, then the stories of the blind man, the palsied man, and the leper, all healed because they had faith. "So I'm saying to you today, come forth! Come forth like Lazarus from the tomb, bound hand and foot with grave clothes. With God's blessed help I will lay my hands upon your affliction, and the scales will drop from your eyes, the obstacles from your ears, and you'll see and hear the fullness of the Lord's power and mercy through signs and wonders. Come! Come! Who'll feel the Lord's power and mercy with me now? Come!" Nobody seemed to want to come. "Come forth, I'm telling you, just as the master bid his servant, Bring in hither the poor and the maimed and the halt and the blind, so I say unto you, bring hither your —"

"Hey, Reverend! We got us here one o' the halt!"

Ty turned to see three big strapping fellows trying to drag the boy named Broom, Carrie Wiggins's friend, through the throng toward the platform. They had him by his skinny arms, one on each side and one in back, shoving him forward with rough blows between his scrawny shoulder blades. "No!" he yelled, "I ain't, I don't wanna!" and even from here Tyler could see the spittle flying out of his mouth and the panic in his eyes.

"Look at that," Stoneman grumbled. "Why don't they leave that poor half-wit be?"

Tyler recognized Eugene Starkey as the one in back, the one poking Broom along like a mule driver. He'd paid a visit to the office a few weeks ago, boasting and swaggering to hide his nervousness, scared to death he had syphilis. He hadn't — and his relief had been so profound that he'd listened to the requisite lecture on conscientious sexual hygiene without a single smart-aleck remark.

All at once Broom wrenched his arms free. Flailing and jerking, he spun to face his surprised attackers. "I ain't gonna!" he shouted, spraying them with spit. Spinning again, he dashed away, bony knees high-kicking, elbows churning. It was a ludicrous sight, and the crowd appreciated it. Laughter erupted all along his crazy, helter-skelter path, and followed him to the edge of the field and into the sheltering pine trees of the neighboring woods.

"Rascally sons of bitches," Stoneman swore.

But Broom's reluctant example seemed to have loosened restraint and uncapped inhibitions, because a moment later a short line of infirm believers began to gather at one side of the wooden platform. First up was a white-haired lady with a cane. Stoneman cackled and rocked on his toes. "Mabel Snowmaker," he confided, elbowing Tyler in the ribs. "Blind as a bat from cataracts. This should be good."

"And the blind man cried out, 'Thou son of David, have mercy on me!' And the Lord said, 'Believe ye that I am able to do this?' And the blind man said, 'Yea, Lord, I believe it!' Say hallelujah."

"Hallelujah!" the reverend's flock complied.

"Do you believe?" he demanded, standing behind Mabel Snowmaker with his hands over her eyes.

"Yes. Yes, I do," she said in a low, strained voice.

The reverend wasn't convinced. "Say halle-lujah. *Do you believe?*"

"Hallelujah. I believe."

"Do you believe?"

"I believe!"

"Oh righteous God, this woman *believes!* Now lift the scales from her eyes and let her see Thy light and Thy power and Thy glory! Pray with me, people! Do you believe? Shout hallelujah!"

The shout went up, and Reverend Ewing took his hands from Mabel's eyes and held his hands up to heaven. "Praise the Lord! Thank Him and shout hallelujah! Great God, it's a miracle!"

People were on their feet, yelling and prais-ing and thanking the Lord for the miracle. Mabel Snowmaker smiled uncertainly and stared up at the sky. "A miracle," she echoed, hopeful.

"A miracle!" thundered the reverend. He snatched her cane from her hand and heaved it far, far out into the crowd. A roar of ap-proval went up at the theatrical, perfectly timed gesture. "The Lord's vouchsafed a mir-acle! Praise Jesus on your knees and give thanks to Him for this powerful gift! Go in peace, and never stop praising the Lord for His signs and wonders!"

Mabel went, hands outstretched, feet shuffling. At the platform's edge, son Todd managed to catch her before she tripped, saving her from a headlong pitch into the front row. Friends took her from there, and she got back to her seat without mishap.

Next came an elderly gentleman with lumbago, then a boy with a limp, then a girl with "galloping consumption" — bronchitis, Ty and Stoneman agreed — followed by a man who swore he had "the plague." Reverend Ewing cured them all, masterfully and with great dispatch. The crowd was delighted, and no one in it more so than Stoneman. Tyler was surprised, therefore, when the doctor suddenly stood up straight and started to swear. Following his gaze, Ty saw Spring Mueller and another girl trying to hustle an obviously unwilling Carrie Wiggins toward the stage. People around them clapped approvingly and made way. Carrie shook her head in speechless misery, hanging back, looking ready to weep. But unlike Broom she didn't fight; Tyler didn't know if it was because of pride or embarrassment or inertia, but she let Spring and her friend bundle her through the crush toward the platform. Even from this distance, he saw the subtle malice at her expense in the girls' giggling excitement.

"Damn it to hell. Wiggins ought to stop

this," Stoneman bristled. "Look at him."

"Where?"

"There. See him? Resembles an ape."

Ty saw him, sitting on a blanket and hugging his knees, big and black-haired and balding. The expression on his wide, pockmarked face looked more like dread than hope. "Does he believe in this business?" Ty asked curiously.

"Hell, yes, he swallows it whole. Superstitious bastard, religious as hell. Except when he's drunk and raving, that is."

Tyler might have pointed out that religion and superstition weren't always the same thing, but at that moment son Todd and his father got hold of Carrie and pulled her up on the wooden platform.

"What ails this child of God?" inquired the reverend, pulling on her hands and drawing her toward stage center.

"She's dumb," Spring called out from the aisle.

"She can't say a single word," her girlfriend amplified.

Reverend Ewing looked thrilled. " 'They brought Him to a dumb man, possessed with a devil,' " he cried rapturously. " 'And the multitudes marveled, saying it was never so seen in Israel.' " Carrie was pushing futilely against his shoulders, straining away from him as far as she could, but he had one hand around the back of her neck and one hand on her throat. In profile, they looked like a man and woman battling each other to the death.

"Child, where's your faith? Do you believe that Jesus is the resurrection and the life? Do you *believe* it?"

Carrie nodded, and hauled on the grip he had on her throat. She was nearly the same height as the reverend, but about seventy pounds lighter. In a swift, unexpected move, he pushed her in front of him and held her by her hair, so that she faced his gaping, wide-eyed congregation head-on. Her shawl slipped off one shoulder; she stood straight and tall and quaking in a patched dress, hatless, bright hair blown awry by the wind. Tyler's hands clenched into murderous fists.

"Don't." Stoneman grabbed his arm and held fast. "You'll just make it worse. I don't think this'll last long."

"Pray with me! Lift your voices up to the Lord for this poor mute girl. She has faith, she believes! Jesus, we beseech You, cast the devil out so that she might speak Your name and praise You. For he that believeth in You, though he were dead, yet shall he live, and whoever liveth and believeth in You shall never die. Believest thou this?" The crowd answered with heartfelt yeas. "Believest thou

85

this?" He gave Carrie a violent shake. Her eyes glittered; she tried to nod.

"She believes! Let us pray!" He pushed her down to her knees. Standing behind her, big hands wrapped around her shoulders, he began to pray in earnest. It went on and on, and every minute Tyler thought he would stop it, rush the stage, and put an end to this ridiculous travesty. Was Stoneman right, would he only make it worse? He couldn't decide, and his indecision tortured him. He glanced back at her stepfather. He'd covered his head with his hands and buried it between his knees; he was either in deep distress or lost in fervent prayer.

"Will she speak?" Reverend Ewing beseeched the multitude. "Lift up your voices for her! Will she speak?" "Yes!" they chanted in answer. He roared out the question again — again — again. Each time, louder and louder, they returned a rousing affirmation.

Stoneman had Ty by the arm again. "Don't. Leave it," he warned. "It's better, I think —"

Reverend Ewing released Carrie and held up his arms for silence. Immediately a hushed, expectant stillness descended. Quiet now, dramatically calm, the reverend asked, "Is your faith strong enough? The Lord is waiting. Heal thyself now, woman." Suddenly he shouted out one word. "Speak!"

In the startled silence Carrie raised her chin. Her face was a white mask of anguish. She opened her mouth, and there was an airless, breathless moment of suspense. Then she dropped her head in defeat, and from the congregation rose a spontaneous wail of disappointment.

Reverend Ewing stepped away from her in haste. "Your faith has failed you," he chided reproachfully. "The whole head is sick, and the whole heart faint. From the sole of the foot even unto the head there is no soundness in it, but wounds, and bruises, and putrifying sores —"

Carrie scrambled to her feet. The reverend made a move to stop her, but she sidestepped him. She saw his son at one end of the platform, whirled, and dashed for the other. A roar went up from the mob, and for a wild second Tyler thought they would try to catch her, drag her back and wring more "faith" out of her. But they leaned away from her panicked flight and let her go. She ran on a mad diagonal toward the pine woods fifty yards away — the same escape route Broom had used half an hour ago.

Stoneman was saying something, but Tyler didn't hear because he was already striding away, shouldering through a knot of snickering young boys, stepping carefully to avoid treading on anybody. But he kept Carrie in sight, and made a straight path for the opening in the thicket at the edge of the woods through which she'd disappeared. Once out of the crowd, he broke into a run, or as much of one as he could manage nowadays on his bad leg. He reached the edge of the field and ducked into the trees. In the sudden dimness he could see nothing but black, blowing branches and dense undergrowth. There was a path of sorts; he trotted along it, limping, trying to see ahead through the coarse tangle. He paused to cup his hands and shout, "Carrie, it's Dr. Wilkes! Carrie!" Silence. He felt foolish when he realized he was waiting for her to answer. He started running again.

The woods ended abruptly. Rounding the last turn in the path, he saw her in silhouette against a dry hillside pasture, yellow in the fading sun and dotted with dark clumps of juniper. She was standing stock still; something in her posture made him halt when he was still a dozen paces away.

In a too-casual voice, he greeted her. "Carrie, hello. I'm glad you stopped." She made no movement, no gesture. He started toward her slowly, limping, holding her gaze. "I haven't seen you in quite a while." Beside her, parallel to the path, the long, rotting trunk of a beech tree made a perfect seat. He kept coming. She didn't move, but her eyes darkened with every step he took. He made a gesture toward the fallen tree with his hand — to indicate his destination. When he was six feet away, he realized she was going to bolt.

Immediately he put an extra hitch in his gait. "Mind giving me a hand?" he muttered, not looking at her. "Sorry — leg still gives out on me every now and then. Damn nuisance." He was hobbling like an old man, probably overdoing it.

But it worked. She rushed toward him and took hold of his forearm, guiding him toward the log. With an exaggerated groan, he sat. Even kneaded his thigh with both hands. It really did ache; he wasn't a complete humbug. Out of the corner of his eye, he could see her standing over him uncertainly, twisting her hands. He smiled at her. "Think I should've let the reverend take a crack at me, too?"

A long army of emotions paraded across her features: dismay and embarrassment, surprise, relief — and finally, miraculously, amusement. Tyler sat back and grinned at her, conscious of an immense relief. "Are you all right, Carrie? Really? Good, I'm glad. Would you like to sit down?"

The idea seemed to intrigue, not frighten

her. She considered it in her forthright way. Presently she gave a little nod, gathered her skirts, and settled beside him.

Her face was almost serene now, but he could see faint trails on her cheeks where tears had recently dried. He spoke tentatively, unsure of his ground — for if she had any faith at all in a man like Ewing's power to heal, then he had no right to shake it. At the same time, he felt a compulsion to comfort her.

"You know, I don't think he really cured anybody back there. Not permanently, anyway. I suppose such things are possible, but something tells me Reverend Ewing's not the man for the job. Of course, some people might say I'm prejudiced," he pointed out, trying to make her smile. "Some might say I'm just trying to keep the reverend from horning in on my territory." She did smile, but he could tell it was an effort in politeness. "Carrie," he said gently, "are you very disappointed?"

She shook her head. Reaching into the pocket of her skirt, she pulled out a stubby pencil and a cheap, dog-eared notebook. She scribbled something and handed the notebook to him. *No, for I knew it wouldn't work.* Taking the notebook back, she wrote something else, crossed part of it out, and wrote again. *I was embarrassed.*

He saw that at first she'd written "ashamed," but then scratched over it. "Because of all the people?" he guessed. "Because of what *they* were expecting, not you."

She nodded faintly. Her cheeks pinkened, as if she were remembering the ugly scene.

"But it wasn't *your* failure." She nodded again — she already knew that. He was glad, but unsure now what to say to console her. A memory came back to him, a private humiliation he hadn't consciously thought of in years.

"When I was about eight years old, Carrie, my mother thought it would be a fine idea to send me away to boarding school in France. The fact that it was the middle of the term and I didn't know a word of French didn't figure in the decision." He faced her, propping his bad leg on the log between them and wrapping his arms around his knee. "On my first day, my very first day, I was late getting to class — I can't remember why anymore. The headmaster stood me up in front of everybody and demanded to know why I was tardy. 'My watch is slow,' I said, or thought I said — *Ma montre retarde.* Only I forgot the word for watch and I said, *Ma morse retarde.* Know what *morse* means?" She shook her head. "It means 'walrus.' *My walrus is slow,* I announced to all my new classmates."

She covered her mouth with her hand, eyes

wide with pity and distress — then laughter. "You think that's funny?" he demanded, taking mock umbrage. She shook her head quickly, anxious to reassure him. He grinned. "No, and it wasn't funny then, believe me. I'll never forget how they laughed at me, Carrie, never, not if I live to be a hundred."

She nodded her understanding. There was no need for him to complete the circle, explain the moral of his little story — that even though it hadn't been in any way his fault, the childhood incident had mortified him, as Reverend Ewing and the crowd had mortified her. In all likelihood they would both take those fiery-hot memories to their graves.

They fell silent. A moment later she wrote in her notebook, *Thank you.*

"For what?"

Telling me that.

"You're welcome."

With the tablet on her knee, she wrote, *People,* then crossed it out. She wrote, *Sometimes,* and crossed that out, too. He could feel her indecision floating between them like a fog, obscuring the faint ties of trust he had thought were beginning to connect them.

She turned the page and scribbled something else.

" 'How are you?' " Tyler read aloud. " 'How is your —' " He bent closer, squinting

92

at the last word. *Nuralja,* she'd written. "Ah!" He glanced up to see her blushing. "Much better," he said quickly. "The neuralgia's all but disappeared; in fact, I haven't had a spell in weeks." She put her hands together in a glad, grateful gesture.

"I wanted to thank you for your gift." She wrinkled her forehead. "The flowers," he reminded her. "I liked them very much." Her smile was enchanting. She really was lovely. "Dr. Stoneman tells me you know everything about flowers and trees and birds and animals."

She made a humorous face and looked up at the blowing treetops, then back at him with a rueful smile. On her notepad she scribbled, *How I wish.*

"I think you're being modest." He glanced around. Across the path, a short clump of bluish, hairy-stalked wildflowers sprouted under a spindly laurel bush. Buttercups, he'd have labeled them, except that they weren't yellow. "What are those?" he challenged, pointing.

She grinned. *Hepatica,* she wrote. *Easy.*

"You see? You know everything. Now me, I'd rather not know what they're called."

She arched her eyebrows in amazement.

"No, I'd rather not know. I tried to learn once, but it was too depressing. Whenever I'd see a really beautiful specimen and look it up in a book, it always turned out to be called 'dogbane' or 'bladderwort.' "

She laughed with her whole face, shoulders shaking, covering her mouth again with her hand. The uselessness of the gesture struck Tyler all at once, sobering him and turning his pleasure in making her laugh into a vague melancholy.

She wrote, *Bastard-toadflax is pretty!* She thought for a second. *So is mad-dog skullcap!* She lifted dancing eyes, and saw his expression. Her smile faltered.

"Has a doctor ever examined your throat, Carrie?" She bent her head; he couldn't read her still profile. He watched her draw tight X's around all the borders of the page she'd been writing on. "There could be any number of reasons why you're not able to speak," he persisted. "An injury to the vocal cords or the laryngeal cartilages. A tumor, a lesion. Trauma from swallowing something corrosive." *Hysteria,* he thought but didn't say. "If you'd let me examine you, I might be able to help you." She stayed motionless except for the compulsive X-making, darker now, the pencil bearing down hard. "There's an instrument we use called a laryngoscope. It's nothing but a little mirror mounted at an angle on a metal stem about this long. It doesn't hurt, I promise you. It gives me a good view of the cords and the trachea, that's all." He waited, but she still didn't look up. "Tell me this. Are you able to whisper?"

She ripped out the X'd-over page of her notebook in a quick slashing movement and scrawled *NO* on a new one in block letters. Then she shot to her feet.

"Wait." He stood up more slowly, not because of his leg as much as to keep her from streaking away like a flushed partridge. "Hold on. Wait now, Carrie, talk to me."

She looked at him for a few seconds, as if weighing the threat. Apparently he didn't present much of one, because she looked away from him long enough to scribble in her notebook again. When she finished, she tore off the sheet and handed it to him.

Thank you for being nice to me. I can't talk I can't, you can't help me.

When he looked back up, she was halfway across the yellow pasture, long legs striding away fast.

6

Gently . . . gently. Don't be scared, little hawk, it's all right. Easy, almost done. There!

Carrie let her breath out in slow relief and laid the panting kestrel on its side in her lap. Despite the seriousness of the moment, she almost smiled because he looked so comical, like a tiny bird-ghost, bound from his neck to his tail feathers in the foot of one of her old white stockings. She'd cut a hole in the top for his head and one in the middle for his poor broken leg, which crooked out at a pitiful angle, snapped in two between the elbow and the foot. The sock would calm him and hold him steady while she tended to his leg. Thank goodness the bone hadn't punched through the skin; at least she wouldn't have to worry about infection. She'd found him this morning, tangled in the burs of a burdock plant behind the springhouse. He'd probably broken his leg thrashing around to free himself. When she'd disentangled him, he'd been too exhausted to move.

Now he was breathing too fast. Using the medicine dropper Dr. Stoneman had given her, she coaxed a drink of sugar water into the sparrow hawk's beak, to settle him down. Her instruments were all ready and laid out on a towel on the flat top of the silvered chestnut stump beside her. She'd cut strips of gauze ahead of time, guessing the lengths she would need, and fashioned and fitted a tiny splint from a piece of cardboard — because wood, even matchsticks, she'd learned from experience, were much too heavy for a small bird. Now she took a thin square of gauze and laid it over the kestrel's head — he'd be calmer if he couldn't see her movements — and set to work.

Steady, quiet hands. Absolutely calm. Firm, but not too firm; a bird's legs were hollow, you could snap a fragile bone yourself if you weren't careful. Slowly and very gently she fitted her L-shaped splint along the outside of the kestrel's leg, from shoulder to claw. He squirmed for a second; she let her hands go still. Her own steady breathing and the warmth of her body soothed him. The little tab at the bottom of the splint curled up perfectly, she saw with satisfaction — she'd wrapped it around a pencil earlier, so it would roll around the stalky leg just right.

Now the hard part: holding everything in place with one hand and winding a gauze strip around leg and splint with the other. This was

97

where the blindfold came in handy, for she had to hold one end of the binding strip in her teeth in order to tie a strong but gentle knot.

Done. She snipped off the extra bit of gauze and surveyed her handiwork. The splint made a little cradle for the kestrel's leg to rest in; now he'd be able to perch, sit flat on the ground, or — by tomorrow — move around without hurting himself. She slipped the square of cloth from his head. *There, that wasn't so bad, was it? Oh, what a handsome boy you are!* The beady eye in his black-and-white face glittered up at her. Lifting him, she carried him to his box and set him on the bed she'd made out of shredded cotton. Using scissors, she cut the sock away. He fluttered his wings feebly for a few seconds, then lay quiet.

So beautiful, Carrie thought. No bigger than a robin, but how much *wilder* he looked with his hawk's beak, his speckled breast, and rusty-red tail. The bluish wings told her he was a male. For a moment she thought of naming him — but no. In two weeks his leg would heal, and she'd set him free. Once you named a wildling you made it yours, and that was wrong; they didn't belong to anyone but themselves. She remembered the big crow she'd taken care of last spring, who'd broken his wing from flying into the cabin window.

She'd kept him for a month and then let him go. *Tried* to let him go, rather. Three times she'd set him free, and three times he flew right back to her. The fourth time, she couldn't stop crying. To tell the truth, if he'd come back then, she'd have had to let him stay.

But in the main it was no good to try to keep wildlings no matter how much you wanted to, because they were happier being free. You could be as kind and gentle as a lamb, but there was no substitute for Mother Nature, and trying to hold on to a wildling could turn out hurtful and not at all what you intended.

She straightened, and covered the hawk's box with a cloth, for warmth. She would come back in a few hours to check on him, give him some water, and try to get a little food into him. If he wouldn't eat tonight, he surely would tomorrow. She couldn't see anything wrong with him except for his broken leg, and she'd fixed that. She had high hopes for his full recovery.

She kept her wildling care log with her other notebooks — her *Record of Specimens of the Wiggins Museum of Natural History*, her bird identification ledger, and her personal journal — wrapped in a piece of canvas and stowed under a corner of the big weathered boulder that made up one whole side of the hospital. With her usual care, she wrote down the details of her discovery of the kestrel, his injury, her treatment and expectations for his recuperation. After that she tidied up, putting things away in the watertight boxes she'd made and fitted into rough, hand-stacked stone shelves.

Even though it was only April, the late-afternoon scent of wildflowers was strong enough to make her pause, closing her eyes on a deep, dreamy inhale. This year she'd worked harder than ever on her flowers, and it had been worth it. She gazed about at the clumps of white Quaker ladies and trillium, heavy-headed and nodding, the low bed of rue anemone, the far-off spread of bloodroot and spring violets. She'd transplanted a tub of yellow wood betony from the patch near the cabin, because thinking of its other name — lousewort — always reminded her of Dr. Wilkes. She smiled now, remembering how he'd tried to make her laugh with his talk of "dogbane" and "bladderwort."

She didn't really need flowers or anything else, though, to make her think of Dr. Wilkes. She'd thought of him every day in the three weeks since the revival meeting, and she knew a lot more about him now than she had then. She'd only been sixteen when the war with

Spain broke out, but she remembered the sinking of the battleship *Maine* in Havana Harbor and how it had outraged everybody in Wayne's Crossing. She'd heard of the Rough Riders, too, and she recalled little boys in town brandishing stick swords and shouting, "Rough, rough, we're the stuff, we wanna fight and we can't get enough! Whoopee!" But now that she had met Dr. Wilkes, she wanted to know more — *everything* — about the war, and especially the First United States Volunteer Cavalry.

So she'd gone to the library, where Miss Fuller had taught her how to look things up in old copies of *The World* and the New York *Journal* and the *Post.* Terrible stories of Cuban peasants starving and dying in the *reconcentrado* camps had made her cry. *Cuba libre!* She remembered the slogan, and wished now she'd been more aware of the war when it was going on. She might have done something to help — although exactly what, she couldn't think.

But the most interesting stories in the old magazines and newspapers to Carrie were the ones about Dr. Wilkes's famous regiment. Twenty-three thousand men had applied for it, she read, but only a thousand had been chosen. Theodore Roosevelt was their leader, and the paper said it didn't take him any time at all to learn every one of their names. They'd come from all walks of life — lumberjacks, college athletes, frontier outlaws, high-society polo players. They'd trained in Texas for weeks, until Roosevelt bragged his regiment could whip Caesar's tenth legion. Carrie loved to look at the photographs of the troopers, posing on horseback in their slouch hats, leather boots, and low-slung gun belts. In one, she thought she saw Dr. Wilkes, looking rugged and nonchalant on a big black horse, in the third row of an endless line of soldiers spread out across the San Antonio plain. She'd stared and squinted, peered and gaped, but she could never be sure if it was really him.

If she could've had one wish, it would've been that she could keep the photograph for her own, whether it was him in it or not, and tack it up on the wall behind the curtain in her sleeping place. But Miss Fuller said it was forbidden to even borrow the old newspapers, much less keep them. So she contented herself with going to the library as often as she could, to read about the Rough Riders and gaze at the grainy smudge of hat and handsome face and wide shoulders that might or might not be Dr. Wilkes.

The sunlight was beginning to drain from the trees. It must be close to six o'clock, which meant Artemis would be wanting his supper. And he'd be wondering why it had taken her so long to clean dead leaves from the roof of the springhouse. But he was used to the not-quite-lies she told him to explain her tardiness and her frequent disappearances — "I was out walking," she'd write, or "I didn't notice the time." As long as it didn't inconvenience him, he didn't really care where she went or what she did. He thought she was crazy anyway. "Hen-headed," he called her, and "feeble-brained." It didn't matter to her what he thought. But if he knew about her hospital, he'd ridicule it or call it "godless" and forbid her to come. No, he'd do worse than that — more likely he'd wreck it, and then laugh at her if she cried.

She took a last look at the sparrow hawk. *You rest and get well,* she advised him. *I'll bring a moth for your supper, after Artemis goes to sleep.* And tomorrow she'd make sketches of the hawk for her Book. Covering the box again, she snatched up her shawl from a branch of mountain laurel.

April on Dreamy Mountain was a trial sometimes. You couldn't trust it, and every good day was still a gift. Nature had played tricks all day yesterday, for instance, with snow in the morning, then rain, dazzling sun, wind all of a sudden, and then *hail,* and finally

103

the prettiest sunset she'd ever seen. Today it was warm and muddy, and the air smelled sweet, and the noise of birds was loud, wild, and constant. She stepped over a soggy, greening carpet of sphagnum moss and started along the path that led down to the cabin. The path was still rough, no one could see it yet, she was sure; but in a few weeks she'd have to begin taking a different route, start a different trail.

Even though it was late, she paused, under the Squeaky Tree, bending over to examine the clear-cut, heart-shaped little hoofprint of a deer in the wet earth. Behind a tangle of wild grapevine a towhee was scratching. She waited for his song, and presently he piped up, "Drink your teeeee!" Beside her shoulder, a green tree caterpillar lowered himself on a silky thread. She touched him with the tip of her finger, and he wriggled up and out of sight before she could blink. Chipmunks raced in the dry leaves; their sharp, steady chipping sent a message: *Go home, Carrie, you're late.*

She thanked them for reminding her and set off, quickening her pace. But at the woods' edge she stopped again, to look at the sky. One star flickered just over the top of the black birch, pale yellow and so faint she could hardly see it unless she looked off a little ways to the side. The first star of the evening was the best wishing star. She made her wish, the same one she'd made every night for three weeks. *I wish I could see Dr. Wilkes again.*

She rounded the side of the cabin, intending to give the mule a hug before she went inside. She stopped short when she saw a horse and buggy standing in front of Petey's lean-to. On the floor of the buggy sat a small black case. A doctor's bag. It renewed her flagging faith in star wishes.

"What would I be wanting with that? Puny little thing, it sure ain't no hunter. No offense, but you can take that back wherever it came from, Doc. I can't hardly keep food on the table for me and the girl as it is, the last thing I need is a useless animal."

Dr. Wilkes turned when he heard her in the doorway, and Carrie saw what he had in his arms — a puppy. She was already smiling from the pure pleasure of seeing him; the sight of the little brown and white dog made her want to laugh.

"Hello," he said in his deep, stirring voice, smiling back at her, and her heart gave a powerful leap in her chest. He looked stronger, she thought; his face wasn't as thin as three weeks ago, and his color was healthier. Men weren't supposed to be beautiful — but he was. Oh, he was.

"A patient gave it to me yesterday in lieu of payment," he was saying, holding the puppy out to her. "I thought you might like to have it, since Shadow's gone."

The puppy had a round baby face, brown with a white spot over one eye and the opposite ear. She loved it already, even knowing she couldn't have it. She took it out of Dr. Wilkes's arms and gave it a soft hug. It was a male dog, she saw. He smelled wonderful. His fat belly was warm and almost hairless. He wagged his tail and started to lick her cheek, and she lost her heart altogether.

"I'm telling you, I won't have it in the house. She can't keep it, and you've got no call bringing useless animals here just because nobody else wants 'em." Artemis planted his feet and got the mule-stubborn look in his face that meant he wouldn't budge if a hurricane hit him. He was so ignorant sometimes, he could take offense at a cross-eyed glance, and now he'd decided to take Dr. Wilkes's kind offer as an insult. Carrie felt her face getting hot from embarrassment, and buried it in the puppy's furry neck.

"I'll take it back with me, then." His voice didn't sound like it, but she wondered if he was angry. "I was in the neighborhood, visiting the Haights' little boy, and I thought of Carrie. Because she lost her dog recently."

She glanced up to see how Artemis took that, if he'd look guilty or angry or what. His cheeks under the stubble of his two-day-old beard turned red, but he didn't say a word about Shadow. "You been to see Haights? What they want with a doctor for?" He laughed his mean laugh. "Bet you got nothing outa them for your trouble, did you? Not even a dog."

"The little boy, Gillie, has a fever," Dr. Wilkes said shortly, and this time Carrie was sure she saw a flick of temper in his blue eyes.

Artemis hawked up some spit and then swallowed it. "Fever, eh? It's nothing but a punishment for the godlessness they live by. The Lord don't allow sinfulness forever, not in this life. There's a payment for it. Gillie Haight is paying it for 'em today. Next time it'll be a different one."

Dr. Wilkes didn't say anything, he just looked at Artemis as if he was some new, strange kind of person he'd never encountered before. The silence went on and on until, to Carrie's surprise, Artemis dropped his eyes and started moving his thumbs up and down behind his suspenders, nervous.

"Where's your manners?" he barked all of a sudden, glaring at her. "Give the doc something to drink. Stay to supper, Doc? Carrie, get the food started. Right now." He turned

107

away toward the fireplace.

"Thank you, but I can't stay. Maybe another time."

Artemis glanced up sharply. "Sure, another time." He looked baffled, as if he couldn't decide if he'd been insulted again or not.

Carrie made up her mind to say good-bye to Dr. Wilkes by herself. Still holding the puppy, she went to the door and stepped outside. Dr. Wilkes followed, and she closed the door on Artemis without looking at him.

Out in the yard, they stood next to each other without saying anything for a minute. She stared at the cabin in horror, wondering how she could've missed seeing how rundown and shabby it looked. What must Dr. Wilkes be thinking of that broken front window Artemis wouldn't fix? She'd covered it herself with a piece of greased paper so some light could get in, but that, she saw now, just made it look worse. Tackier. How *backward* they must seem to him! His house had electricity and even a telephone. And how puny her garden must look; she wanted to explain to him that it was too shady and cool right here for much besides onions and lettuce, cabbage and beets. But did he notice how healthy her herb garden was, and did he think it was clever of her to plant it between the rungs of that old ladder on the ground? *Drat*

— why hadn't she swept the porch this morning, and gotten those cobwebs out from under —

"I'm sorry about the dog, Carrie."

Sometimes his voice could go clear through her, all the way to the soles of her feet. She gave the top of the puppy's head a sorrowful little kiss and handed him over. He started squirming, half in her arms and half in Dr. Wilkes's, so they set him on the ground between them. Immediately he waddled over to the side of the house and peed on the violets and the lily of the valley that hadn't bloomed yet. She and Dr. Wilkes looked at each other and grinned.

Carrie got her notebook out and wrote him a message. *Thank you for thinking of the puppy for me. I wish I could've kept him.*

"I'm sorry it didn't work out," he said after he'd read it. He was looking at her with such a warm expression, she could've melted right where she stood. "I didn't think about your stepfather. Stoneman told me a few things about him, and now I realize I shouldn't have brought the dog. I apologize if I've made you feel worse — that wasn't at all what I intended."

She reached out and touched his sleeve, anxious to set him at ease. Scribbling quickly, she wrote, *I don't feel worse. Honest! Will you*

109

keep him for yourself? The puppy?

He smiled, and her heart did the little dance in her chest again. "I guess I might have to. Mrs. Quick will not be pleased. Which is reason enough to think about keeping him, don't you think?"

She touched her hand to her mouth, laughing with her eyes. It thrilled her to be taken into his confidence like this, to hear him talk about his housekeeper in that humorous way — as if they were really friends and Mrs. Quick was someone they could joke about together.

The puppy was over by the buggy, snuffling around the horse's feet, yipping at it, and worrying it with little make-believe attacks. Dr. Wilkes walked over to him, scooped him up, and set him on the seat inside the buggy. *"Stay,"* he commanded. It didn't surprise Carrie at all when he stayed.

In her notebook she wrote, *Is Gillie going to get well?*

"Yes, I don't think it's anything serious." He hesitated. "The Haights haven't got much good to say about your stepfather, have they?"

She nodded unhappily. *Bad blood,* she wrote. *Willis Haight and Artemis — enemies.*

"So I gathered. But they all think you're an angel. Gillie said he wished you were his real sister."

She flapped her hand in the air and made a face.

"Mrs. Haight told me — out of her husband's hearing — that they might not have made it two winters ago without your help. Secret help, I think. And dangerous for you if your stepfather knew of it. Am I right?"

She shook her head. *Nothing,* she wrote hurriedly. *Really, nothing.* The disbelief in his face made her write, *Really,* again, dark and bold. Quickly she wrote, *How are you feeling these days?*

"Much better." He sounded impatient. "Carrie —"

You look wonderful, she scribbled, and held the paper out for him to see. He grinned. She blushed. *Much healthier,* she clarified, beet-faced.

"Thank you very much. I think it's this wholesome country air."

She nodded, and started to write, *It's very* — when he reached out and put both hands on her throat. She was so surprised, she didn't move. His touch was light and gentle — she could've taken one step back and been free of it. She stayed still. She felt like she was under a spell. But he must've seen something in her eyes because he said, so quiet, "Don't be afraid, Carrie, I'd never hurt you. You know that, don't you?" *Yes.* She moved her chin a

111

little, to tell him. He smiled, and she had to close her eyes for a second. He slid one hand to the back of her neck, steadying her, and started to move the fingertips of his other hand up and down her throat. She stopped breathing entirely. "How does this feel?" he murmured. "Is there any pain when I press here?" *No.* "Or here?" *No.*

His eyes were the same color as gentians, blue-violet and brilliant. Carrie's legs started to tremble. She couldn't look at his mouth any longer. She closed her eyes again and all her senses, everything in her focused on the soft, sure feel of his hands on her bare skin. No one had touched her, not like this, with kindness, almost with tenderness — not since her mother died. Tears burned behind her closed eyelids. Her heart burst open. She loved Tyler Wilkes.

"Open your mouth, Carrie." He had his fingers on her lips, pressing softly, persuasively. "Let me see what I can see. Open up, that's my girl."

His smile shattered her. She almost — almost — obeyed.

She batted his hand away and ran.

"Wait!"

He grabbed her shoulder before she could go three steps and pulled her around to face him. His hands weren't so gentle now. "What is it? Carrie, why are you frightened? *Tell me.*"

All she could do was stare at him, miserable, both hands pushing against his chest.

"Listen to me, I want to *help* you. If I can't, I'll find someone who can. I know a doctor in Baltimore, he specializes in ailments of the larynx and the vocal cords, he could — Carrie, wait —"

She twisted away, too quick for him this time. She started to bolt for the house — and skidded in her tracks when she saw Artemis in the opening door, poking his head out and scowling at her.

"Were you planning on making supper tonight? Get inside, girl, *now.*"

He looked more than mad, he looked suspicious. Forcing her body to relax, Carrie made herself turn around and give Dr. Wilkes a friendly, casual wave. He stood stock-still, watching her. Then he said her name, quietly so Artemis couldn't hear, in a tense question. But of course, she couldn't answer. She waved again, turned, and fled.

7

Carrie could hardly believe she was here. In fact, the louder the music played and the more crowded the fire hall got, the more unlikely it all seemed. But she was here, all right, dressed in her old yellow pinafore, patched blouse, and worn-out shoes, trying to become invisible against the farthest wall of the fire hall at the Wayne's Crossing Annual Spring Heel-and-Toedown. Wondering what in the world had possessed her to come.

She must not have been in her right mind. It hadn't been her idea, that was for sure. It was Eppy's fault, really, because she wouldn't take no for an answer. Carrie had spent the day taking care of the four little Odell girls while Eppy went to Chambersburg to visit her mother, and when she came home she'd insisted that Carrie go with her and Frank to the dance. Nothing Carrie had done had made the least bit of difference. Eppy looked sweet and gentle, and people who didn't know her made the mistake of thinking she was a docile, even a meek sort of person. Ha! She didn't have a meek bone in her body. Most people did what she said, just to avoid getting bullied, and more often than not Carrie was no different.

Still, she might have disobeyed her tonight, considering how much she hated public gatherings or any other occasion, even church, that gave people a chance to look at her and whisper about her. She guessed she would never understand what was so interesting about a person who couldn't talk, or why people hadn't gotten used to her by now. Being mute had set her apart from the day she and Artemis had come here four and a half years ago, and she hadn't helped any by being shy, private, and nearly always alone. Things were better now that she was through school — adults didn't torment her the way children did, and by now most people had figured out that she was harmless. Except for a few, though, no one had much to do with her. That was partly her fault, because of her bashfulness and isolation, and partly Artemis's fault. Nobody liked him, and when they thought of him, naturally they thought of her, too.

But tonight she'd let Eppy browbeat her into coming, and the reason wasn't because she was too shy to stand up to her. The reason, silly and exciting and all but unmentionable, was the secret hope that if she came, she might see Dr. Wilkes again.

Eppy caught her eye just then — she was dancing with Mr. Odell, in a green Mother Hubbard that didn't hide from anybody the fact that she was in the family way — and Carrie waved and sent her a big smile back. She put a lot into the smile, to set Eppy at ease; otherwise she was just as likely to leave Frank where he stood, march over, and demand to know why Carrie wasn't having fun. Sometimes, as much as Carrie loved her, Eppy was a trial.

"Well, hi, Carrie."

Spring Mueller smiled at her, even gave her a friendly pat on the arm. She had her friend Sarah Staples with her, who nodded to Carrie and then went back to scanning the dance floor. "I'm surprised to see you here," said Spring. "I don't believe I've ever seen you at one of these dances before."

Carrie smiled, shrugged, nodded. She found her notebook and wrote, *My first time.*

"Mm." Spring barely glanced at the note; her attention had already wandered. The two girls reminded Carrie of kingfishers hovering over a fast-moving stream, trolling for prey. Spring had on a pink and white flowered dress Carrie knew she'd ordered out of a catalogue. She was the lawyer's daughter — too rich to ever have to make her own clothes. She had yellow-white hair she wore in ringlets, with little curls on her forehead that were always neat, round, and perfect. If Carrie lived to be a hundred, she could never get her hair to look like that.

"I mean to *do* something with my life," she was saying to her friend Sarah, continuing a conversation they must've started earlier. "Not just marry the first boy who asks me and then settle down in Wayne's Crossing." She turned slightly. "I was just telling Sarah that I've been accepted at the Whitson Teachers' College, Carrie. I'll be leaving in July, to stay with my aunt in Harrisburg until the fall term. I'm *terribly* excited about it. Educating young minds is my calling, I truly do believe."

Carrie smiled, trying to communicate congratulations. Spring smiled back, even as she flicked a glance at her that Carrie had seen before: an up-and-down once-over that pitied and dismissed her at the same time. Just then Walter Baugh tapped Spring on the shoulder and asked her if she cared to dance. Walter's father owned Baugh's Pharmacy. Spring excused herself prettily and went off with Walter, and a few seconds later Sarah wandered off, too. "Bye, Carrie," she remembered from twelve feet away, calling over her shoulder. Carrie lifted her hand, but Sarah didn't see, she'd already turned away.

117

Why was being alone in a crowd so much worse than being alone by yourself? Nobody was looking at her — why should they? — but if they did they'd see she was alone, and then they'd either think, *Well, what else?* or they'd feel sorry for her. Either way, she didn't think she could stand this much longer.

If she forgot about the people and just concentrated on the music, she could almost enjoy herself. Through the bobbing heads of the dancers she could see the band, the "Blue Ridge Shufflers." It consisted of Mr. Dattilio, the barber, sawing on a fiddle; Max Hummer playing the banjo; Chester Yeakle, the shoe, boot, and harness repairman, dancing by himself while he squeezed an accordion; and — most wonderful of all — Miss Essis, the Sunday school teacher, sitting in a chair and stroking the most beautiful music out of a great big harp between her knees. Carrie's toes began tapping; she closed her eyes and let the lively melody come right into her, the same way she could let birdsong or the sound of wind in the trees flow into her whole body. How *pretty* it was — how lucky Mr. Dattilio and Miss Essis and the others were to be able to make music whenever they liked. She thought of the time when she could sing, when she and her father had sung "Nellie, Don't Let Me Down" at the top of their lungs, while he drove the wagon to the next town they were going to live in. Her mother would say, "If you two don't stop that screeching, you'll paralyze the horse." But before long she'd join in, too, and in the end they'd all be laughing and singing as loud as you please.

The music stopped, and Mr. Dattilio called out that the Shufflers were going to take a little break. Couples started drifting off the floor. Carrie saw Eugene Starkey with Teenie Yingling; they were holding hands. And here came Eppy, heading straight for her and looking put out about something. Carrie put on another bright smile, anticipating what the something was.

"Carrie Wiggins, you haven't moved from that spot since you got here! How do you expect to have any fun if you don't mingle? Now's a good time, now that the band's taking a rest."

Eppy only meant to be kind, but oh Lord, this was *awful*. With her arm held tight so she couldn't slip away, Carrie let Eppy drag her around two sides of the empty dance floor. They had to stop every few feet so Eppy could greet friends and chat for a minute. She did her best with each group to include Carrie in the conversation, but of course it didn't work. It didn't seem like such a hard notion to grasp, not to Carrie — why couldn't Eppy see that a person who couldn't talk could never "mingle"? She wanted to disappear, fall through the floor and get swallowed up and never be seen again, she hated, hated, hated this . . .

She heard the warm, rumbling sound of a man's laugh, and the skin on her arms got tight and began to tingle. He was here.

She had to give Eppy's hand a little jerk to get her to let go, so she could turn around and look for him. There he was — beside the punch table in the corner. He wore a dark brown coat over tan trousers, and a yellow shirt with a white collar. Ordinary clothes, but they looked anything but ordinary on him. They were richer-looking than other people's clothes, that was one thing. But mostly it was the way he stood, strong and tall and graceful, and the easy, confident way he moved that set him above all the other men she'd ever seen. He had one hand in his trouser pocket, and he was using the other to gesture with. Whatever he was saying was making the half-dozen men gathered around him laugh and grin and slap each other on the shoulders.

"Why, there's Dr. Wilkes," Eppy noticed, hearing all the hilarity. She caught Carrie's arm again and started toward the men. Carrie wanted to hang back, but Eppy squeezed her way right into the middle of the knot and said how do you do to everybody.

It was clear to Carrie that they were interrupting a purely masculine conference of some kind. She recognized most of the men; they said hi to Eppy and nodded to her. But when Dr. Wilkes smiled, looked her straight in the eye, and said, "Hello, Carrie," a jolt of excitement streaked through her like an electric shock.

"So anyway," Hoyle Taber said, sounding impatient. "Tell what it was like charging up that hill, Doc. Bet you pinked plenty of them Spaniards. Come on, tell it again."

"Oh hell, Hoyle," Dr. Wilkes laughed, "you could tell it yourself by now."

"Well, Ed here hasn't heard it, or Taylor either. Come on. Doc. You're runnin' up San Juan Hill, minus your horse because it drowned swimming ashore, while the ship's band was playin' 'There'll Be a Hot Time in the Old Town Tonight.' "

"That's right —"

"And Roosevelt wouldn't ride his horse because he wanted to walk with his men, sweatin' like a pig in his yellow mackintosh."

"He walked with us from Daiquirí to Siboney, that's right. And —"

"And you slept on your ponchos in the hundred-degree heat, beatin' off red ants and mosquitoes, eatin' fried mangoes, and drinkin' fire-boiled coffee and black market rum."

"Who's telling this story, Hoyle?"

"You are, Doc. So, go on. You routed 'em at La whatever it was, and then —"

"Las Guásimas. We didn't rout them, we survived an ambush and outlasted them." Carrie thought his wide, handsome mouth got a fixed look to it, and his eyes, which had been laughing before, turned somber. "Hamilton Fish was the first man to die. A fellow named Capron was the second. Six more fell after that, all hit by high-speed Mauser bullets. Thirty-four troopers were wounded before it was over. We buried our dead the next day in a common grave."

Nobody said anything for a minute.

"Okay, but get to the part about the charge," Hoyle urged. "Teddy's on his horse, even though the bullets are rainin' down like — like —"

"Rain," Dr. Wilkes continued obligingly. He folded his arms. "Thousands of them, ripping down in sheets through the grass and the reeds. We couldn't see the Spanish snipers up in the palm trees because their uniforms were green and their powder was smokeless. There wasn't any cover except the mosquito bogs. We kept waiting for the order to charge, men taking hits everywhere around us." He got that odd expression in his eyes again and looked straight at Hoyle. "Bucky O'Neill took one in the mouth, about a minute after he bragged to his mate, 'The Spanish bullet ain't made that'll kill me.' It blew the back of his head off."

Even Hoyle got pale for a second. "Okay, but then Roosevelt says charge, and that's when you gave 'em hell."

Carrie thought Dr. Wilkes looked exhausted all of a sudden. He dredged up a half smile for Hoyle, though, and said, "That's when we gave 'em hell. We just kept coming, crawling up the grass slopes, pounding and pounding, until they could see we weren't going to go away. When we saw them jumping out of the trees and running, we knew it was over."

"And you took a shot in the leg, but you kept on running."

"I what?"

"Didn't you? And when you got to the top, the trenches were filled with Spanish corpses, and the rest of 'em were runnin' away like ants. And our guys —"

"When I got hit, Hoyle, I didn't do any more running. It was a glorious victory, but it got celebrated without me."

"Oh, yeah. Okay, but you *heard* what happened afterward."

"Yes, I heard. Eighty-nine Rough Riders died that day. We lost more men than any other regiment in the cavalry."

"And then Santiago surrendered without a fight," Hoyle insisted. "Right? Come on, Doc. Finish it."

But Dr. Wilkes pushed away from the table where he'd been leaning and stood up straight. "You finish it, Hoyle," he said shortly, but still smiling. "You tell it better than I do anyway." He gave Hoyle a slap on his scrawny shoulder. "Besides, I'm parched from all this bragging. I need some punch — that is, if Stoneman hasn't already spiked it."

That brought a relieved-sounding laugh, and the group of men started to break up.

The Blue Ridge Shufflers had returned and were tuning up their instruments — a pretty kind of music all by itself, thought Carrie. Eppy let go of her arm and went straight over to Dr. Wilkes, who was standing by himself now, drinking a glass of punch. *Go over with her,* Carrie ordered herself; *maybe he'll talk to you.* But she couldn't make her feet move. *Carrie Wiggins, you are the backwardest, bird-heartedest mouse brain in this whole town!* The story he'd told had moved her, at the same time it had made her feel silly, for until now she'd been as guilty as Hoyle Taber of wanting to believe that the war had been nothing but glorious, thrilling, and splendid. So she was a ninny as well as a mouse brain.

Maybe she could write him a letter. Except for her spelling, she was good at letters. She could thank him for his bravery and for the sacrifices he'd made for his country. She might even confess that she hadn't realized before how little "glory" there might be in a brutal, bloody battle, even if in the end your side won.

Well. She'd seen him, even heard him talk; the evening was a success. She could go home now, and tomorrow she really might write him a letter. She clasped her hands under her chin and stared hard at Dr. Wilkes one last time; this memory would have to last and last, for she might not see him again for weeks, maybe months.

Her fervent gaze wavered; her cheeks started to burn. Was he looking at *her?* No — behind her, surely; she stayed motionless and resisted the urge to turn around and see who he was smiling at. He and Eppy said last words to each other, and then he started walking toward her. She didn't move a muscle; she felt like a rock with moss growing on it. He *seemed* to have her in his gaze, but if she was mistaken, standing motionless as a stone was the best defense against humiliation she could think of.

"Hello."

He didn't say it in passing; he came to a full stop in front of her and didn't look around at anybody else. Her throat dried up; she felt herself blushing like a child. He was so tall, as tall as Broom; but unlike Broom he was strong and vigorous and athletic. *Elegant,* that was the word. His dark hair curled a little at the ends, and it was longer than the last time she'd seen him. She bet he thought he needed a haircut, and just hadn't had time for it. But she didn't think so; she liked that friendly shagginess, because it made him look young and carefree. And handsome. But he was already the handsomest man she'd ever known.

"It's good to see you. I didn't know you came to these things. Are you enjoying yourself?"

She nodded automatically. She was enjoying herself now.

"I've still got that puppy. Couldn't get anybody else to take him. He hasn't got a name yet. I've been calling him T.B.D., thanks to Mrs. Quick. B.D. for short."

She looked quizzical.

" 'That Blasted Dog.' "

She grinned, and covered her mouth with the knuckles of one hand, then fumbled in her pocket for her notebook. *You could name him Lou,* she wrote.

"Lou?"

126

Because of how you got him.

Now it was his turn to look puzzled.

Pressing down a smile, she scrawled, *In lou of payment,* and then blushed to the roots of her hair when he threw back his head and laughed, long and loud.

"Lou it is. I like it. Here, Lou!" he called experimentally. "It works. Thanks, Carrie."

She mouthed, *You're welcome.* Her delighted heart felt light as a feather.

He looked past her shoulder. She stood straighter, girding herself for good-bye. "Would you like to dance?"

She couldn't believe her ears. Her blood beat faster — it was celebrating. Unable to stop smiling, she shook her head.

"No?" He looked surprised.

She wrote in her notebook, *Thank you. I wish I could but I can't.*

"Why can't you? Your new shoes pinch your toes?"

She looked down at her tattered old brogans, then back up with a grin. *No,* she mouthed.

"You're tired because you were out all last night dancing?" he teased.

She wanted to laugh at that. She mimed *No* again.

"You don't like me?" His eyes twinkled; he tried to make his lips droop in a pout, but they

127

just wouldn't go that way.

That was the silliest guess of all. Carrie flushed, and bent her head over her notebook to hide her face. *I can't dance,* she wrote.

He scowled down at the message. Then he took the pencil out of her hand, closed it inside the notebook, and slipped them both back into her skirt pocket. "I'll teach you."

She stepped back, startled, heart pounding. While she was shaking her head, he reached out and took her hand.

"It won't hurt," he said in his low, thrilling voice. They were the same words he'd said that day he'd touched her throat and made her fall in love with him. "I'll show you right here. Nobody will look at us." He took her left hand and put it on top of his shoulder, still holding her right. When he slid his other hand around her waist and rested it on the small of her back, she had to quit breathing.

"This is a waltz," he told her. "This is the easiest dance of all. Nice and slow." She was only dimly aware of the soft, sad song the band was playing now. "Move back when I move toward you, Carrie. That's it, your right and my left. Now over here. Up again, that's it, and now over here, back where we started. Perfect. I think you're a natural at this. Shall we do it again?"

She beamed at him briefly, then frowned

down at her feet, concentrating. They were making a little box, she saw. She didn't step on his toes, but she was stiff, too conscious of herself, and of every inch of herself that was touching him. But gradually she started to relax, beguiled by the music, and his jokes, and his constant encouragement.

"Don't look at your feet anymore. Look at me."

She did — and immediately stumbled. He caught her and pulled her closer, until she could feel the whole front of his body against the whole front of hers. After that she never missed a step, which was strange because she completely lost track of what her feet were doing.

"This isn't so bad, is it?"

It's wonderful, she wished she could say. She never wanted it to end. His blue-violet eyes were dark now, and in them she saw the deep down kindness she was used to, and something else, too — an attentiveness that was new, a special concentration on her alone.

His lips curved in a smile, and all at once she realized she was staring at him like a dreamy-eyed fool. But she couldn't look away. She smiled back, giving her heart away. She didn't know a thing about flirting or hiding her real feelings. What did he think of her? She'd have given anything to know. Her impossible love welled up, like a creek flooding its banks — and finally she did have to look away, to save herself from drowning.

You are a melon-headed fool, Carrie Wiggins. He doesn't think of you at all. He asked you to dance because he's a nice man and you were standing right next to him. When this is over he'll forget about it, he won't lie awake all night remembering it, second by second, and tomorrow he won't think of every detail all over again.

He stopped moving. She came to an awkward halt in his arms, perplexed because the music was still playing. "What's wrong?" he asked, not letting go of her.

She had no answer, nothing to tell him. Even if she could speak, what would she say? *Loving you makes me sad.*

Then the music did stop. There was an odd little pause before he stepped away from her, letting his hands fall.

"Hello, Tyler. You haven't forgotten our dance, have you?"

Spring Mueller's radiant smile and china doll eyes were dazzling. Carrie blinked in their brightness, backing up fast. Mr. Dattilio was announcing something called the "Cumberland Reel," and parties of dancers were starting to form on the floor in some complicated pattern that dismayed her. Without waiting for Dr. Wilkes to say "Good-bye" or "Excuse me," Carrie spun around and escaped into the crowd.

Eppy caught her at the edge of the dance floor, before she could reach the door. "I can see you're having a good time now," she laughed, "because your cheeks are red as apples. Did you enjoy your dance? I don't believe I've ever seen you dance before, now that I think of it. That Dr. Wilkes, isn't he an interesting man? I've invited him for supper next week. Did you see Frank waltzing with Erma Stambaugh? I told him he had to, so she'd take out another ad for her restaurant in the paper."

She kept on gossiping about her friends and neighbors, cackling at her own jokes. At last she ran out of talk and craned her neck over her shoulder. "Lord, Erma's setting out the pies already, and I said I'd help. See you later, Carrie. You have fun!"

The minute Eppy was out of sight, Carrie turned and hurried out of the fire hall.

The night air was fresh and almost chilly after the hot closeness of the dance floor. She paused in the middle of the street and looked up at the sky. Tomorrow night the moon would be full; tonight it nearly was. A scuffling noise behind her made her whirl. There — a figure came away from the dark side of the building. She heard the fast crunch of gravel as the figure scrambled away and ran down the alley toward Wayne Street.

Broom — she knew him by his height and his rail thinness, but mostly by his peculiar jerky gait. She wanted to call out, tell him to stop. He'd been standing under the window, watching the dancers inside the hall, too shy or too scared to come in. Well, maybe it was just as well; he wouldn't have liked it. She knew people who would have stared at him — at best. Laughed at him and made fun of him at worst. But the thought of him standing out here by himself for who knew how long made her feel like crying.

She started up Broad Street, walking toward the moon. It was rising over High Dreamer tonight, outlining the gentle curve of the summit with a silver glow. Almost always the sight of the moon coming and going behind wispy clouds could take her out of herself and make her forget all the little worries and sorrows she might be carrying. Not tonight. She was full of some strange, unnameable feeling, bursting with it, and it was so heavy on her that even the beautiful night sky couldn't touch it. She heaved a troubled sigh and turned her face up to the moon, eyes closed. If she could bathe herself in its cold silver rays, as if it were the hot golden sun, maybe it could make her feel peaceful.

"Hey, Carrie, hold up!"

She whipped around. Eugene stopped running and walked the rest of the way toward her. Swaggered, more like, hands in his pockets, chin jutting at that smart-aleck angle; but when he got to her, he was still breathing hard. She could smell the alcohol on his breath.

"You going home so soon? I saw you before, but I was with somebody and couldn't talk. I've never seen you at a dance before. You didn't come with anybody, huh?"

She guessed he meant a man, and she shook her head. He looked "spiffy," as Eppy would say, in a checkered jacket with a vest, and his thick brown hair slicked down with oil.

"You look good tonight, Carrie. What kind of flower is that?"

Eppy had pinned it to her dress — she'd forgotten all about it. She held up two fingers, then touched them to her lips, to tell him it was a tulip.

"Huh?"

She put her hand in her pocket for her notebook.

"Never mind, it don't matter. Come on, I'll walk with you a ways."

Before she could nod all right, he took her

hand. She was surprised, but she didn't draw away. They were friends, after all. Sort of. They went along quietly for a little ways. She began to think there was something he wanted to tell her, because he was so silent and alert. His huge hand squeezed around hers hard, and she could feel the nerves jumping. She was more than surprised when he pulled her to a stop under the street lamp at Truitt Avenue and took hold of her other hand, too. She'd never seen this earnest, watchful look on his face. His eyes were black, and for once there was no mischief or goading in them.

"You look so good, Carrie," he repeated, in a voice she'd never heard before either. "You're really pretty." Before she could think about that or anything else, he put both arms around her and kissed her on the mouth.

She was too startled to do anything except stand there and let it happen. Her first kiss. It didn't seem quite real; her brain wouldn't settle down enough to let her feel it. It's not too *bad*, she decided. His arms felt good around her, strong and secure, and it was nice to be hugged. His lips pressed too hard, though; surely a kiss ought not to hurt. His mustache was scratchy, and she could smell the wax he'd put on it. He had her arms pinned to her sides, but she managed to free one and lift her hand to his cheek, pulling her mouth away.

"Carrie," he muttered, still in that funny voice. He looked like he wanted to devour her. She pushed against his shoulder with her free hand, but he shifted his grip and kissed her again, and this time he opened his mouth wide over hers and licked her with his tongue. Her eyes widened in amazement. Then she felt his hand close over her breast, and amazement changed to shock. She started to struggle, pulling on his wrist and twisting her face away. He slid his wet lips along her cheek, making her shudder. Finally she got her other arm loose and pushed at him with both hands. With a grunt, he let her go.

His face changed from glazed to cocky while she watched. He put one hand in his pocket and jingled his change, grinning like a fox. "That's been a long time coming, hasn't it? I been saving it up for you." He stepped toward her again, and she moved back quickly, realizing he wanted to do it again.

"Evening."

They both whipped around. Dr. Wilkes was sauntering toward them down the middle of Broad Street. Carrie flushed hot as fire and hugged herself. Had he seen them? He must have! *Lord, take me right now, I'm ready to die.*

"Evening, Doc," Eugene said, casual as anything. "On a call or something?"

"Not tonight." He was watching her carefully. "Everything all right, Carrie?" he asked, just as casual.

"Everything's fine." Eugene stepped sideways, closer to her. Their arms touched, and she shied away. "Anything we can do for you?"

"You could let Carrie speak for herself."

Eugene gave a fake-sounding laugh. "Well, that'd sure be a good trick, wouldn't it?"

Maybe it was the light, but she thought Dr. Wilkes looked angry. But he sounded nothing but pleasant when he said, "You left the dance so quickly, Carrie, you didn't give me a chance to ask if I could walk you home."

She could not believe her ears. Eugene couldn't believe his either, because when she glanced at him his mouth was gaping open like a carp's. Both men were looking at her, waiting for her to do something. She put her hand on top of her head, staring between them, floored by Dr. Wilkes's offer — and aware that if she accepted it Eugene's feelings would be hurt. Even though he hadn't treated her in a gentlemanly way tonight, and even though he'd hide the hurt behind nastiness and bad temper, she didn't have it in her to embarrass him. But she couldn't go with him, either.

He solved her dilemma for her. Maybe he

saw her answer in her face before she knew what it was going to be herself, because he didn't wait to hear it. "Yeah, you go on with the doc, that's a good idea. I got somebody waiting for me anyway, so I better get going." He smirked at her, and winked at Dr. Wilkes. "You know how women get when you keep 'em waiting." He backed up a few steps, gave a cheeky salute, and slouched off down the street in the direction of the fire hall.

Carrie didn't know where to look or what to do with her hands. Dr. Wilkes wasn't feeling very comfortable either, she could tell. Sometimes it was a blessing, not being able to talk. She couldn't decide if this was one of those times or not. Something needed to be said, but even if she was the chattiest girl in Wayne's Crossing, right now she didn't think she'd know what it was. She was relieved when he said, "Well, Carrie," whatever that meant, and started walking toward the mountain.

They went along for a long time in silence, even after the street lamps gave out and there was nothing to light the way except the moon. Try as she might, she couldn't fathom just what kind of silence it was. She'd gotten used to Dr. Wilkes's easy, lighthearted conversation, designed, she knew, to set her at ease. When she shot secret glances at him, she saw him frowning and looking straight ahead, and all she could think was that he'd seen her and Eugene kissing, and it had put him in a bad mood. She still wanted to die — that he might think her a light sort of girl made her burn with embarrassment — but she also wanted to know why, if he disapproved of her now because he thought she was loose-moraled and easy, why he'd gone to the trouble of walking her home. No man had ever done such a thing before — Broom didn't count. What was he thinking of her right now?

The track they were walking on curved between long pastures and fragrant fields; the smell of turned earth mingled with the faint scent of a distant skunk. The sky to the east was invisible now; Dreamy Mountain blocked it out, dark and somber and lovely. The fields gave out, and the last of the wild cherry fencerows; the scents of bittersweet and elderberry gave way to honeysuckle and pine. When they came to the bridge over South Creek, Carrie stopped.

Resting her notebook on the handrail, she wrote — hard, so he could read the message in the bright moonlight — *I'll go on by myself now.*

"No, I'll go with you," he insisted — rather shortly, she thought.

No, but thank you. Too far for you. I'm used to it.

He scowled. "You shouldn't be out by yourself this late. What does your stepfather think? Doesn't he mind it when you're out alone at night?"

She almost laughed. She sent him a look, but in her notebook she just wrote, *No.*

He muttered something, one side of his mouth twisting in disapproval. She thought he looked disgusted, and her spirits sank even lower. "I'll go with you," he repeated.

She shook her head vigorously. *No. Thank you. You might get a call — somebody sick.*

He read that, and put the notebook back on the railing. "All right, then," he said after a long time.

Another pause. The low, bubbling rush of the creek below the wooden bridge sounded cheerful and indifferent. A scuffling in the brush along the far bank might be a ferret, or maybe a weasel, and in the distance she could hear the eerie wheeze of a barn owl. Gradually the realization struck her that Dr. Wilkes had something to say, but for some reason he was having trouble saying it.

She wrote in her notebook, *What?*

He bent close to read the word, and when he'd read it he almost smiled. "I'm not sure how to ask you," he said.

She scribbled again.

" 'Just ask,' " he read out loud. He pulled

on his earlobe. "All right. I saw you with Eugene, just now. I thought — I couldn't tell if you were in difficulty or not. I didn't mean to interrupt — something. If I butted in where I wasn't wanted, I apologize."

Carrie went pink again. How to explain? What had happened was new to her — a man's touch, a man's interest in her as a woman; she didn't know the words to describe it even to herself. She wrote, *Never mind*. Lord, what a stupid thing to say! *Eugene*, she wrote — then crossed it out. She handed the notebook over, feeling idiotic, knowing that "Never mind" didn't really get to the bottom of things.

He set the notebook down with a little slap. "Did you like it when he kissed you?"

She felt so relieved by the directness of the question, she shook her head violently — and was astounded when, for the first time since he'd found her in the street, Dr. Wilkes smiled. For the life of her, she thought he looked glad. An amazed warmth spread through her. A miracle might be happening. Dr. Wilkes might care for her.

She smiled back, lit up with hope and a fledgling joy. She couldn't write what she was thinking. So instead she showed him. She put her finger to her lips, then reached out and touched it to his.

He looked floored. "You want *me* to kiss you?" he guessed.

Every ounce of her courage went into the slow nodding of her head, with a little left over to keep her from burying her hot face in her hands.

"Carrie. Listen."

But he didn't say anything after that, and the awful truth of what she'd done hit her like a fist. She got one long, panicky stride away before he caught her, first by one arm, then the other, and turned her back to face him. She'd never thought he could do a cruel thing, but he was making her look at him, making her show all the stupid, stupid shame she felt. *Let me go,* she begged him, *don't look at me.*

"Carrie, wait. No, listen." Now he had her face in his hands, holding her still. "Believe me, because it's true — there isn't anything I'd rather do than kiss you."

His face blurred because her eyes were swimming, but she was acutely aware of the soft brush of his lips on hers and the warm whisper of his breath on her cheek. She closed her eyes, feeling her heart pound and her blood race. A minute passed and she pulled back, thinking it must be over now. But he kept his hands on her face, touching her cheeks and her lips with just the tips of his fingers, and then he put his mouth on hers again.

This one was different. Better. He held her closer and his mouth pressed harder; she thought of Eugene's kiss for half a second, then forgot about it. Dr. Wilkes stroked the back of her neck and slid his fingers into her hair, cradling her head while he kissed her and kissed her. She held onto his arms and tried not to shake, all the while a million different feelings streamed through her. His mouth glided to her jaw and then her throat. "What is that?" he whispered. "That sweet smell. It's right here." She felt his lips move at the back of her ear; his deep inhale sent a delicious shudder through her whole body.

She couldn't stop trembling. She made a blind, one-handed grab for her notebook, to answer his question.

A low laugh rumbled in his throat. "Tell me later," he murmured, and kissed her mouth again.

She slipped her arms around his neck and pressed into him. Her lips parted under his. He drew his breath in with a sudden hiss and pulled back.

Oh — *now* it was over, she realized, and tried to steady herself, get her feet on the ground again. Breathing hard, she gazed up at him, searching for a clue to what it had meant to him. But his face was a mystery, she

142

couldn't read it. She took his hand from her shoulder and laid it against her cheek; she kissed his fingers, then his warm palm.

He pulled his hand away — gently — and she understood that kissing was all right with him, but cherishing was not. She took a step back.

"Yes," he said in a low voice, "you'd better go. It's late." She started to turn. "Carrie." He rubbed his neck with one hand. "I —" She waited, watching him. "I beg your pardon. That should not have happened. It was entirely my fault. I'm very sorry."

She fumbled for her notebook, wretchedly aware that he must be sick and tired of waiting for her to write her little notes. She shouldn't write anything — she should run — she'd made a fool of herself tonight as many times as she could stand.

She scribbled in haste, tore out the page, and thrust it into his hand. Without waiting for him to read it or — worse, worse — say anything back, she turned and walked off fast. But she thought of her message all the long way home. *I'm sorry you are sorry. It was so lovely to me. Good-bye.*

8

"You're sayin' bring 'em all?"

"All."

"All *six?*"

"And bring your husband, too."

"Willis? Hah! Now I know you're kiddin' me, Doc."

He wasn't, but he could see her point: Willis Haight was snoring on his back in a patch of sunlight on the Haights' falling-down front porch, passed out from corn liquor, and apparently it was no uncommon occurrence. Getting him and his six children to come down off the mountain for diphtheria inoculations understandably struck Mrs. Haight as a joke.

Tyler gave her a bracing pat on her mammoth arm. "I'll see you next Tuesday afternoon — that's when I'm doing vaccinations. In the meantime, speak to Willis again about the new well. As long as you're using the old one, you can expect Bad and the others to get these intestinal ailments again and again. And they might not recover as easily as Bad did."

He bent over the sleeping two-year-old

with the unfortunate nickname. Bad was quiet now, but a few hours ago he'd been convulsing with a temperature of 105. Castor oil, two enemas, and continuous bathing had settled him down; salol and bismuth had finally put him to sleep.

"I can ask 'im till I'm blue in the face, and he'll still say we ain't got money for a new well."

"He'll have to find it somewhere."

"And we can't keep askin' Carrie for spring water."

Ty straightened. "How's that?"

"Carrie Wiggins brings buckets o' water from her place sometimes, but if her pa found out she'd catch it. Heck — if Willis found out *I'd* catch it." Mrs. Haight hitched seven-month-old Gracie higher up on her huge, apron-covered hip and blew a flutter of dirty hair out of her eyes. "I reckon we could use the crick till Willis thinks of something. And that's just what I need, Dr. Wilkes, one more extra chore to do around here." Her baleful glare conveyed the clear implication that this was all his fault.

He began to put his medicines and instruments back into his case. "I'm sorry, but I don't know what else to tell you. The well's bad, and it's making your kids sick." He glanced around the dirty, cramped cabin.

Over the course of the long afternoon, he'd gotten used to the smells of garbage and sewage, dirty linen and unwashed bodies; but the clutter and filth still shocked him, even though the Haights were hardly the first — and not even the worst — mountain family he'd visited whose house looked more suitable for pigs than human beings. Mrs. Haight sewed her scabby, undernourished children into their "winter clothes" every November, after which they wore them day and night, without bathing, until she "cut 'em out" in March. There were no screens on the windows, no ice, no sanitation. The miracle was that the Haights weren't all dead, or sick constantly instead of only half the time.

"Ma! Ma! Hey, Ma!"

Harried mothers had a wonderful way of ignoring their children. Gillie Haight kept yelling at his mother from the doorway until Tyler was ready to ask him what he wanted himself.

"What?" Mrs. Haight finally barked, straightening up from wedging the baby between two pillows in the center of the sprung couch. Immediately the child started to wail.

"Look what Carrie brung."

"What."

"Come an' look."

"I said *what*."

146

Gillie pointed at something out of sight on the porch. "Great big kettle o' berries."

"Well, bring it in, don't just stand there. Shoot. Never mind, I'll do it myself."

The floorboards shook under her thunderous footfalls. Tyler understood the dietary causes, but it still amazed him when he encountered people as grossly overweight as Mrs. Haight, in families so poor they had barely enough food to keep from starving.

"Is Carrie here?" he asked Gillie, who was poking a finger at the screaming baby.

"Nuh uh."

"Where is she?"

"Gone home."

"When was she here?"

"Huh?"

"Was she here just now?"

"Yuh." He scratched his rear end unselfconsciously. "She seen your buggy and writ a note. Took off."

"She wrote a note?"

"Yuh." The blank look in his vacant face sharpened with glacial slowness. At last he reached into the pocket of his filthy, hand-me-down dungarees and withdrew a folded piece of paper.

Exasperated, Tyler all but snatched it out of his grubby hand. But the sight of Carrie's loose, graceful scrawl had him smiling to himself before he'd read the message.

Dear Dr. Wilkes,
    Yesterday Artemis stepped on a nail at the mill and it looks bad but he won't have a doctor. Since you are here and so close, would you please pretend you are stopping by in a friendly way and then look at his foot if he says you may? Thank you for your trouble.
                                Sincerely yours,
                                Carrie Wiggins

Hoyle Tabor had rented Tyler a mule today instead of a horse. It wasn't Poison, but the animal was almost as lazy and dim-witted. As a consequence, Tyler had plenty of time to think about Carrie on the half-mile journey between the Haights' cabin and the Wigginses'.
    He'd never had any intention of touching her that night at the bottom of Dreamy Mountain. He thought of the kiss, of how it had gotten away from him at the end, and of her bittersweet note afterward. What a callous lout he'd been, to kiss her and then *apologize* for it. But she'd misunderstood his apology. It wasn't the kiss he'd been sorry for — that had been nothing but a pleasure; in ten days he hadn't quite gotten it out of his mind. What

he'd meant to apologize for was leading her to think there could be something between them, something serious. There couldn't, of course. He liked her; he'd never met anyone remotely like her; he was attracted to her. All the same, a romantic relationship was out of the question. Carrie was barely more than a child, and they had nothing in common. They were worlds apart in every way, there was no conceivable future they could share — but exchanging intimacies on a bridge in the moonlight must have conveyed a very different message to her.

He'd tried to correct his mistake afterward, but all he'd done was hurt her. *I'm sorry you are sorry. It was so lovely to me.* To him, too — but that was beside the point. He'd had no right to take advantage of her innocence and her loveliness, and then insult her by apologizing for it.

The sturdy little cabin came into view; it was situated in a cluster of pine trees behind an ancient, crumbling stone wall. Today he would set things right with Carrie, Tyler promised himself. Return their relationship to the pleasant, casual footing it had been on before he'd spoiled it. She'd been his friend, after all, albeit a shy, reclusive one, and until now he hadn't realized how much he'd enjoyed their friendship. Today he'd repair the damage. He pulled the slow-footed mule to a halt in front of the cabin's tidy, slightly sagging front porch.

The door was open; Carrie appeared in it a second later, neat as a pin in a faded pink dress with a high white collar. All her clothes had a homemade, handed-down look; he suspected she was the original seamstress and she handed them down to herself, with alterations, time after time as she outgrew them. She'd tied her reddish hair up in the usual careless knot on top of her head, from which a few thick strands had fallen and now hung on her shoulders. Her serious face was a study: she looked worried, nervous, guilty, and glad to see him all at the same time.

He felt like a conspirator himself. "Miss Wiggins!" he called out, springing down from the buggy. "I was hoping to find you in. I've a message for you from Eppy Odell." He stood in front of her in the doorway and said in a loud voice, "She told me she spoke to you about sitting with her children one day next week. Well, now she says to tell you she won't be needing you after all, she's not going to — wherever it was she was going."

Carrie looked impressed, and under the concern in her sober gray eyes he detected a hint of amusement. She mouthed, *Thank you,* and he couldn't resist reaching for one of her hands and giving it a quick squeeze. Her smile was instantaneous and dazzling. Whatever constraint was between them melted away as if it had never been; with a queer twist of pleasure, he knew they were friends again.

She gestured him inside. The small cabin was sweet-smelling and spotless, as it had been the last time he'd visited. This time he noticed a curtained alcove to the right of the front door, and through the curtain, a narrow, quilt-covered mattress on top of a bench. With a slight shock, he realized it must be where she slept.

Her stepfather was slouched in a chair at the scuffed wooden table, one leg propped up on another chair beside him. "Mr. Wiggins," Tyler greeted him, with a feigned note of surprise. "How are you today?" *Resembles an ape,* Stoneman had said. An exaggeration, but there was something undeniably simian about Artemis Wiggins's hulking, long-armed, hair-covered physique. And Carrie lived with him in this cabin on terms of domestic intimacy, cooking his food, washing his clothes, suffering his surly, disagreeable company day after day. The thought was unsettling; something perverse lingered around the edges of it, something close to obscene.

"I've been better," Wiggins growled from his chair. He had bright black eyes, but the brightness came from skepticism and distrust, not good humor.

"Oh?" Tyler made no move toward him and kept his glance away from his propped-up foot. He had the uneasy sensation that protecting Carrie's innocent ruse was more important than he'd known. More important than it should be.

He could almost hear the creaky turning of suspicious wheels in Wiggins's brain as he stared between Ty and Carrie, undecided. At length he crossed thick arms across his block of a chest and said belligerently, "Since you're here, you might as well take a look. At my foot," he specified impatiently when Tyler looked dumb. "The Lord'll heal me in His own time, but I guess there's no sin in letting one of His minions hasten it along."

"You've hurt your foot, have you?" He came forward, wearing the grave and modest demeanor he and Stoneman liked to brag to each other they'd perfected. He couldn't wait to tell Stoneman he'd been called a "minion" of the Lord. "Yes, I see. A puncture wound. How did you do it? Miss Wiggins, would you mind going out to the buggy and getting my case?"

The wound was clean — he could thank Carrie for that, he felt sure — and a simple perforation, fairly deep but non-purulent and uncomplicated. While he waited for Carrie to fetch his case, he glanced around the cabin, taking unwilling note of its sparseness and poverty, its almost pathetic neatness. His gaze fell on a stack of worn-looking notes on the table beside him. Carrie's distinctive handwriting caught his attention. They were messages, he saw, thumbing them surreptitiously. "Are you going out?" said one; "Supper now?" asked another — homey, commonplace inquiries and announcements she must use over and over. They depressed him.

"Mr. Wiggins, have you ever asked a doctor to look at Carrie?"

"Why?"

He stared. The question had to be facetious. "Because she can't speak," he answered slowly.

Artemis rested his bad foot on his knee and hunched forward, squinting at his wound. "No, I ain't taken her to no *doctor*. The girl's affliction is the will of the Lord, and no *doctor* can change that."

"You must be joking," Tyler shot back, forgetting his bedside manner. "You can't seriously believe it's God's will that your daughter spend the rest of her life cut off from the world, locked up in a cocoon of silence that a good throat doctor could probably —" He broke off when he heard Carrie on the front porch. Common sense told him he couldn't win this argument, especially not in his present frame of mind. When he calmed down he'd speak sensibly to Wiggins, out of Carrie's hearing, and convince the son of a bitch that occasionally doctors actually *implemented* the Lord's will.

He cleaned the wound and put a light gauze bandage around it, then set about filling a hypodermic syringe with fifteen hundred units of tetanus antitoxin. "Lucky I happen to have this with me," he mentioned conversationally. "I don't usually carry it, but I was visiting the Sussmans last evening — their hired man fell on a pitchfork in the —"

"What's that?" Artemis barked, finally seeing the needle.

"It's for tetanus. It's —"

"You're not sticking that in me. No, put it away! I'm telling you, I won't have it!"

Tyler laid the syringe on the table and leveled a speculative eye at Wiggins. Children always balked at needles, but occasionally adults did, too. Most just feared the pain, but a few objected on quasi-religious grounds — like Hoyle Taber and his distrust of pills because they weren't "natural." He could see a self-righteous lecture coming from Wiggins about the arrogance of doctors and the will of the Lord. To forestall it, he folded his arms and asked calmly, "Have you ever watched tetanus run its course through a human being, Mr. Wiggins? It starts with a little stiffness in the throat muscles, a little yawning, some difficulty in swallowing. Pretty soon the lower jaw becomes spasmodically fixed — that's why they call it lockjaw — and after that the spasms spread to the face, then the neck, the trunk, and finally the whole body. The pain is indescribable. The victim looks like he's grinning, or screaming. He can't move his head or his neck, he's *locked* in place. Sometimes he's bent backward at the waist, frozen that way. But his mind's clear the whole time. What finally kills him is exhaustion — that's if he doesn't strangle to death because of the chest spasms. If he makes it beyond ten days, his chances of surviving increase. It's not something you'd wish on a dog, Mr. Wiggins, and I can virtually guarantee it won't happen to you if you'll agree to let me stick this little pin in your arm for about three seconds. What do you say?"

He said yes, with little grace and no gratitude, and after the injection he lumbered out of his chair and hobbled toward his room. "I'm going to sleep, I want peace and quiet," he snarled without turning, and banged the door shut behind him.

"Give him one of these when he wakes up,"

Tyler told Carrie with a sigh, measuring out four fifteen-grain doses of calcium bromide. "It'll keep him quiet. Another tonight and one in the morning. He'll limp for a few days, but I expect he'll be good as new by the end of the week. If you should notice any of the symptoms I described, come and get me immediately."

For the first time, he noticed her agitation. She had both hands over her mouth; when she lowered them to nod, he saw a haunted, abstracted fear in her face that struck him as extreme and inappropriate in the circumstances.

"I'm sure he'll be *fine*," he repeated. "The tetanus injection was just a precaution, Carrie."

She nodded again, still pale, and walked over to the kitchen area, where she took down a clay jar from a shelf over the cook stove. When she began to take money out of the jar, he closed his case with a snap and said, "That's not necessary. You asked me to come over 'in a friendly way,' and that's what I did."

She shook her head firmly. Marching back to the table, she snatched up a small slate and a piece of chalk and started scribbling.

"Oh hell, give me a dollar and be done with it."

She glanced up sharply, surprised by his tone. But she gave a brisk nod and went back to the jar. Apparently there were no bills inside; it took forever for her to count out a dollar in nickels, pennies, and a couple of dimes. His impatience gathered; he didn't want the money, and the longer it took her to parcel it out, the more he wanted to stuff it all back in her damn jar. When she finished, she needed both hands to give it to him. He slid the heavy pile of coins into his pocket, annoyed with the lopsided sag it made in his coat.

But Carrie looked so pleased with herself, he had to smile — which brought on one of her rapturous smiles in return. He was beginning to find them unsettling. On the chalk tablet she wrote, *Do you have to go right away?*

He had no office hours today, and no other patients to see on the mountain. "No, not really. Why?"

Would you like to see something?

"What?"

A secret, she wrote. Her eyes flashed with excitement. *A surprise.*

He folded his arms and grinned at her. "How can I resist?"

Whirling, she all but skipped out the door. Tyler picked up his bag and followed more slowly, intrigued.

At first he thought they were going for a

walk on the meandering deer trail that led into the woods behind the cabin's outbuildings. But before long, with nothing to mark the sudden turnoff except an immense weathered boulder, Carrie plunged into the trees and set off eastward on a rugged, overgrown path he wouldn't have noticed if she hadn't been guiding him. They climbed steeply for about forty feet and then turned south, following approximately the wandering track of a stream. Trees bordered it on both sides; he recognized sassafras and oak and hickory, but the names of the others eluded him. Carrie, of course, would know them all. After a little while they left the stream to cross a boulder field seamed with deep ravines and thick, tangled undergrowth.

The three o'clock sun blazed hot in a corner of the cloudless sky; Tyler took off his coat and slung it over his shoulder, and marveled at the fluid, long-legged grace with which Carrie moved across a terrain that had him panting and sweating to keep up with her. He didn't even have his bad leg to blame it on, either, because his wound had troubled him hardly at all in the past few weeks. It chafed a little to be bested by a slip of a girl, who moved like a healthy young doe through the stony woodland.

When they reached the top of a narrow

ridge, the going got easier. There was even a path he could see, although just barely. The trees thickened, became all but impenetrable at precisely the point where the vague sometime-path gave out.

They stopped. Carrie faced him, breathless with something other than exertion. He had never seen her so animated before, so lit up with anticipation. Or so beautiful — there really was no other word for it. "See-through skin," his mother called that kind of fragile, almost translucent complexion, the cheeks deepened by excitement now to the shade of rose petals. She put both hands over her shining eyes, then took them away and looked at him expectantly.

"Close my eyes?" he guessed. She nodded; he obeyed. He felt her hand on his arm, light and shy, and a second later she reached around his back to take his other arm. Urging him forward, moving beside him, she led him in a direction that seemed to be straight into the trees. He felt a branch slide past his shoulder, a leaf graze his cheek. She went slowly so he wouldn't stumble, holding his arms in her gentle grip; he had the sense sometimes that she was pulling tree limbs out of his path and guiding him around unknown obstacles on the ground.

They stopped. Her hands dropped away. A

moment passed, and then he felt the light touch of her fingers on his cheek. He opened his eyes.

Color and light. The dazzle of a butterfly flickering in and out of sun bars. Bird music. Water rushing. The perfumed odor of flowers.

An involuntary sound escaped him, a heady, wondering laugh. He had to blink to believe his eyes. Carrie clapped her hands once and gripped them tight under her chin, beaming at him, tense with excitement.

She'd made paradise. Everywhere he looked there was beauty and brilliance and wild, exquisite symmetry. He was in a glade, a natural clearing surrounded by woodland, where flowers burgeoned and flourished in banks and cunning tiers on every side. Colors dazzled — violet and lavender, amethyst, azure and jade, scarlet, gold, lemon and ivory. And lush, voluptuous greens, aquatic, almost overwhelming. Luxuriant ferns and emerald-green mosses sprawled under the low branches of mountain laurel and wild azalea, while overhead the sun filtered down through the spines of a colossal spruce in slants of dusty golden light. Somewhere close by a stream splashed and bubbled, cooling the air with the smell of damp earth.

He began to pick out details, to separate

one object of inexpressible loveliness from the rest. "Those, Carrie," he said, soft-voiced, "what are they?" He pointed to a low, cloudy heap of pink, orchid-like flowers. *Dragon's mouth*, she wrote in her notebook. "And those?" *Indian pipe*. She knew them all, and scribbled their names as fast as he could ask them: wild columbine, meadowsweet, bloodroot, mayapple, lady's slipper, wild geranium. The ancient limestone boulder was a chair, he realized, the long fallen pine with its bark peeled away a bench. She'd strung a canvas hammock between a wild apple tree and a chestnut oak; from it her view of the sky would shift with the seasons, lush and tangled in summer, stark in the winter. Bird houses, bird feeders, bird baths stretched the length of one leafy wall of the glade; the feathered tenants had scattered to the treetops, but birdsong sounded from everywhere, excited and — he fancied — welcoming.

Carrie wrote a new note — *This is my hospital!* — and now he could see that what he'd taken for a low stone wall was a line of handmade shelves; and under the cover of fresh pine boughs he'd thought belonged to a tree lay a rubber tarpaulin that sheltered half a dozen wooden boxes, elevated from the ground with piled stones. Beds for her patients?

Yes. She slid the nearest box toward her and separated the two boards covering it far enough apart so he could see inside. A bird squawked and fluttered its wings — startling Ty and causing him to jump back. Carrie laughed her silent laugh. *Grackle,* she wrote. *Broken beak.*

"What are you doing for it?" he asked, fascinated.

Nothing — feeding him till he heals by himself.

"Who's in here?" He pointed to the next box.

Her smile dissolved. *Gray squirrel. Dying. Old age? Just keeping him comfortable.*

He felt like comforting her. "And this one?"

She shook her head and gestured, indicating that the other boxes were empty — her hospital was sparsely populated today. She wrote, *Sit down!* and led him to a tree stump with a canvas-covered pillow on it — the seat of honor, he could tell, in her beautiful glade.

Beside him on a wooden crate rested something small under a covering of gauze. Carrie peeped underneath the gauze, and Ty caught a glimpse of three sky-blue eggs in a nest of twigs. She shook her head and carried the nest to the limestone boulder, which still caught the full afternoon sun. *Robins,* she scrawled for his benefit. *Orphans.*

"Will they hatch?"

162

I don't think so. Still — The note trailed off with a hopeful flourish.

He watched as she rummaged among her shelves and drew out a cloth-covered object, which proved to be a heavy green glass. She disappeared with the glass in the direction of the splashing stream or brook, and returned with it full of water.

He took it from her gratefully and drank it down without stopping. "That's the best glass of water I've ever drunk in my life," he told her, with perfect truth, and had the pleasure of watching her blush.

She sat down on the wooden crate and folded her hands in her lap. Her cheeks were still flushed with excitement; she couldn't seem to stop staring at him. She began to write something in her notebook, but he stopped her by saying, "Carrie, it's beautiful. It's perfect — exquisite. Heaven couldn't be any more glorious than this place you've made. Thank you for showing it to me."

The last blush was nothing compared to this one — hot, crimson, disconcerting. She bent her head, and the message she wrote was even more disconcerting. *No one has ever seen it before. You are the first* — she crossed out "first" — *the only one.*

Her lovely, guileless gray eyes gave too much away. What could he say to her? "Then

I'm honored as well as grateful," he managed lightly. Her brilliant smile took his breath away.

She jumped up and went to her rock-shelves again. She brought him two composition books this time, holding them out diffidently.

"What's this?" He read aloud the title printed neatly on the cover of the first one — *"Record of Specimens of the Wiggins Museum of Natural History"* — and looked up at her in amazement. Pride and self-doubt warred in her face, stifling the laughter on his tongue. Opening the book, he saw that it was a naturalist's sketchbook arranged according to the seasons, full of studies and field notes on birds and flowers and all manner of creatures — the original subjects for which were presumably stored away on her stone shelves.

"Carrie, this is wonderful!" The pencil drawings were simple but sure-handed, careful but also spontaneous, revealing genuine talent as well as unmistakable love of her subjects — moles and turtles, caterpillars, frogs, butterflies and hornets, a bat, a chickadee, acorns and horse chestnuts, witch hazel, tansy, primrose, and cinquefoil — and snowflakes. All meticulously labeled, many by their Latin names, with a short text indicating where the specimen had been found and

sometimes a note regarding its discovery —
"Little hoary bat, *Lasiurus cinereus.* Flew into
house at dusk. A. killed it before I cd. catch it
in coffee can."

The second book was entitled, *Wildling
Care Log,* and it was nothing less than a detailed casebook record of every sick or injured
bird, mammal, or reptile she'd ever treated in
her hospital. "Incredible," he marveled, skim-
ming the lucid accounts of a barred owl's BB
shot wound, a baby skunk's bout with pneumonia, a crow's broken wing. Her last patient
had been a sparrow hawk, he read; she'd put
his fractured leg in a cardboard sling, fed him
bugs and kept him quiet for two weeks, and
set him free last Thursday, "good as new."

She was saving the best for last. *I'm writing
a book,* she confided, shy, eyes shining; she'd
retrieved it from a special place on the stone
shelf, wrapped in double layers of canvas.

"Another book?"

She shook her head. *A Real Book.* Re-
suming her seat beside him on the wooden
crate, she hugged the book to her chest
briefly, then wrote in her dog-eared notebook, *Would you care to see it?*

He almost laughed again. "Of course."

She placed it on his knees with great care.
" 'The Summer Birds of the Appalachians in
Franklin County, Pa.,' " Ty read aloud.

165

"Well, well." Her anxious face moved him in a strong, unexpected way. "This is quite an undertaking." She nodded heartfelt agreement and began scribbling a long message while he leafed through the pages of her masterwork. Again he was impressed with her skill, and captivated by her unique style. The drawings were much more detailed than the ones in her specimen book, and so was the painstakingly printed text accompanying them. Under an astonishingly graceful portrait of a cardinal, she'd written, "The male cardinal [*Richmondena cardinalis*] glows like a live coal among the blossoms of a white dogwood [*cornus florida L.*]."

She waited for him to turn the last page — she'd completed about thirty sketches so far; at least a dozen more were half-finished — and then handed him her notebook. *I showed it to Mr. Odell, he's the Editor of our paper, and he said he knew someone who might print it like a real book and even pay money for it!!! He's also helping me with the writing, for I can't spell, and sometimes my sentences get all TANGLED UP.*

"So many of the pictures are unfinished," Tyler observed, leafing through the pages again. "Did they fly away?" He knew her too well to believe she'd kill the birds in order to study them — even though that was the common practice of most ornithologists including the great Audubon.

Yes, flew away, she wrote. *Or else too far away to see.*

Too far away? "You have binoculars, don't you?"

She shook her head.

He stared, dumbfounded. "You mean you draw them without field glasses, just — *looking* at them?"

She nodded. *Warblers are the hardest. They all look so much alike.*

He was speechless, and presently she penned another note.

Do you know if Mr. Roosevelt is a bird-watcher? I read that in a magazine.

"Yes, it's true. He's got a place in Virginia called Pine Knot where he goes to relax and look at birds. He's a great conservationist, you know, always making speeches and writing papers about irrigation and reforestation and land reclamation."

Carrie's awed face made him smile. *Do you know him? Are you FRIENDS?*

"We're acquainted, yes."

From the war?

"That, and we share an alma mater." When she looked blank, he explained, "We went to the same college. He was about ten years ahead of me, of course."

167

She took her bird book back, shaking her head, still impressed. After she'd stored the book away, she sat down beside him again, clutching her knees, smiling up at the sky. She hunched her shoulders in a beguiling gesture of wonder and contentment, then recommenced staring at him. He'd never known anyone whose emotions were so close to the surface, or so easily understood. Happiness transformed her, made her look truly beautiful. Her normally solemn eyes were dancing, and the straight, elegant mouth that rarely smiled was smiling now with fragile elation.

What he had to tell her would break the mood, but that couldn't be helped. It was important. The longer he knew her, the more important it became.

"Do you remember the doctor in Baltimore I told you about, Carrie? The otorhinolaryngologist?" He couldn't help smiling at her consternation. "A specialist in ailments of the throat." Ignoring the flicker of alarm in her suddenly frozen face, he said quietly, "I want you to go with me to see him." Predictably, she shook her head and kept shaking it. "Why not?" A premonition of failure caused him to say the words too sharply.

She flinched at his tone and wrote in her notebook, *$$*.

"Then you'll have to let me help you. If you

won't take money, I'll lend it to you. Dr. Peterson is a friend of mine; I've explained the circumstances to him, and I can promise you he won't charge much." Through all of this she continued to shake her head. She was as stubborn as her stepfather, and he'd had enough. "Why?" he demanded. "Why won't you let anyone help you?"

Her hand shook slightly when she wrote, *No use.*

"*Why* is it no use?" More head shaking; she looked everywhere but at him.

"Damn it, don't you *want* to speak? What's wrong with you, Carrie? Are you *happy* this way?"

She bolted up, spilling notebook and pencil on the ground. He caught her before she could twist away and held onto her wrist. She was ashamed of her tears; she kept her body angled away from him so he couldn't see her face.

He was ashamed, too. "I'm sorry, that was a stupid thing to say. I was angry — I want to help you and you won't let me. Don't cry anymore." He put his handkerchief in her hand. Her face in profile was tragic and forlorn; he silently called himself a number of vulgar names and touched his fingers to her damp cheek. "Just say you'll think about it — seeing the doctor in Baltimore. Will you? Just consider it, and decide later. All right?"

She nodded miserably.

"It's not for me," he said inarticulately. "Do you think I don't like you the way you are? Carrie — it doesn't matter to me if you can speak or not. I can't imagine liking you any more than I do now."

Fresh tears; her cheeks went bright pink with distress. When she made another move to escape, he put his arms around her and held her still. "Carrie, Carrie," he murmured, "no more crying now. This is not such a tragedy. Don't run away from me."

She stopped straining and let him hold her, but she kept her face hidden against his chest. "What is it about being with you that makes me say stupid things, do you think?" he wondered, feeling the tears and her warm breath through his shirt. She moved her head negatively. "No, I don't know either," he said, deliberately misunderstanding her. She looked up, anxious to tell him he didn't say stupid things, and he took the opportunity to stroke the wetness from her cheeks with his thumb. He recalled the stupidest thing he'd ever said to her, that he was sorry for kissing her, and thought about kissing her now. Not a good idea. Reckless and ill-advised. Why, though? The reason had been clear and immediate not long ago, but just now it seemed to have lost its urgency. Carrie's lashes were dark and spiked from crying; beneath them her troubled eyes shone like wet silver. She had her hands on his shoulders, light and trusting. She sighed, and her soft breath fanned his throat like a caress.

He put his lips on her forehead. A compromise kiss, brotherly, consoling. Except that a minute passed and neither of them moved; he didn't think either of them was breathing. He kept his hands still, but under them he was acutely conscious of the bend of her waist and the long, sleek curve of her hip. She wore no corset, no stays — he knew that from the last time they'd done this. The same faint, flowery scent he'd noticed that night on the bridge came to him now. She wore it behind her ears, and he thought of putting his lips there again. But no — that wouldn't be brotherly. His fingers flexed and spread across her back.

She lifted her head. He made a mistake then: he looked at her mouth. Wide, generous, the top lip tipped up ever so slightly; a subtle architectural miracle of sweetness and proportion. He gave up. They both wanted it. He kissed her.

Immediately all the reasons why it wasn't a good idea came back to him. How could he have forgotten how seductive her shy, tentative eagerness was? Her arms came around

171

him; her lips moved, opened, as if she found his mouth delicious and she wanted more. He gave it to her, sliding his tongue slowly around the passionate oval her lips made, and the tasty wetness of her aroused a hard, aching need he had almost managed to convince himself wasn't there.

He moved one hand into her hair, the other between her shoulder blades, pressing her close so that he could feel her breasts. She seemed to melt, go liquid in his arms. He stopped kissing her long enough to look at her. Her mouth and the incredulous, undisguised pleasure in her eyes defeated him again. He whispered, "Carrie, I wasn't going to do this." And then, "I wish you could say my name."

She wished it, too, she told him with her tremulous smile. His fingers played over the silk of her cheekbone, her jaw, her parted lips. He toyed with the redgold wisps of hair at the side of her face and traced the shape of her ear, intimately aware of the soft tremor that quivered through her with his touch. She stood on her toes to brush her mouth to his in a thankful, reciprocal kiss, her eyes open and alive. In return, he skimmed his lips across hers, back and forth, varying the pressure and the friction until she gave a breathy gasp and pushed her fingers into his hair. Holding his head in a gentle vise, she kissed him with all her new knowledge, tenderly, greedily, unreservedly. Blind need had him sliding his hands down her back to her buttocks. She didn't resist; she strained against him when he pulled her up, in instant sympathy with his craving to be closer.

Through the heat, he had a glimmer of an insight that what had begun with pleasure was going to have to end in torture, and the longer he kept this up, the harder it would be to stop. But that was later — a minute later, maybe; all that mattered now was pressing his palm against the fullness of Carrie's breast, her soft, perfect breast, and watching the flutter of her eyelashes and the faintly agonized pout of her lips. He traced ardent circles around the hard little point her nipple made through her cotton dress, murmuring her name, layering warm, openmouthed kisses against her lips.

Why wasn't she helping him? Why did he have to end this lovely torment all by himself? It was supposed to be — always had been, for him — the other way around. But she was shaking, she was lost, she was taking soft, hungry bites of his lips and kneading his shoulders with her clenching hands.

It hurt, physically hurt, to pull away and take his hands off her. And she was literally coming up for air, drowned-looking, her wet mouth bruised, round with surprise. "I won't say I'm sorry this time," he got out hoarsely. "I wasn't the last time either — that was all rot. But, Carrie — can't you see we have to stop?"

He didn't know what he expected, but it wasn't a simple nod and a huge, blinding smile. He brought his hand to her cheek, unable to help himself, and she closed her eyes, still smiling; after a moment she turned her lips into his open palm.

Then she stepped away and looked at him expectantly. "Yes, I'd better go," he thought to say. "I don't like to be away from the office too long unless I'm on a call." Funny he was just remembering it, though.

She'd recovered much faster than he; he still felt like a starving man chained inches out of reach of a banquet. Was it possible she didn't *know* what they'd just barely avoided? It would explain her unnerving composure.

"You'll have to show me the way back," he told her. She nodded readily and reached for his hand. "Thank you for bringing me here. It was a beautiful gift. I'll think of you in this magical place you've made, Carrie, and it'll make me smile."

Her eyes misted. She touched her lips to his fingers in the lightest, swiftest kiss, then pulled him out of paradise and into the darkening woods.

9

He ought to have waited for Carrie to come home. Pulled that cane chair with the broken bottom into the shade on her slanting front porch, sat down, and waited for her. If he had, he'd be cool and comfortable now, feet propped up on the peeling porch rail, sipping from a glass of cold well water. Not panting for breath, using a beech sapling to help haul himself up another steep, slippery, rock-mined ridge, at the top of which he would look around and see nothing, absolutely nothing, that looked familiar. That was the worst — not the bugs or the sweat or even the dull throbbing in his thigh. The worst was the sneaking, gathering suspicion that he was lost.

Wouldn't Frank Odell love this? If he didn't print it in the *Clarion*, he'd *threaten* to print it, and Tyler could already picture the headlines he'd think up to torture him with: "Doctor Caught Dreaming on Dreamy"; "Jungle War Hero at Sea in Woods of Pa."

He muttered an earthy cavalryman's curse as his toe snagged in a low-growing vine and he came close to pitching face first onto the nonexistent path. His shirt was sticking to him and he was ready to murder everyone, including Carrie, who had ever told him it was always ten degrees cooler on the mountain than it was in the valley. It might be a *little* cooler, he'd concede that, but the bug quotient was about ten times higher. On a steamy June afternoon, there really wasn't all that much difference, he decided sourly, between getting lost on High Dreamer and getting lost in the Cuban jungle.

He halted beside a fallen log and mopped his face with his handkerchief. His leg hurt and the log looked inviting; he sat down. Every rich green vista was starting to look the same, but didn't that line of pine trees forty feet dead ahead have a familiar shape? He remembered trailing behind Carrie toward a thick barrier of trees just like that. She'd stopped in front of it and made him close his eyes. If he was right, her secret glade was just beyond those trees.

And she'd better damn well be there, because if she wasn't he was going to feel even stupider than he did now. Not to mention disappointed.

He was aware that he wasn't behaving like a man trying to discourage an innocent girl's unrequited crush. He'd told himself he was only visiting Carrie so soon after their last meeting so that he could give her a present — his old army field glasses. But the truth of the matter was, he wanted to see her.

See her. Not touch her. Touching her was dangerous and irresponsible. It dismayed him that on two separate occasions he'd kissed her without intending to, and that the last time he'd come close to not stopping with kissing. It wasn't fair to Carrie, and he cared for her too much to hurt her by raising unrealistic hopes. It was past time to recall that he was a responsible, professional adult, not an undisciplined boy. He was calling on Carrie today — if he ever found her — for only two reasons: to give her a gift, and to let her know that Dr. Peterson had set a date for a consultation.

It hadn't been easy nailing Peterson down. He was a busy, overworked specialist, and it was only after several letters and a bullying telephone call that Tyler had convinced him he had time to examine a mute country girl whose problem might not even be physical.

Getting to his feet, he stuffed his handkerchief in his pocket and hefted his field glasses back onto his shoulder. The longer he stared at the pine trees in the distance, the surer he grew that they marked the secret boundary line of Carrie's hospital. If she were there, she'd be tending to her flowers, or maybe one of her wounded wildlings. She would smile her enchanting smile when she saw him, and write him one of her ingenuous notes. He'd ask for a drink, and she'd bring him an icy-cold glass of water from the stream he'd heard but not yet seen. The binoculars would amaze her; she'd try them out immediately, and she'd be overcome with gratitude to him for giving them to her.

He was counting on that. His conscience didn't bother him a bit that the field glasses were as much a bribe as they were a gift. She was afraid of something, but he wasn't going to be put off this time by her odd, incoherent excuses. One way or the other, Carrie was going with him to Baltimore to see Dr. Peterson.

The woodchuck was still peering at her. Beady-eyed, flat head resting on his forepaws on top of the big boulder. Unblinking, perfectly still. The scratching of Carrie's pencil and her occasional sighs didn't bother him. She'd already sketched him twice; it was time to get out of the hammock and feed the rabbits. But she delayed, knowing he would disappear as soon as she moved, and she liked his company. She liked looking at his little round ears, his bushy tail, and his tiny black feet. Farmers down in the valley killed groundhogs, as they called them, every chance they got. *You're lucky you live up here on Dreamy,* she told her silent, staring friend.

High overhead in the dark spruce tree, a bird called. *You again,* Carrie thought, with more than a touch of frustration. For weeks she'd been trying to identify the bird, but he kept eluding her; try as she might, all she could ever seem to see of him was a flash of red feathers. He sounded like a robin with a sore throat, but she'd narrowed him down to either a scarlet tanager or a summer tanager. She was tempted to get up and try for another look now through the branches — but of course, if she did, her woodchuck would desert her.

Before he'd come, she'd been writing in her journal. Reading over the last page, she could feel herself smiling and her cheeks getting warm all over again with self-conscious plea-sure. "And then he kissed me on my fore-head," she'd written, "and all that sadness in me flew away like a startled bird. We stood to-gether so still and quiet, and I didn't know what he was thinking. He has eyes like wild hyacinths, and his lips are strong and firm — but so warm! And then — then — he kissed my mouth. I thought my heart would burst out of my chest, it felt so full. I don't have any words to say what it was like when he touched me, but it's a memory I will keep forever. And afterward he said he wasn't sorry. And he said my hospital is 'magical.' He likes me, I know it, and I will love Tyler Wilkes until I die."

Carrie closed her eyes and pressed the open journal to her chest, as if she could press the words into her heart. "Always," she vowed, feeling the love swell and rise like bread, until she couldn't contain any more. Tears wet her lashes, and she laughed and called herself a spoony goose. How could she cry when she was overflowing with happiness? For two whole days she had lived in a spell, lit up from the inside like a flame in a lantern. Could this be how other people felt *all* the time? No, of course it couldn't be. This was rare, special, and if everybody went around feeling the way she did right now, they'd never have time to be mean or sad or scared. Besides, there wasn't anybody else in the world like Dr. Wilkes (even though they'd kissed, she couldn't quite call him Tyler yet), so even people lucky enough to be in love with *someone* weren't in love with *him*. Which meant they couldn't be as happy as *she* was. Poor people!

She sat up suddenly, bubbling over with energy — and the woodchuck shot straight up in the air. In a scrambling rush, toenails skittering on the slippery rock, he vanished. "Oh, excuse me — !" But then she had to laugh because he looked so funny. And he'd come back another day.

She got up from the hammock and stored her journal away. She'd brought two biscuits, an apple, and a carrot for her hospital's newest residents: five baby rabbits. They could feed themselves now, thank goodness; giving them infant cereal every three hours yesterday and the day before had worn her out. Eppy had rescued them from her two oldest daughters, who'd found the nest in an empty lot and couldn't resist poking and playing with the babies until the mother rabbit disappeared and never came back.

Carrie kept them in an old bird cage when she was here, and in a box with a window screen and a rock on top when she was absent. Four inches long, that's how big they should be, she reckoned, before she could let them go. Sitting down on the dry moss, she reached through the bird cage door and lifted the littlest baby out carefully — jumping escapes were easy for them but a nuisance for her when she had to track them down and put them back. Holding the squirmy brownish ball on the flat of her palm, she judged him to be about three and a half inches from his twitching pink nose to his white cottontail.

Not much longer now, she told him, stroking between his petal-soft ears with her fingertip. *Sylvilagus floridanus* was his Latin name. In about two more days, she'd set him free. Not here, though — in the meadow by the bridge at the bottom of the mountain, because the hedgerows there would be much better for foraging than here in the dark woods.

Back you go. But she kept her hand in the cage so she could pet the others. *Oh, you like my biscuits, do you? Well, I made them just for you — don't tell Artemis.* She was surprised to hear herself laugh — even thinking about her stepfather couldn't spoil her happiness today.

Would Dr. Wilkes like to see the rabbits before she let them go? Maybe. But he was so busy, it wasn't likely he'd be coming up the mountain for a visit in time. Well — what if she took them to him? To his house some evening, when he was through with his work. Would he like that? She stared off into space, imagining it. He'd invite her into his kitchen and make her a cup of tea, like he had that night after Shadow died. They'd sit at the table and he'd talk to her, say things to make her laugh, and she'd write him a note telling him all about the rabbits. Maybe he'd walk her to the foot of the mountain when it started to get dark, and they could set the babies free together.

Carrie hugged herself, letting the wild delight surge through her again. She could remember, just barely, feeling this way as a child when something wonderful would happen — Christmas morning, or the time her father had said she could keep the calico kitten. Sheer happiness, absolute perfection. Now, for the first time in years, she thought of a song her mother used to sing. How did it go? It wasn't a hymn but it sounded like one, the tune slow and stately and almost sad, which made the joyful message all the sweeter.

"Sing out, oh my heart, all the love deep inside, like a lark raise your voice to the sky. Let delight fill you up till a drop overfills you, set the joy in you free and let it fly."

How her mother had loved to sing. And she'd had the prettiest voice, bright and clear and full of laughter. Not rusty like Carrie's. She cleared her throat and tried again. "Sing out, oh my heart, all the love deep inside . . ."

She stopped, caught her breath. The skin on the back of her neck went prickly hot, then cold. *Oh God.* Someone was here. But she couldn't move, couldn't make herself turn her head to see who it was. *Please, please, please, don't let it be him,* she pleaded in terror.

"Carrie? My God — Carrie?"

Dr. Wilkes! Clumsy with panic, she scrambled to her feet and whirled around to face

183

him. He moved slowly but steadily toward her across the clearing, shock in his eyes, one hand stretched out in a baffled, questioning gesture. *Oh God, help me!* she thought, in a daze of fear and shame. The rock shelf was at her back. She slid sideways, step for step with him, stealing toward the corner so she could run. He must've seen her plan in her face, for at the moment she reached the edge he lunged for her. She cried out, even though his grip on her arm wasn't painful. He said something — she hardly knew what, but she heard in his voice that he was bewildered, not angry. The message that she was safe almost penetrated the fog of fright blanketing her mind. But she squirmed and twisted and tried to run again, and this time he caught her hard by her elbows and didn't let go.

"Talk to me, Carrie. *Talk* to me, explain this to me. Hold still — damn it — I'm not letting you go."

She finally stopped struggling. But after that, for the life of her, all she could do was shake her head.

It made him mad. "Damnation, Carrie, I *heard* you. What the hell is going on?"

She started to cry. If she kept on shaking her head, there was no telling what he might do. So at last she said something — "Dr. Wilkes!" — in a hopeless, desperate whisper.

The first words she'd spoken to a human be-ing in five years.

His fingers softened on her arms. "Tell me," he said soberly. "Trust me."

She nodded, *I do.*

"I know you're afraid of something."

She shook her head violently; without thinking, she fumbled in her pocket for her notebook.

"No, talk to me, tell me why you've been pretending. Who else knows you can speak? How long has it been going on, Carrie?"

She couldn't tell him anything, of course. She wriggled out of his grip and took a step back.

"No, by God, you're not running away this time." He caught her wrist and held it too tight. Now he was angry, and she wanted to die. "You're going to stand there and explain it to me, all of it."

"No, I'm not." She barely murmured the words, meant nothing defiant by them, but her answer made him even angrier. "Don't be mad," she whispered. "I couldn't stand it."

"Don't be mad?" His voice made her quail. "What should I be, happy for you? Thrilled because apparently you've been playing a nasty little game with the people who care about you?" He gave her wrist a rough shake. "Just tell me why. Did you want us to feel

185

sorry for you? Was it some twisted way to get attention, make people —"

"Yes," she croaked, seizing on it. "Attention. People noticing me."

It was his idea, but now he didn't seem to like it. "No, that's not it. I don't believe you."

"Yes. Pity — it's close to love," she said wildly.

"No. No, you're lying."

"It's true, don't you see? I was so lonesome."

"Carrie, for God's sake, tell me the truth. Is that all it was? Because you were lonely?"

She nodded.

"Talk to me!"

"Yes! And you were nice to me, so it worked. Please — couldn't you forgive me?" She couldn't look at him; she could scarcely speak past the misery in her throat. But through her tears she finally saw his face harden, go from disbelief to dislike, and she knew she'd convinced him.

He let go of her wrist, and this time he was the one who took a step back. He was looking at her as if he'd never seen her before, and the cold disapproval in his eyes made her feel naked and dirty. "Well." There was a long, awful pause. "You're right — it worked. If you're telling me the truth, you must be pleased with yourself, Carrie, because you got

186

what you wanted. I didn't feel sorry for you before, but now I do." He took something that hung on a strap from his shoulder and laid it on the ground at her feet.

"Wait!" she cried when he turned away.

"Well?"

"If you would — oh please, if you . . ." How to ask? She twisted her fingers until they hurt.

"What is it you want?" he snapped.

"Don't tell anyone about me. I'm begging you."

He didn't answer; he just stared at her until it was hurtful to look at him any longer. She dropped her head and didn't look up until she knew from the dreadful silence that he was gone.

10

"He's not here. Can't you read? Didn't you see the sign downstairs?"

Yes, she'd seen it, a framed slate hanging on his office door: "Dr. Wilkes will return at ——." Nobody had filled in the blank. Carrie found her notebook and scribbled, *When will he be back?*

Mrs. Quick squinted her eyes in that distrustful but fascinated way some people took with Carrie because she couldn't talk. "Well, I'm sure I can't say. He got called away on an emergency." She pursed her lips, enjoying herself because she knew where Dr. Wilkes was and Carrie didn't; but before long she couldn't stand it, she had to gossip. "If you want to know, Emma Rindge's boy come galloping up an hour ago, yelling about his poor mama's appendicitis. *Appendicitis,*" she scoffed. "Anybody knows Emma's eight months gone if she's a day, and nobody there since old Rindge passed on except that Italian farmhand she hired to help out. *Farmhand.*"

She put her hands on her hips when Carrie kept her face a blank and didn't look interested. "What do you want with Dr. Wilkes anyway? Are you sick?"

Yes, she thought, *I'm sick inside, my heart's shriveled up to nothing.* She slipped the heavy leather case from her shoulder and handed it to the housekeeper.

"What's this?"

She wrote in her notebook. *Please give it to him.*

"What is it?"

After a long, motionless moment, while anger and grieving coiled inside her like garter snakes, she made herself write, *Binocyulers;* crossed it out, wrote, *Binoculers.* That wasn't right either. She thrust the paper at Mrs. Quick, embarrassed and defiant.

"Well, I can see that. What're you giving 'em to him for?"

Now, that was too much. Carrie made a sharp gesture with the flat of her palm and turned away, clattering down the wooden porch steps in her noisy shoes. Mrs. Quick hollered something after her, but she pretended not to hear. She wanted to stop and put the violets in her pocket on Shadow's grave, but Mrs. Quick would be watching and Carrie didn't feel like having anybody look at her right now. She went around the side of Dr. Wilkes's office and hurried up the half block toward Broad Street.

Mondays were quiet in Wayne's Crossing, which was why she always made it her shopping day. There weren't as many people on the streets and in the stores to look at her and speculate on her. Feel sorry for her. She blew her nose, amazed that she could still have any tears left after two days of doing hardly anything else except shed them. She couldn't help it, though; that Dr. Wilkes thought so badly of her that he believed she *wanted* people to feel sorry for her broke her heart whenever she thought of it. She'd lost her love, her dearest friend, and she couldn't seem to do anything about it but weep. But she put her handkerchief back in her purse and squared her shoulders, because she wasn't going to walk down Broad Street in the middle of the day with tears streaming down her face. People who already thought she was a little queer would decide she was completely crazy, and she didn't need any more of the kind of attention she already attracted.

"Hey, Carrie."

She looked beyond the cross street to see Eugene Starkey coming out of the drugstore with Teenie Yingling. Eugene grinned, showing the toothpick he had clamped between his big teeth, and waved to her. She waved back. He stood still, as if he was waiting for her to catch up, and she quickened her step. Teenie gave his hand a yank and said something in his ear. Just then the ice wagon turned off Broad onto Truitt, cutting off Carrie's view. When it passed, Eugene and Teenie had turned their backs on her and were walking away fast.

She was used to being snubbed, especially by girls, but that didn't make it sting less when it happened. She didn't want to talk to Eugene anyway, but it annoyed her that he liked to flaunt Teenie or some other girl in front of her every chance he could, trying to make her jealous. She *wasn't* jealous, but sometimes he could make her feel sadder and lonelier by showing off how much fun he was having with one of his girlfriends. She thought of the night he'd kissed her and told her she was pretty. He'd been drinking, of course, but that didn't explain everything. It was hard to say whether Eugene liked her or hated her, and sometimes Carrie didn't think he knew which it was himself.

She'd left Petey and the wagon in front of Eppy's house while she did her errands. As she turned the corner onto the Odells' quiet street, a familiar bobbing figure caught her eye. Going closer, she recognized Broom, bent double over an enormous trash can beside the curb. She knew what he was doing as soon as she saw the pile of tin cans on the ground at his feet.

She had to touch his raggedy sleeve to get his attention. When he straightened up, he smacked his head on top of the can. "Ow! Hi!" That fast, his pained expression turned into a wide, gap-toothed grin. "Hi, Carrie! I'm working! See? I'm hard at work."

She nodded, showing how impressed she was. Mr. Needy, who owned the metal salvage yard, was paying Broom a nickel for every hundred tin cans he collected. Carrie didn't think it sounded like a very good deal, but Broom was so pleased because he had a "job," she didn't have the heart to tell him.

"Guess what happened! I thought Mrs. Hawbaker's gate was scrap and I tried to take it, I *did* take it, and she found out and come after me! Mr. Needy was gonna pay a dollar, Carrie, a *dollar* for the whole thing, but in she comes runnin', carrying on, yellin' about her gate, her gate!"

Carrie made an amazed face.

"I thought it was *junk!* You seen that gate, Carrie? All bent and rusty and spokes gone and dirty and all?" She nodded, although she couldn't really picture Mrs. Hawbaker's gate. "So they made me take it back and put it where it was, and I could hardly make it stand up. And then Mr. Needy said I wasn't to look for nothing but cans from now on. Say, you

192

got any cans today, Carrie?"

She shook her head; she was saving some for him, but she hadn't thought to bring them down today.

"That's okay, I got plenty anyway. Listen, write down how many this is, okay?" She raised her brows, asking why. "Because, just because." He shuffled his feet and stuck his finger in his ear. "Sometimes I might get mixed up. Sometimes I might think I got more than he pays me for. That's what he says."

Carrie frowned, wondering if Mr. Needy was counting wrong on purpose. She counted the cans on the ground, and then the ones in the burlap sack Broom had already collected. She wrote *64* on a page of her notebook and handed it to him. She wished she could caution him about her suspicions, but she didn't know how — Broom couldn't read. But he would surely show his boss the paper and tell him all about how she'd counted the cans for him, and maybe that would make Mr. Needy think twice the next time about shorting him — if he was even doing that. Maybe he wasn't. Maybe Broom was the one who was counting wrong.

He started telling her about all the places where he'd found cans today and yesterday, and all the places he had in mind to try tomorrow. She listened as long as she could, but finally she had to go. She put her hand on his skinny arm. He shut right up and grabbed her into one of his fierce, jerky hugs. She hugged him back, feeling how pitifully thin he was. There was hardly enough meat on his bones these days to keep him standing up straight. She worried about him often, but she could never think of what to do to help him.

"Bye, Carrie! I'll see you!"

She waved until he was out of sight, and then she went through the high privet hedges and up the Odells' walk to the front door. It was open, as usual, and through it she could hear the sounds of chaos that were a standard, everyday thing in the Odell household. From the sweet cinnamon smells, she guessed Eppy was in the kitchen, making something with apples. Through the parlor door she caught sight of Charlotte, the oldest child, trying to play one-a-cat with a pillow instead of a puck. Upstairs, Emily and Jane were having a shouting match, and from somewhere in the back of the house Fanny, the baby, was squalling. All the Odell children had literary names, and Frank Odell said if the next one was another girl he was going to call her George. That had mystified Carrie until Eppy explained that George Eliot, who was a famous writer, was really a woman. For the child's sake, Carrie hoped Mr. Odell was joking.

There wasn't any point in knocking, nobody would hear, so she walked right in and started down the hall toward the kitchen. Charlotte saw her from the parlor. "Carrie!" she yelled, dropping the stick she'd been beating the pillow with and dashing out the door. Her sturdy, seven-year-old body almost knocked Carrie over. "I was hoping you'd come soon, I haven't seen you in *ages*. Do you like my dress? Mama made it so I could wear it to Gramma Odell's birthday party, but now I can wear it anytime I want. The party was lots of fun, we got to stay overnight, and Jane threw up in the bed. The next day Gram made fried pears for breakfast, and Jane threw up again, right at the table. Come on, Mama's making apple butter, and it's almost time for the tasting!"

Carrie let herself be pulled into the kitchen, where Eppy was standing in front of the stove, trying to stir the big iron kettle with one hand and hold Fanny with the other. As soon as Carrie took her, the baby stopped screaming.

"Praise God," laughed Eppy, pushing damp hair back from her forehead. "I'll never question the power of prayer again, Lord, and that's a promise. Carrie, you are a sight for sore eyes. That child's not wet, is she? She couldn't be, I just changed her ten minutes ago. Is this butter dark enough, do you think? It's been six hours. Charlotte, get *down,* I told you, before you pull that kettle over and scald yourself to death."

The baby wasn't wet, just cross, and Carrie had already coaxed a smile out of her by tickling her belly button. Wonderful smells came from the oven, where fresh biscuits were baking; soon it would be "tasting time" — an excuse to spread hot apple butter on warm bread and pretend to consider whether the apples were a rich enough brown or the cinnamon was overpowering the sugar.

Eppy gave the pot a final stir, then dropped into a chair at the big kitchen table, wiping her face with a towel. "I swear, this is the last time I put up apple butter in the middle of summer. What possessed me? Charlotte, move that chair over so I can put my feet up. Sit down, Carrie, I haven't seen you in weeks. What've you been doing?"

She tried to shrug, but it was hard with Charlotte standing behind her, hugging her around the neck. Eppy, who loved to talk, didn't wait for Carrie to fish out her notebook; she launched right into a recitation of all the Odell family doings in the last two weeks, including the trip to Chambersburg for old Mrs. Odell's birthday, progress on the renovation of the pantry downstairs into a tiny bedroom for Charlotte and Emily after the new baby came, the female typesetter Frank had hired last week at the *Clarion*, the string bean blight, Emily's new tooth, Jane's sleepwalking, and how hard the baby had kicked last night. "I swear, I thought I was going to fall out of bed. Frank woke straight up and said, 'What the devil was *that*?' "

"Gram says it's a boy this time," Charlotte told Carrie. "Oh, I hope, hope, hope so! I'm so tired of girls, I really, really hope it's a boy."

"We'll love it whatever it is," Eppy said automatically, as if it was something she'd said many times before.

Carrie looked down at the apple-cheeked child in her arms, thinking she could have a *hundred* girls and never get tired of them, or boys either. Would there ever come a day when she was so old, she wouldn't care that she had no children? She hoped so. But she couldn't really imagine it.

"And now Frank's talking about turning that old two-horse stable in the backyard into a study for himself. Can you beat that? He goes to his nice, quiet office every day of the week while I'm home with four and a half children, and *he* needs a study."

Carrie shook her head in sympathy.

"You'll stay to supper," Eppy announced,

getting up to stir the apple butter again. "Frank's coming home early, he *says,* so we can probably eat early. You can't? Why not?" She leaned over to peer at the word *Artemis* Carrie scribbled in her notebook. She scowled. "How is he?" Carrie lifted her shoulders and made a noncommittal face. Eppy said, "Hmpf," but nothing else. She never had a good word to say about Carrie's stepfather, but when her children were around she tried to keep her opinion to herself. Carrie wondered what she would say if she told Eppy that last night Artemis had gotten drunk on the front porch with one of his shiftless friends from the sawmill. She'd overheard them plotting mean things to do later to Willis Haight — burn his outhouse, trample his garden, kill his chickens — but they'd both passed out cold before the moon rose.

She stood up, reluctantly handing the baby over to Eppy.

"You have to go *now?* You can't even stay till the butter's done?"

"Please, Carrie," begged Charlotte, "can't you stay?"

No, she really couldn't, but it took a long time to persuade them. She'd only stopped by to say hi, and to let Charlotte and Emily know what had happened to the rabbits. She'd come prepared with a page-long explanation already written, telling how big they'd gotten, how smart the dark one was — their favorite — and when and where she'd let them go. She gave the folded paper to Charlotte, who took it and immediately ran off to look for her sister.

"What do you say, Charlotte?" her mother called after her.

"Thank you, Carrie!" she screamed back, and kept running.

"You look tired," Eppy told her at the door, jiggling Fanny on her hip. "Are you all right? Sure? I don't like the way your eyes look. Would you tell me if anything was wrong? I'm coming up there if you two don't quit!" she yelled over her shoulder. "Jane's still sick, and Emily's bored and can't quit pestering her. Dr. Wilkes says it isn't anything serious, so I'm not worried. Well — bye!" she called when Carrie turned away abruptly. "Come back soon, you hear me? Don't wait so long next time!"

Carrie waved to her from the wagon. Envy was a sin, but it was hard not to feel a pang of it when Eppy kissed her baby's fat cheek and disappeared into her noisy, sweet-smelling house. Was self-pity a sin, too? Probably. Then she'd try not to think about who was waiting for her at her own house. Try not to miss Shadow. Not remember that her hospital was empty today because the rabbits were gone, and the grackle, and the old gray squirrel. But sometimes she got scared when there was no one to take care of, no one to love. Petey was just a mule, and he didn't like it when she hugged him too much anyway.

She turned Petey off Broad and onto East Street, heading for the back alley between town and Stoops's field. Nobody would see her there, or nobody much. Maybe this sadness wouldn't last. Things could never go back to the way they were before she'd met Dr. Wilkes, because she would always love him and she'd always know that he didn't even like her. But some sick or wounded wildling would need her soon — she never had to wait long — and then she'd feel better. If that meant she was peculiar, well, there was nothing she could do about it. She had a heart, there was still love in it, and it had to come out somehow. She gave Petey's rump a swat with the reins and started the long climb up Dreamy Mountain.

"Hm. Ha! Hmmm."

Tyler looked up from the weak mixture of gin and lemon juice he was swirling in his glass and glanced over the kitchen table at Dr. Stoneman. "What does that mean?"

"Shut up, I'm not finished."

Tyler slid lower in his chair and leaned his head against the back, smiling tiredly. Stoneman must've driven his patients insane during examinations with his incessant humming and hrumphing. He wasn't examining Ty now — he was reading his paper on the etiology of erysipelas — but he was doing a good job of driving him crazy all the same.

He flexed his shoulders, trying to ease the ache between them. His day had begun at four-thirty this morning with Morton Bittner banging on the door, yelling that his wife was dying in labor. She very nearly was, but it was the postpartum hemorrhage twelve hours later that almost carried her off. Things got complicated when she remembered, somewhat belatedly, Ty couldn't help thinking, that her religious beliefs wouldn't allow her to accept medical treatment. Either luck or divine providence had intervened when she'd finally passed out from blood loss, and her distraught husband had lost no time in overriding her scruples. Now she was resting comfortably, with a clear conscience and a healthy new son named Tyler.

A happy ending, but the baby's namesake was tired to the bone. He'd quailed when he'd come home and found Stoneman leaning on the back porch railing, sipping gin from his flask in the pitch-dark. Ty didn't want a drink, and he didn't want to chat; he wanted to fall into bed and sleep until the sun came up. But Stoneman was going away in a few days, off to a Harrisburg sanatorium for an indefinite stay, so his nighttime visits to Tyler's kitchen were numbered. Trying not to sound grudging, he'd invited him in, and now he was waiting for Stoneman's unasked-for opinion on the manuscript Ty was about to send off for publication in next month's *Transactions of the Association of American Physicians.*

"Hmm," he intoned for the fifth or sixth time. "So."

"Hmm, so, what?"

Stoneman turned the last page and pulled his half glasses to the end of his beaky nose. "It must be good. I don't understand one word of it."

Tyler laughed. He didn't believe it, but if that was the tack Stoneman wanted to take, it was all right with him. "Do you want anything to eat? A sandwich, a glass of milk?" The old man's gray flesh hung on his bones these days like rags on a scarecrow.

He snorted and waved the suggestion aside, as usual. "Tell me, Doctor, do you like it here? Are you satisfied with the work you're doing in our little town?"

Tyler eyed him in surprise. "That's two different questions," he hedged.

"I'll take two different answers."

"All right. Yes. And no."

"Ha! Just what I thought."

Tyler held his glass up and peered through watery gin at the kitchen light. The subject of his professional dissatisfaction was one he'd put off thinking seriously about for months; he felt little inclination to confront it this very minute for Stoneman's benefit.

"Don't take this wrong, but I never did think you were cut out for country doctoring. I'm not saying you aren't good at it; you're better now than I was when I quit, and I did it for forty years. And if you repeat that to anybody, I'll call you a damn liar and sue you for slander."

"Your secret's safe." Ty grinned. "But I don't agree with you — I think you were a fine doctor." It wasn't a polite lie; he'd been here long enough to have heard a hundred stories about the old doc's tirelessness and dedication. If good doctoring were measured by devotion to duty, Benjamin Stoneman had been one of the best.

"I thank you for that." Stoneman's sallow cheeks turned faintly pink. He poured more gin into his glass and lifted it in a toast. "But you, now, you ought to be practicing in a big city, Washington or New York, treating high-society hypochondriacs for astronomical fees. You could join all the prestigious medical societies and boil yourself down to a specialty, like diseases of the right thumbnail or the anterior earlobe. Think how rich you'd be! *Richer*, I should say."

Medical specialties were another of Stoneman's reactionary pet peeves. But Ty was too tired to rise to the bait tonight; he got up and went to the sink to throw his drink away and pour a glass of water. "If you want to know the truth, I don't want to practice the clinical side of medicine anywhere anymore," he decided to admit. "If I did, I'd do it right here, because the need is greater and the life suits me. But the fact is, I don't want to be a country doctor *or* a city doctor."

"Well, what the hell do you want?" Stoneman's irritation came partly from puzzlement, partly from watching good gin go down the drain.

Tyler looked at him speculatively, gauging his likeliest reaction. "What do I want to do? I want to look for cures for diseases," he said combatively, "not treat the symptoms after they've already been contracted. I want to eliminate typhoid fever by finding out what causes it and then developing an antitoxin. And malaria and yellow fever and tuberculosis — they can all be prevented, we know that now, if we could find the bacteriological keys to their causes. That's what I want to do." He folded his arms, preparing himself for his colleague's cynical rebuttal.

But Stoneman disarmed him. "Then do it! You want to study epidemiology, is that it?"

"Yes."

"Then study it! I haven't any doubt that you'll succeed. It pains me to admit it, but you've got too good a mind to spend your life lancing boils and setting bones and delivering babies." He poked a stiff finger at the air to make his point. "A man with ideas has no business wasting his time treating sick people. The best that can happen is that once in a while you'll save a life. But truth is eternal, and besides that; it's got more applications."

Tyler almost laughed, he was so surprised. And gratified, and inexplicably moved. "If I didn't know better," he said gruffly, "I'd say you just gave me a compliment."

"You must be hearing things."

They smiled at each other.

Stoneman pushed his chair back abruptly and got to his feet. "You look tired, Doctor," he observed almost gently. "You ought to get more rest."

"Look who's talking." He stopped himself from reaching out for the old man's arm and helping him up. "When do you leave for Harrisburg?"

"Monday, ten o'clock train." He slanted him a sardonic look. "Think you'll still be here when I get back?"

"Of course I will."

"Maybe not. I might be up in that hawker's prison for months and months, and when I get back you could be long gone."

"Oh, I doubt —"

"Then again, they might ship me home in a pine box in a week or two."

"That's true. Or an urn. An urn wouldn't take up as much room in the boneyard."

Stoneman made a sour face. He hated it when Tyler undercut his morbidity by parodying it.

But Ty didn't miss the faint gleam of optimism in his emaciated countenance, hard as he tried to hide it. It had been like pulling teeth to convince him the Winslow Sanatorium had something to offer, not only because Stoneman's nature was deeply cynical but also because, as a physician, he'd arrived at the impartial conclusion that his time was up. He'd all but reconciled himself to dying, and resurrecting hope at this late hour was a responsibility Tyler didn't take lightly. All he could do was trust that Dr. Winslow knew what he was doing, and pray that he himself hadn't set his friend up for a tragic disappointment.

As if reading his thoughts, Stoneman rumbled, "I'm holding you personally accountable for my full recovery, you know. You and this Winslow friend of yours."

"Colleague, not friend."

"I'm sorry you told me he's on the 'cutting edge.' That's an expression I've never much cared for."

"Now, Doctor, squeamishness doesn't become you." He followed Stoneman to the door. "You know the first thing Winslow's going to insist on is that you get rid of that." He nodded at the flask Stoneman was sliding into his coat pocket.

He snorted; the very idea put him in a bad mood. "I should never have let you talk me into this. You know they make you sleep in little revolving shelters out in the open, all the doors and windows wide open? And they make you drink *beef juice* all the time." He swore softly but foully. "I'd rather die in my own town, where at least a few people know me, than up there with a bunch of spitting, hacking strangers." He started down the porch steps, ignoring Tyler's hand. "Turn the damn light on before I break my damn neck."

"Good night, Doctor."

"Hah."

"I'll see you before you go."

"Maybe!" His gaunt figure merged with the darkness and disappeared.

A low half-moon floated behind pink clouds and the fat leaves of the sycamore tree in Tyler's backyard. Leaning on the railing, he watched the fireflies flicker on and off, mirroring the flickering stars over his head. To his left, the soft outline of High Dreamer, vaguely breast-shaped, rose into a mist. Carrie lived about three-quarters of the way up, right about . . . there. He wondered if she was sleeping now, on that narrow bench behind the curtain in her little cabin. It was late; he hoped she was sleeping.

Stoneman's abrupt departure had taken the decision he'd been trying to make — whether or not to tell him about Carrie — out of his hands. Remembering her desperate plea for secrecy, he was glad now he'd missed the opportunity, even though the need to share the astonishing truth about her with someone, especially someone who cared about her, was still strong. But his anger was gone, dissipated in the night sometime between yesterday and today, and he'd spent most of the day asking himself *why* his first reaction to her amazing revelation had been indignation.

The answer didn't flatter him, which was why he'd resisted looking at it as long as he had. What it boiled down to was hurt pride. It had pleased him to be among the pathetically small number of people whom Carrie trusted; when she'd shown him her hospital and shyly confided that he was the first person to see it, he'd felt at least as much self-satisfaction as uneasiness. But discovering she had an even bigger secret that she had no intention of confiding in anyone, *even him,* had wounded his vanity. Simple as that.

The binoculars and the cryptic note he'd found tonight from Mrs. Quick — "Wiggins girl left this" — deeply distressed him. After the things he'd said, it couldn't have been easy for her to come here and return his gift. He could imagine her state of mind and the mix of her emotions when she'd encountered his surly housekeeper instead of him. Now all he could think about was seeing her and making her understand that he was *glad* she could speak, not morally outraged. He didn't care anymore what had compelled her to begin living such an intricate, life-involving deception; whatever it was, she'd suffered for it, and he'd callously added to her pain by scorning her. He had failed Carrie at a time when she had never needed him more, and the hours between now and the next time he saw her were going to be his penance.

Lou was scratching in the ivy at the side of

the house. It was very late, time to bring the dog in and go to bed. "Here, boy," he called. "Here, Louie, *come.* Come on, boy!" Lou ignored him, as usual. Whistling and clapping had no effect. Sighing, Tyler descended the porch steps, located the puppy in the dark ivy, snatched him up, and carried him back up the steps. It wasn't the dog's fault he wouldn't mind; Ty's schedule left him no time to train him. He should've found him a real home after Wiggins wouldn't let Carrie keep him.

He yawned, and Lou tried to lick his face. With his chin on the puppy's knobby head, he took a last look at the glimmering firefly spectacle, a last sniff of the flower-soft air. Tomorrow was another all-day inoculation day — he scheduled them every other Tuesday — but with luck he could be finished by five or six. He'd have a quick dinner at home, hire a horse from Hoyle Taber's livery. Then he'd ride up to Carrie's cabin on High Dreamer and make her his friend again.

11

But at seven-thirty the next evening, he was still vaccinating children, and by eight-fifteen he was too tired to do anything but fall into a chair in front of the cold coal stove and try to work up an interest in a leathery chicken pie Mrs. Quick had left for him in the icebox.

He was twenty-eight years old, in the prime of his manhood; all he'd done today was stick needles in the arms and buttocks of people under four feet tall. It infuriated him that he was exhausted from his so-called labors, and it frustrated him that he couldn't shake off the pitiful last vestiges of his disease once and for all. Even his damn leg ached — because it was raining. He felt like an old man with "the rheumatiz." When would he be whole again? The fact that he *was* improving, that every day he got infinitesimally stronger, brought him no consolation at all in his present mood. Each time he thought he was finally well, some petty setback inevitably occurred, proving he'd been deluding himself. He was sicker than ever of being sick, and "physician, heal thyself" was a gibe of Stoneman's with too much ironic significance to be amusing any-more.

Stoneman's sense of humor must have been at work when he'd told Tyler that Mrs. Quick was a good cook. He poked at the gluey, tasteless piece of pie for a few more minutes, then put his fork down and stood up — stiff-legged — to carry his plate back to the kitchen. Halfway there, he heard a knock at the back porch door. *No,* he vowed, grinding his teeth, *not tonight.* If that was Stoneman, he'd tell him he couldn't come in. Enough was enough. If it was a patient —

But the willowy, long-legged figure under the disreputable-looking umbrella wasn't Stoneman or a patient; it was Carrie.

"Come in," he urged when she hesitated, even though he was holding the door open for her. She wore the same plain blue frock he'd seen her in many times, but tonight she'd fastened a bouquet of wildflowers to the cheap lace collar. Her unruly hair, misted from the rain, stood out around her head like a springy halo. For all that she made a damp and im-poverished-looking angel, the sight of her filled him with pleasure and a vast relief. "Carrie?"

Still she hesitated. She stood on her toes to look over his shoulder. "Are you alone?" she asked in a raspy whisper.

"Yes, it's all right. Come in, I'm very glad to see you. If you hadn't come tonight, I'd have gone to see you tomorrow."

"Really?" Disbelief changed slowly to delight. She sent him one of her blinding smiles, closed her umbrella, and stepped over the threshold.

"What's this?" he asked when she handed him a small package wrapped in coarse paper and tied with a sprig of wilted honeysuckle.

"Nothing," she demurred, still whispering. "Something for you."

Under the paper he found a corked glass bottle full of an amber-colored liquid. "Mint vinegar" read the carefully printed label. "Thank you very much. Did you make it yourself?"

She nodded. A few seconds passed before she seemed to remember that she could talk now. She cleared her throat self-consciously. "Yes, I made it. It's spearmint and sugar in cider vinegar. You put it in iced tea."

"Do you?" He was intrigued by her voice, which was low and unexpectedly husky. "Shall we try it? Mrs. Quick left me some tea in the icebox, I think. Will you have a glass with me?"

The gladness in her expressive face almost undid him. "Yes, thank you," she acquiesced with grave politeness. "Shall I get it?"

"No, you sit down."

213

She obeyed, taking the same chair at his kitchen table she'd taken on that long-ago day in February, when they'd buried her dog together. She folded her hands demurely, the perfect guest, and watched as he got glasses out of the cupboard and filled them with cold tea. He sat across from her, and she added the mint vinegar to their glasses herself. "Delicious," he pronounced, and she beamed.

"Are you busy right now?" she asked, still shy. "Were you doing something?"

"No, nothing at all."

"Is it all right if we talk?"

"Yes, of course."

She sat back a little in her chair. Her eyes shone; her cheeks were flushed, but not from exercise. He sensed the same diffident excitement in her as on the day she'd first shown him her hospital in the woods. She wet her lips, fixing him with a purposeful look, and cleared her throat again. He readied himself for a revelation.

"I wouldn't be surprised if this rain kept up all night."

He blinked. Shifting in his chair, rearranging his expectations, he remarked, "Yes, and we can certainly use it."

"Yes, we certainly can. It's been dry for June."

"Very."

She took a small sip of tea. "I saw trout lilies beside the bridge over South Creek tonight."

He raised his eyebrows.

"Did you know they're also called dogtooth violet?"

"No, I didn't." He folded his arms, smiling. She didn't have anything specific to tell him, he realized, charmed. She just wanted to talk.

"Yesterday," she said deliberately, "I saw a possum drop dead."

He registered a suitable amount of amazement.

"I caught him trying to pull down a suet bag I'd hung up for the birds behind the springhouse. He dropped eight feet to the ground and fell flat on his back, dead as a doornail. I couldn't revive him, he was gone. So I got out the shovel, to carry him into the woods and bury him. And guess what."

"What?"

"While I was carrying him, one of his eyes popped open!"

"No!"

"Just for a second, and then he went back to playing possum. I put him down on the moss under some laurel trees, and when I went back a little later to look, he was gone."

Ty grinned appreciatively, enjoying himself. Her new voice was raspy, sultry, seductive, completely at odds with everything he knew about her, and the incongruity fascinated him.

"Did you read the *Clarion* yesterday?" she inquired next.

"No, I missed it. Didn't have time."

"There was an interesting article about death."

"About death?" He stroked his chin.

"It said that sometimes when a husband or a wife dies, the spouse dies, too, not long after. From a broken heart. Do you think it's true?"

He nodded slowly. "Yes, sometimes." She looked at him expectantly, and he saw that now it was his turn to talk. "I treated an elderly couple for pneumonia," he offered. "They were both very ill; there was never much hope. The old woman went first. 'Is Mother gone?' the husband asked me. But he already knew, I think. A few minutes later he closed his eyes and let go, too."

Carrie sighed, and stared into her glass.

"But it doesn't always happen that way. I lost a woman not long ago — abdominal tumor, too far gone for surgery — and I was offering condolences to her husband. 'Well,' he said, 'Letty was a good wife, she kept a clean house, and she took good care of the children. But I never liked her.'"

To his delight, a tickled laugh burst from

Carrie before she thought to clap her hand over her mouth — and now he understood the motive behind a gesture that had once puzzled and depressed him. "That's the first time I've ever heard you laugh," he chuckled.

"Sometimes I came close, with you," she admitted, "when you'd say funny things." But then her smile faded. "I — I —" She stopped, and visibly gathered herself together. "I apologize for what I did, Dr. Wilkes. For fooling you, I mean. It wasn't right."

"No, Carrie, I'm the one who should apologize — and stop calling me Dr. Wilkes. I shouldn't have been angry, I should've been nothing but happy for you."

She waved a hand in the air, absolving him. "No, it was *my* fault. At first I didn't think I was doing anything wrong, because I couldn't really believe we would be friends. Then when we were, I was too happy and I didn't want anything to change. I might have told you — no, I *would've* told you, soon probably, if you hadn't found out for yourself. Yes, I would have, I'm sure I would, but just not so early. It was such a big secret, you see, and I wasn't brave enough yet to tell you. But I would have. And I had to come here tonight and tell you that, and just — talk to you. I had to." She ran out of breath.

"I'm glad to know you'd have trusted me enough to tell me eventually." He reached across the table and took one of her slim hands. "Do you trust me now?" She nodded without a second's hesitation. "Then tell me why you did it, Carrie. Why you've been pretending for so long."

Her gray eyes darkened with distress. She looked down and whispered, "Please."

"Carrie —"

"Please," she repeated, urgent, her hand in his suddenly stiff with tension. "I want to tell you, truly I do. If I could tell anyone, it would be you. But I *can't*. Tyler —" She said his name experimentally, and something jolted between their hands when she uttered it. "If you would be my friend and not ask me that question, then I would have everything. It would be a matter of trust."

A matter of trust. He owed her that. He remembered how she'd seized on his suggestion that she'd feigned muteness so that people would notice her. It was all that had made sense to him at the time, but now he saw how much his hasty, ungenerous conclusion had hurt her.

"All right," he agreed softly. "I won't ask you." She closed her eyes in relief, then snapped them open when he added, "On one condition."

"What?" She was wary again.

"That you tell me what you're afraid of."

She pressed her lips together and preserved a stony silence.

He squeezed her hand hard, until her eyes widened and she had to look at him. "Tell me this, then, or we have no bargain: Does your stepfather hurt you?"

"No."

"In any way?"

"No."

Her answers were immediate and uncalculated — he had no choice but to believe her. He was relieved, of course; but somewhere in the back of his mind a prickly unease lingered.

"So, will you?" she urged in a shy murmur when a long minute passed and he didn't speak.

"Will I what?"

"Be friends." She kept her hopeful gaze on their clasped hands, waiting.

He wanted very much to kiss her. "I'm honored to be your friend. I'll keep your secret, and I promise not to press you to tell me anything else until you're ready."

Her smile reminded him of sunlight breaking through clouds on a dark day. "Thank you," she breathed, brushing a single glad tear away. Then she let go of his hand, sat back in her chair, and inquired, "Did you know I was born in North Carolina?"

"No, I didn't."

"A little tiny town called Walnut Cove. I don't remember it at all. But we didn't live there for long; we left when I was only six months old."

He rested his elbow on the table, his chin in his hand, and asked, "Do you remember your parents?"

"Oh, yes. My father's name was John Hamilton, my mother was Rachel. We traveled all over — Georgia, Tennessee, Virginia — because he was a photographer and he went from town to town, taking people's pictures. My mother was beautiful, she had light-brown hair and the kindest blue eyes, and she could sing like an angel. And my father was tall and handsome, with a big, dark mustache and black hair. I still have pictures of them both — would you like to see them sometime?"

"Very much. Whom did you lose first, your mother or your father?"

"My father, when I was ten years old. He was only thirty-four."

"How did he die?"

"He was struck by lightning." She looked down at her hands, and for some reason he thought of the brave little note she'd written Stoneman after his daughter died. "We were living in Spaulding that summer — that's in West Virginia — and Papa had set up a little studio right off the main street. One day some people hired him to make a picture of their whole family, for a reunion out on their farm. Almost as soon as he drove out of town, the sky started to change. I remember Mama and me looking at it through the screen door after he left, shaking our heads and worrying that he'd get drenched before he even got there, and then all for nothing when they couldn't go outside to make the picture anyway on account of the storm. But the rain held off and held off, and we began to think it wasn't going to come after all." Her eyes filled with unselfconscious tears. "Some men brought him home at nightfall in a wagon. They'd found the horse first, lathered and frightened, the harness all broken. Then they found Papa, lying beside the wagon in some weeds by the road."

"Ah, Carrie."

"They said he must've died instantly, and that that should comfort us because he didn't suffer. So." She pulled a handkerchief from her pocket and blew her nose. "So then my mother and I stayed on in Spaulding. But we were poor, so about two years after that she got married to my stepfather. And then she died, too, and then Artemis and I moved to

221

Dreamy Mountain."

"How did you lose your mother?" he interjected, aware that she'd coasted over the last
eight years of her life in two bald sentences.

"She had appendicitis, and then she got
blood poisoning."

"How?"

"I don't know, no one ever told me."

"How long did you and Artemis —"

"Guess who was the first person I met when
we moved here," she rushed on, cutting him
off — and he understood that speaking of her
stepfather, before or after her mother's death,
was going to be out of bounds.

He leaned back in his chair. "Who?"

"Broom. That's not his real name, of
course; people just call him that because of his
hair, and because he's so skinny. He scared
me when I first saw him — I was only thirteen, and he was already tall as a tree. But he
liked me right away, and it never mattered to
him that I couldn't talk. We had in common
that we were both different from other people, so it was easy to be friends. He's been my
friend even longer than Eppy or Doc
Stoneman.

"Did you know he lives by himself in his
own house? Outside of town on the
Chambersburg Road. It's not much of a
house, but it's his. He used to live there with

his mother — she wasn't quite right in the head; she took in people's washing for a living — until one day she disappeared. Nobody knew what happened to her, and then finally somebody thought to ask Broom. Why, she died, he told them. He found her dead and cold in the bed one morning. So he buried her in the backyard, and kept on as if nothing had happened. They dug her up, of course, and found out she'd had a heart attack. Everybody thought it was silly and wrong, but they went ahead and reburied her anyway in the indigents' graveyard outside of town, because of the law against burying kin in your own yard."

She paused to wet her throat with another sip of tea. "After that, nobody wanted to take Broom in, but they didn't want to send him away, either, so finally people just stopped worrying about him and let him stay where he was. He still lives in his mother's house, and he gets jobs sometimes, but they don't usually last long. People like the minister and Doc Stoneman look out for him as much as they can, but mostly he's on his own. He's like a child, pretty much. He'd never hurt a fly, even when the children torment him. Most folks are so used to him, they don't even see him anymore."

No wonder her hair was always falling

down from the knot she tied it in, Tyler mused, gazing at her through half-closed lids; she had that shiny, slippery kind of hair that wouldn't stay put no matter how many pins she stuck in it. The kind of hair a man wanted to set free with his fingers. And then bury his face in. Her voice still beguiled him, and so did the sensual play of her lips over her white teeth and her pretty pink tongue. Everything she said enchanted him. But the minutes ticked by, and the fog of fatigue in his brain thickened. He encouraged her with appropriate noises and movements of his head, but he heard less and less of her fervent, soft-voiced soliloquy on the baby rabbits she'd set free, her prayers for Doc Stoneman's recovery in the Harrisburg sanatorium, Eppy Odell's exceptional qualities as wife, mother, and friend. He'd never associated sensuality with somnolence; nevertheless, as physically stirred as he was by Carrie's subtle loveliness tonight, he found himself unable to resist the strong, gently sexual pull of languor that stole over him while he tried to make sense of her words. The last thing he heard clearly before sleep swallowed him up was, "His name's Old Crutchy, and he looked so pathetic I had to give him a nickel, even though I knew he was spoofing. He comes every few months and begs for pennies, or sometimes it's eggs, and each time he pretends he's got a different handicap. Today it was an ulcer on his elbow, but he'd just smeared pokeberry on it, you could tell by the smell."

Carrie watched Tyler's eyelids flutter closed for the final time, his chin sink to his chest and stay there. "Doc Stoneman says Old Crutchy's a tramp, and tramps aren't the same as hobos," she said softly, experimentally. His breathing stayed slow and heavy; he didn't move. "Hobos will work if they have to, he says, but tramps are just friendless outcasts who'd rather starve than work. And bums are somewhere in between." She set her glass on the table without a sound and stood up carefully. "Artemis says there wouldn't be any beggars if there weren't any givers. He made a sign once that said, 'Cross Dog Here,' but it didn't work. Doc Stoneman said tramps have a gossip network, and they're always telling each other which houses they can get a handout from and which they can't."

She smiled, partly because she felt silly, and partly for the pleasure of looking at Tyler — she guessed she could call him that now. *Tyler Wilkes. My friend, Dr. Tyler A. Wilkes.* She wrapped her arms around herself and squeezed.

He was as beautiful asleep as he was awake, though in a different way. She cocked her head, studying him. Artemis looked slack and empty-headed when he slept; Broom looked like a little boy, more childlike and defenseless than ever. But Dr. Wilkes — Tyler — looked serious and grave, as though he wasn't sleeping at all but pondering some knotty problem with his eyes closed. He wore no jacket or vest, and no collar on his clean white shirt; he'd rolled his shirtsleeves over his elbows, and she could see that his forearms were tan and muscular, the soft hair on them a lighter shade of brown than the hair on his head. He still needed a haircut, and she still liked the shaggy curls that fell on his forehead and tickled his neck. The bones in his face were proud and fine, which must be why he always looked handsome no matter how weary he was. His lips, so clean and strong, stirred memories of the first time he'd kissed her. And the second time. She sighed.

She drew her notebook out of her pocket without making any noise. *Dear Tyler,* she scribbled, then paused for a full minute to stare at the word she'd never written before.

I bet you wish I was still mum! Before, when I could talk, though, I never was such a magpie as tonight, so I think it will go away and the next time you see me, I will be normal! I'm sorry to have kept you awake this late, but to tell you the truth, I'm pretty sure I'd do it again. I'm so very glad we are friends now.

Sincerely yours,
Carrie Wiggins

Stealing to the screen door on tiptoe, she saw that the rain had stopped and a milky fog was creeping in, swirling low on the ground, ghostlike. She stepped outside, wincing when the door hinge squeaked — but Tyler didn't wake. Dr. Stoneman had once told her that a tired M.D. could go to sleep anywhere, in any position. She threw a last look back through the screen. "Night," she called in a secretive whisper. "Good night, Tyler Wilkes. I love you." She touched her fingertips to her lips, then to the rusty screen. Then she set out for home through the mist.

12

Carrie had names for everything.

Tyler discovered this by accident on a hot June afternoon when she suggested, after a long walk on Dreamy Mountain, that they sit down for a rest on Watch-From Rock. Her husky voice definitely capitalized the words, and for a moment he looked around for a sign or a plaque near the high, flat limestone boulder she was indicating. There was none — but there was a fabulous, unobstructed view of South Creek and the wide valley through which it wound, and beyond them both the spectacle of the sun dropping down behind the Tuscaroras forty miles in the distance.

As June turned into July, she introduced him to other points of interest in her personal landscape: Butterfly Field, Come-Upon Pond, Possum Stump, Nighthawk Hill. She made an expert guide, and part of the pleasure he took in her company nowadays was the opportunity to absorb the naturalist's lore she dispensed with effortless abandon. Carrie saw everything, and her ability to observe the patterns and minutiae in nature impressed the scientist in him. Wherever they went she would repeatedly warn, in a gentle, motherly tone that always enchanted him, "Careful, Ty, don't step there," thus saving the life of the snail, baby turtle, or pink lady's slipper he'd been about to trample. A five-toed smudge in the stream bank, she informed him, was a muskrat's footprint, but that four-toed one on the trail was a fox's. "Oh, look, chipmunk trails," she'd exclaim, pointing to nothing but an overgrown tangle of weeds, through which there were never any visible highways that he could see. That sharp *chicking* sound in the underbrush was a white-eyed vireo — which was similar to but not to be confused with the *chicking* of the crested flycatcher. Crushed jewelweed stems were an antidote to poison ivy, she explained, politely hiding her amazement that he, a *doctor*, didn't know that. She taught him the interesting lesson that scooping up a handful of whirligig beetles from the surface of Come-Upon Pond made your palm smell like apples for an hour afterward.

Birds seemed tamer around Carrie, squirrels less inclined to scamper away, and it wasn't his imagination. Once he watched her pet a bumblebee's back with her fingertip while it gorged, oblivious, on sweet clover nectar. The world was simultaneously simpler and more complex when he was with her, for she taught him a new way to see. And she taught him to listen for the loveliest, most haunting music on the mountain: the song of the hermit thrush.

Today, while he waited for her in a buttercup-covered field at the foot of High Dreamer (what would she call it, he mused, Wildflower Meadow? Honeybee Pasture?), he made an attempt to take careful sensory note of the sights, sounds, and smells around him, the way Carrie would; but without her sharp-eyed, beguiling presence he lacked the initiative. "What are you *looking* at?" he was always asking her, watching as she stared, minute after minute, entranced, at something completely unremarkable in the distance. She'd look at him in mild surprise and answer, "Why, the sky," or "the sun on that tree." Then he'd see it: the extraordinary cinnamon color of oak tree branches in the hour before dusk, the elegant silhouette of green-gold leaves against an opal horizon.

Carrie, Carrie. She was on his mind constantly. How flat his life in Wayne's Crossing must have been — he could hardly remember it — before she'd shared her secret with him and they'd begun to meet in fields, beside brooks, and on meandering mountain trails. Innocent though it was, they kept their friendship hidden from other people because they both knew it would be misunderstood — and also, of course, because Carrie was in constant dread of being seen or heard speaking. And speak was what she did now at fervent length. Ty clasped his hands behind his head and peered up at the drifting clouds, wondering how he'd have fared if she'd been any less engaging or fascinating a confidante — because, like it or not, he was the bemused recipient of all the dammed-up thoughts, emotions, questions, and convictions she'd been collecting for years. The dam had burst, and he was standing alone in the path of a rushing, gushing flood of words.

Luckily, she was a delight. She lit up his days like winter sunlight; fatigue, boredom, impatience, and career dissatisfaction were far from his mind when he was with her. The real Carrie was sociable and generous beneath her habitual reserve, and expansive, inquisitive, and free-spirited under the constraints of loneliness and self-inflicted silence. He couldn't see that he'd done anything to deserve the privilege of knowing and enjoying the truth about her, but it was a gift he didn't take for granted.

Only two clouds marred the clear sky of his content: the possibility that whatever dire circumstance had compelled her to adopt her radical disguise in the first place might still threaten her; and the worry that if he allowed the intimacy between them to progress naturally — the way it became increasingly clear each day they both wanted it to progress — Carrie would end up getting hurt. Regardless of his own needs, he had an obligation to save her from that. His privileged world was wide and full of opportunities; hers was unique and full of wonder, but at the same time narrow and inescapable. Occasionally he was clear-sighted enough to see a day coming when he would have to protect her from himself.

Something, maybe a note-change in the steely drone of insects, made him sit up and turn his head. Carrie was sailing toward him across a sparkling lake of yellow flowers, legs swinging in the long, graceful glide he loved to watch, already smiling at him. He jumped to his feet. Sunlight glinted on metal — his field glasses, swaying from her shoulder; she never went anywhere without them. "Hello," she called, still twenty feet away. "Am I late? I hurried, but at the last minute I had to pack a supper for my stepfather to take with him to Porterstown — he's going now and staying overnight, to help pull stumps out of a farmer's field." She came to a halt in front of him, pink-cheeked and beaming, her red-gold hair a lovely windblown tangle.

He took the hand she held out and smiled back at her. "Look at you, you have on a new dress." White and flower-sprigged, a pretty, impractical dress unlike any of her others. She'd made it for him. He was sure of it, and the certainty filled him with a guilty delight.

She stepped back, pulling the full skirt out to one side to show him. "Do you like it?"

"It's very pretty. You must be a good seamstress."

"I'm not, though. No one ever really showed me how." She lifted her head and took a sniff of the air. "Isn't it a *beautiful* day? How are you, how long can you stay? Should we sit here or in the shade?"

"Shade," he voted. Holding hands, they sauntered toward the edge of the meadow, where a sycamore tree threw enormous shadows on the grass.

"Look, I brought you watermelon cake," she said, rummaging in a cloth sack she was carrying. "How long can you stay?"

They sat down on the grass, resting their backs against the peeling tree trunk, shoulders touching. "Only an hour. Every one of Anna Shindeldecker's children has the mumps, and I have to go look at them at three o'clock."

She looked disappointed, but only said, "I've never had the mumps."

"Then you'd better stay away from the Shindeldeckers for the next three weeks. What in the world is watermelon cake?"

Cake batter tinted red, she informed him, surrounded by regular white batter, with raisins mixed in for "seeds." It looked peculiar but tasted delicious; he ate it all, including her piece when she insisted because he'd missed lunch, and then licked his fingers.

"I'm glad you liked it," she said when he complimented her. She took out the little hand lens she always carried and began to examine a green bug making its way along the rough bark between them. "How did the pennyroyal work on Louie's fleas?" She looked up when he didn't answer, and laughed out loud when she saw his face. "It worked, didn't it? I knew it!"

"There seems to have been a moderately beneficial effect, which may or may not be a direct result of —"

"It worked," she crowed, "admit it! 'Folk medicine,' you called it. I guess that means it works for folks." She stuck a finger in his ribs, making him jump.

"All right, all right, his fleas are better," he admitted grudgingly. "Now have you got anything to make him stop digging holes in the yard? He doesn't *look* Chinese, but he sure wants to go there." Carrie laughed gaily.

"Yesterday he left a little surprise for Mrs. Quick on the sitting room rug. I could hear her yelling at him from downstairs, and so could my patient. She chased him down the back steps with a broom."

"Poor Louie," she tsked.

"Poor Louie?"

She put her magnifying glass away, plucked a blade of grass, and carefully positioned it between her thumbs. "Yes, poor Louie. Nobody tells him what they want him to do till after he's done it wrong." She took a deep breath and blew hard against her thumbs and the grass blade, emitting an ear-piercing shriek.

"Ow!" he complained. "Cut that out."

She laughed again and looked smug; she'd tried for half a day once to teach him how to make grass whistles, but it remained an art he couldn't master. "Oh," she said suddenly, sitting up, "I just remembered — I brought you a present. Close your eyes."

"Why? This present better not be alive." He was thinking of the glowworm she'd brought him last week, another "close-your-eyes" kind of present.

"No, this is a gift for your nose. Come on, close your eyes."

Grumbling, he obeyed. He heard her rustling in the cloth sack again, and a moment later he felt something tickle the end of his nose.

"Guess what it is," she challenged.

He inhaled something tangy-sweet and pungent. "Mmmm. I'll say . . . white birch?"

"No."

"Ivy?"

She tsked again. "No."

"I give up."

"Sassafras. Like it?"

"Mm hm."

"Now, what's this?"

Something sweeter this time. "A rose?"

She snorted. "No, bayberry. I guess you can open your eyes." Her way of saying he'd never guess the rest.

She laid something on his palm, and he blinked down at a motley collection of leaves and twigs and wildflowers tied together at the stalks and spread out like a fan. "Well, look at this. It's . . . um . . ." He didn't have the slightest idea.

"An olfactory bouquet," she enlightened him. "Sassafras and bayberry, and this is sweetfern — smell. And this is spicebush, here's yarrow, and this is catnip."

He sniffed each one, humming appreciatively. "Very nice."

"I used to leave them sometimes for old Mrs. Urquehart until she passed away. She

236

was blind," she added in explanation.

"Left them for her?"

"In her door." Her sweet smile turned a trifle wistful. "Well, I couldn't talk and she couldn't see, so there didn't seem any point in trying to make friends."

He touched the back of her hand with his finger. "Do you think she knew who was leaving her the bouquets?"

"Oh, no, she couldn't have, she didn't know me at all." She cocked her head to one side. "Listen. Hear it?"

He heard a bird, making a gurgling sound somewhere on the other side of the meadow.

"It's a redwing." She leaned toward him. "The males take more than one wife, you know," she said in confidential tones.

"Why, those heathenish rascals." Diverted, he watched her unlace her shoes and shuck them off, toe to heel, then matter-of-factly strip off her cotton stockings. He caught a flash of cream-white calf, long and slim and startling in a bar of golden sunlight. Then she shoved her skirts back down and curled her toes, which were long and bony, into the cool grass, sighing with contentment.

He swallowed, and popped a handful of blackberries, still warm from her pocket, into his mouth. "Got a letter from my mother today," he mentioned.

"You did?" Her face lit up with interest. "That's nice."

"Ah, well. Not altogether."

"Oh, no? Is she sick?"

"Mother is never sick. Did you bring your scissors today, Carrie?" She nodded. "Do you still want to cut my hair?"

"Yes, if you like." She ducked her head, coloring with pleasure, and Tyler got that fresh, cool, heart-racing feeling in his chest that assailed him at odd times in her company.

She found the scissors in her bag while he took off his collar and stuck it in his trouser pocket. He crossed his long legs, and she came up on her knees beside him. "I didn't bring a comb," she explained shyly as she pushed her fingers through his hair to straighten it. The soft, soothing sensation made him close his eyes and moan. "Feel good?" she murmured.

"Mmmm. Don't let me fall asleep on you again, Carrie." He opened one eye to see her smiling. "Did I ever apologize for that?"

"No, you didn't, and it was very rude. Here I go for years without saying a word, and the first person I finally talk to starts snoring in the middle of my life story."

That tickled him. He started to chuckle, and she leaned against his shoulder to laugh with him; the sound of their hilarity flushed a bird out of the sycamore tree — a warbler, Carrie guessed, craning her neck to follow its flight, maybe a yellowthroat. Bees and crickets droned in the clover. Crows cawed crankily, skulking along a line of trees at the meadow's edge. Tyler could easily have fallen asleep under the gentle ministering of her hands, but presently she broke the contented silence with two soft-voiced, uncharacteristically personal questions. "What's your mother like, Ty? Don't you like her?"

He smiled. "Yes, I like her very much. But she's what's called a 'formidable woman.' If I let my guard down for half a minute, she'd eat me alive." Carrie's fingers stilled; he turned his head and saw her look of amazement. "I take it your mother never tried to gobble you up," he said blandly.

"My mother? Oh no, my mother was *wonderful*."

"Lucky girl — being eaten isn't any fun at all. Carolivia swallowed my father whole. All he wanted to do was read books and write scholarly papers nobody would ever read, but she had other plans."

She went back to cutting his hair. "What plans?"

He closed his eyes, savoring the flutter of Carrie's breath behind his ear, soft as a caress;

the elusive fragrance she used activated another pleasant chest spasm. "My mother was a Morrell before she became a Wilkes. Do you know the Morrell name, Carrie?" She shook her head. "It's famous, at least in Philadelphia."

"What does it stand for?"

"Money," he smiled. "Specifically, *old* money. The Morrell Company is one of the oldest shipping lines in the country; it imports and exports commodities all over the world. When my parents married, the idea was that my father would learn the business and eventually become its head. But he was completely hopeless, a dreamer instead of a schemer. My mother, on the other hand, was a natural. So the inevitable happened: he became a lovable figurehead, and Carolivia ran the company."

" 'Carolivia,' " she repeated, drawing out all the vowel sounds. "How important it sounds. Is your father still alive?"

"He died when I was fourteen."

She made a sympathetic sound. Because it was Carrie, he knew it came from the heart, no reflexive gesture of compassion. "And now," she guessed, "your mother wants you to be the head of the company."

"She's given up on that, although it obsessed her for years. No, she's finally become reconciled to the deplorable fact that I'm a doctor. Now she has something else in mind for me."

"What?"

"She wants me to be president."

"President? Of the company, the —"

"Of the United States."

Carrie sat back on her heels and gaped at him.

"Well, I can see I won't be able to count on your vote."

"Oh — no — you'd make a *wonderful* president, I'm — I just —"

He laughed at her. "Relax, Carrie, I'm not running."

"Oh." She laughed, too. "But — what a strange thing, Ty, for her to have in her mind! Isn't it? I don't know, but I thought presidents were always senators first, or lawyers at least, or generals —"

"Usually, yes. But both the Wilkes and Morrell names are very old and very well connected, politically and socially. Stranger things have happened, as Mother likes to say. And her master plan begins on a smaller scale, with me being elected to something in Philadelphia first and then Congress, she doesn't care which House. You're not cutting too much off that side, are you?"

"What? No, I'm almost finished." She was leaning close, frowning with concentration,

241

the tip of her pink tongue between her teeth. The breeze blew a long strand of her hair across his throat, and he wondered what it would be like to trace the delicate outline of her ear with his fingers, or his lips. She bent closer to blow hairs off the back of his neck, and his whole body tightened.

"And so — when she writes you letters, it makes you feel sad? Because you love her but you don't think you can ever please her, not if you please yourself at the same time?"

"That's it," he said softly, half his mind on what she was saying, the other half on the shapes her mouth made when she spoke.

She shook her head, perplexed. "But how could she not be proud of you — you're a *doctor.*"

He chuckled; she might as well have said, "You're a *god,*" her voice sounded so awed. "But my mother thinks of herself as part of an enlightened aristocracy, Carrie. She wouldn't admit it — she thinks she's a Republican — but personal power is important to her. She wants her only son to be a leader of men, she wants the Wilkes name to be venerated. Power, glory, noblesse oblige — you can't achieve them by taking care of sick people, so she doesn't value that profession."

Carrie thought about that in silence. "Does

your sister have to fight against her all the time, too?"

"No, Abbey stays out of it, above it, I'm not quite sure how. I suppose she got the best of both my parents — my mother's strength and my father's gentleness."

"But you're strong. And gentle." She'd laid her scissors in her lap; she was resting her hand on his shoulder. "I think you're the kindest man I've ever known. I wish . . ."

She didn't finish. Her gray eyes were wide, luminous with emotion, and utterly without guile. He couldn't look away. He didn't ask her what she wished because he already knew, and it was time to end this risky, tantalizing moment. There were many reasons why an emotional entanglement with Carrie was out of the question, and remembering them had always — eventually — swamped his desire for her at dangerous times like this. She was too young for him, much too innocent; something from the past had wounded her, and he couldn't take responsibility for her; they came from different worlds, and one day, perhaps soon, he would go back to his and leave her here.

But she tempted him so powerfully. He reached out to touch the whitish wildflower, wilted now, she'd threaded through the buttonhole of her new dress, beneath the low collar. Her fingers on his shoulder tensed. He drew the flower out and brought it to his nose. A revelation. "This," he murmured wonderingly. "Carrie, this is your scent."

"Honeysuckle," she confirmed, lips curving in a slow, unknowingly seductive smile. "My mother taught me to use it. I put some here, and here." She touched the back of one ear, then the other. "Do you like it?"

Her shy coquetry was new and disarming, and her throaty voice was devastating. He slid his fingers along her jaw to the back of her neck and bent toward her, nuzzling wisps of her hair aside with his lips and breathing in the faint, subtle fragrance that was part honeysuckle, part Carrie. "I like it better on you."

"Oh, Ty," she whispered, and closed her eyes. She started to tremble. "You can kiss me if you want to."

The sun gilded her hair and the fragile line of her cheekbone; her soft, delectable mouth was an invitation he was weary of refusing. He grazed the pad of his thumb across her lips. Her lashes fluttered, dainty and nervous, casting elegant shadows on her skin. "Carrie," he breathed, "how beautiful you are."

She opened her eyes — and the undisguised wanting in them finally brought him back to earth. When she touched his cheek, he took her hand away and kissed her fingertips, then straightened away from her. "But if I kiss you," he said, in a rough approximation of his normal voice, "I'll be late. You wouldn't want all those swollen Shindeldeckers on your conscience, would you?"

For a long moment, she didn't return his determinedly lighthearted smile; she studied him gravely, alert for the faintest sign of rejection. She was too intelligent for guessing games; *words* were what were needed between them now, if he was to be honest with her at all. But he didn't know his own mind well enough to explain himself to her, and all the reasons he could give for turning away from her would hurt her. So he didn't speak. And when she finally smiled — because he'd reassured her, or because he'd taught her to play his game? — he knew a coward's relief.

She put her stockings and shoes on in silence, gathered her belongings, and rose gracefully to her feet. He grasped the hand she held out for him and stood with her. As soon as he was upright, she dropped his hand and moved back a step. She swatted a fallen lock of hair back over her shoulder and cocked one eloquent eyebrow at him. "Of course, I'm new at it and maybe I'm wrong, but I can't help thinking."

"What, Carrie?"

"That kissing must be like anything else —

quick sometimes, other times slow. You must've had in mind the slow kind, Ty, but to tell you the truth I wouldn't have minded a quick one. Those Shindeldecker children wouldn't even have noticed."

She sent him a twinkling look, spun on her toes, and danced away across the wildflower meadow.

13

"To you, Carrie. To the start of your new career." She lifted her glass and touched it to Tyler's mug of beer. The pride in his eyes warmed her all the way through to her bones; a glass of French champagne couldn't have tasted any sweeter than Erma Stambaugh's ice-cold buttermilk did right at that moment.

"Well, look at this, now. What're you two celebrating?"

She glanced up to see Mrs. Stambaugh herself, carrying a wide black tray with two plates of food on it — ham steak for Ty, honey-dipped chicken for Carrie; "honey-dipt," the menu read — and smiling at them while she tried to pretend she wasn't wild to know what they were doing together in her restaurant. Other people were wondering, too, Carrie could tell from the stares they'd gotten when they'd come in, and were still getting when people thought they weren't looking. Well, they couldn't be any more surprised than she was, for she'd never been in a restaurant before, and now here she was in Pennicle's, Wayne's Crossing's finest, at a table with a white cloth on it, sitting across from — this was the best part — Tyler A. Wilkes, M.D.! She folded her hands in her lap and squeezed tight, nearly quaking with excitement.

"We're celebrating the imminent purchase and publication of Carrie's new book," Tyler spoke up, answering Mrs. Stambaugh's question.

Mrs. Stambaugh used the minute it took to set their plates down to get her face in order, and say with less astonishment than she surely must've been feeling, "Carrie's what?"

Ty beamed across the table at her, and Carrie could feel her cheeks getting hot from pleasure and embarrassment. "You mean you didn't know Carrie's an author?"

"Why, I declare. No, I can't say I did. What kind of a book did you write, honey?" She rested her hands on her big hips and looked at Carrie as if she'd never seen her before — as if she wasn't the mute girl she passed in church every Sunday, or the shy, backward girl her son Carl used to throw mud balls at every day after school.

"She's written and illustrated a book about the birds in Franklin County," Ty answered for her. "It's not quite finished yet, but it soon will be. Frank Odell's been acting as her agent, and he's pretty sure he's found a buyer for it."

"Why, I declare, isn't that something? That is purely something, mm mm mm."

Carrie was half-afraid she might laugh out loud because it sounded so funny to hear Ty call Mr. Odell her "agent." She smiled up at Mrs. Stambaugh — who was looking at her now as if she was Sarah Bernhardt, come to sample the cuisine at Pennicle's. She might've stood there all night saying, "Mm mm mm," if Ty hadn't asked her for the mustard. She pulled herself together and went off to get it, still shaking her head.

Ty had a conspirator's grin that told Carrie he knew everything that was going on in her head. "How's your chicken?" he asked, and she nodded that it was fine. The mashed potatoes surprised her, though; she'd never seen so much butter on just one food in her life. So this was how people ate in restaurants. Ty had been sure she was joking when she'd told him that, except for the counter at the drugstore, she'd never eaten in one before. That was after she'd told him the miraculous news about her book and he'd said they ought to do something special to celebrate. He'd made a joke — she *hoped* it was a joke — that he wanted to take her some place public for a change so she'd have to shut up and he could finally get a word in edgewise. But what a luxury talking to him was, and how fast she'd gotten used to it! The habit of muteness was old and ingrained, though, and she had no real fear that she'd unthinkingly blurt something out to him in front of everybody at Pennicle's. Just the same, it felt strange that she couldn't say to him straight out, right now, "Oh, Ty, I forgot to tell you in all the excitement — I got a letter today from Dr. Stoneman." Instead she found the letter in her pocket and handed it to him across the table.

"What's this?"

She made a gesture that said, *Open it.* She watched him unfold the one-page letter and begin to read, admiring his long eyelashes, his cheekbones, the way his jaw muscles worked when he chewed his food. He had on a striped gray coat that made him look serious and wise, not to mention broad-shouldered and handsome. His dark, shiny hair, if she said so herself, had never looked better. She liked his wide maroon tie; a "Windsor" tie, he called it. But her favorite touch was the bright orange marigold in his buttonhole — a gift from her; she'd snipped it from Eppy's garden an hour ago.

He started to smile, then chuckle in that low, rumbling way she loved, and she guessed he'd gotten to the part in the letter about "Ingrid the Impaler." That was the nurse who was making Dr. Stoneman obey all the rules and regulations at the sanatorium. He said *terrible* things about her, but in such a comical way that Carrie had had to laugh, too. But what she liked most about the letter was the optimistic sound of it, at least if you read between the lines. Dr. Stoneman was the least hopeful person she'd ever known, so he must be improving if he could find even halfway cheerful words to say about his stay at the hospital.

"I got a note from him, too," said Ty, folding the letter up and giving it back to her. "Not as nice as yours, I must say. You should feel flattered, Carrie, that he cleans up his language for your benefit."

Her notebook and pencil were beside her plate. *Do you think he'll get well?* she wrote. She'd asked him the question before, and he always said he didn't know, but maybe now he had new information to go by.

But he only shook his head and said, "I honestly don't know. At least he's finally getting the kind of care he needs if he's to have any chance at all. If he'd done this a year or even six months ago, I'd like his prognosis better. As it is, all we can do is hope."

And pray, she added to herself. Did Tyler believe in God? She'd never asked him. Dr. Stoneman didn't. That had shocked her when she'd first found out. *Thank you for telling me the truth,* she wrote in her notebook. *You know — not trying to spare me.*

He nodded, and started to say something, but at that moment they both saw Spring Mueller, of all people, walking toward their table. A feeling came over Carrie that she didn't have very often but which she recognized easily enough as jealousy; it got stronger when Spring raised her perfect blond eyebrows and looked back and forth between her and Ty as if she couldn't quite put the two of them together in her head. As if she were looking at a beautiful lady in an ugly dress, or a handsome prince on an old broken-down horse.

"Good evening," she said in that affected way she'd had since she was fourteen — or before, for all Carrie knew; maybe she was born that way. "How are you, Tyler? No, please, sit down. I can only stay a second, I'm dining with my parents. Carrie, hi. You're not sick, are you?" She laughed a false, tinkly laugh, not trying to hide her perplexity. She was worse than Mrs. Stambaugh, Carrie decided, because she was smoother, and because her supposedly humorous disbelief that Ty could know Carrie any other way but professionally was a subtler insult.

But the look on her face when Ty told her

what they were celebrating went a long way toward easing all the mean, envious thoughts Carrie had ever had about her. For a minute Spring couldn't even speak, she was so confounded. Finally she managed to say, "Well, isn't that nice, I couldn't be more surprised," and then she launched right away into a speech about how she was leaving in two days for the Whitson Teachers' College in Harrisburg, and she wanted to be sure to say goodbye to them — looking only at Ty, of course — and how excited she was because molding young minds was a noble calling, and she only hoped she had the sensitivity and the intellectual capability for the difficult but worthy task that lay ahead of her — et cetera, ad nauseam, as Dr. Stoneman would say. Carrie stole furtive glances at Ty while Spring droned on, and at first all she could see in his face was friendly politeness; but then, in the depths of his beautiful blue eyes, she could've sworn she saw a flicker of impatience. A bright, unholy, completely wicked glee came over her. Even guilt couldn't make it go away.

Finally Spring stopped talking about herself. "I hear you're going to be getting some competition soon, Tyler."

"I heard that, too," he said agreeably.

When Carrie looked blank, Spring said, "Oh, didn't you know? Wayne's Crossing is about to acquire *another* new doctor. Do you think this means our little village is finally coming into the twentieth century after all?" She laughed the tinkly laugh. "Daddy's doing some legal work for him before he gets here. His name is James Perry, he's from Richmond, and he has three children and a wife named Maria."

"He did his residency at Bellevue Hospital," Ty added, "and he'll be here by the end of the month. He's buying the old Jansson house on Wing Street."

Spring looked put out because Ty knew more gossip than she did. "Daddy says he sounds very bright. I hope he doesn't take *too* many of your patients away, Dr. Wilkes," she said archly, batting her eyelashes.

"Me, too. If he did, I might have to lower my fees."

She finally said good-bye, shaking Tyler's hand — he never had sat down — and giving Carrie a wave. As soon as she was gone, Carrie scribbled worriedly,

Might Dr. Perry really take your patients away?

"I hope so," he said, spooning a big bite of applesauce.

But — don't you care?

"He's welcome to as many as he can handle, the sooner the better." She looked at him quizzically. "The town's long overdue for another doctor, Carrie," he explained. "We could really use three. My work load's always been too much for one man." He added more softly, "Especially since it's not what I want to do anyway."

She nodded in sympathy. He wanted to be an "epidemiologist," which was someone who studied diseases and thought up ways to cure them. That was certainly a "noble calling," as Spring would say, but Carrie couldn't help thinking it would also be a shame, because Ty was so good with people. Everybody in town thought the world of him.

Mr. Bridgers, the town undertaker and furniture upholsterer, was a perfect example. Tyler paid the check, and he and Carrie were on their way out of Pennicle's when Mr. Bridgers, who was coming in, grabbed him by the arm and started pounding him on the back. "Dr. Wilkes! Just the man I wanted to see. You know those pills you give me for that bladder problem I was having? They worked like a charm. Lemme tell you —"

Carrie moved off down the street a ways to give them more privacy, not that Mr. Bridgers seemed to want it. The mannequin in the window of Kline's Ready-to-Wear caught her eye, and she drifted over toward it. She was staring at the rose-colored dress on the mannequin, trying to imagine the kind of life a woman who wore a dress like that would lead, and then trying to picture herself wearing the dress, when she saw Eugene Starkey's reflection looming up behind her. She whipped around just before he reached for her shoulder to turn her.

"Hey, Carrie, I thought it was you. What're you doing in town so late?" He grinned as if he was glad to see her, and she smiled back, pleased to see him. "I've been in a meeting for the last two hours," he said importantly. "Yeah, the work never stops. All the foremen and assistant foremen get together once a month, see, to talk about problems on the job. I had to give the shop superintendent a report on the turning department. Yeah, he said we're doing great, we're eleven percent above production from this time last year."

She made an amazed, congratulatory face.

"Yeah. So." He put his hand on the glass behind her and leaned against it, bringing their faces close. "So how've you been? Good, good. Me, I've been fine. So listen, what are you doing next Sunday? Want to go on a picnic? Some of the boys at work are going up to High Rock for the afternoon. The girls make the food, and the guys bring the beer." He grinned humorously. "What do you say?"

She said no, as politely as she could, in a

rather long, explanatory note in her notebook.

"Aw, come on," he wheedled when he'd read it, bracing his hand on the window again and bending over her. "Sunday's your day of rest, ain't it? You need to get out some or you'll turn peculiar, up there on Dreamy with nobody for company except old Artemis. *Anybody'd* go crazy living with that lunatic. Come on, Carrie, let's have some fun."

She shook her head again, looking regretful and apologetic. Footsteps sounded behind her. Eugene looked past her shoulder and straightened up, and a second later Tyler joined them.

"Hello, Eugene," he said pleasantly, coming to stand beside Carrie.

She could tell the instant Eugene realized they were together, because his face closed up and his dark eyes turned cold and hard. "Oh, hey, don't let me keep you," he said in a slow, sarcastic voice. "You two have a real nice evening." He turned on his heel and stalked off down the sidewalk, stiff-legged and tight-shouldered. But for once, Carrie thought he looked more hurt than angry. The idea troubled her — all the way to Ty's house.

"No emergencies — we're in luck."

Carrie nodded, peering through the dusk at

the blank message board on Tyler's office door.

"Do you want to come upstairs and have something to drink?" he invited. "We can sit on the back porch and watch the fireflies."

"That sounds perfect." The perfect end, she mused as they walked around the flagstone path to the back of his house, to a perfect day.

Louie greeted them with a lot of joyful barking and ecstatic rolling around on his back. He was still an adolescent and he didn't have much dignity yet, but Carrie thought he showed a lot of promise. He lay with his chin on her shoe as she sat beside Ty in one of the kitchen chairs they brought out onto his back porch. They sipped lemonade in peaceful silence, staring off at the dipping, rising, winking lights in the trees across the way, listening to the katydids and the crickets. But Carrie's thoughts kept going back again and again to Eugene, and once she sighed so heavily, Tyler asked her what she was thinking about.

"Eugene," she answered readily.

He grunted. "What about him?"

"He asked me to go on a picnic with him. I said I couldn't, and I think I hurt his feelings."

He'd taken his coat off and loosened his Windsor tie; he had his feet up on the railing, his hands folded over his stomach. She loved to see him at ease like this. Sometimes the fact that she was actually one of his personal friends, someone he spent free time with on purpose, struck her as too good to be true. It was the sort of thing so much more likely to happen to someone else, not Carrie Wiggins. "I'll take your word for it that Eugene's got feelings to hurt," he said dryly.

She looked at him in surprise. "Oh, no, Ty, he's very sensitive."

He looked skeptical, but didn't say anything for a while. "You're fond of him, aren't you?" he finally asked her.

"Yes. In a way."

"Why?"

"Because . . . he's not really a bad person."

"Probably not. But I think there must be more to it than that."

How clever he was; she wondered what it would be like to try to keep a secret from him. "There's another reason," she said slowly, "something that happened a long time ago. I've never told anybody." There was a long, long pause, while they both waited to see what she would decide. "I'll tell you if you like," she offered in the end.

"Do you want to?"

"Yes. But . . ."

"But?"

"It's embarrassing to say it out loud."

He reached across the little bit of space between them, offering his hand. "Don't look at me, then," he suggested. "Look off up there and say it to the lightning bugs and the tree frogs."

She could do that. She put her hand in his, and the wide warmth of it comforted her. She could tell Ty this. She loved him — he was her best friend. And he wouldn't think less of her afterward.

Still, he was right about it being easier to look straight ahead, not at him. "It happened three years ago," she began, her voice soft to accommodate the quiet night and the story she had to tell. "I was fifteen and Eugene was a little older, but he was still in my grade at school. Some of the kids used to laugh at me, you know, because I couldn't talk, and — Eugene was one of them. He was one of the worst, to tell you the truth. He was the one who first started calling me 'dummy,' and after that they almost all did.

"It wasn't too bad," she rushed on, leery of Ty's pity when his palm tightened around hers. "I just got farther and farther away from people and kept to myself, and then I was all right." She risked a glance; what she could see of his profile in the dimness was stony and grim. "Anyway, one day I was walking home from school. When I got to the bridge at the bottom of Dreamy, I saw two boys I didn't know — older boys, they worked at the mill, I think — standing at the other end. I didn't see them till I was in the middle. I stopped, and they started coming toward me, walking very slowly and snickering to each other in a nervous, nasty way. Well" — she tried to laugh — "I knew they were going to do something to me. I turned around to run, but Eugene had come up behind me and he was blocking the other end of the bridge. They'd all been waiting for me."

She took a drink of lemonade and set her glass down on the porch floor. Without knowing she was going to, she got up all of a sudden, letting Ty's hand go, and went to stand by the railing, not facing him but not quite turning her back on him. She hadn't expected it to be *this* hard to say. Why was it? It was an old, old memory, she hardly ever thought about it anymore. She should've just said it all at once, not set the scene and told it like a story, because all the feelings of fear and shame were coming back, and she was afraid she might cry.

"So." She had to swallow to clear her throat. "They caught me. In the middle of the bridge. Eugene said, 'Hold her,' and one got my arms behind me and held me still, and the other one started — he — opened my dress

261

and touched me, my —" She put her hand on her chest. "I was crying, but they just laughed and kept saying, 'Why don't you scream, dummy, why don't you scream?' "

She heard Ty get up, and a second later she felt his big hands on her shoulders. "Eugene was behind the one who was touching me. It was him I kept begging — with my eyes — to please, please make them stop." She took a quick swipe at her eyes. "And he did. He stopped smiling all of a sudden, and the meanness went out of his face. He made them quit, Ty. He said, 'Come on, leave her be, she's just a kid.' He was the leader, so finally they did what he said. And that's the end, that's all there was to it."

Tyler's arms came all the way around her, and she leaned back against his hard, solid chest. "After that, Eugene stopped teasing me at school," she finished quietly. "Started calling me Carrie instead of — the other name. Pretty soon, the others did, too. Things got much, much better after that, and I knew I had him to thank for it."

She couldn't have been more surprised when Ty swore — softly, under his breath, but she could hear the vulgar words clearly. He bent his head so their cheeks were touching, her right and his left. He still had his arms around her, locked together beneath her breasts. The need to burst into tears went away slowly, and after a while she didn't feel anything except safe.

"Carrie," he murmured against her hair, "what can I say to you? I'm sorry you were hurt."

"But it's all right now. It's all in the past, Ty, I don't think about it."

He sighed. "Stoneman told me a long time ago you were too good for this world. I think he was right."

She laughed softly, tickled.

He gave her a gentle, impatient shake. "Eugene brutalized you. How can you just *forget* that?"

"I'll never forget it. But he changed his mind, he did something *good*, not bad. And ever since then — it's not that he watches out for me, it's more that he's *aware* of me. He's a part of my life, Ty. Whatever happens to either one of us, we'll always . . . Oh, I don't know the words to explain it."

They stood still, looking down at their twined arms and feeling each other's soft breathing. Louie got up suddenly, toenails loud on the wood floor, and ran down the steps to investigate something only he could hear. Carrie thought Ty would let her go now, now that he knew she was all right. But he didn't. She could feel his breath in the curve between her shoulder and her neck, and a second later she felt his lips there. She stopped breathing, to savor it. She hadn't let herself hope for this. Just a comfort kiss, though, that's all it was. She closed her eyes and tried not to tremble when his lips glided so slowly across her skin, coming to rest in the sensitive spot behind her ear. But she gasped when she felt his tongue there. And shivered when he said, "Honeysuckle," in a breathy whisper.

"No," she finally remembered to say. "Rose petals. You must . . . you must need another olfactory bouquet."

He laughed, a warm explosion on her throat, and turned her around. "Is that what I need?" She held still, didn't lift her hands to touch his face, even though she was longing to. He stroked a finger across her lips, urging them apart with gentle pressure, and lowered his mouth to hers for a long, slow, sweet kiss. He let his hands drift into her hair, combing it with his fingers; the raspy sound of his touch on her scalp blended with a whispery roar in her ears, and she thought that must be what desire sounded like. She didn't move, but she let the pleasure flow all the way through her, like rain filling up a barrel.

"What's wrong?" he whispered, trying to read her face in the dim starlight. "Are you thinking about what happened, what those boys did?"

"No. When you kiss me I can't think about anything," she answered truthfully.

He smiled. Her heart stuttered. His hands on her waist tightened and relaxed, and then he slid them around to her back and pulled her closer. His mouth came down again. She couldn't help it, she opened her lips so that he could kiss her the way he had before, that day on the mountain.

He sleeked his warm tongue in, and somehow he managed to whisper her name and stroke her inside her mouth at the same time, like a painter with a soft, wet brush. His mouth tasted like sugar, like lemon candy. Her blood flowed thin and hot, and her muscles felt weak and powerful, leaden and weightless, all at the same time. Everything he did made her want more, and what she wanted now was the feel of his hands on her breasts. But still she didn't move, didn't let him know how completely she was his, because then he would stop.

"Carrie?" he urged, taking soft sips of her lips, holding her face between his palms as if he treasured her. One of his hands coasted down her neck, her chest, his fingers playing in the hollow of her collarbone. Slow heat burned where he touched her so deftly, little circles lower and lower. Then he caught her bottom lip between his teeth, to hold her still while his fingers gently pinched the tight tip of her breast. Live sparks shot through her. She swayed, forced back a moan. The porch railing creaked when she leaned against it. Ty reached behind her and pressed his hand against her bottom, pulling her up tight against him, and everything she wanted narrowed and focused and became one thing: to join with him in an act of love.

I love you, she told him, with everything except her voice. He muttered something, maybe her name again, and undid the top button of her dress. He fumbled with the second one; she could feel his impatience through his fingers.

Then he took a deep breath and held still.

"Don't stop." She whispered it so softly, she could barely hear the words herself. Part of her hoped he hadn't heard them either, because they were so forward. But most of all she hoped he wouldn't say he was sorry, because if he did she would cry.

What he said was, "I don't want to hurt you."

"Oh, Ty, you couldn't. How could you?"

"Easily." He was whispering, too, his forehead resting against hers. It was easier to talk, she guessed, if they couldn't see each other's eyes.

"Nothing you could ever do could hurt me," she said bravely, wishing it was true.

"Sweet Carrie. You're so young."

"I'm almost nineteen."

"I'm almost twenty-nine."

"That's not so much." She wished she hadn't said that, too, because it wasn't dignified to argue. "Is that what it is? That you think I'm too young?"

"Partly."

She didn't have the courage to ask what the other part was. A terrible confession was welling up inside, filling her chest like a balloon. "Is it . . . are you . . . careful with me because you think I'm a maid?" He didn't answer. "I'm not." Her cheeks flamed; she felt glad for the darkness. "I'm not. . . . So . . . you wouldn't be the first. If you wanted me."

He didn't move and he didn't say a word. Aghast, she listened to the echo of what she'd just told him; the longer the silence between them lasted, the harder it got to believe she'd really said it.

She stepped away, breaking contact. "Don't hate me, Ty, I couldn't stand it."

"Never."

"But you're surprised. Aren't you?" He couldn't deny that. "And — disappointed."

"No, of course not. It's none of my business."

She rubbed her arms, which were suddenly as cold as if she'd stuck them in ice water. "No, it's not." She started backing up.

He put his hand out to stop her. She flinched and kept moving, started down the stairs.

He caught her on the third step. "Wait — Are you leaving? Carrie, I'm —"

"I really have to go," she cried, before he could say the hateful word.

"No, wait, listen to me."

"I know what you'll say already. I'm all right, Ty, I'm fine, you didn't hurt my feelings. I have to go home now, so please let go of my arm." He did, and she clattered down the rest of the steps.

But he followed. He didn't touch her again, but he moved fast to get in front of her and block her way. "Don't go. Please. I hate it when you run away from me like this."

"I'm not running."

"Then stay and talk to me."

"Sometime outside — in a field someday, in the sunshine —" She wasn't making any sense. With a great effort, she made her voice sound very calm. "I wouldn't say things the right way if we talked now," she explained. "But you were right, Ty, I am none of your business, and I have to think about everything before I can see you again."

"That's not what I meant. I *swear* that's not what I meant. Do you think I care who's touched you before me?"

"No. I know you don't." She sidled around him, desperate to be gone.

"Wait, Carrie. Wait!"

Lou started barking and dancing around his feet. Carrie saw her chance and walked away, as fast as she could without running. She heard Ty curse, and hoped he hadn't tripped over the dog. He called to her one more time, but she kept going and didn't answer.

14

The last rays of the sun warmed a line of limp laundry hanging in the cabin's side yard — yellow work shirts and wide-waisted denim trousers; towels and pillow cases and three narrow sheets; a cotton nightgown, long, skinny stockings, a woman's drawers. Tyler approached the cabin slowly, tired from the climb; he'd come on foot, wanting the time to put his thoughts in order. The smells of hot pine and bleach and wet earth mingled in the humid air. Beside the porch, the flowers and low shrubbery were dark and wet — from a recent dousing with wash water, he surmised.

He stopped with his foot on the porch steps when he caught sight of Carrie through the screen door, seated in profile at the table, poring over something. She didn't see him; the hand she was resting on her temple shielded him from sight. Something about her still posture, her fluid angularity or the long, gracious curve of her neck, arrested him. Sexual heat engulfed him in a fast, spiking wave, taking him by surprise. Small, soft, helpless young women had attracted him in the past, rich men's pampered daughters who flirted and promised secret things with their eyes. Carrie was nobody's daughter, she couldn't flirt, she wasn't helpless, and her elegant body was sleek and reed-slim, practically boyish. He wanted her more than he'd ever wanted anyone. She wasn't a "maid," she'd said. Who had her lover been? His curiosity was as low-minded as it was uncontrollable.

She lifted her head. When she saw him, she laid down the pen she'd been using and stood up. "Hello," he said from the doorway. She didn't answer, only watched him. "Is your stepfather here?" he guessed, in a different voice. He hadn't considered that possibility, even though it was Saturday.

But she said, "No, he went into town."

"Ah. May I come in?"

"Yes."

The spare, small room was shadowy; it was time to light a lamp. It smelled of soap and furniture oil; the bare floor looked freshly swept. There were no pictures on the walls, no ornaments or mementos anywhere. If he didn't know her, he might have made the mistake of thinking that Carrie's spirit, the vital, imaginative center of her, was as barren as this room.

He moved toward her, uninvited by her

manner, drawn anyway by a sudden ungovernable tenderness. She didn't retreat, but behind her smile he glimpsed a remnant of the half-wild wariness he'd thought was gone between them for good. He reached for her hands, resisting the urge to embrace her because she was skittish, and because of the news he'd come to tell her. He'd sent her enough confusing messages; now, clearly, she was the one paying for his confusion.

"I was writing you a letter," she murmured, sidestepping, sliding out of his hands like a cool, slippery fish.

"Were you?"

She gestured toward the table. "It's not finished." She brushed a wayward lock of hair behind her ear. She was tense, but she looked aimless and indecisive; something had gone out of her.

"Do you want me to read it?"

"It's not finished," she said again; then, "Yes, if you want to."

"I'm sorry about last night, Carrie," he blurted out. "Even though you don't want to hear it. What happened was entirely my fault — again."

"No, it wasn't," she said gently. Her eyes hinted at some dark awareness that disturbed him. He wanted to argue, but she glided past him to stand in the doorway, leaving him

272

alone. He picked up her letter.

Dear Tyler,

Thank you for the loveliest summer of my life. Dreams fade when you wake up, even the magic ones you think you'll hold on to forever, but this was a dream I'll never forget, even when I'm an old, old lady.

I don't want to write about last night except to say that many things got clearer to me afterward, and the main one is that it's going to get harder and harder for me to be with you anymore. This has nothing to do with you. I've been not seeing what I didn't want to see. I took your kind friendship and pretended it was something else, and I embarrassed you. Always you say you're sorry, but the fault is really mine.

Do you think we could be friends the way Dr. Stoneman and I are friends? We could see each other every once in a while, and sometimes I might write you a letter — just a note to say how I am doing and so forth. You know a secret about me now, but you should understand that that doesn't mean you have any responsibility for me. I know that you will keep the secret, even though you don't know

273

and have never asked

That was as far as she'd gotten. He reread the second paragraph, amazed at how completely she'd turned everything around backward. Now it was *her* fault she was miserable — she'd misread his "kind friendship" and "embarrassed" him. He was embarrassed, all right, but by his own selfishness, and his arrogance in thinking he could control a volatile situation involving Carrie's deepest feelings. He crumpled the letter in his fist and stuffed it into his pocket.

She started at the violent noise. The anxiety in her storm-gray eyes made him cross the room to her in four long strides. Everything in him clamored to comfort her, tell her he was free to give whatever she needed from him. Failing that, he just wanted to touch her, and tell her anything that would take the tragic shadows out of her face. Last night he'd told her she was too young — cravenly skirting the real issue, of course. She looked much older now, almost world-weary, and disillusioned by her ruined hopes. The dream had indeed died, and there wasn't a damn thing he could say — truthfully — to resurrect it. Worse, what he'd come to tell her would bury it deeper.

She was resting her chin on her clenched

hands, watching him, waiting for him to decide whether or not they could be "friends." His discomfort made him say, too harshly, "Carrie, that's all rubbish and you ought to know it."

"What do you mean, Ty?"

"I mean *nothing* was your fault, you didn't do *anything,* and taking all this on yourself is ridiculous. You make me angry."

She said, "Oh," and tried to escape, but he prevented it by putting his arms around her. He couldn't help himself.

But she was inconsolable; her slender back stayed poker-stiff, her forearms crossed over her breasts to keep him away from her. It occurred to him that it might be more charitable to tell her the truth immediately, not ease into it gently with reassurances that would be shown up soon enough for the lies they were. Her body felt brittle, untouchable. Nevertheless, he kept her in his embrace as he gazed out across her pathetically neat yard, to the dark line where the pines and hemlocks started, and told her the worst.

"Carrie, love, I've come to tell you that I'm going away." He kept talking, even though he could feel the tension draining out of her like grain from a sack. "A letter's come, offering me a chance I can't turn down. An opportunity to do what I'm best at."

"A letter?" Her voice was muffled; she had her hands over her mouth.

"From George Sternberg — he's the U.S. surgeon general. He's asked me to serve on a commission charged with investigating the causes of infectious diseases in Cuba. That means yellow fever. It's what I'm trained for, my best hope of doing anything worthwhile with my life. Carrie, I can't say no."

She nodded her head in agreement. He didn't think she was crying, but he wasn't sure.

"It's the kind of work I've wanted to do for a long, long time. To be asked as a civilian by the surgeon general — do you see that it's an honor, a —"

"Yes, yes."

"Sternberg says he read my paper on erysipelas and asked Major-General Wood about me — Wood's in the Army Medical Corps; he's military governor in Cuba now, and he was Roosevelt's superior in the war. I'm sure it was Roosevelt who told him to recommend me. And" — he tried to laugh — "I imagine it didn't hurt that I've had yellow fever and survived it. I'm an 'immune' — a handy man to have around on a board investigating what causes it."

She pushed away from him at that. Her dry-eyed, grief-stricken face alarmed him.

"Oh, Ty, I'm glad for you," she said, with heartbreaking sincerity. "Of course they want you, you're brilliant, the only mystery is why they didn't ask for you sooner. Will you be an epidemiologist?"

Her careful pronunciation made him smile. "I'll be a sort of junior pathologist, I imagine, who does everyone else's dirty work." It was true, but he doubted Carrie would ever believe it. "The board's headed by Major Walter Reed — he's in Havana now with the rest of the team. They've been there since June." He was letting his excitement show through, he realized with a guilty start. But it was hard not to: Sternberg's summons was his own dream come true.

"When . . ." She trailed off. He started to answer, but she got the rest of it out. "When will you come back?"

It wasn't the question he'd been expecting. Consternation tied his tongue. "I — Carrie — it's —"

That was answer enough, and what was left of her composure collapsed. Her face turned bright red. She hurried to the cold fireplace and stood before it with her back to him, and he had to close his eyes against the painful spectacle of her bowed head and the incessant, aimless pressing of her fingers against the mantel's edge. *Your fault, you bastard,* he swore at himself viciously. It could have been worse: at least he'd stopped short of seducing her. If they'd become lovers, this moment, agonizing already, would have been intolerable.

She said something; he went closer. "I didn't hear you. What did you say?"

Her husky voice sounded thick, gluey. "I always knew that you would go away someday. I didn't think it would be this soon."

"I didn't either. I'll advertise for the practice," he told her, for the sake of something to say. "But I'll have to go whether anyone buys it or not. If not, I'll turn it over to Mueller or somebody to sell for me. I won't just let it go, though — the town needs another doctor."

"When will you leave?"

That was the question he'd expected before, but the answer wasn't any easier. "As soon as I can manage it — a week or two. Carrie, you do see that I have to go, don't you?"

"Yes, of course."

The clomp of hooves and the creak of harness leather sounded through the open door.

"Artemis," she whispered, stiffening. "He's back."

Tyler swore. He went to the table and got his hat, stood rotating the brim in his fingers. "I'll write to you."

Her smile wobbled. "I'd like that."

He whispered, "I'll never forget you," and her shadowy gray eyes darkened. "Carrie — meet me somewhere," he said rashly. "Meet me tomorrow in the wildflower meadow."

"No, thank you."

"Carrie —"

Artemis stomped up onto the porch and halted abruptly in the doorway. Whatever he'd been doing had caked his shoes and his coarse trousers with mud, and stained wide crescents of dark sweat under the arms of his dirty work shirt. His brutish body struck Ty as an encroachment, a profoundly inappropriate invasion of Carrie's pristine cabin, and her innocence, and the gentle essence of her. He saw Ty, and his small, berry-black eyes narrowed in suspicion. "What're you doing here?" he asked, without a trace of welcome.

Tyler hesitated, unsure how he should answer. "I've been visiting with Carrie," he said evenly.

"Why, she sick?"

"No." Tension hovered in the air; he couldn't get a grip on it, couldn't fathom what it meant. Artemis squinted at Carrie while she looked at nothing, hands fidgeting at her sides. Tyler moved toward the door reluctantly. "How's that foot these days, Mr. Wiggins?" he asked, stalling, trying to sound like he gave a damn. "Giving you any trouble?"

"No."

"Good, glad to hear it." Something was wrong, but for the life of him he couldn't define it. He watched Artemis go past him to the table to light the lantern. He tried to catch Carrie's eye, but she was staring fixedly at her stepfather. "Well," Tyler said. "Good evening to you." Artemis looked up once from the lantern and nodded, dismissing him. Carrie shot Ty a lightning-fast glance, but he missed the message, if there was one, because he was distracted by the white flutter of her hands, a quick rise-and-fall gesture that disturbed and confused him. In its wake, her face was completely expressionless.

All the way down the mountain he pondered the indecipherable gesture, haunted by its veiled urgency, and by the persistent worry that he had missed something. Twice he stopped short in the middle of the darkening track and debated going back. His helplessness ate at him. But it was a fitting punishment; she'd said it herself — he wasn't responsible for her.

"I'll never forget you," he'd told her, in his infinite arrogance. It was true as far as it went, but how much worse it was going to be for her — abandoned, dropped back into her silent world like a too-small fish. Carrie was an unfinished story, and what he'd just told her, what she'd just *forgiven* him for, was that he had more important things to do than stay around to find out the ending.

15

Artemis didn't go to work at the mill the next day. Instead, all morning long, he kept on doing what he'd done most of the night before: stare at Carrie. Last night she'd stood it for as long as she could. At nine o'clock, before it was even full dark, she'd crawled into her alcove and pulled the curtain across it to escape his black, steady watching. She'd lain awake for hours worrying about Artemis and crying because of Ty. It wasn't until ten o'clock when she heard Artemis snoring that she finally felt safe, and even after that she lay sleepless till nearly dawn.

Now, washing his breakfast dishes at the basin, she could feel his eyes on her again, from the table where he sat mending a piece of Petey's harness. She wished with all her heart that he would say something, go ahead and accuse her of whatever it was he thought she'd done. They habitually spent their days and nights together without speaking, so why was this silence so different? She knew: because he suspected her of something. But what? What could he know?

A soapy plate slipped out of her nervous fingers, clattering in the sink. She'd better get out of the house. She'd work in the garden, she decided, stacking the last dish and drying her hands on her apron. To reach the door, she had to pass behind Artemis's chair. He had his head down for once, scowling at a knot in a strip of rawhide. She was almost by him when, quick as a snake, he twisted around and grabbed her wrist, yanking on it to stop her. Her heart hammered from shock — and then from realizing how close she'd come to crying out. Trying to pull out of his grip got her nowhere; he was too strong. He hauled her up against his chair until her hip touched it and her breasts were grazing his shoulder.

When he spoke, his lips rolled back over his big yellow teeth in a snarl. "What're you up to? Huh? What're you up to, you and that *doctor?*" He jerked her so violently, her arm ached in the socket. "You keep away from him, you hear me?" She nodded quickly, embarrassed by her fear and the hot tears spilling from her eyes. "I won't tolerate filth in my house. I see that devil around again, I'll shoot him for trespass, and I'll beat hell out of you till you're clean. Understand me? *Understand?*" She nodded again, not able to look at him any longer for fear he'd see how much she despised him. He shoved her away, and she ran for the door.

She spent the rest of the morning in the vegetable garden, weeding and watering, one eye on the cabin to see when he left — because she wasn't going to go back inside until he did. The August sun beat down on her hatless head, baking her; by noon she was sweating and tired. But by one o'clock he still hadn't come out, except once to use the privy. She had a dozen chores to do in the house; she couldn't stay out here much longer. Had he fixed his own dinner? What was he doing in there? *What did he think he knew?*

He frightened her. Her wrist was livid and sore; how could she have forgotten how strong his hands were? The look in his mean black eyes when he'd held her and railed at her was that same look of crazy fury she hadn't seen in years but would never forget, not if she lived to be a thousand. Crouched between two rows of peppers, she wrapped her arms around her knees and rocked. *Please don't let it be starting again. Oh, Mama, help me —*

She caught herself and broke off the pitiful half prayer, made herself unwind, sit up straight on her knees, and not cower. She wasn't a child anymore, she was a woman. She'd written a *book*. And she had friends now, she could get help if she needed to. Whatever happened, she had to keep remembering that she wasn't little Carrie anymore, thirteen years old and terrified.

The cabin looked the same, silent and squat and surely harmless. But her unwillingness to go inside was growing, not diminishing. She tried to tell herself she was silly, she was letting her imagination run wild. *Artemis is taking the day off, that's all. He's in there reading his Bible right now.* He was angry with her about Tyler because he'd never seen her with a man like him before. He was jealous. Why, even a real father, a *normal* father might have feelings like that if he saw his daughter changing before his eyes into a woman.

But how could he know, how could he tell so fast that she and Ty had been something more than friends, at least for a little while? Did it *show?*

She stored her tools away in the shed, dawdling at it. Stalling. *Quit being foolish,* she scolded herself. *He can't drive you out of your own house.* At the well, she pulled up a bucket and splashed water into a copper can to take in with her. Straightening up, she squinted at the cabin, shielding her eyes with her hand. Nothing to see. *Don't be a baby.* All the same, it felt like walking through molasses to put one foot before the other and go in her own front door.

After the bright sun, the cabin was dark. That sour-sweet smell should've warned her, but it didn't. All she noticed was Artemis sitting at the table, hunched over his Bible. She took a deep, relieved breath and went toward the kitchen basin to wash. Passing behind him, she saw the blue Mason jar beside his elbow, half-full of liquor. She almost dropped her water can.

Instinct made her turn her head and keep moving, smoothly, not too fast — he would strike if he knew she was afraid. She felt his eyes boring into her back as she unbuttoned her sleeves and rolled them up to her elbows. *Maybe he's not drunk. Or not yet, maybe there's still time to get out.* The chill of the water on her hot skin made her shudder but she kept at it, bathing her face and throat, hands and forearms, not hurrying. But then she heard the scrape of his chair on the floor. She froze.

"Getting prettified?"

The slur of his words told her everything. She couldn't turn around. Couldn't move.

"God will not hear vanity. The generation that's not washed from its own filthiness will perish."

His footsteps came to a stop behind her. She saw herself rinsing the washcloth over and over, paying minute attention to the shapes it made when it bloated with water and when she squeezed it dry in her fists. She heard the clink of Artemis's teeth against the whiskey jar and the sound of him swallowing, the sharp exhale of his breath afterward. In her side vision she saw him put the jar on the drain board next to her. Dropping the washcloth, she turned slowly around to face him.

The look in his eyes, cruel and righteous and full of the black lust, answered all the questions she had left.

" 'God is faithful,' " he quoted to her. " 'He'll not suffer you to be tempted above that ye are able, but will make a way to escape, that ye may be able to bear it.' "

He wasn't any taller than she was, a part of her mind observed in surprise. Funny she'd never noticed that before. But she never got this close to him if she could help it. Holding his rabid gaze, she glided one sideways step toward the door.

"Every man is tempted when he's drawn away of his own lust and enticed. But you won't draw me into sin again, you fornicating slut, and I'm God's punishment on you."

She bolted.

He reached the door before she did, slammed it shut with a giant paw, and lunged for her. Even though he was staggering drunk, he was lightning quick and ten times stronger, and she was too panicked to move fast. He had her in a strong-armed hug, grunting and breathing his whiskey fumes in her face. Why wrestle, why fight? This was fated — it had happened before and it was happening again. But the second she got one hand free, she hit him as hard as she could on the side of his beefy neck.

He struck her across the face, using his knuckles. She sailed backward and crashed against the cook stove, scattering pots and pans. The cast-iron skillet wobbled near her hand; she picked it up. Artemis came at her like a charging bull. She took a mighty swing. The skillet thunked him hard on the shoulder, and he howled. She couldn't back up any farther. He yanked the pan out of her grip and flung it at the wall behind her.

"When lust hath conceived," he panted, "it bringeth forth sin, and sin bringeth forth death." He wound his enormous hands around her throat and squeezed.

She flailed out at him, kicking, scratching. He had her bent backward over the stove. She couldn't see anything but dots, black and white and streaming. But suddenly he let go of her neck and started to tear at the buttons on her dress. She rolled to her side, trying to throw off his vile weight, but it was no use.

When he pawed her bare breasts, she snarled at him like an animal, blind with rage, yanking his hair, biting at whatever part of him came within snapping distance of her teeth. Keeping silent was the last thing in her mind, but it didn't matter; she could've screamed in his face and he wouldn't have noticed. He'd gone mad.

Her knee missed his groin by an inch. He jerked back, and she scrambled out from under him, running blind. He came at her from behind, bringing her down on top of the table. It crashed beneath them, the legs splintering, sending them both sprawling. Carrie got one knee on the floor, but before she could spring up, Artemis leapt at her, taking her down again. His weight crushed her; she couldn't get her breath. Pulling on her hair, he got her turned around; he wanted her facing him. He was battering her with his knees, trying to get between her legs, struggling with apron and skirt and petticoats. She raised up to sink her teeth into his throat. He screamed. When she tasted his warm blood, she had to let go, repelled by it.

He arched over her. She saw his raised fist; he was going to kill her with it. She twisted her head, and then she felt the score-settling *smash* against her temple. She dropped down a deep hole into nothing.

★ ★ ★

At first it was just a feeling, lurking beyond the shifting rock wall between her and consciousness, beyond the pain and confusion. A feeling that he was watching. Time crawled, or raced; somehow it passed. The rock wall began to shift. She had a glimpse of gray denim — a trouser cuff. Now a mud-caked shoe. Everything in her rebelled — uselessly. She let her eyelids slide closed again, feigning unconsciousness; a second later she slipped into the real thing.

The rock wall crumbled, and the fragments of her mind began to reassemble. The next time she opened her eyes, all she could see were scattered marsh violets and larkspur, mule harness, notebook papers, a copper pot — the toppled remains of their struggle. Artemis was nowhere in sight.

She sat up. The room whirled and buzzed like a bottle full of bees; she held onto her head so it wouldn't go flying off her shoulders. Since the table was broken, she had to stand up on her own power. Nausea passed in its own time, but her vision wouldn't clear. The least movement of her head caused pictures to flap into place sideways, like somebody thumbing a deck of cards. By focusing ferociously, she made out that the mantel clock said ten minutes to four.

A noise — from Artemis's room. Panic snaked along her scalp, skittered down her spine. She stumbled against the door, fingers gone numb, scrabbling at the knob. Wrenching at it, she got the door open and staggered outside.

Wobbling crazily, she made it to the lean-to and got that door open, too. But she didn't think she could hitch Petey to the wagon. She'd ride him, then. She'd gotten the bridle bit in his teeth when she heard a crash from the cabin, then a drunken shout. She jerked the harness over Petey's ears and somehow got it buckled. Using the stall rail to stand on and mount him bareback, she kicked him into a startled jog, out into the sunny yard.

Artemis was lying sprawled on the porch step, legs spread, arms waving. When he saw her, his vacant eyes burned, and he let out a bellow of rage. She slapped Petey's rump with the long rein and dug her heels into his sides — but he was trotting toward the cabin, *toward* Artemis, and he wouldn't turn. Now Artemis was only twelve feet away, hollering about concupiscence and fornication and idolatry. But he was stuck like a bug on his back, elbows and heels slithering helpless against the porch step. Slowly, like a scene from a nightmare, Carrie finally turned the mule and got him moving, barely, on the narrow track that led down the mountain.

Everything hurt, and Petey had the bumpiest gait of any creature God ever made. All that kept her from despair was knowing she was going to see Tyler, and every jolting step the mule took carried her closer to him. When she reached the town's outskirts, she had enough presence of mind to take the alley, not Broad Street, so she wouldn't be so conspicuous. The few people who did see her looked startled, but she didn't know them and nobody stopped her. She couldn't imagine what she looked like, but it must be a sight, with her hair down and her face bloody, her torn dress held together in one hand.

Turning left on Antietam, she spied Broom on the far corner, bent double under a sackful of cans. He saw her a minute later and immediately dropped the sack in the middle of the sidewalk. Petey snorted and stepped sideways, scared of the noise. Broom shouted out, "Carrie!" and scampered over, arms and legs churning like broken umbrella spokes, while she tried to quiet the mule. She felt lightheaded, and she couldn't make her legs stop shaking, but she was glad to see Broom.

"What happened? How'd you get hurt? Are you hurt bad, Carrie? What happened to you? Was it Artemis done it? Was it, Carrie?" She finally nodded, and Broom burst into tears.

He pressed his face against her thigh and sobbed, clutching at her skirts. "I'm all right," she whispered, reaching a hand down to stroke his head. His dirty hair had the feel and the color of grass in wintertime. "Help me, Broom. Take Petey's reins and help me get to Dr. Wilkes."

Broom never was any good with horses or mules; they scared him to death. But he took Petey's reins without a second's hesitation and pulled him all the way to Dr. Wilkes's office. If he thought anything about the amazing fact that she'd just spoken her first words to him ever, he didn't mention it.

"I swear it never fails," grumbled Mrs. Quick, setting Tyler's plate of sausage rolls and scrambled eggs down with an irritable smack — as if it were *her* dinner the pounding on the door downstairs was about to interrupt. She made no move to see who it was, though. Cooking and cleaning were her jobs, and hell could freeze before she offered to do anything extra. Holding in a sigh, Ty got up from the table and headed for the sitting room stairs that led down to his office, shrugging his coat on as he went.

The banging got louder, but he didn't race to the door; experience had taught him that nine out of ten "emergencies" were no such thing, and that the more theatrical the messenger's arrival — upon a foaming steed, for example — the less urgent the call was likely to prove.

He pulled the door open. Carrie's friend, the boy named Broom, tumbled in and almost tackled him.

"Doc, Carrie's pa beat her up! Look, look!" He pointed to the street behind him. Over his flailing arms, Ty saw Carrie standing on the far side of her mule, resting her head on its withers. He shook Broom off and ran.

She put her arms out when she saw him. Bruised face, bare breasts, wild hair — he took it all in at a glance, and snatched her up in his arms before she could fall. Her hand on his chest was unsteady but her eyes were clear. "I expect I look worse than I am," she said faintly, trying to smile — trying to reassure *him.*

"Don't talk. I'll tell you how you are." But she was clearheaded and apparently not mortally hurt. His panic subsided.

Broom danced around them all the way back to the house, babbling and weeping and wringing his hands. In the waiting room, Ty told Carrie, "I'm going to put you here because it's more comfortable than on my examining table." He laid her down on the sofa. "Mrs. Quick, bring my medical case down here now!" he called up the stairs. "And a blanket!" Kneeling beside Carrie, he stroked the hair out of her eyes and asked in his best professional voice, "What hurts you the most?" Her hand went immediately to the abraded black bruise on her right temple. He skimmed it lightly with his fingertips. No sign of a broken bone spicule to cause bleeding into the brain. "Were you unconscious?" She nodded gingerly. "For how long? An hour?"

"Longer, I think," she whispered.

"Did you vomit?"

"No."

"Are you cold now?" She shook her head. She wasn't shivering; her skin felt warm but not hot. She wasn't in shock — yet. "You're going to be fine," he assured her. But when Mrs. Quick appeared with the blanket from his own bed, he threw it over Carrie quickly and tucked it snugly around her feet.

"Lord have mercy! What happened to you, child?"

Ty said, "Thank you. Mrs. Quick, I won't be —"

"Artemis done it," cried Broom. "Artemis beat her, lookit her face. Aw, Carrie." He fell to his knees and pressed his head against her arm; his body shuddered convulsively from the spasms peculiar to his disorder, worse now because of his distress.

295

Tyler put two firm hands on his shoulders and hauled him to his feet. "Broom, you want to help Carrie, don't you? Don't you?"

It took a second to get his complete attention, but then he answered eagerly, "Yes, sir!"

"Well, what she needs right now is rest and quiet. Rest and quiet, hear me? She needs to lie in this room by herself and be quiet so she can get strong again. Do you know what you can do to help her?"

"What?"

"Take her mule to the livery and tell Hoyle Taber to stable it overnight. Tell him I said so. Can you do that?"

"Yes, sir, I think I can, I'm pretty sure I can."

Tyler wasn't sure at all. But he said, "Good boy," and gave him a manly thump on the shoulder. "Go along now. You can see Carrie tomorrow, and I bet she'll be good as new."

"No, tonight," he protested, the tears starting again. "Let me see her tonight, please? Please, Doc, I'll —"

"All right," he cut him off hastily. "Come back tonight, and I'll tell you how she's doing."

"Okay! Now I'm going to the livery."

"That's right."

"I'm taking Petey, and he's gonna stay there till tomorrow."

"That's it." He got Broom through the door, and closed it on him before he could start in on a new subject.

Carrie's pulse was rapid but even. Her pupils weren't dilated, but it seemed impossible that she could have avoided concussion after such a blow. "What else hurts you?" he asked, after making sure no bones were fractured. She rolled her eyes and made a face. "Hurts all over," he guessed, smiling in sympathy. "Did he hit you here?" He pressed lightly against her spleen, her pelvis, her kidneys. She made a negative gesture with her hands that said he hadn't hit her in the body at all. The bruises must have come from falling, then, or struggling with the son of a bitch.

"Is this girl staying here overnight, Dr. Wilkes?" Mrs. Quick asked from behind him. He'd forgotten she was there.

"Yes."

She gave an unpleasant adenoidal sniff. "Then I guess I'll have to stay, too."

Tyler looked at her over his shoulder. "How's that?"

"For decency's sake. Can't have a young woman in your house all night and no chaperone."

He made a private face at Carrie of exaggerated revulsion. She put her hand over her mouth and turned her head into the sofa cushion — a reaction that heartened him so much he almost laughed out loud. "Thank you, that's very kind and thoughtful of you, Mrs. Quick, but it won't be necessary." He stood up and put a solicitous hand on his housekeeper's massive shoulder. "I wouldn't think of troubling you," he said as he walked her toward the staircase. "It's after six now, you don't want to be late getting home. Miss Wiggins is fine where she is, I assure you. She'll rest here tonight. I'll be upstairs, of course, within calling distance if she should need me. There will be no proprieties flouted, you can be sure of that. Thank you very much, though, that was indeed a gracious offer." He was practically pushing her up the stairs now.

She went, but he couldn't flatter her into approving of it; if there was one thing Mrs. Quick knew, it was her duty. "All right, I'm going," she conceded with a disapproving *hmpf*, "but don't blame me for the consequences," and clomped up the stairs to get her things. A minute later he heard the screen door slam, then her heavy feet on the back porch steps, descending.

Tyler crossed to Carrie's sofa and knelt beside her again. "I don't know about you, but I feel better already." Her answering smile was wavery. "Does your throat hurt, love? You've got some bruises here, over the larynx." Artemis must've used his thumbs.

"It hurts," she whispered.

He got alcohol and cotton from his case and began to clean the worst of her wounds. "Feel like telling me what happened?"

She shrugged, looking away. "Not right now."

"Okay. Are you sleepy?"

"No." She winced when he swabbed the jagged scrape over her cheekbone.

"Sorry, almost done. That's a good sign, that you're not sleepy. It means you probably don't have a concussion. Are you hurt anyplace I can't see, Carrie?" She shook her head. "Good. Now I want you to lie quietly for a while. Would you like me to bring you a cup of tea?" She shrugged again. He stood and went toward the stairs.

"Ty?"

"Yes?"

Her voice was huskier than ever because of the injury to her throat. After a moment's hesitation, she asked, "Do I have to stay down here?"

He stopped with his hand on the banister. "No," he realized sheepishly, and came back to her. "No, you sure as hell don't."

"I can walk," she protested when he bent to lift her, blanket and all.

But he wanted to carry her. Her flimsy weight felt solid and substantial in his arms. He wanted to give her the comfort of touching, and he needed it for himself.

He carried her upstairs and into his bedroom. When he laid her on the bed, she sat up awkwardly, glancing around the room. "Am I going to stay here tonight?"

"Yes." He went to his bureau and took out a clean nightshirt. "Put this on while I make the tea," he instructed.

"Thank you," she said when he laid it on her lap.

"Do you need any help?"

She shook her head, stroking the soft cambric. "Do you sleep in this?"

"Sometimes." He couldn't quite fathom her mood. He watched her for another minute. "Put it on, Carrie, and then get under the covers. All right?"

"Yes."

"I'll come back in a little while."

"It's a good thing . . ." Her voice trailed off; she stared into space, seeming to have forgotten what she was going to say.

"What's a good thing?" he prompted.

"It's a good thing I don't have any patients in my hospital. Since I'm staying here tonight."

"Yes, that's fortunate. Crawl into bed, love. I'll be right back."

But when he returned ten minutes later with a pot of tea, a plate of biscuits, and an ice bag for Carrie's head, she was sound asleep. Curled up at the edge of the bed, her hands, invisible under the long sleeves of his nightshirt, folded under her cheek.

"Carrie?" he murmured, cupping her shoulder.

She said, "Mmm?" and blinked up at him sleepily.

"Nothing. Go back to sleep."

She did, easily and naturally, and for the first time he relaxed. She'd wake up with a headache, but he could give her something to soothe it. The main thing was that she was sleeping normally, not reacting narcotically to trauma. She would be all right.

Broom came back a few minutes later. It took time and patience to make him understand why he couldn't see Carrie again, and firmness to make him go home, not sit outside by the door all night, keeping a vigil. His devotion was touching, even if his doggedness was exasperating. Tyler took the opportunity to ask him how long he'd had tics.

"I ain't got no ticks!" he denied, chin jerking, wrists twitching. "Once I got fleas, but they went away when winter come."

Tyler patted his shoulder and told him to come see him next week. They'd talk.

It was a perfect summer night. He dragged a chair out onto his back porch and sat down to watch the sun set and wait for Carrie. Relief that she wasn't seriously hurt was giving way to slow-burning anger and a deadly longing to make Artemis pay. It was convenient to direct his fury outward, and he did that for as long as he could. But honesty wouldn't permit him to enjoy that escape indefinitely. The bitter truth was that if he'd troubled to trust his instincts, Carrie wouldn't be hurt. Last night he'd *known* something was wrong, but he'd walked out and left her alone, ignoring the question in his mind because it was easier. Above all, he'd wanted to get away from her sadness. Not being *responsible* for her — that was the great thing, that's what had been paramount in his mind. He'd wanted to cut the messy ties between them early and cleanly, to avoid unpleasantness. What he'd done was hand her over to a brute.

He didn't notice when the sun set, saw nothing of the rising moon. He sat on in the dark, brooding, reliving the scene in her cabin last night and imagining different endings — fighting Artemis to some bloody conclusion, or ignoring him and bearing Carrie off down the mountain to safety. But what happened after that victorious scene was harder to imagine because he couldn't get past one inescapable barrier: in two weeks he'd be gone. The circumstances that had brought their two different and incompatible lives together would no longer exist. Walking hand in hand with Carrie into the golden future was a hypocritical dream, because they had no future. Not together.

The screen door squeaked on its hinges. He turned and saw her silhouetted in the doorway by the yellow kitchen light. "There you are," he said softly, going to her. "How do you feel?" His hands went out automatically and began to roll up the long sleeves of his shirt over her slim wrists. She looked frail and insubstantial, hair tousled, her expression a little lost. But he could see the provocative outline of her body, backlit through the linen shirt, and the view caused him to forsake any sentimental comparisons between her and a sleepy child.

"I'm better," she said rustily.

He stroked her jaw with his thumb. "Head hurt?"

She gave a faint nod. "Not too bad, though. The ice helped. Thank you."

"You're welcome." He'd thought to make her smile by mocking her odd formality, but he only succeeded in discomforting her. "Sit down, I'll bring you something for your head. Are you cold?"

"No."

"Not at all?"

"No." She sat on the chair he'd just vacated, back straight, hands clutching her knees. She started slightly when he smoothed her hair back and covered her forehead with his hand. Her skin was cool and dry; no fever. Frowning, he left her and went inside.

He made a powder of phenacetin and quinine sulfate, and gave it to her in a paper with a cup of hot tea. She swallowed it down the way most of his patients took their medicine: trustingly, not even asking what it was. Afterward he leaned against the porch rail, alternately watching Carrie and the starlit sky, waiting for her to speak.

She didn't. Too much time passed; her silence was lifeless, not companionable.

"Tell me what happened," he said at last.

She spoke to her knees. "You already know. He hit me."

"Was he drunk?"

"Yes."

He reached out to touch her — her hair or her shoulder, just to offer some kind of solace; her body didn't move away so much as shrink. Diminish. The message was the same, though: she didn't want his hands on her.

A subtle chill prickled his skin. He whispered, "Talk to me, Carrie," but she didn't move. He didn't know what to do; he couldn't even see her face. The melancholy silence flooded back between them, much worse now because of the dreadful possibility taking shape in his mind. A rustle of leaves distracted him, followed by the familiar sound of toenails on wood — Louie, back from his nightly prowl, scrabbling up the porch steps. As usual, he went into a delirium of joy at the sight of Carrie. She slipped from the chair to the floor and embraced him, to his unbounded delight, while Ty sat on the railing, chin in his hand, and smiled with humorous resignation. "He never greets *me* like that," he complained, "and I'm the one who feeds him. I guess he likes girls better. Pretty ones, though; he's got no use at all for Mrs. Quick. Lucky I'm not the jealous type . . ." He stopped, appalled; he'd been trying to draw a laugh from her, and now he realized she was sobbing.

He went down on his knees beside her. She shifted away when he touched her, but she wouldn't let go of the dog — who was subdued now, as if he sensed that she was grieving. Ty pushed his handkerchief into her hand and stayed where he was, listening to her heartbroken weeping, watching her trying to smother the sound in Lou's furry neck. Her anguish and his helplessness caused him an almost unbearable distress. He'd consoled the bereaved, the pain-racked, the hysterical — a hundred times, but he'd never felt this desolated by another person's sorrow, or more hopelessly inept at soothing it.

He thanked God when she stopped crying. She mopped her face and blew her nose, and fell back against the shadowy clapboard wall of his house as if she were exhausted. Lou settled himself along the length of her outstretched thigh, and heaved a sigh that sounded for all the world like relief. Because it was impossible now not to touch her, Ty wrapped his fingers around her long, skinny foot. Her face was a delicate pale oval, indistinct in the dimness. He wanted to hear her voice; but there seemed to be only one question in his mind, and he wasn't ready to ask it. Stalling, he slid his fingers between her cold toes, in and out, reconciled to the gently sexual pull the contact aroused in him. He heard her light sigh. Squeezing her bony ankle, voice soft, belying the tension in every muscle of his body, he put the question.

"Carrie, did he rape you?"

Her head went back against the wall; she appeared to be looking up at the sky. The answer he dreaded came out on a wispy, disembodied breath. "Yes."

He made some sound. He felt her hand pressing against his and realized he was hurting her. Releasing her ankle, he was about to reach for her, and to hell with whether she wanted it — *he* wanted it — when her hopeless voice came again and arrested him.

"But not today. Five years ago."

Five years ago.

"And — only once."

Only once.

Tyler put a hand under Lou's belly and lifted him bodily up and away, then shuffled on his knees into the dog's place. Carrie pressed back against the wall, her body a white blur of mortified resistance, but he snaked his arms around her and held on, dragging her up against him. He said her name repeatedly, holding tight until a measure of calm came back and helped him see what he ought to do. Rocking her, working against the stiffness in her he couldn't seem to defeat, he chanted, "Darling, darling, it's all right, you're safe now. Tell me — no — Carrie, let me hold you —"

But she would not allow it. She scrambled to her knees, pushing back at him with her hands. "Don't, please. I don't want this."

"What do you want? Carrie —"

"I can't bear your pity."

He was floored. *"Pity,"* he repeated stupidly. *"Pity."*

"I can't bear to have you touch me the way you touch the others, all your — patients. I don't want kindness or friendship from you anymore. I want everything. But you don't want me that way, Ty, and it's killing me. You have to let me go."

She stumbled up, batting aside the arm he put out mechanically to stop her. Stepping past him, she jerked open the screen door and disappeared inside the house.

He felt as if he'd been racing up a hill and had just achieved the summit. Head down, hands on his knees, he waited for his heart to slow and his breathing to steady. His body knew before his brain that he'd come to a decision.

Louie was guarding the screen door, staring inside at the bright, empty kitchen, ears cocked. Tyler put his shoe across the dog's chest to hold him back. "Sorry," he muttered, sidled inside, and shut the door in his face. Flicking out the porch light and the kitchen light, he headed for his bedroom.

She'd turned on the bedside lamp, but she was standing in front of his bureau, gazing down at a framed photograph of his parents. He moved toward her cautiously, but she didn't turn or step away when he stopped behind her. Her head was bowed; he couldn't read her expression in the mirror over the bureau.

"Your mother and father?" she asked, fingering the silver frame.

"Yes."

"They look . . ." She hunted for the word. "Formidable. And very handsome." She exchanged the picture for the one beside it. "And this is your sister, Abbey."

"Yes."

"Is she always laughing?"

"Very nearly."

"She'll miss you. When you go away."

He put his hands on Carrie's waist. Her head shot up. "You were wrong about me," he said in a low, level tone. "I do want you, in the same way. Just as you said — everything." Her eyes softened indulgently; she didn't believe him. He slid his hands to her hips and gripped them hard. "I want to lie with you and make love," he said starkly, enjoying the shock in her face when he said it. "I've wanted us to be lovers since that night on the bridge, the first time we kissed." Her eyes shone; her mouth widened enticingly with surprise. "But, Carrie, I —"

She heard only "But" and tried to twist away. He gripped her harder and kept her still. "But I'm going away," he whispered, his lips grazing the crown of her head. "Carrie, my darling, I have to leave you. I must."

Her bright, gentle smile, at once hopeful and forbearing, took his breath away. "I don't care," she whispered back. "I love you. I never thought you would stay. Did you think I thought you would marry me? Oh, Ty, I just love you. I just love you."

She defeated him. Circling her in his arms, he held her close, and buried his face in her sweet-smelling hair.

16

He wanted to look a little longer at their reflection in the bureau mirror, because the view of his big, suntanned hands sliding across Carrie's stomach and stretching the white fabric of his shirt tight over her hips was an erotic pleasure he wasn't ready to relinquish. But she pivoted in his arms and embraced him, and then kissing her seemed like an even better idea.

For Carrie, it was as if they'd never kissed before and this was their first, or at least their first free, uncomplicated kiss, with neither of them holding back or trying to ignore a guilty conscience. Her mouth opened under his gentle probing and welcomed his warm, sleeking tongue, sucking on it softly until he growled low in his throat and pressed his hands against her spine to bring her nearer. "I don't want to hurt you, Carrie," he whispered, "and I might, inadvertently. So you must tell me if I do. Promise."

She ran the tip of her index finger along the furrow between his dark eyebrows. "I promise," she said dreamily.

"I mean it." He frowned harder at the spreading, blue-black contusion at her temple. "How do you feel?"

She licked her lips delicately, tasting him. "How do you think?"

He couldn't help smiling. "Seriously."

Her arms around his neck tightened. "Oh, Ty. I think you must've given me happiness medicine." She laid her head on his chest and closed her eyes, to enjoy the feel of his fingers smoothing the hair back from her forehead. He had the cleverest hands. "We're going to make love, aren't we," she said on a long sigh, a statement more than a question — but needing to make sure.

"Yes." It didn't feel like capitulation to him anymore; it felt like a gift. He pressed his mouth to her hairline, letting stray wisps tickle his nose.

She lifted her face. Behind her shining eyes lurked a question, shy but also bewitchingly matter-of-fact: *Well, what now?*

What, indeed. Of course he must handle her with great care and utmost tenderness, go slowly, lead her along this new, risk-strewn path with deliberate consideration, for in every way but technically Carrie was a virgin. But behind her, in the mirror, his hands had hiked the nightshirt up to the tops of her long thighs, and he could see the narrow white crescents of her buttocks gleaming like smooth marble under the hem. In the unexpected flash of lust that scorched him, he wanted more than anything to strip her bare and take her where she stood.

Instead he took her hand and led her to the bed; they sat down on the edge, side by side. He smiled at the prim straightness of her back, and trailed his fingers up and down to relax it. She smiled back, enjoying that, but behind her sensuously drooping lids blinked the eyes of a very alert and attentive pupil. He slipped his fingers inside the square neck of the shirt and stroked them softly across her chest, discovering that her skin was as smooth as warm glass. "Amazing how much better this shirt looks on you than me," he observed.

Carrie tried to take a deep breath, but her lungs weren't expanding quite right anymore. "Shall I take it off?"

He shook his head slowly. "I will."

Her heart gave an extra heavy pound, then missed the next beat entirely. Even kissing him, she'd never felt like this before. Ty taking her clothes off was a powerful thing; it would've scared her to death if it hadn't been so thrilling. Every button he unbuttoned gave her body a new jolt; it started behind her ribs and shot all the way down to her feet, making her go soft as butter inside. The last button was right over her woman's place, and the feel of his fingers there made her flex her thighs together. He slipped his hands in and coasted his warm, dry palms slowly over her pelvis, her stomach, right between her breasts, across her collarbone and up to her shoulders. He pushed the open shirt behind her arms, and when he looked at her bare breasts, she felt the tips pucker and crinkle. Just for a second, she was embarrassed. She might've tried to cover herself, but her arms were stuck to her sides in the nightshirt's long sleeves. But then Ty put his fingers on her breasts and made little circles, and then he pinched the peaks ever so gently. Her head fell back. It felt like shooting stars were popping and sparking in her nipples and then zinging away, down to her vitals. It didn't last long enough, though — he stopped, and when she opened her eyes he was scowling at her throat. "Bastard," she thought he muttered.

"Don't look there, Ty. Don't think about it," she advised, whispering. "We won't let him spoil this."

He took her face between his hands, holding her jaw and feathering his thumbs across her cheeks. "Sweet Carrie, I'm sorry for what he did to you. I'm so sorry."

"I'm all right, though. I'm so happy right now."

He kissed her with all the tenderness in him, over and over, each kiss taking them deeper, binding them tighter. She was drawing deep gulps of air when she could, her breath coming fast and hot in his mouth; he felt her move under his hands, and opened his eyes to see her squirming the rest of the way out of the nightshirt. He began to unbutton his own shirt, but she put her fingers over his to stop him. "I will," she said in her husky voice, and his whole body tightened.

She started out boldly enough, but about halfway down his chest Carrie got pudding-fingered, because shocking pictures of where all this undressing was leading to kept flashing in her mind's eye. But she finally did it, got every last button undone. "Oh, you're beautiful," she breathed, pulling his shirt wide open. "I always knew it, and now . . ."

"Now?"

"Now I get to touch you." She spread her palms across the hard, horizontal ridges of muscle that lay over his stomach, amazed at how soft his skin was there — she hadn't thought he'd be soft anywhere. He wasn't covered all over with hair, like Artemis; he only had a downy, light-brown sprinkle in the center of his chest. It narrowed at the bottom to a fascinating arrow that trailed down his flat belly and disappeared into his trousers.

She didn't have the nerve to explore that — yet — but she couldn't resist putting an index finger on one of his flat nipples, the way he'd done for her. But it didn't do a thing for him — not until she gave it a little flick with her fingernail. Then it turned to a hard bead, and Ty sucked in his breath. "Aha," she murmured. "So."

"So," he agreed, beguiled by her keen-eyed, gentle-handed exploration.

"I don't know *anything*," she wailed, suddenly dismayed. "Nothing at all. All the things to do, all the differences between a man and a woman — Ty, I'm not going to be any good, I'll just —"

"Be quiet," he commanded, kissing her to make sure she did. "It's all right not to know anything. You can't hurt me — everything you do pleases me. It's all good between us, Carrie. All good." He took her down in a long, drugging kiss, pressing her into the feather mattress. When she tried to protest, offer more reasons for why she wasn't going to be any good, he seized her wrists. "Don't talk with your mouth full," he instructed, nudging her lips apart and slipping his tongue deep inside.

She was delicious; he tasted and stroked and teased until her mouth turned greedy and tried to devour him, too. The sounds she was making — low moans, whimpers, incredulous gasps — drove him up too high, much too fast. Using his teeth on her jaw, he took voracious bites along the way to her ear; he opened his mouth wide and sucked it in, giving it a sharp, darting tongue bath. Carrie squealed and shuddered and tried to squirm away, but he held on, burying a heady laugh against her neck. "I'll stop," he promised, panting. She was driving him crazy.

"When you kissed me before," she finally managed to say, "those two times before you knew I could talk — do you remember?"

"Mm, yes, I seem to remember."

"I was so scared."

"Scared? Why?"

"I thought I'd make a sound — a noise! I wanted to. I came so close, especially when you . . . you know."

"What?" He smiled, knowing the answer but wanting to hear her say it.

"Touched me," she whispered.

"Touched you? Where?"

"Here." She made a vague gesture at her chest.

"Where?"

A dawning smile replaced the consternation in her beautiful face. His own smile faltered and froze as he watched his shy, innocent Carrie cup her left breast with her hand, and then slide the hand away in a slow, uncannily knowing caress, uncovering a pert and very erect nipple. "Here."

He'd never been offered a more tantalizing invitation. He accepted it instantly, using the flat of his tongue first, then the edge of his teeth, and finally the rough-soft tug of his whole mouth, while Carrie arched upward and clutched at the sheet. Still suckling her, he shoved the bunched-up nightshirt past her hips, and she wriggled the rest of the way out of it herself.

He raised up over her, to see her. "Ah, Carrie, look at you. You're so . . . lovely," he said, inadequately. She had long, fine bones and smooth, feminine flesh and muscle under skin the color of clean sand. Gently curving hips — nothing boyish about them after all — and perfect breasts with pink-tipped nipples, one of them rosier now than the other. Dimpled knees and long, elegant shin bones, gleaming like white blades through the satiny skin. Delicate ribs, a shallow, enticing navel, reddish curls set in a seductive triangle between thighs the shade of sunlight on snow —

"I am?" she quavered.

"You are. Very, very lovely."

It amazed her. *Lovely.* Would he say that just to be kind? Yes, certainly — but she almost believed him anyway. It was a marvel-

318

ous possibility, and it filled her with a shivery, tentative joy. *Lovely.* It would be enough. Oh, it would last her forever.

Tyler stood and stripped off his clothes, swiftly, with no wasted movements. When he was naked, he stood still, waiting for her to look up at him. Finally she did — but only his face; it was as if the rest of him had been chopped off at the neck. He put one knee on the edge of the mattress, tipping it, and her, a little toward him. "Look at me, Carrie. It's just me. My body won't hurt you. Artemis hurt you, but I never would. Never could."

"Oh, Ty, I know that." She pondered for a moment *how* she knew it, and why what her stepfather had done hadn't poisoned her against all men for good. Because it was Ty, of course. But part of it might also be because of her real father, whose memory was still strong, who had loved his women — her and her mother — and been a gentle man until the day he died.

"Then look." He smiled to reassure her, careful to come no closer; and at last, with an air of valiant fatalism, she sat up and faced him. He expected a shy peek or two, just to break the ice, accompanied by a lot of maidenly blushes. She might be blushing, he couldn't tell, but what started as a shy peek turned very quickly into something else entirely. She studied him minutely and intently, taking her time, missing nothing. "Well?" he finally had to ask, breathing unsteadily. Her fascinated scrutiny unnerved but didn't unman him. In fact, quite the opposite.

"Well," she echoed. She finally raised her wide gray gaze to his eyes. "My goodness, Ty, aren't we different?"

He threw back his head and laughed, an easy, solid, real laugh. "By God, we are," he agreed heartily. Tugging the covers out of the way, he lay down beside her.

"All right," she said after a few quiet seconds.

He turned his head on the pillow they were sharing. She had her arms at her sides, chin pointed to the ceiling. "Hmm?"

"I'm ready, Ty. Go ahead."

He turned on his side, propping his head on his hand. He mustn't laugh again, but her fearful bravery tickled him. "Well, you know, I'm not quite ready," he confessed softly. That seemed to surprise her. He could understand why; he'd warrant he looked ready enough to her. He traced her tense profile with a finger, forehead to chin and back up again. Her nostrils were thin and fine, and her nose ended in a sharp but elegant point. It was her mouth that captivated him, though. The sensitive lips quivered when he caressed them, from nerves and desire and self-consciousness. He kissed the corner nearest him, working his way across the dainty arch to the center. Her pink tongue was lying in wait, and flickered out at his when he got there. She bit his lips, both of them and then one at a time, without a trace of shyness. She was learning very quickly.

He let his slow hand drift to her stomach, pressing and kneading her there until she groaned, head turning on the pillow. But she went still when he twined his fingers into her soft pubic hair. "Open your legs, Carrie," he breathed against her mouth. Her thighs were trembling; for all her brave words, she was afraid. Petting her, softly squeezing the firm flesh of her mons pubis, he waited.

It was what she wanted. It was all she wanted. But she held back, constrained by a lifetime of propriety. To — to *open her legs* so a man could touch her there went against everything she'd ever been taught or instinctively guessed about proper female behavior.

But this was Ty. And — God help her — he'd just stretched out one of his long, sensitive fingers and touched a tender spot on her that reacted like a switch: it turned her mind completely off. But it left everything else humming and alive. Shuddering, whimpering his name, Carrie spread her thighs wide.

She was slippery and hot — so small — sleek as a wet silk glove. He fingered her softly, ardently, eyes shut tight. He pictured her: dark and swollen and slick with wanting, her lips pulsing softly around the two fingers he had inside her. He spread them a little, stretching her; a sound like "Nunh" burst from her throat. He could take her over the edge now, he realized. Right now. Was that the way? No. Selfish — maybe, but he wanted to go with her the first time. With excruciating reluctance, he withdrew his hand.

Carrie put both of her hands over her heart. "Oh, Ty," she breathed in a high, frustrated quaver. "That was wonderful."

She thought — it hit him hard, and once more he had to swallow euphoric laughter — she thought it was *over*. "Darling," he muttered, "oh, sweet, sweet Carrie," kissing her cheeks and her eyes, her pretty nose. He reached for her far shoulder to pull her onto her side, facing him. "Your turn," he whispered, watching her drugged eyes clear quickly and then widen in apprehension. "Touch me, love."

"Oh," she said, the word rising and falling with false enthusiasm, "would you like me to?"

"Yes," he said emphatically. "I'd like it as much as you did."

That got her. "Well, then. All right."

She was trying mightily to hide her distaste for this job, and clearly preparing for the worst. He wished he could help her, ease her into it gradually — but he was fast losing his capacity for finesse. He caught her fluttering hand and led it directly to his jutting, rock-hard member, wrapping her fingers around it and urging her to move in the basic, uncomplicated way that pleased him best.

After a few aghast seconds, Carrie had to admit to being pleasantly surprised. *Well, what did you think, silly,* she scolded herself, *a — a snake?* She didn't really know what she'd expected, but it wasn't this warm, silky stalk, thick as a tree limb and throbbing with life. Then she looked at Ty's face. She softened her hand instinctively and stroked him as she would any wild creature she wanted to gentle — a bird, a fawn. "Is it right?" she whispered. "Do you like it?"

"Yes."

Even she could tell that this was an understatement. He had an expression she'd never seen, half rapture and half torture, his heavy-lidded eyes following the slow movements of her hand as if she was hypnotizing him with it. She smiled, and all her trepidation vanished. The big dread — which she hadn't even known was there, not for sure — was sud-

323

denly gone. This was Ty's body, and this amazing part of him could be touched by her in a way that thrilled him. What had she been afraid of? It was only him, and her, loving each other with their bodies. So simple! She'd known it already on some level, and now she knew it straight out, bone deep and whole-hearted.

"Oh, Ty, I do love you," she had to tell him. "I love you so much."

He came out of his trance and stopped the provocative slide of her hand with his. The thought crossed what was left of his mind that he ought to stop everything now. It was humbling to discover that he couldn't. "Sweetheart," he began, some fraudulent, grandiose sentiment taking shape on the tip of his tongue —

"Oh, you don't have to say it back," she assured him hastily, winding her soft arms around him. "*That's* not necessary."

God, she meant it. She was offering her lips to him, generous as always, still slightly too shy to kiss him first. His heart turned over. Covering her, he took her mouth in a rapacious kiss designed to deprive her of reason, and him, too. Lost, blind, his fingers found her again. "Carrie, darling, let me —"

"Yes —"

But he could feel the tension quivering in

her stomach muscles, and it gave him the grace to enter her carefully.

Alive to everything, intent on every nerve ending in her body, Carrie got another surprise: it didn't hurt. He'd said it wouldn't, and she'd believed him — until the last second. Then the perverse memory of her stepfather's battering cruelty had come swimming up out of nowhere, soaking her with anxiety. Ah, but this, this was Ty and he was her lover; he rode high inside her, swelling and filling and completing her. And yet — how amazing! — already she was almost used to him there. When he moved in her, just a little, she couldn't keep from crying out from the unbelievable pleasure, coming from a place in her own body she hadn't even known existed. Minutes ago she'd imagined she would lie quiet and passive in his arms when this moment came, while he did something to her vaguely resembling this, after which they would be "lovers." But it wasn't like that at all. She was *in* on this, the most intimate and intense experience of her life; every tiny movement, every beat of his pulse sent sparks of exquisite sensation glittering through her. Just then he pushed his hand beneath her thigh, pulling it up and then pressing her knee out to open her even more, make her feel even more *possessed*. How could he know what she wanted before she knew it herself? She gasped out her all but unbearable pleasure, clutching at him with clumsy hands, hardly able to return his slippery, ravenous kisses. Flexing both knees to brace her feet, she arched up at him, frantic.

The effect was electric, and he was perilously close to the brink already. *Slow down*, he commanded his body. But she was so very tight, and her hot sheath nipped the tip of him in an innocent but incredible way he associated with women who took money for this and knew everything. Muttering fervent endearments, he buried his hands in Carrie's wild hair and tried to hold her still, stroking her shallowly to regain control, kissing her to divert her.

Carrie didn't know anything about control. Subtlety was lost on her. She writhed and twisted, pressing his buttocks, the small of his back, wanting him deeper, lost in the urgency, so close, so close —

Something intense and inevitable launched her striving body out into space; she floated there weightless, saturated in perfect pleasure. It was excruciating, it was too much — it was over. Too soon she slid over another edge and toppled into a different space, a black one shattered in pulses with brilliant bursts of light. Each one lifted her up for a second, then dropped her gently down to the next. Everything thrummed and vibrated; when her body came back to her, her blood was singing.

The exquisite contractions tapered away; she felt herself softening, going liquid all around him. She felt Ty's mouth on her closed eyelids, and the sweetness of it almost made her cry. She might have — but he hooked his hands around her shoulders then and rasped against her cheek, "Carrie, hold tight." She did, and felt him surge and plunge inside her. He went still for an unending moment, buried deep; everywhere she touched he was hard and tense and straining. His breath came out in a whoosh and a second later his body convulsed, driving into her with a force that ought to have been painful but wasn't. And now she did weep, because her impossible love was too big to hold inside. Offering herself, arms and legs banded tight around him, she took what he could give, and counted it enough.

But in the sweet, whispering aftermath, while he rested in her arms and gave her his slow, lazy kisses, the shadow of a fear ghosted across Ty's heart — that he would never have enough of her.

Carrie was singing. Ty finished shaving his top lip before letting himself smile at the novel sound, a gravelly but lovable contralto not perfectly on pitch. "What is that?" he asked, glancing at her in the mirror over the sink.

She leaned back in the bathtub and stuck her big toe inside the spout of the cold water spigot. "It's called 'Wild Mountain Gal.' "

"I've never heard it before. It's very . . ." He searched for a polite word. "Soulful."

"It was one of my father's. I think he made it up. He liked to make up tragic songs, but he couldn't sing any better than I do. My mother was the one with the beautiful voice in our family. Ty?"

"Hmm?"

"Have you, um —" She paused, sitting up to study her knee. "Have you done what we did with lots and lots of women before me?"

The razor nearly nicked his jaw. He took a long time swishing it around in the basin, considering how to answer. "Lots" was such a relative word. Compared to Carrie, he was a veritable Don Juan. "Why would you want to know something like that?" he asked, delaying.

"Oh, well, you know. I was just wondering."

"No," he decided to say. "Not lots." And certainly nobody like her. There had been prostitutes and "loose girls" in college, and in medical school he'd had affairs with women

328

who were in "the arts" — actresses and opera singers, and a woman who'd fancied herself a sculptor. But the young, single women in his own social set were usually too respectable — or too discreet — to jeopardize the brilliant marriages their families had been planning for years, certainly not for anything as frivolous as mere physical passion.

Carrie listened to the silence after his answer and assumed he was remembering an old favorite. *Well, you had to ask, didn't you?* she jeered herself. And then came another question she ought not to ask, bubbling up like a spring in March. "How do you . . . Why don't you . . ."

He turned his head to look at her. "What?"

"I was just thinking, since you see ladies all the time and sometimes they're naked and you have to, um, you know, look at them and touch them and everything, how do you . . ." She squinched all her toes, exasperated with herself because she just couldn't seem to get past that.

"Keep myself from ravishing them?"

Glancing up to see him grinning, she put her hands over her face and giggled.

"I'll tell you, it's not easy. A man needs nerves of steel."

"Really?"

He sent her a mock disgusted look and

went back to shaving.

Oh, he was joking. "No, but really," she prodded. "Why isn't it the same? I'm sure it's not, but *why* isn't it?"

"The same as what *we* did? Oh, Carrie." He shook his head at her in the mirror. "Think about it."

She didn't have to think for long, the answer was so obvious. But now she wanted to hear him say it.

Tyler set his razor down and came to sit beside her on the edge of the tub. The bath towel around his waist slipped; he retied it absently, his mind on the alluring spectacle Carrie's bobbing breasts made, just breaking the top of the sudsy water. Her long, lithe, angular body inflamed him now; he wanted her incessantly. But she was soaking away her bruises and soreness in hot water and epsom salts on doctor's orders, and it would be unprofessional, not to mention ungentlemanly, to interrupt the treatment solely for the doctor's pleasure. Not for a little longer, anyway.

"How did you get this?" he asked, tracing an old, double-sided white scar at the top of her trapezius muscle.

"I'll tell you," Carrie said softly, after a little pause. "But you didn't answer *my* question yet." She was thinking how beautiful he was, like a statue of a god or a king in a book. He had a gentleman's occupation, and yet he was strong and muscular — not brawny like Artemis or Eugene, but fit in a refined, athletic way that suited her much better than beefy strength would have.

"Move your feet," he warned, reaching for the faucet nozzle and turning the hot water on again. "Well, if you must know, I've never had a lady patient as beautiful as you are."

She laughed gaily, genuinely amused.

"If I did, I'd probably lose control and take her right there on my examining table."

"You would not."

"Why wouldn't I?"

She beamed at him. "Because you're strong. And honest." She searched for the right word. "*Ethical.* But what makes you not even *want* to 'take' a pretty patient on your examining table?" she persisted.

"Because one thing has nothing to do with the other. A patient's body doesn't even look the same as a woman's body to me."

"No?"

"No." He rested his forearm on his thigh, leaning in. "When I look at you, Carrie, what I see is silky skin and soft, luscious breasts. Tasty little nipples that pucker up when I kiss them. A flat belly to press mine against, thighs — such long white thighs, and they open for me with such lush, feminine eagerness." Her lips were parted; she'd gone pink in the face, eyes wide and rapt on his. His hand went to her bent knee and rocked it softly — No, enough of that.

He leaned back, folding his arms. "Do you know what I see when I look at one of my 'naked ladies'?"

She shook her head.

"I see the sweat ducts in her epidermis. I take careful note of her areolar glands and her lactiferous ducts. Her transverse colon fascinates me, but it's nothing compared to her rectus femoris or her pharyngeal orifice, the graceful curve of her innominate bone —"

Carrie whooped with laughter. Cupping her hands, she splashed a wave of bath water over the side of the tub, drenching him.

Her took her shoulders and pressed her firmly back against the tub's sloping end. "Understand?" Before she could answer, he gave her a loud, smacking kiss, which turned gentle before it was over.

"Yes," she said, breathless, eyes glowing.

Back at the sink, Tyler smiled at his steamy reflection, pleased with his answer, even though it didn't quite cover the whole truth. Occasionally his humanity got in the way of his professionalism, and he actually *did* see a woman as a woman, patient status notwithstanding. No need to bother Carrie with that little detail, though. Especially since there was no conceivable possibility that he would ever act on those feelings and touch a woman under professional circumstances in any other way but professionally.

Moistening the lather drying on his chin, he thought how easy it would be to get used to this domestic harmony he and Carrie were sharing. He was quite sure she had never enjoyed an intimate hour in a bathroom with a lover before; but the truth was, he never had either. It was an unexpectedly agreeable experience, nearly as seductive as lovemaking. She was a good companion, interested and interesting, unaffected, open and confiding, talkative but by no means the chatterbox he liked to tease her she'd turned into. He felt relaxed and mellow in the expanding silence between them now, content to let it go on indefinitely. So he was unprepared for the shock when Carrie broke it.

"My stepfather raped me when I was thirteen," she announced in a low voice, crouched in the tub, holding one foot and staring fixedly at her toes. "It was about six months after my mother died. I was taking a bath in the kitchen of the house where we were living in Spaulding." She gave a quick laugh. "It wasn't a bit like this bathtub — it was a little wooden basin, you could kneel in it but you couldn't sit. I didn't think Artemis was coming back that night, because he was drinking a lot by then and most times not getting home till morning. I'd learned to be scared of him, and usually I could stay out of his way. Sometimes I wasn't quick enough, though, and he'd slap me or hit me — but only if he was drunk, so it wasn't as bad as it could've been."

There was a stool beside the tub, next to the wall. Tyler dried his face and sat down on the stool, just behind Carrie's left shoulder.

"He's religious, you know, in a peculiar way, so he'd always be sorry afterward, and beg forgiveness — God's, not mine — for losing control of himself and hitting me. Anyway, on this night he came home early, while I was still bathing. He was drunk. When he saw me he started raving about how I'd tempted him long enough, quoting things from the Bible about Eve and Adam and the serpent. I didn't know much, but I knew he wasn't just going to beat me this time."

She leaned forward, wrapping her arms around her calves. "He grabbed me and pushed me down on the floor. I shouldn't've bothered to fight him, I just hurt myself worse, but I couldn't help it. And I couldn't stop screaming. He kept hitting and hitting, he bit me — there." She reached back and touched the white scar on her shoulder. "But I still wouldn't give up, and I kept on screaming. So he put his hands around my neck and started to squeeze. Then I stopped. But I was awake when he raped me. I didn't pass out till he finished, still choking me. I thought sure I was dying."

Tyler couldn't think of any words. He laid his hand on the back of her neck and held it there.

"When I woke up, I could barely move. Everything hurt — the back of my head from where he'd slammed it on the floor, and the bite on my shoulder, all covered with dried blood. My throat — I couldn't swallow at all, and it was even hard to breathe. And — where he'd raped me. That pain seemed the worst, because I felt so ashamed."

She dropped her head to her bent knees just for a second, then sat up, drawing a deep breath. "I tried to get up and cover myself, but I was too sick and dizzy. So I just stayed in a ball in front of the cold stove, drifting in and out of some kind of dream. The next thing I remember, it was getting light out, and Artemis was crying and praying out loud in his room. I was hot — I had a fever. I tried to get up again, but I fell, and he heard me. He came in and covered me up with a blanket, blubbering and carrying on like a crazy man.

"I was really sick, and neither of us knew what was wrong with me. It was two days before we figured out that I couldn't speak. By then he'd prayed himself into a frenzy. I remember when it happened, when he found out I was mute. He dropped down on his knees right there beside my bed and started praising God, thanking Him for saving him."

"Because you couldn't tell anyone who hurt you," Ty guessed.

"That's what he thought. He said the Lord had used me as an instrument to wrest his soul back from the devil. He swore he'd spend the rest of his life in prayer and acts of contrition, and dedicate himself to God for saving him from earthly retribution for his sins.

"I only understood part of it — the part that attributed his salvation to me not being able to talk. Right after that I got even sicker. I had tetanus, although we didn't know what it was then. It was just like you said, Ty, that day in the cabin with Artemis after he hurt his foot. The pain and the rigidity, the exhaustion — everything you said. It was horrible."

"Ah, Carrie." He started a gentle massage up and down the back of her neck, trying to ease the tension.

"It lasted for two weeks. I think I almost died. After it was over, a doctor came — Artemis was too scared to call one before, for fear of what I might do. But when the doctor asked me what happened, who hurt me and everything, I didn't tell. I truly *couldn't* speak — he'd hurt something inside my throat, you know, when he choked me — and I really believed his — his — reformation was a *miracle*. I thought for some reason God had sacrificed my tongue for Artemis's sake. So I didn't tell. And I felt safe then, because he'd thrown all his liquor bottles away and gotten very pious."

She splashed water on her face, rubbing her eyes. "But the doctor was suspicious anyway, because he knew — everybody in town knew what Artemis was like. He couldn't prove anything, though. Once the deputy sheriff came and asked me a lot of questions, but I wouldn't answer. It was right after that that Artemis decided we should move away from Spaulding. So we packed everything up in the wagon and came north. He bought the cabin on Dreamy and got work in the sawmill in Wayne's Crossing."

"How long did the muteness last?" He was squeezing a sponge full of water down her back over and over, to keep her warm.

"About two months. Exactly as long as he stayed sober. One day I found out by accident that I could talk, and that night he didn't come home. When he came back the next morning, still half drunk and stinking of alcohol, I didn't say a word. It was so *clear* to me that there was a connection." She twisted around, looking at Ty for the first time. "Even now, you know, I'm not *sure* it was a coincidence. It seems too strange for it to be pure chance. Don't you think?" When he didn't respond, she faced forward again. "Well. I thought so, but I was only thirteen. Anyway, from that day on, I pretended. And it worked — he never touched me. He didn't keep liquor in the house, and whenever the urge came on him he always went away, to town or to a friend's house, or just in the woods by himself. He had to fight his lustful thoughts, and me not speaking kept reminding him that once God had granted him a miracle."

"Until yesterday," Ty said grimly.

"It — was starting before that," she admitted. "He was drinking at home the day he hurt Shadow." She twisted around again, smiling. "The first day we met." He didn't smile back. "And — other times, lately. I'd stay out of the house when it happened. One night I slept in the woods."

She leaned forward abruptly and pulled the chain on the plug. "I think I'm turning into a prune," she laughed, grasping the sides of the tub and climbing to her feet.

"How much longer would you have kept it up, Carrie?"

She heard the anger in his voice and stepped out of the tub carefully, not answering.

"Forever?"

There was a dry towel on a hook by the door. She reached for it, but Tyler shot up and snatched it out of her hands. "Answer me, how long? Forever? The rest of your damn life?"

"I don't know."

He pulled her against him and hugged her too hard, until the fury and distress snarling inside him collapsed under a wave of tenderness. They leaned against each other, swaying, soothing each other with their hands. After a long moment, he said, "You can't stay there anymore."

"No, I know."

"What will you do?"

She moved her shoulders. "Something. I can't think." She didn't say it, but she'd thought many times before now that there wasn't much an unlearned mountain girl with no skills but bird-watching could do to earn a living.

He didn't say it, but he was thinking he would support her in any way she would let him, for as long as she needed help. Tilting her chin, he touched her lips with his, as gently as he'd ever kissed a woman. Her hands crept to his face, and she held him in the tender, cherishing way she had that always undid him. But fragments of her dreadful story haunted his mind; it was too easy to see Carrie at thirteen, screaming in fear, locked in a hopeless struggle with her drunken, loutish stepfather. His own hands on her hardened, then relaxed.

He still had the towel, and he slid it down the lean length of her spine to her buttocks, stroking them through the soft cotton in a way meant to soothe but also to excite. Beads of water still glistened on the warm, flushed-pink skin of her breasts and her abdomen. He blotted her dry, teasing her nipples with a gentle, ruthless friction, relishing the sharp sound of her breath catching in her throat. The stool was behind him; he sat down, dragging her close, rubbing her hips, her flanks, her long, sleek calves. And then the pretense that he was drying her fell away with the towel.

Her uncertain laugh turned into a gasp when he buried his nose in her damp pubic hair and blew on her. He moved his mouth to her navel and sucked on it delicately, while Carrie's fingers in his hair clenched and pulled. Cupping her lush pelvis, he kneaded her softly, urgently, while his other hand clasped one warm buttock to hold her still. The need to arouse her was a compulsion now; a mute dread consumed him that if he didn't try to erase the brutal legacy from her mind and her body now, this moment, while the vicious story still corrupted the very air between them, then something irretrievable would be lost, something vital not only to Carrie but to himself. To both of them, equally. His big hands spanned her hips; he spread them across her belly. Using his thumbs, he opened her, and pressed his mouth to the warm, pulsing core of her.

Carrie lost her frantic grip on his shoulders when he sank to the floor on one knee. Grabbing for the wall behind him, she braced against it, stiff-armed. What was this? What could it be? *It's all good between us, Carrie.* He'd said that. *All good.*

Yes. Oh, God.

"Ty?" she gasped. But the edge rushed up before she could say anything else, and she tumbled over it headlong. She heard her own voice making the most extraordinary sounds, like singing in harmony with her body while it flew off on another wild journey. When it was over, she could barely stand. Ty had to support her, her head lolling against his shoulder, her legs shaking.

"What on earth?" she quavered in a faint voice, not really expecting an answer. What could possibly explain *that?*

He scooped her up in his arms. "There's more," he promised, smiling down at her and looking proud as a peacock.

She wrapped weak arms around his neck. "I doubt it," she said frankly.

Slowly his smile faded. "I'll make you forget him, Carrie. Never think of him again. Never." Impossible, of course; he knew it as he said it.

But halfway to the bedroom, he had to laugh when she bit his ear and asked in a husky murmur, "Forget who?"

17

A sound woke Carrie. She sat up in bed, confused for a second. Then she saw Tyler standing in front of his bureau, tying his tie, and everything came back to her. Gray light shimmering around the curtain told her it was morning, so wishing it would never come hadn't done any good. She put her hand on the rumpled sheet beside her and stroked the empty, still-warm space where he'd lain. *Good-bye,* she told it. *Good-bye,* she said to his straight, strong back.

He turned.

"What time is it?" she asked.

"About eight-fifteen." He came toward her, pulling his suspenders over his shoulders. "Good morning, sleepyhead."

"So late!" She sat up straight, stunned. She couldn't remember sleeping this late in her whole life. She started to get up, but Ty sat on the edge of the bed and pulled the covers back over her legs. Her naked legs. He kept his hands on her waist and his eyes on her breasts and said, "Yes, it's very late. But I want you to stay in bed today, Carrie."

He smelled like soap and tooth powder. "But doesn't your housekeeper come this morning? Eight-thirty, you said —"

"Yes, but we won't worry about her. I'll tell her I slept downstairs and gave you the bed. Or you came up this morning, early — you had to vacate my waiting room sometime, after all. I'll tell her —"

"But I have to get dressed. I have to go, I can't stay here."

"No, I want you to stay. I want you to rest, don't do anything today."

"But Mrs. Quick —"

"Mrs. Quick can be damned," he interrupted mildly. "I've got inoculations all day, starting at nine, but I'll be finished by five or so, and I'll take you home to get your things then."

"Oh, Ty, you don't need to do that. I'll be all right — Artemis won't even be there."

"How do you know?"

"He has a two-day job in Lesterstown starting today, picking apples, and he won't miss it because it's double pay." He'll be mad, though, she mulled in silence, because I took Petey and he'll have to walk.

"No," he said firmly, finally raising his gaze from her naked body to her eyes. "I don't want you to go there again without me, Carrie. It's too dangerous."

344

"But I wouldn't stay, I'd just get my clothes and a few things and come back. I can sleep tonight at Eppy's, and by tomorrow I'll have figured out what to do with myself." At least for a few days. Maybe she'd stay in Dr. Stoneman's empty apartment over the hardware store — Ty had said last night he'd call him on the telephone in Harrisburg if she wanted him to, to make sure it was all right.

"No," he said again, and she could see he meant it. "You stay here today and be quiet. I'll take you home tonight, and after that to Eppy's or anywhere you like."

She looked up at him through her lashes. "You didn't care anything about me being 'quiet' last night," she pointed out, in a tone of voice she would not have believed could come out of her mouth. His slow smile made her skin tingle.

"No, you're right," he said softly. "And I feel just terrible about it."

"You do?"

"Terrible." His kiss took her all the way back down to the pillow. The way they kissed now, with such longing and skillfulness and fast results, was nothing like the way she'd always thought people kissed. All night they'd been doing it, and other things, until she was almost as good at it as he was. She certainly liked it as much, and she felt the same way about it that he'd whispered once in a tender confession that he did: "addicted."

"It's late," she murmured, but taking little nips of his tongue, secretly hoping he wouldn't stop. He was rubbing her bare stomach, and all of a sudden she wanted him to do everything to her that had completely exhausted her and made her fall fast asleep in his arms about two hours ago.

But he sat up, groaning, and said, "Yes, it's late, I have to hurry."

He started to kiss her again, a good-bye peck on the lips, but Carrie slipped past him and sat up, too. "I'm getting up. Where's my dress? Oh, there" — on the chair where she'd left it. She started to wriggle into her torn shift.

"What are you doing? I thought we just —"

"I want Mrs. Quick to find me downstairs!" she hissed in a stage whisper. He looked amused. "It's *important*, Ty," she insisted. "I'm going."

"Go, then." He grinned, still watching her from the bed. "She goes home for the day right after lunch. Then you can have the whole house to yourself."

"My shoes!" she said, remembering just in time. She blew him a kiss from the hall and hurried downstairs, feeling guilty and excited, just like a criminal.

346

Seven minutes later, Mrs. Quick found her on the sofa in the waiting room, rumpled and sleepy-eyed, stretching and yawning in her tattered dress.

"Well, how're you feeling?" she asked — grudgingly, but her curiosity was even stronger than her disapproval. Carrie signed that she felt pretty good. "What happened to you? It was your pa, wasn't it, like that boy said? I heard he drinks like a duck. What all did he do to you?" When she realized she wasn't going to get anything out of Carrie past shrugs and vague gestures, she put her hands on her fat hips and said, "Well, you can't stay down here any longer, I got to clean and sweep these rooms, and I only got thirty minutes to do it in. So you'll —"

Had he been listening? At that very second, Ty hollered down the stairs, "Mrs. Quick, ask Miss Wiggins if she'd care to come up and have a cup of tea in the kitchen, will you?"

Mrs. Quick gave a sour-faced sniff and watched Carrie go.

Carrie spent the morning moving from one room to another, trying to stay out of the housekeeper's way while she went about her cleaning and straightening. At lunchtime, Ty came upstairs and ate a bowl of soup in the kitchen. Mrs. Quick wouldn't let Carrie help serve him, but it was plain that she hated the idea of waiting on Carrie even more; so Carrie ended up not having anything until Ty left, and then serving herself a quick bite and eating it standing over the sink. Mrs. Quick's humor didn't improve when Ty told her Carrie was staying alone in his house all afternoon, and tonight he was personally escorting her home. "And tomorrow I'll have a word with Billy Stonebrake," he added. "So there's no need for you to concern yourself about the unfortunate incident at all anymore, Mrs. Quick. You've been very kind. I appreciate it, and I'm sure Miss Wiggins does, too."

He certainly had a way about him. Carrie had to look away so Mrs. Quick couldn't see her eyes twinkling. The mean old goose actually looked *flattered.*

But what wasn't amusing at all was Ty's determination to "have a word" with Officer Stonebrake, who constituted the entire police department of Wayne's Crossing. Last night she'd tried her best to talk Ty out of the idea, but he wouldn't budge. All she wanted was to find a way to support herself independent of her stepfather, and she didn't care scat about justice or due process or retribution. She particularly didn't care for the idea of telling a stranger all about how Artemis had beaten her. But if Ty wanted her to, she guessed she'd have to go ahead and do it.

After Mrs. Quick left, Carrie was alone in the house. Every once in a while she'd hear a high-pitched holler from downstairs, which upset her until she considered that each yell might mean one less child coming down with diphtheria or smallpox. After that, every outraged shriek almost made her smile.

She found a needle and thread in Ty's bathroom cabinet and sewed up the long rip in her dress. After that she felt sleepy and lay down on his bed for a nap. Waiting to fall asleep, she thought back over a conversation they'd had sometime in the middle of the night. He'd asked her where she was in her "cycle," and it had taken her an embarrassingly long time to figure out what in the world he was talking about. When she'd given him the answer, she could tell he was relieved, but she hadn't understood why until he explained about the different times of the month when it was harder for a woman to conceive a child. For some reason the conversation had depressed her, almost made her feel ashamed. No — not the conversation, she realized. Ty's *relief* was what had depressed her. Even now, the memory of it brought a cold, scary loneliness she knew would stay with her for a long, long time. She fell into a restless sleep.

Loud barking woke her up — Louie at the kitchen door, wanting to come in. He was a silly, gentle dog, gawky as a new calf. She'd have petted and played with him all afternoon, but he had too much energy to stay inside for long. She let him out again and wondered what to do with herself next.

Ty's sitting room fascinated her. Books and magazines were always scattered around everywhere — although in neat piles for a while after Mrs. Quick left — and they were the kinds of books and magazines Carrie had seen in the public library but never in real people's houses. Not even Mr. Odell or Dr. Stoneman had as many books as Ty did, and certainly none with titles like *Studies in the Psychology of Sex* or *Naturalism and Agnosticism* or *Das Kapital*. The magazines he read were different from other people's, too; he didn't get the *Saturday Evening Post*, he got *Scribner's* and *Harper's*, which were ninety-nine percent words, no pictures at all to speak of.

The book lying open on his desk now was called *The Scourge of Yellow Fever*. Thumbing through it, she saw that most of it was too technical to comprehend, but the preface was in plain English. The extent of the disease and the devastation it caused surprised her, even though Ty had spoken of it to her before. In the last hundred years, she read, in the Caribbean alone, it had killed a *hundred thousand people*. And it wasn't just a tropical disease: in bad years it could spread as far as Philadelphia or even Boston; in 1878, four years before she was born, twenty thousand people in the Mississippi Valley died of it.

Ty had told her about the different theories there were nowadays for what caused it — that a mosquito carried it, that dirty water and poor sanitation spread it, that germs in the air were responsible — but he'd never once talked about what it had felt like when he'd nearly died of it. The description she found of the disease's progress explained why. It was horrible. She wished she hadn't found it; once she had, she had to read to the bitter end. The sickness came on all at once with a chill or sudden dizziness or a headache so violent it could jerk you out of bed, retching. The second stage lasted about three days, when your fever could reach a hundred and ten. Your muscles and joints felt as if they were in a vise, you were nauseated, your headache was excruciating, and all the while a strange excitement made you act as if you were mad or drunk.

Then, miraculously, all the symptoms disappeared; the vise released you and at last you could rest. You woke up refreshed, thinking the worst was over. But it was a trick. The toxemia had destroyed your liver, and now the terrible hemorrhaging, the "black vomit" of blood and digestive enzymes set in. Jaundiced, bleeding from everywhere, you died in a coma, or from convulsions, or by fainting from heart failure.

Sickened, Carrie slapped the book shut and put it back where she'd found it. Ty said he was an "immune," he couldn't get the disease again because he'd already had it. What if he was wrong? Doctors didn't know everything — they didn't even know what caused it! What if he got it again, even a milder case of it? Or what if, having a *weakness* for it now, he got a worse case and died? She wound her arms around herself, shuddering. Oh, God! All the dreadful images would stay in her mind forever now. She wouldn't mention it to Tyler, though; he would only worry because *she* was worried, and she already knew all the things he would say to try to make her stop. And none of them would do any good.

She shouldn't have looked at the dratted book, and a few minutes later she'd have the joyless satisfaction of saying the same thing to herself again, this time after opening a small, leather-bound photograph album that lay on the table by the window. She'd never seen it before. She was restless, bored, disturbed; the book was fat, intriguing, harmless-looking. The inscription inside, under a recent date, read, "For Ty, lest you forget us utterly! With all our love, Abbey." Leaning against the windowsill, Carrie began to turn the pages.

She'd always known — she'd have to be blind not to — that Ty's world was different from hers, or for that matter anyone else's in Wayne's Crossing. But these photographs, lovingly pasted in the book by his sister with humorous captions and sayings, widened the difference from a gap to a chasm. There was Ty in 1881, tall already at nine years old in his knee socks and knickers and Russian blouse, posing with his classmates on the steps of a building called the Delancey School. There he sat in a sled with his baby sister, in front of a great, snowy, four-story castle — "Christmas at the Camp, Scarborough, 1882," read the caption. There were pictures of him standing among rows of distinguished gentlemen, members of the Racquet Club, the Rittenhouse Club, the Philadelphia Club. Here he was playing cricket, here tennis, here baseball. "Schuylkill Regatta" showed him in a straw hat and a striped jacket, young and unbearably handsome, holding a trophy on the deck of a sailboat. "Summer '89, the Cape May cottage" made Carrie gape, for the "cottage" — like the "Camp" — was a mansion, three floors of porches and chimneys and turrets stretching across a wide, perfect lawn that ended at a cliff right over the ocean. The faces of his mother, father, and sister were familiar to her now — elegant, distinguished people in their graceful clothes, smiling and refined, so quietly self-confident. Ty's best friend was someone named Scottie, a stocky, sandy-haired young man who showed up first in pictures from Harvard, and regularly from then on. "Ty and Scottie in Scotland, Potting at Defenseless Animals," read one caption; "Ty and Scottie Losing to Adele and Me!!" read another — a blurred badminton foursome.

There were more of "Adele" after that. In "Ty and Adele in the Caboose," they were waving from a train; "Ty and Adele *in flagrante*" showed them holding hands on a porch swing; in "2nd Phila. Assembly, 1897," they posed in gorgeous formal clothes with more beautiful young people.

But worse was the last picture in the album, a solitary portrait of the dark-haired, light-eyed Adele. Her soft, mysterious smile might mean anything. She was so beautiful, Carrie ached. For once the caption wasn't in Abbey's handwriting. "Nothing's the same without you, Ty. Come home soon. Your Del."

Have you done what we did with lots of women? she'd been idiotic enough to ask him last night. If she knew anything at all, she knew with total certainty that he had never, ever done what they'd done with Adele. Not

354

Adele, with her high lace collar and her cameo brooch, her gleaming upswept hair and intelligent forehead. A woman like that wouldn't let a man touch her the way Carrie had let Ty. Had begged Ty. She wouldn't lie naked in a bathtub for him to stare at, or spread her legs so he could kiss her the way men must kiss whores in exchange for money —

White-faced, nearly faint with shame, Carrie closed the album and put it back exactly where she'd found it. Rather than cry, she went back into the bedroom, lay down, and fell instantly asleep.

When she woke up, the clock on the bedside table had run down. She sat up groggily, rubbing her eyes. She couldn't hear anything from downstairs — maybe he was finished for the day. Maybe he was waiting for her to wake up so he could take her home.

But he wasn't in the house. The sitting room clock said six-ten. She got a glass of water in the kitchen and drank it over the sink; then another. She was washing the glass when she heard footsteps on the porch stairs. Ty came through the screen door with a panting Louie on his heels. He was in his shirtsleeves, hair disheveled, face damp and flushed. He grinned when he saw her. Her heart turned inside out.

"So, you're awake. We went for a run, we

thought you'd never —"

She went to him and put her arms around his shoulders. She'd only meant to hold him, but the fire jumped between them, and he pulled her head back and kissed her with a rough, unsmiling urgency that went straight to the center of everything she was feeling, too.

"When does it stop?" she gasped, hanging on with clutching hands. "I thought I could have enough, but —"

He wouldn't let her talk; he just wanted to kiss her. She pulled her mouth away with a half-hysterical laugh. "Ty, does it just keep on and on? How do people get any *work* done?"

He had her against the table, the edge hard against her hip. His sweeping arm dashed salt shaker, napkin rings, newspaper to the floor. She let him press her backward till her shoulder blades struck the hard wood.

"Stay the night," he said.

"Yes."

"I'll take you home in the morning."

"Yes."

"Early. No one will know."

They managed her skirts together, and he came into her at once. It was wanton and lewd, sinful. It was unrefined. But it went on and on, and when it ended the image of Adele she'd never stopped seeing shattered into as many pieces as her body. She heard herself cry out Ty's name, and words that made no sense, and on an exhausted sigh afterward, "I don't care, I love you, I don't care."

A colorless dawn was graying around the edges of the curtain. The Carolina wren who nested in the forsythia bush was already up and singing. Carrie kept her fingers light and caressing in Ty's hair, dreading the moment when he would wake. He'd only given in to his exhaustion a little while ago, and it helped a little to know that he was as unwilling to let the night slip past as she was. But it was over now, everything. What a lovely dream, but when he awoke it would be gone for good. So she soothed him the way a mother would soothe a sleeping child, to hold back the morning — the end.

His face, pressed against the side of her breast, was pale from fatigue but still beautiful. She would not have thought any man, not even Ty, could touch a woman the way he'd touched her in the night, with such gentleness and generosity. She hadn't felt ashamed in his arms, not for a minute, even though they'd been as intimate with each other's bodies as she believed it was possible for two people to be. Thoughts of Adele — "your Del" — had come and gone and come again as the hours went by. But even with her new knowledge, Carrie couldn't feel regret for what she'd done. She would do it all again, even if it was a sin, even if afterward Ty would never confuse her with a lady, because she belonged to him now with her whole self. Giving him her heart and soul without her body would've been wrong, *more* of a sin — God forgive her — than holding back and staying chaste. And if she went to hell for it . . . well, then she would go, with no defense except that she loved him. But she'd lost him, too, and that was a different kind of hell in advance.

A violent pounding noise startled her so much, she jerked upright, jolting Ty out of his sleep. "What — ?" she started to say, her heart tripping.

"Downstairs," he mumbled, already sliding away from her. With the speed of practice, he had his trousers and shirt on in half a minute, and then he was gone.

She didn't have long to miss him — but she didn't need long. Resentment, anger, jealousy flooded through her; she actively hated the person banging on the door. Then she *did* feel ashamed.

"Emergency," he told her when he returned. "A child, I have to go." He sat on the bed with his back to her, pulling on his shoes and socks. "Stay here until I come back. I don't know how long. It might —"

"No, Ty," she said, quiet but firm. "I've got to go home." He turned around, but she wouldn't let him interrupt. "If he's there, I'll know before he sees me, and then I'll just turn around and come back. I promise I won't see him without you. It'll be all right."

He kept shaking his head; she thought he was going to argue, but finally he said, "All right, Carrie. But swear to me again that you won't go near him, no matter what."

"I swear. I'm telling you, I'll know if he's there and I'll come back. Don't worry."

He took her by the shoulders. "I'll do nothing but worry until I see you again." He gave her a quick, hard kiss. "Leave the mule at the livery and walk. It's only half-light; be careful and don't let anyone see you. Remember — you weren't here, you went home last night."

"I'll remember. But what shall I do about Petey?"

"I'll get him for you later today. I'll tell Hoyle you remembered he had a stone in his foot and decided to leave him. Or — something, I'll think of something." He straightened his hair with his hands. "I've got to go."

"Yes, hurry." It hurt her throat to say the words, though. She didn't cry. He took her hands; she could see it in his eyes that he knew what everything meant — that it was over now.

"Don't stay here long, Carrie. Go right after I do."

"I will."

His smile twisted inside her. "See you soon."

She nodded.

His last kiss was soft, and afterward he didn't look in her eyes. He was trying not to make it feel like good-bye. He got off the bed, went to his wardrobe for something — she didn't know what, she couldn't look at him either. A moment later she thought he said, "See you" again, but when she glanced up he was gone. His fast footsteps faded. It seemed to Carrie that one of them ought to say it. So, into the gray dawn silence, she whispered, "Good-bye."

No smoke from the chimney. That was a good sign. If Artemis was here, he'd have lit the stove by now to heat up his coffee. And it was barely full light, but there was no lamp burning — another good omen. He wasn't here. She'd told Ty he wouldn't be, and now she was looking at the proof. Odd, then, that she couldn't shake this skittery, uneasy feeling inside. Even if he *was* here, and still asleep because he'd never stopped drinking, she was safe. He wouldn't wake, and if he did, she could simply outrun him. There wasn't a single sensible reason for this peculiar prickly fear. She told herself that several times, standing in the quiet yard. But it didn't help.

The sun hadn't burned through the morning haze, and fog still swirled like ghosts on the ground. Towhees were scratching in the underbrush; nearby a woodpecker drummed. The spiderwort under the window needed watering, and the dayflowers needed thinning again. But Carrie wouldn't be staying long enough for that. More than likely she'd never live here again. Would she have to close her hospital? Yes, probably — but maybe she could move it somewhere else, someplace closer to her new home. Wherever that might be.

With a silent, fog-muffled step, she moved to the porch. The door wasn't closed tight, she saw — it stood about two inches ajar. A strong shock of fear gripped her then; she came close to turning around and running. But she steadied herself by will power and made her legs stand still. *Don't be foolish, it doesn't mean anything,* her mind scolded. *He's not sitting inside cleaning his gun, waiting for you.*

Oh God! — the image of it had her ready to bolt again. *What if he is?*

He's not. This is your house, too, you can go in and get your own belongings. Anyway, he's not here. How can you let your fear of him keep you from going into your own house?

She put her hand on the door and pushed it slowly open. The room was empty, but the sight of the flattened table and all the debris around it shocked her again, calling back the sickening memory of how it had gotten that way. She hung on hard to the doorknob, needing its stability, and stepped inside.

She noticed the rank smell and the buzzing of flies at the same instant, and in the next she saw the muddy shoe. On the floor behind the door, preventing it from opening any farther. She jumped back, too panicked to scream, expecting anything.

But nothing happened, and when she craned her neck, she saw a splayed leg clad in gray denim. Artemis — drunk and unconscious. She took one more step, and saw the blood.

Everywhere. A great pool of it under him, as if he was swimming on his back in it. His eyes and mouth looked like wide black holes of amazement. And where his stomach used to be was nothing except red and gray meat, shiny as wet rubber, with green bottle flies swarming all over it.

Backpedaling, Carrie felt her shoulder

smack the door frame, and then she did scream. Twisting away, she floundered back out on the porch. Fog and silence — just as before. She grabbed her skirts in both hands and ran down the mountain as fast as she could.

18

Tyler's emergency was a twelve-year-old girl with a perforated appendix. He operated immediately, on the family's kitchen table, with nothing but the instruments he'd brought with him boiled in a dishpan and no surgical linens except the clean sheets and towels the girl's hysterical mother found for him. But he worked clean and fast; as appendectomies went, this one was a success. If he'd been called six hours earlier, he might have saved her. After the operation, he stayed with the family for the thirteen hours it took her to die, of acute peritonitis.

His exhaustion was so complete, he could hardly bring himself to detour from the direct route home and stop by the livery stable on Wayne Street. He found Hoyle Taber in his tiny office, going over the day's receipts. They greeted each other tiredly — working until nine o'clock made it a long day for Hoyle, too — and then Ty asked how Carrie's mule was doing. "Did you notice anything in the right front foot, Hoyle?" he fabricated. "She said he was gimpy coming down the mountain, and she thought he ought not —"

"Carrie Wiggins?" Hoyle butt in. "Ain't you heard? No, you couldn't've, you been up at Ettermans' all day. I heard about their little girl. Say, Doc, that was a damn shame."

Ty acknowledged it with a nod, but it was a subject he had no heart for right now. "Yes, I know about Carrie, I treated her on Monday evening. She's all right now, Artemis didn't —"

"No, no, what happened today! You didn't hear this, I'll bet."

"Hear what?"

"She killed her pa! Least, that's what everybody's saying over at the town hall."

Tyler dropped his medical case on top of Hoyle's littered desk. "What?" was all he could say.

"Yeah! She come runnin' down the mountain this morning, claiming somebody killed her pa. Billy Stonebrake went back up with her, and then they got deputies and the county sheriff down from Chambersburg, and now they're all over at the town hall figuring out whether to arrest her. She's got Peter Mueller for a lawyer, I heard, and Frank Odell's up there, too, trying to get 'em to let her go. Hell, half the town was standing around outside till it begun to get dark, but now I heard — Hey, Doc! Wait, here's the damnedest part," Hoyle shouted, jogging after Ty to the stable doors. "The Wiggins girl? She can talk now! Good as you and me! Ain't that —"

The rest was lost as Ty raced up Wayne Street toward Broad. Town hall was a squat, two-story brick building with an incongruous pseudo-Greek portico taking up space across the narrow front. In the glow of a street lamp, two or three scattered knots of people still loitered, waiting for news. A solitary figure lurched away from the curb, and Ty made out Broom's form bearing down on him.

"Doc," was all he could say at first. Impatient to get away, Tyler jerked on his skinny arms, but the boy held on like a spider monkey. "Carrie," he got out, choking on tears and spittle. "Locked her up. Oh, mercy." His body shook as if he had palsy.

At a minimum he needed a sedative, but Ty had no time for him now. "Let me go so I can help her," he said distinctly, finally getting a grasp on the spindly shoulders. He pushed Broom away and gave him a shake to get his attention. "I'll go in now and fix it. You wait here. Understand?"

"You'll fix it?"

"I'll get her out."

"You will?"

"I promise."

"Okay."

But he wouldn't, or couldn't, relax his grip, and in the end Ty had to pry him off with rough hands. "You wait here," he said again and left Broom in the street, crying like a child.

Frank Odell stopped pacing the linoleum-covered foyer when he saw Tyler come through the door. "Hey, Ty," he greeted him, the grimness in his boyish face lightening a little.

"Where is she?"

"Carrie? They pulled a drunk out of the lockup and put her in there."

His hands curled into fists. "Who do I have to talk to to get her out?"

"Well, it's too late for that. Peter's been —"

"Why?"

"They arrested her, they're going to keep her overnight. Tomorrow they'll have the arraignment and set bond. Peter and I figure we can get up about five hundred dollars between us by then. He thinks that'll be enough, but if you'd like to help us out, Ty, we'd —"

"Who's still here? I want her out *now*."

Frank's blue eyes widened at his adamance. "You can't now, I'm telling you. They've arrested her, she's —"

"Why? Why do they think she did it? Tell me what the hell happened!"

A door opened down the hall; he whirled to

see Peter Mueller close it behind him and come toward them, already shaking his head. Mueller was a large, bald-headed man with a bulbous nose, as ugly as his daughter Spring was pretty. He smiled when he saw Ty, no doubt remembering last Thursday night, when he'd won four dollars from him at the weekly poker game. "Well, Doctor, what brings you here? Heard about the Wiggins girl's trouble, did you? They'll probably want to talk to you about her tomorrow, since you saw —"

"Frank says they've arrested her," he cut in.

"That's right. There wasn't much I could do about it. The sheriff's a hardhead," he said, lowering his booming voice a trifle, "but in this case I couldn't much blame him. Why, what's wrong, Ty? Do you know something about this?"

"Tell me what happened, Peter. I've been out on an emergency all day. I just found out about Carrie."

Mueller smoothed the front of his vest with both hands. "Well, she says her stepfather — *says*, mind you," he interrupted himself to point out, still amazed, "she can *talk* now. Must've been the shock. Anyway, she says her stepfather knocked her out cold, night before last. Your housekeeper corroborated that, and so did the boy — what's his name?"

"Broom," answered Frank.

"Broom. She stayed overnight — this is Monday night, now — at your office. That's right, isn't it?"

"Yes."

"And she didn't leave the next day till six or so — this is according to Mrs. Quick again — when you took her home. Got there about seven, Carrie says, and you left soon after. She says you were worried, but she convinced you there was no need because Artemis was away on a job and wouldn't be back till late today. That right so far?"

"Keep going."

Mueller glanced once at Frank, but went on obligingly. "Well, then it gets bad." Reaching inside his coat pocket, he took out a leather-bound notebook. "As near as they can tell right now, Wiggins died between ten and fourteen hours before Sheriff Butts and the deputies first saw the body, which was around noon today. They'll know more tomorrow, but for now they're thinking he was killed around midnight, give or take a couple of hours on either side. Now, what Carrie says is that she was fast asleep when she heard him come in last night, and she has no idea what time it was. She says he didn't even know she was there — she sleeps behind a curtain, evidently, in the main room of their cabin. She

369

says they never argued, they never even spoke, that he went to bed as soon as he got in and that's the last she saw of him. Till the next morning when she found his dead, fully clothed body by the front door."

Mueller pulled on his ear and started thumbing through his notebook. "Not unnaturally, Butts doesn't find this too convincing, and he starts hammering at her. Did she hear a shot? No. Why not? She went for a walk, she suddenly remembers. A walk, in the middle of a moonless night? Yep. Where did she go? Just a walk, she says, there's trails up the mountain behind her house, she knows them well even in the dark. How long was she gone? All night." He looked up from his notes and shook his head, unable to hide his own skepticism at that. "Says she slept in the mule's stall; says she's done it before, to get away from Artemis when he's drunk.

"Did she hear a shot? Butts asks her again. No. Why not? She's a sound sleeper, never hears anything once she's out. Meanwhile, that mule's stall is all of thirty-forty feet from the house, there's no way a dead man could've missed a shotgun blast."

He closed his book with a snap and stuck it back in his pocket. "She's making it all up — that's my *confidential* opinion — and she's the worst liar I ever heard."

"It's pitiful to listen to her," Frank agreed, "especially since there's no way in the world she would've done this, and I don't care how many times the son of a bitch beat her. Carrie wouldn't hurt a fly. *Literally*," he insisted. "I don't know how many times I've seen her carry 'em outside the house so Eppy can't swat 'em." He ran his hands through his carrot-colored hair. "Eppy's fit to be tied. She told me not to come home without her."

"Butts thinks Artemis beat her, and she went back and shot him with his own gun," the lawyer concluded, "and there's nobody to say she didn't." He took out his watch and flicked it open. "Well, gentlemen, it's late. My wife —"

"Is Butts in there?" Ty pointed to the door Mueller had just come out of. The lawyer nodded. "Then you two had better come in with me. I've got something to tell him."

The sheriff's makeshift office was a tiny room furnished with a desk, two chairs, and a filing cabinet. At the moment both chairs were occupied, one by the sheriff and one by Officer Stonebrake; that meant the two deputies had to stand. When the door opened and three more men came in, the room shrank even further.

Sheriff Butts scowled at the interruption. Like most elected officials, he had supporters

371

and detractors. The former said he was a proud man; the latter said he was a horse's ass, and an aptly named one at that. In any case, his dignity meant a lot to him, and he didn't suffer affronts to it graciously. He didn't care to be contradicted, and he particularly disliked admitting he was wrong.

But he had a soft spot in his heart for Dr. Wilkes, who had drained an abscess from Mrs. Butts's rectum last spring and put an end to her month-long, highly vocal suffering in about half an hour. So his frown disappeared when he looked up to see who had burst into his temporary headquarters in the town hall without so much as knocking. "Doctor!" he exclaimed, standing up to shake hands. "Nice of you to come by this late. I'd have sent a deputy over to see you tomorrow if you hadn't, just to nail down a few details. You've heard all about the Wiggins murder, I take it?" He glanced at Mueller and Odell.

"Yes, I heard," Tyler said shortly. "You've made a mistake, Sheriff. Carrie Wiggins is innocent, you'll have to let her go."

The two deputies glared at him. Billy Stonebrake's freckled face turned red. The sheriff let out a hearty, artificial laugh and glanced around at his subordinates with an expression of fatuous tolerance. "Hear that, boys? We've got the wrong person! Well, I've said it for years — what the sheriff's department needs is a good doctor to help us put the criminals away." Forced chuckling greeted his quip.

Tyler made a terrific effort to relax his combative stance. "Listen to me," he said more calmly, "she couldn't have shot her stepfather because she was with me."

The sheriff stroked his upper lip in an attempt to appear thoughtful. "Well now, how can that be? She told us you took her up the mountain and left her there — she says you were gone by seven last night."

"That's not what happened. I — don't know why she told you that. The fact is, she stayed at my house last night, all night."

"Why did she do that?"

Tyler didn't blink. His brain stayed an instant or two ahead of his tongue, no more, and so Butts and the others learned of Carrie's alibi at almost the same moment he did. "She said she felt dizzy. Her head began to hurt again in the late afternoon, and I was concerned about the possibility of cerebral irritation, a condition which sometimes follows concussion. I wanted to monitor her for fever and nausea in case there was frontal lobe damage that hadn't been evident earlier."

Butts peered at him across his half glasses; Tyler tried, but he couldn't read the expression in his steel-gray eyes. But the rest of his face looked skeptical.

"She signed a statement, this one right here —" Butts thumped a paper on his desk with blunt fingertips — "and there's not a word in it about spending the night at your house. If she was sick, why didn't she say so? Why would she make up a story that was bound to get her arrested?"

Tyler's creative tongue chose that moment to desert him. He stared back at Butts, toying with the idea of telling him that memory loss sometimes accompanied head trauma. He hadn't committed perjury yet because he wasn't under oath, but visions of the revocation of his medical license wouldn't go away. And how the hell was *Carrie* going to confirm any of this unless they let him talk to her first? Before he could answer, Peter Mueller spoke up.

"Why don't you ask Carrie?"

Ty didn't like the sound of Mueller's voice; it was too quiet, too deliberately expressionless. An instinct told him the lawyer had already guessed the truth, all of it; if he had, the others wouldn't be far behind. "What difference does it make why she said what she said?" he demanded, trying the offensive again. "I'm *telling* you what happened. Carrie didn't kill anybody, and you're going to have to let her go."

The sheriff leaned back in his chair and twined his stubby fingers over his potbelly. Another thing he didn't like was being told what to do. "Where did Carrie stay in your house last night, Doctor?" he asked mildly. He wasn't stupid, either.

"Where?" Ty pretended the question threw him off, took him by surprise. "In my waiting room, same place she stayed the night before. There's a couch down there, it's fairly comfor—"

"What time did she retire for the night?"

"What time?" He had to stop repeating Butts's questions. "I'm not sure; I'd say around nine, nine-thirty. No later than ten."

"And you stayed upstairs?"

"That's right."

"What time did you turn in?"

"Me? Around ten-thirty, I think."

"Ten-thirty. Sleep well, did you?"

"What? Yes, as well as —"

"Didn't hear anything in the night?"

"No. Hear anything? No. Like what?"

Butts sat up in his seat fast and glared at him. "Like the sound of Miss Wiggins getting up and going out."

"Going out? — Don't be ridiculous, she —"

"I've seen your office — the door to your

375

waiting room faces the street. How do you know she didn't get up and leave by that door while you were upstairs snoring? It would take her about an hour to walk home. She could've shot her stepfather and been back on your waiting room sofa by one o'clock, and you'd never have known the difference." He smiled unpleasantly. "Nothing you've said gives her an alibi at all, Dr. Wilkes."

He heard the dare in the sheriff's voice, and understood perfectly what he wanted him to admit next. Instead he asked, "Are you saying you're not going to let her go?"

Mueller broke in before Butts could answer. "I'd like to talk to Dr. Wilkes alone for a minute, Lowell."

"Fine, talk to him, I've got no —"

"No," Tyler said flatly. He took two steps toward Butts and planted his fists on the edge of the desk. "Carrie didn't go anywhere."

"And how would you know that?"

"For God's sake, Lowell," Mueller tried again, "can't you just let it go now? If Ty says —"

"No, I can't just let it go! Damn it, this is a murder investigation. If the doctor's got evidence that bears on the case, then he can damn well say it, right here and now."

Mueller sighed, raised his arms, and dropped them back to his sides. "Say it, then," he muttered, resigned.

Besides Tyler, there were six men in the room. If he'd thought it would make any difference, he'd have asked everyone but Butts to leave, so he could ruin Carrie's reputation on a smaller, less public scale. But the time for discretion had come and gone. He hadn't chosen it last night or the night before, and it was a little late to start wishing for it now. He took his hands off Butts's desk, stood up straight, and told the truth.

"Carrie couldn't have gone anywhere last night because she was with me. All night. We were together."

The pause that ensued was hostile but not shocked, which confirmed his suspicion that he'd only corroborated what they'd all figured out by now anyway. Butts looked profoundly disgusted. Frank Odell, mild-mannered to a fault, muttered a string of obscenities that left everyone on edge. Ty and the sheriff engaged in a brief staring contest.

The sheriff looked away first. "Get her," he snapped, jerking his chin toward Officer Stonebrake. The startled policeman mumbled, "Yessir," squeezed past the others, and left the room.

Everyone stared at Stonebrake's empty chair as if it were a unique and fascinating artifact. Motivated more by duty than hope, Ty finally broke the silence by asking, "I don't suppose there's any chance of this remaining confidential, is there, Sheriff?"

Butts didn't trouble to hide his dislike. "If the girl confirms what you've told us, she won't be charged with a crime. Naturally people will want to know why. There'll be talk —"

"You're saying no?"

"I'm saying people will be wondering —"

"Not even a gentleman's agreement, for Carrie's sake?"

Butts put the tips of his fingers together and looked at them. "Reports have to be filed. You'll have to make a statement and swear to it. And don't forget that Frank here runs a newspaper —"

"Damn it, Lowell, you won't be reading about this in the *Clarion*!" Odell's voice was reedy with anger.

"Well, fine, that's fine. All I'm saying is that this is a small community, gentlemen, and we all know it. A thing like this, there's bound to be talk, you can't contain it, and once —"

"Forget it," Tyler snarled, turning his back on him. But it wasn't the sheriff he was disgusted with, it was himself.

Butts bristled with antagonism. "Maybe you should've thought about what was best for 'Carrie's sake' a little sooner, Dr. Wilkes.

Eh? What about that?" His voice rose as he warmed to it. "Maybe where you come from this kind of thing doesn't mean much, maybe it's an everyday occurrence, but around here it's a little different, see?"

"Gentlemen," Peter Mueller interjected smoothly, on the verge of a diplomatic lecture.

Ty spun around. "This 'kind of thing' means exactly the same where I come from as it means here. Not that it matters, and not that it's any of your business, but Carrie and I are engaged to be married."

The floored silence didn't last long. In a matter of seconds the door opened again, and Officer Stonebrake ushered Carrie into the room.

She held herself carefully, but the long day of deception had begun to tell. She was waxy-pale from fatigue and strain; her eyes looked haunted and her mouth made a tight white line. How much longer would she have been able to keep it up, Tyler wondered, forcibly resisting an all but overwhelming need to touch her. She looked close to breaking — but she was strong; she might have gone on indefinitely. For five years she'd convinced the whole world she was mute, after all. He thought Carrie knew altogether too much about self-control.

She jolted when she saw him. Her carefully composed features gave way, and she took a step toward him, then halted, recollecting herself. It was painfully obvious that she was attempting to pretend he was nothing to her but her doctor, someone only peripherally involved in her unfortunate predicament. She even said, "Hello, Dr. Wilkes," trying to feign surprise. Frank was right: she was the worst liar he'd ever seen.

"Have a seat, Miss Wiggins," invited the sheriff, stern-faced. "Here, if you please." He placed her in front of the desk, with her back to Ty — deliberately, so he wouldn't be able to coach her. Butts sat back down and leaned his bulky torso toward her, his version of an intimidating posture. He nodded to one of his hovering deputies, who began to write in a tablet. Mueller, standing at Carrie's shoulder, gave her a comforting pat. She looked up, but the smile she tried to return was unsuccessful.

Not a man to mince words, Butts went straight to the point. "Miss Wiggins, Dr. Wilkes has given us some new information and we'd like you to confirm it — or not — if you can. It concerns your whereabouts last night, especially during the time between 10 P.M. and 2 A.M. Is there anything you'd like to add to what you've already told us? Or anything you'd care to change?"

"You weren't under oath before," Peter Mueller pointed out carefully, "so if you weren't being totally truthful when you made your statement, even though you signed it, you won't be in any trouble. Understand, Carrie?"

She nodded slowly.

Tyler couldn't see her face, just her rigid back, and her long neck looking thin, taut, and breakable. A wayward vision materialized unexpectedly, of her in his bathtub; he saw his fingers massaging that slender neck while she told him about the rape of a child. "Tell the truth, Carrie," he said softly.

"That's enough out of you," Butts snapped.

But Ty didn't give a damn. "Tell him," he instructed her, louder.

The deputies shifted, restless, looking to Butts for direction. "Fine, then, tell me," he barked. "The truth, Miss Wiggins, *now*. Where were you last night?"

Carrie's hands flexed and relaxed on the arms of her chair. Ty imagined the debate going on in her mind, the guessing, the weighing of unthinkable alternatives. When she bowed her head, he knew she knew the game was up, because she'd figured out what he'd told them. Damn it, he thought with a flash of irrational anger, she'd *better* know.

"I stayed at Dr. Wilkes's house," she said,

in a voice so low he could barely hear it.

Butts couldn't either. "You stayed where?"

"At Dr. Wilkes's. I . . ." There was a long pause. "I wasn't feeling well." The next silence was a curious one, as everybody waited to hear what interpretation she would decide to put on her tale. She didn't know *exactly* what he'd told them, so she was thinking it was still possible to put a different complexion on things. Nobody uttered a sound; suddenly it was as if seven gentlemen were deferring to a lady.

"I wasn't feeling too well," she resumed, in a murmur still so low they all had to lean toward her to hear. "I — my — head was hurting again. Dr. Wilkes thought I should stay quiet for one more night. And so . . ." She couldn't finish. She wanted to leave it vague, to accommodate whatever he might've said. Specificity was the enemy.

No one looked at anyone else. But Ty had a feeling they were all smiling the same slight, sad, faintly amused smile that he was. Carrie was a terrible liar, but he wasn't much better; it seemed comically ironic, now that it was over, that they'd both tried exactly the *same* clumsy lie. But her fragility had affected them all, he saw, including the sheriff, who didn't even ask her why she hadn't told this harmless story in the first place. They were all in on the

382

conspiracy now: the conspiracy to save her from any more pain.

"Well, Sheriff?" Peter Mueller said, subdued. "Any further need to hold my client tonight?"

Butts cleared his throat and said after only a moment's hesitation, "No, I guess not." He frowned, no doubt thinking of all the work that lay ahead of him now to discover who had really killed Artemis. He glared at Carrie, annoyed with her — but still not enough to chastise her. "You can go, Miss Wiggins. We'll want to speak to you soon about your stepfather's acquaintances, his habits, and so forth. But for now, you're free to go."

She mumbled something that sounded like thanks, and stood up.

Tyler felt the accusing, ice-cold glares of every man in the room. His character had plummeted in their eyes, and no belated betrothal announcement was going to change that. But all he cared about now was getting Carrie out. When he took her hand, she started in surprise. He felt another surge of irritation. Did she think the charade could go on? Did she really think anyone had *believed* her? Her simplicity wrung his heart, at the same time it made him want to shake her.

Out in the dim vestibule, he said, "Wait here for a second, Carrie. Don't go outside without me." She nodded readily, but he hoped his precaution wasn't necessary. It was after ten o'clock; surely the last of the gawkers had dispersed by now.

"Frank?"

Odell stopped in front of him. "This is a hell of a thing, Tyler," he said in a grim, low-pitched voice. "A *hell* of a thing."

"I'm aware of that. Is it all right if Carrie stays at your house tonight?"

"Of course it's all right. Damn it, if she'd stayed with us in the first —"

"Thank you. I think we should go now." With Frank trailing behind, he went back for Carrie. "You'll be staying with the Odells tonight," he told her. She looked startled, but he gave her no chance to respond. Taking her arm again, he guided her out the door, with Frank on her other side.

Miraculously, the street was empty. Even Broom seemed to have disappeared; if he was lurking somewhere, Tyler couldn't see him. All the way down Broad Street to Truitt Avenue, nobody said a word. But when they reached the Odells' small, clapboard-sided house, Ty said tersely, "Frank, would you mind giving me a minute alone with Carrie?"

He looked more uncomfortable than angry now. "Sure," he muttered. "Sure, go ahead." With an awkward salute, he turned and trotted up his porch steps.

Frank was barely through the front door when Carrie reached for Ty. "I wish I could stay with you," she began, but he cut her off by unwinding her arms and leading her away from the dim pool of light the street lamp cast and into the blackness beside the privet hedge.

"Carrie —"

"Hold me," she whispered.

This wasn't part of the plan; he had to keep his head now. But when he felt how hard she was trembling, he gathered her up and held her fast. "Darling," he heard himself call her, "are you crying? It's all right, don't cry anymore. It's over now, it's all right."

"I know, I *am* all right, I just need — this —"

He let her cry. She wasn't hysterical, and her weeping was more exhausted than despairing; but there was something desperate in the feel of her and in the shaky tension of her embrace. He thought of what she'd been through in the last three days, and wondered if she would break down now. But even as he thought it, he could feel her calming. At length she stopped weeping and began snuffling.

"How long were you locked up?" he asked, while she whiffled and blew into his handkerchief.

"Not long. They weren't cruel to me. But they thought I killed him, and that was the worst. I found him, his — corpse." She went stiff and began to shudder. "They never found his gun. They thought I shot him and hid it in the woods. I'll never —" She choked and started to cry again. "I'll never be able to forget how he looked, Ty. Oh God, I wish I could go home with you! But I can't." But a half-second later, she whispered, "Can I?"

"No," he said gently. "Carrie, why didn't you tell them the truth?" What he wanted to say was, *How long would you have held out, till they hanged you?*

"I *couldn't,*" she retorted, with a sudden hint of spirit. "And you shouldn't have, either. In a way, it's lucky that you're going away now, because people are going to think badly of you. You don't understand what it's like here," she explained patiently, wiping her eyes again. "You're admired and respected, you're a *hero*. But they'll think less of you now that they know you've been with me . . . You know, *been* with me." That was the best she could do. "Because I'm not respectable, Ty. I'm common. And even though —"

He shut her up with a rough hug. He felt numb and humbled, realizing all at once that she'd lied for the sake of *his* reputation, not hers!

"Carrie, Carrie," he breathed into the air over her shoulder. "What am I going to do with you?" But of course, he already knew.

Releasing her, he kept her hands and bent close, wishing the light were brighter so he could see her face. "Listen to me, love. There's no hope of any of this staying a secret. I had to tell Butts the truth, not that gallant lie you made up to protect me." Which I tried on him first, he added to himself, with no better success.

"Oh." She sounded dismayed but not surprised. "I'm sorry, I didn't know what you'd said. You told me to tell the truth, but I couldn't be sure how much you'd already told them yourself. So — that means they didn't believe me?"

"Not for a second."

"Well, I didn't think so, either. Nobody said anything, but I — had a feeling."

He decided against letting her in on the general consensus that she was the most dismal and inept liar anyone had ever met. "The whole town's bound to know everything within a few days, I'm afraid," he said.

"Oh, by tomorrow, I think."

She sounded reconciled to it, and she was probably right; she knew the town better than he did. He squeezed her hands tighter. "So there's only one thing to do. We'll get married."

387

She was shocked into silence for a full ten seconds. "We'll what?" she got out, on something between a laugh and a gasp.

"Dr. Perry arrives tomorrow, the last I heard. I can have my affairs settled within a week, and then we can leave. We'll marry in Philadelphia, or" — it just occurred to him — "or here, if you'd rather, it doesn't matter to me. You'll stay with my mother and sister while I'm in Cuba. I wish I could tell you how long that will be, but I can't. It could be a month, six months, a year — I just don't know. I'm not sure where we'll live afterward, either — Washington or Philadelphia, maybe Baltimore. But it'll have to be a city, Carrie, if I'm to do my work. I'm sorry, I know the country suits you better, and I know it's not what you'd have chosen. But we'll find a quiet place, and it won't be so bad, I promise."

He paused to let her speak. She didn't. "Well?" he prodded, trying for a lighthearted tone. "Aren't you going to say something? I've never proposed to anyone before. If I didn't do it very elegantly, there's inexperience to blame. Carrie?"

She drew her hands out of his. "You do me a great honor, Ty," she said with husky formality. "I thank you for it with all my heart. My answer is no, but I'll never forget that you asked me. And it'll be the happiest memory of my life."

She'd whispered the last words, as if she were crying again. "Wait," he said. She was moving back, away from him.

Behind her, a widening rectangle of light in the doorway silhouetted the diminutively pregnant figure of Eppy Odell. "Carrie, will you come in now, please?" she called out in a high, emotional, tightly angry voice. "Dr. Wilkes, will you say good night to Carrie now, please?"

He ground his teeth and uttered an oath. "Wait, Carrie. Listen to me, don't say no like that. Think, what else can we do? I can't leave you like this, to suffer the town's disapprobation by yourself. It might not be the life either of us had in mind, but things are different now, the circumstances —"

"Does 'disapprobation' mean disapproval?" she interrupted, soft-voiced.

"What? Yes. The circum—"

"Then it doesn't matter, Ty. I've lived with disapprobation for years and years, and I'm not afraid of it. Don't worry about me, *please* don't." Her voice got fainter as she moved back. "I have to go inside now. It's not good for Eppy and her family for us to be together like this. I didn't think of that before." She drifted farther away.

"Wait," he said for the third time. "Damn it, Carrie, we have to talk!"

"We can't. Let me go, Ty. Thank you, but I decline your proposal. Good night!"

She turned and fled, leaving him alone in the dark with his sadness, and his shamefaced relief.

19

Carrie stayed with the Odells for almost a week, sleeping on a folding cot in what had been the pantry but was now Charlotte and Emily's tiny first-floor bedroom. She never went out, except to weed Eppy's vegetable garden or cut flowers for the house, so if there was "disapprobation" toward her in the town, it never touched her directly. She felt it, though, and from an unexpected source: Eppy herself. Her friend of five years, her only female friend, couldn't hide how much she disapproved of what Carrie had done, even though she tried.

"I'll leave," Carrie had offered on the day after her arrest and release from jail, when it was already clear to her that her presence made Eppy uncomfortable.

"Where will you go?" she'd snapped. "You can't go home, there's a murderer on the loose. If you go to Doc Stoneman's and stay there alone, people will talk worse about you than they already do. You're stuck here, Carrie, and that's that."

So she tried to make herself useful around

the house, taking care of little Fanny, playing for endless hours with the older girls, cleaning, making breads and cookies and great pots of beans — all the while trying her best to stay out of Eppy's way.

True to his word, the sheriff came to see her after two days, and asked her a hundred questions about her stepfather. He particularly wanted to know about Willis Haight. She couldn't lie, but she dreaded what would happen to all the Haights, Frances and the six children, if Willis got himself arrested. They lived on the edge of ruin every day as it was. Willis didn't make much money doing whatever it was he did — selling the distilled whiskey he didn't drink up by himself, from what she could tell — but if that source of income dried up, the family would be truly destitute. Luckily the sheriff asked her about four or five other acquaintances of Artemis, some she'd never heard of. In a way, it was a relief to find out he'd had even more enemies than she'd thought.

Broom visited her every day, sometimes more than once. His solution to her troubles was for her to come and live with him in his house, where they could be a family. Once, lying on her hard cot and listening to the soft breathing of the little girls sleeping nearby, she actually considered doing it. Not for her sake — she didn't want to live with Broom — but for his. He needed somebody to take care of him. It was a miracle he hadn't burned down his house yet, or accidentally poisoned himself, or fallen victim to a thousand other disasters he was too simpleminded to avoid. But she guessed she was just too selfish and mean, because she couldn't bring herself to do it. Now that Artemis was gone, she could help Broom out a lot more, she told herself, in ways her stepfather would never have allowed. She could bring him nutritious meals, for instance, and sew up his raggedy clothes. It wasn't enough, but it was all she could think of to do right now. Heaven help her, she just didn't want to be Broom's mama.

One morning she was out in the front garden, weeding and pinching back the dead blooms of snapdragons and strawflowers in Eppy's annual border. It was a job she loved, even though it made her homesick for her own wildflowers up on Dreamy. Maybe it was a sound that made her stand up and turn around, shading her eyes with her hand under the brim of her borrowed sunbonnet, but it seemed more like a sensation, a *feeling* that somebody was watching her. She was surprised when she saw that it was Eugene. Not so much because she wasn't expecting him, but more because of the way he held himself

— still and watchful and maybe a little tentative, and the way he didn't move for a few seconds even though he knew she'd seen him. It took a wave of her hand to get him out of the middle of the street, and a smile to move him through the privet hedges and up the slate walk to where she was standing in the yard.

"Hey, Carrie," he greeted her, hands in his pockets, swaggering only a little. "How you been? Heard about your pa and all. Guess he finally got what he deserved."

He couldn't seem to look at her directly. When she'd look at him, he'd look away; but when *she'd* look away, she could feel him staring hard at her, almost as though he'd never seen her before. She didn't know exactly how to respond to his remark about Artemis, so she just said, "How've you been, Eugene?"

"Fine," he answered automatically, but now he *really* couldn't take his eyes off her. "God damn, Carrie," he whispered. "I heard you could talk now, but I couldn't hardly believe it. God damn."

His swearing had always made her cringe a little. "Yes, I can talk now," she said with a small smile. "But people get used to it fast, I've found out. Eppy and Frank, and especially the children — everybody just takes it for granted now."

"How come you can do it all of a sudden?

Must've been the shock, huh? Of finding your pa shot and everything. That's what folks are saying, anyway."

"I expect that's what it must've been," she said, running her work gloves through her hands. Strangely enough, nobody had asked her the question straight out yet, not even Eppy; everybody just assumed it was "the shock," whatever that meant, so she hadn't even had to try to make up a story.

"So." Eugene rocked up and down on his toes, one hand in his belt, the other smoothing his mustache. "So they buried Artemis yesterday, I heard. Must've been a pretty small funeral."

Very small, she thought, nodding. Just her and Reverend Coughan, who'd had a hard time finding nice things to say about the deceased. Eppy had been planning to come, just for the company, but the baby's croup got worse the night before, and she didn't want to take her outside. All through the short ceremony, Carrie had wondered if Ty would come. But he never had.

"Did your pa hurt you bad, Carrie?"

She looked up in surprise at the genuine concern in Eugene's tone. "No, not very. He hit me" — she touched her temple unconsciously — "but I'm fine now. Thank you for asking."

"Damn son of a bitch. I'm not sorry he's dead. I'm sorry for what he done to you, Carrie."

"Thank you," she repeated, startled by his vehemence.

"So. What're you gonna do now?"

"I'm not sure. I haven't quite decided." Now there, as Ty would say, was an understatement.

"Heard the doc's leaving."

She kept her eyes on her gloves, twisting them in her hands. "Yes."

"First I heard that you and him were getting together, but I guess that was just a rumor."

She didn't say anything.

"Reckon our little town's not good enough for the great *doctor* after all."

Her head jerked up. "He's going to Cuba to help find out what causes yellow fever, Eugene. The surgeon general himself invited him to go."

His eyes finally got the dark, hard look she was used to. "Oh, yeah, I forgot. It's an *honor*."

"It *is*."

"Yeah, well, any way you look at it he's still leaving, though, ain't he?"

After a long minute, she had to admit it. "Yes, he's still leaving."

They stared at each other, and Carrie had a feeling that something was being communicated between them without any words. Then Eugene's voice went soft again. "Well, I'm staying right here. So if you need any help, anything you need a man to do for you, you can always ask me. Because I'm not going anywhere. Understand, Carrie?"

She nodded, and murmured, "Thank you, Eugene. I appreciate that." But she didn't really know how she felt about it.

"Except to work," he cracked suddenly. "Can't stand around jawing all day, can I?" He looked cocky and sure of himself once more, and she couldn't help feeling relieved — that other Eugene confused her.

"You take care now, and I'll see you soon. So long, Carrie."

"So long," she echoed, watching him saunter back to the street and walk off west toward the Wayne Tool & Die. She thought about him, off and on, for the rest of the day.

Ty came to see her that evening. It was the third time he'd come since she'd been with the Odells. Eppy never left them alone together until the very end, and then only for a few minutes so they could say good-bye on the front porch. Each time, he asked her again to marry him, and each time she politely refused. Tonight it was the same, except that this time he took a folded piece of paper out of his pocket after her polite refusal and pressed it into her hand.

"What is it?" she whispered, feeling guilty already.

"Your *duena* won't give me a chance to say anything to you," he whispered back, with a smile that broke her heart, "so I'm reduced to this. Furtive love letters to plead my case. And I thought it was the twentieth century." His blue eyes turned somber. "Read it, Carrie, and give me your answer quickly."

"But I've already —"

"It's time to be practical."

"Oh. Practical," she repeated, forlorn.

"I leave on Thursday."

She looked down at the letter to hide her face. Today was Monday. She couldn't speak a word.

"I'll come again tomorrow, and we'll talk. But time's running out, you've got to —" He broke off, muttering, when the porch light flicked off and on — Eppy's unsubtle way of saying their time was up.

"Ty," Carrie said quickly, "I've already given you my answer. Please, it would be so much — easier for me if you'd accept it."

He reached for one of her cold hands and squeezed it. "Carrie, the last, the very last thing I want to do is hurt you."

"I know, I do know that. So isn't it better if we just say good-bye?"

The humid air had curled the tips of his dark brown hair; it looked soft, in contrast to the hard, handsome bones in his face and the straight lines of his firm mouth. "Read the letter. I'll come and see you tomorrow." Dropping her hand, he murmured, "I wish I could kiss you."

She put her cold hands over her hot cheeks. "Good-bye, Ty —"

"Good night, Carrie."

A "love letter," he called it. For a little while — before she read it — the possibility lifted her, made her feel like she was floating. But they must have different ideas about what went into love letters, because Ty's didn't have any words in it about love. It was all about her honor and his duty, and the responsibility he felt to protect her. She answered it in a letter of her own, trying to use the same tone he had, although it sounded stiff and unnatural to her. So this was how educated people's letters sounded. She thought of all the notes she'd written to Ty in the past — silly, half-literate jottings that must've amused him no end. She tingled with embarrassment.

Later in the evening, she told Eppy and Frank she was going home. Their opposition took her by surprise; they were violently against it. It almost came to a quarrel, but Carrie held out and finally they gave up trying to talk her out of it. Frank made her take a gun, though — a *gun,* a Colt something or other he had to go down in the basement to find — and she had to act like she was paying attention when he took her out in the back-yard and taught her, by moonlight, how to load it and pretend to shoot it. But the thought of pulling the trigger and actually shooting somebody seemed so ridiculous to her, she felt like giggling the whole time.

Jiggling Fanny on her hip, Eppy followed her out onto the front porch the next day to say good-bye. The other girls were playing upstairs, and for that Carrie was thankful. Poor Charlotte had taken it the hardest, yelling at first and then turning sullen when she heard the news that Carrie was leaving. Emily and Jane had both cried. Now Eppy scowled at her and said, sour-voiced, "This is *stupid,* anything could happen to you up there. I can't understand why you're doing it."

"Because I'm homesick," Carrie explained, as she'd tried to last night for an hour and a half. "I just want to go home."

"Because it's noisy and crazy in this house, that's the real reason."

"That's not —"

"It's *chaos* here, don't you think I know it? And when this baby comes, it'll get even worse." She rubbed her hand over the seven-month bulge of her stomach, and shut her eyes for a second. It was only eleven in the morning, but already she looked worn-out.

"I'll come help you every chance I get," Carrie said quickly, "every day if you want me to. But there isn't room for me to stay, and it was just pure kindness in you to squeeze me in as long as you did. I'll never forget it, and I thank you for it."

"Oh, hush, Carrie," Eppy said, half-embarrassed, not looking at her. "Listen. I . . ." She stopped, and took a long time wiping the sticky remains of breakfast off Fanny's face with a cloth. Carrie waited, struck by her uncertainty, which was rare. "I, um . . . I haven't been much of a friend to you the last few days."

"You have, too."

"No, I haven't and you know it. Before you go, we might as well get it out in the open."

Now it was Carrie's turn to look away.

"I can't say I approve of what you did, and I won't say there wasn't a part of me that wanted to keep you away from my girls when I first heard about it."

That hurt; oh Lord, that cut deep as a knife.

"Because I'm a bad influence," Carrie said miserably.

"Well, there you are," Eppy said in her practical voice. "Sounds pretty silly, doesn't it? Think this one's ruined for life because you fed her her pears this morning?" She gave Fanny a bounce, and they all three laughed — two of them with tears in their eyes.

"I know what I did was wrong —" Carrie started.

"Wait now, hold on, I haven't finished. What I'm trying to say is, friends don't always do exactly what we'd like them to do. I guess if they did, they'd be us instead of themselves, which wouldn't be very interesting. But I know you, Carrie. If you did anything wrong, I know you did it out of love and nothing else, because that's the kind of person you are. And if that's a sin, it's the easiest one to forgive that I can think of. I should've done it much sooner."

"Oh, Eppy." Carrie set her old cardboard traveling bag down and put her arms around her friend, and Fanny, too. They stood that way, snuffling and squeezing each other, until the fidgeting baby let out a squall in Carrie's ear.

"Well," said Eppy, blotting her nose with the baby's towel, "what do you plan to do now? Keep on telling him no? He leaves the day after tomorrow." She shrugged at Carrie's look. "Shoot, what'd you think I was doing in here while you talked to him, sticking wax in my ears?"

With a wan smile, Carrie reached into her skirt pocket. "Give him this note for me, will you? He said he'd come by tonight. For my answer."

"Your answer? This is it?"

She nodded. "I better go now."

"Well, if you're going, I guess your answer's no. Just be sure, Carrie. Have you thought about it long enough? If you want to talk to me, I know I'm offering late —"

"I've thought about it, and I'm sure."

"But you love him, don't you?" Eppy asked gently.

She swallowed. "But it's —" What was that word Ty used? "Irrelevant. It's neither here nor there." She bent down for her bag. "I better go," she said again.

Eppy shook her head at her, kept shaking it and didn't answer. Finally Carrie gave her a quick kiss and went down the steps.

"I'll come see you soon," she called from the walk. "Tell the girls I love them!"

Eppy waved back, and kept on shaking her head.

Five Cooper's hawks soared in lazy circles

high up in the sky. Watching them from her hammock, her sketchbook on her knees, Carrie tried to capture the feel, just the *feel* of their slow, gliding, effortless flight. *So beautiful.* After a few minutes, she put her pencil down and just looked. They were what they were; no matter how carefully or how deeply she tried to see them, she could never get inside and *be* them. She thought of a time, before Ty knew she could speak, when he'd asked her why she kept logs and journals, constantly recording and sketching birds and animals and the changing of the seasons. She'd never really thought about it before. *To hold it?* she'd written. *Stop it. Keep it.* She remembered that he'd smiled, and said, "Ah, so you're trying for a form of immortality, I see. Freezing things in time." Was that it? She still didn't know. She thought it might be as simple as the fact that she loved the hawks — or the dew on a flower, or ice on a bare oak branch.

It felt good to be home. Last night it had finally rained, after a week of drought, and now the dripping forest looked shiny and fresh and clean. The sphagnum moss was a bright green, and the droopy ferns stood upright and shaggy, bursting with health. A robin chanted, "Clear up, clear up!" and the late-afternoon sky was just starting to obey.

Soothing the soul could take a long time, and Carrie allowed that she might've been hasty in thinking just being in her hospital again could soothe hers, in only one afternoon. But it was starting. The air smelled like perfume. The clouds were stretching and blowing away beyond the five beautiful hawks, and from somewhere she could hear the sweet, jubilant gibberish of a mockingbird. It was starting.

She got up and put her sketchbook and journal away among her rock shelves, because it was time to go. And then, with a start, she remembered: she didn't have to go home, not if she didn't want to. Artemis wouldn't be there. He wouldn't be waiting for his supper, moody and impatient, and asking what godless, time-wasting foolishness she'd been up to while he'd been working to put food on the table. But with a little laugh, she realized she wanted to go home anyway, because she was tired after a day of cleaning and washing inside, clearing and weeding outside. It was a good kind of tired, though, better than the kind she'd felt after a long day at the Odells'. Not that she'd ever admit it to Eppy, but it *was* chaos there, and she wasn't used to that. She thought maybe she needed peace and quiet more than most people. How interesting it was going to be, though, finding out what changes were in store for her life now that Artemis was gone. She couldn't imagine *missing* him — but wouldn't it be funny if it turned out she didn't do much of anything different? Wouldn't that be a laugh on her, considering how many times she'd dreamed of being free of him?

She was still smiling to herself when she saw Ty. Standing beside the fallen pine log she used for a bench, and watching her with a kind of startled sadness that she'd never seen on his face before.

"I was trying not to hope you'd come," she said before she could think, not quite realizing it was true until she said it. They came to each other and touched hands.

"I remember the first time you brought me here, Carrie. I thought it was paradise."

"It was May then. There aren't as many flowers now."

"Tell me what they all are," he said softly. "I like to hear you say the names."

She wanted to put her arms around him and just lean against him, feel his flesh and bones and the beat of his heart. They turned together as she pointed, naming her flowers: twayblade orchids and blue lettuce, touch-me-not, wild sweet William, lady's thumb, ox-eye daisy and wild chamomile, jewelweed and goldenrod and the last of the pink dame's rocket. "I didn't have to water them after all, and I'd been worrying all week. Because of the drought. Oh, Ty — look what I found."

She let go of his hand to get the little box off the chestnut stump and open it. "Look," she said, carrying it to him. He looked inside and jumped. "It's dead," she said hastily, remembering that some people didn't like bats. "I found it on the steep path, coming up the last rise." He made a polite humming sound. "It's a brown bat," she explained, "just a baby. *Myotis lucifugus*. You know, bats are the only mammals that can fly. Don't you think he's pretty? Look at his wings, like crepe paper." Why was she talking so much?

"He's very nice."

"I'm taking him home to sketch him. Artemis would never let me before."

"Wouldn't let you what?"

"Bring anything home. Now I can."

"Why wouldn't he?"

"Oh, he hated my wildlings. Once he — well." That memory wasn't pleasant. "Let's not talk about him."

"No."

He'd put his hands in his pockets, and was standing tall and straight, watching her. In the softening twilight, he was as beautiful to her as a picture of a saint. "Did you get my letter?" she finally had to ask, because looking at him had become too hurtful. "I left it with

Eppy to give to you."

"I got it. It sounded . . . final."

"Yes," she agreed softly. "It is. So — if you've come —"

"I've come to say good-bye."

"Oh." She nodded, dry-eyed, not looking away. "I was just about to go home, but if you're tired or you'd like to rest first —"

"No, let's walk," he said, and she thought he sounded relieved. "Besides, I left Louie in your house. I hope you don't mind. And I hope he doesn't disgrace himself."

They both smiled, and set off together along the path he knew almost as well as she did by now, Carrie carrying the box with her little brown bat inside. The cicadas were deafening, taking turns trading their coarse, scratchy messages from tree to tree. When they came to Wet Weather Stream, she stopped to point out a bright island of goldenrod close to the far bank — so pretty, and sometimes Ty missed things like that. On the spiky ridge top, while a family of rusty crows scolded and complained, she showed him the small cleared spaces in the dead leaves, eight or nine of them, where a herd of deer must've slept last night. All together in a group, except for two spots a little ways away, next to each other. "Lovers?" she guessed, and Ty smiled back at her.

The soft, gentle rise and fall of the dark hills in the distance was lovely tonight, and as familiar to her as the lines in her own hand. Layer after layer of dark green fading to light, then disappearing into the sky. She'd live and die here, she expected, and never go beyond the hills. Well, there was safety in that thought. But sadness, too.

"How many days does it take to get to Cuba?" she asked, pausing by a tangle of wild blackberry vines on the steep side of the last ridge.

"It depends on the weather, but usually about five."

Amazing, thought Carrie. It took her half a day to go to Chambersburg! "Do you sail from Philadelphia?"

"No, New York."

"But you'll go home first?"

"There isn't time, I'm afraid."

She thought of the formidable Mrs. Wilkes, and felt a stab of sympathy for her. "And what does your mother think of *that*?"

"She thinks I've lost my mind. She's ready to wash her hands of me once and for all."

But she could hear the fondness in his voice, and she knew he was joking. She thought of the elegant, smiling faces of the people in the photograph album — Mrs. Wilkes, Abbey, Sandy, and the others. Adele.

They would miss him and worry about him while he was away. But they didn't know how lucky they were, for they could wait for him at home, and no matter what happened, he'd always come back to them.

His rented buggy was tied up by Petey's water trough, and the horse was dozing. Ty went to let Louie out of the house while Carrie pulled a bucket of water up from the well. They sat on the porch step because it was cooler outside, sharing the dipper and petting the dog till he settled down. She wondered if Ty was thinking the same thing she was — of the times they'd sat out on his back porch at night, watching the sky and talking and talking. There were long pauses between their words this night.

"Eppy said Frank gave you a gun to protect yourself," he mentioned. "I told her that set my mind completely at ease."

She smiled back, loving his sarcasm, and feeling a fierce rush of emotion because of the simple but precious fact that he understood her. "Don't you think I could shoot somebody?" she teased.

"Oh, I think you're a regular Jesse James."

"It doesn't matter anyway, nobody's going to hurt me. Artemis had enemies, but I don't."

"But you'll be careful anyway, won't you?"

he said seriously. "They still have no idea who shot him."

"Yes, I'll be careful. But nothing was stolen. It wasn't a vagrant, I'm sure of it." She kept it to herself, but she was thinking about Willis Haight again. They'd passed on the mountain yesterday, she coming up on Petey, he going down on foot. He was a little, bald-headed man, strange and silent; he hardly ever said boo to anybody. But he'd touched his hat and said, "Carrie. So you're back." She decided to take that as an expression of sympathy, or at least an acknowledgment of Artemis's death. Which she sincerely hoped he'd had nothing to do with.

"I wasn't afraid at all last night," she told Ty, after another pause. "It felt odd being here alone, especially at first. But I wasn't frightened."

They were sitting side by side; their shoulders touched sometimes when one of them moved. "And not lonely?" he asked presently.

"Oh, lonely." She dismissed that with a smile. "Everybody's lonely."

He didn't answer, and they fell back into silence. A peewee drawled in the hot woods and a wheezing, unmusical starling sang to its mate. Then Ty asked, "How will you live, Carrie?" and there was something in his voice that made her feel anxious to reassure him.

"I've thought it all out. I have my own house now — how many people are so lucky? — and I can live on very little. I'll make a bigger garden next year and cut down on expenses for food. And there's my book, don't forget. I've only got a few more sketches to do before it's finished, and then I can send it off to the publisher Mr. Odell knows. They'll pay me for it, Ty. After that, maybe I can do another one, on wildlife or the flora in our area. There's no way to know what opportunity might turn up. It's the only thing I can do very well, and if the first one's a success, who knows what might happen?" He nodded, but she couldn't tell if he was just being tactful or if he agreed with her. "And — children like me, I could probably find work taking care of people's babies if I wanted to." She tried not to sound defensive, but she felt goaded a little by the idea that he might be humoring her. "What's wrong with that?" she asked when, instead of reassuring him, her last suggestion made him frown.

He traced the outline of an old crack in the porch step with his long index finger. "I needed some clothes for my trip — work shirts and some socks — so I went to Patterson's this afternoon. I saw some women poring over the catalogues at the counter. They didn't see me. I knew one of them; you

412

probably know them all."

She had an inkling where this was heading. "Believe me, I don't care —"

"They were talking about you. Not *me*, Carrie, you. Just you. As if I hadn't even *been* there during the two nights we spent together. As if I had nothing to do with the 'sin' they're so self-righteously convinced we committed."

She wasn't surprised. Sorry, but not surprised. She pressed her hands between her knees and waited for him to finish.

"The point is," he said more calmly, "I don't think there's much chance of the good women of Wayne's Crossing hiring you to watch over their children."

"Eppy would," she said faintly. "She tried to get me to take money for it before, but I wouldn't. If I really needed it —"

"It still wouldn't be enough to live on," he insisted.

She had to laugh. "Ty, I really don't think you have any idea how little it's going to take!"

He got up and stood over her. "Listen to me," he said with his hands on his knees. "You didn't hear them, I did. I don't want to leave you here, Carrie, because they'll rip you to shreds."

"No, they won't," she said positively. "I won't hear them, so it doesn't matter what

413

they say when my back is turned. I don't care about them, truly I don't."

But she couldn't help thinking of the time he'd taken her to Pennicle's, and that lovely sense of belonging she'd felt. Proud to be with him, of course, but even more proud to be a member of the community. A regular person. For one night in her life, she'd felt respectable.

She got up too and stood close to him, to emphasize her point. "Don't waste time worrying about me because it's silly. You're going to do so much good where you're going. I want you to go there with a clear mind and a heart that's unburdened. Don't think about Wayne's Crossing or anything else except saving lives. *I'm so proud of you.*" She took his hand and held it. "I'll be fine. I'm happy now, I swear it."

He touched her, just the side of her throat with his fingertips, and she almost lost her careful balance. But she held his eyes without faltering, until finally he broke the spell by letting go of her and reaching into his pocket. "Take this."

She looked down at a long white envelope. "What is it?"

"It's money."

"No."

"Take it. If you don't need it, don't spend it."

She wouldn't let him put it in her hands.

"Ty, I can't," she whispered, appalled.

"Yes, you can. Do it for me, Carrie. Yes." He slipped it into her skirt pocket.

She kept shaking her head, almost weeping. "Please, I don't want it, I don't."

"I know. Keep it anyway. Will you, Carrie, for me?"

She hung her head, wretched.

"Carrie?"

"All right." She felt old and tired all of a sudden.

"Thank you." He put a gentle kiss on her forehead. "Now I've got something for you you'll like."

She watched him cross the yard toward the buggy, and come back carrying something square and bulky wrapped in brown paper. Her foolish heart lightened; she wondered how old she'd have to get before she got over her childish love of surprises.

"Sit," Ty ordered, and she sat. He laid the package in her lap.

"What could it be?" she wondered out loud, trying to gauge its weight on her thighs, rubbing her hands together like a miser.

"Open it and see."

But she waited another full minute, loving the suspense, dragging out the anticipation as long as she could.

"Will you *open it?*" he finally barked, pretending to be exasperated.

So she did.

No amount of anticipation could have prepared her for what was inside. A book. No, not a book. A miracle. *Birds of America* was the title, by John James Audubon. She knew him, of course, had even read parts of his *Ornithological Biography* in the big library in Chambersburg. This was his *real* book, though, and what rested on her knees was the 1871 edition of the lithographs. Hundreds of them, life-size, the colors so real she could hardly breathe and look at them at the same time. She was afraid to turn the pages, but she did, and each view filled her fuller and fuller until she couldn't bear it. Swallow-tailed hawk. Sparrow falcon. Snowy owl. Purple martin. Thrush. Herons, egrets, puffins and grebes, so many ducks. Dusky albatross! Goldfinches on pink thistles. A barred owl sinking silently down beside a doomed squirrel. Cardinals on wild almond trees, an Oriole family in a tulip tree, kinglets on a branch of laurel. Then she couldn't see the pages anymore because she was crying.

"Carrie?" Ty was kneeling beside her, trying to see her face.

She lifted it, unashamed. "Oh, Ty. Oh, heavens, what have you done?"

"Like it?"

All she could do was move her head and make helpless gestures with her hands.

"I thought you might."

She closed the book before a teardrop could wet it, and sat for a while staring at the leather binding and running her fingers over the gilt edges. "Thank you," she managed at last. "I don't know what to say. It's beautiful — *beautiful.* You shouldn't have, it must've cost —" She stopped on a half laugh, and waved her fingers in the air again. "I wish I had something to give you."

He made some sound she couldn't interpret. "Will you take Louie for me, Carrie? You don't have to. If you don't want him —"

"I want him."

"Good." He looked relieved. "He'll get some sense one of these days, quit chasing birds and squirrels."

"I'll teach him."

"I know you will."

They stopped talking. Carrie finally laid her book aside with great care, and they both stood up. "When does your train leave?" she asked, feeling brave.

"In the morning. Early. Carrie, I wish . . ." He didn't finish.

"I wish you happiness." She smiled, trying to relieve the sorrow in his eyes. "It's late. I guess you should go now, Ty." Neither of them moved. "You could kiss me," she whispered.

He did. Nothing but their hands and mouths touching, for a sweet, endless time, while inside she made herself say, *Good-bye, good-bye, good-bye* to keep from holding him. And when she felt him start to give in to the same temptation, she was the one who pulled away.

"I'll never forget you, Carrie."

She put the words in a special place, to save for later.

"I'll write to you from Quemados. I put the address in the envelope I gave you. If it changes, remember you can always reach me through my family in Philadelphia — I left that address as well."

She said nothing.

"If you ever need me for anything, promise you'll let me know. Promise."

She nodded.

"No, say it."

"I promise."

The next silence was excruciating.

"If you don't go now, it'll be dark before you get home," she reminded him.

He nodded once, impatient. "Carrie . . ."

"Be safe, Ty."

He whispered, "Will you remember me?"

She had to look down at their clasped

hands. She felt his soft breath on her hair, and heard him say words that sounded like, "Forgive me for that. Ah, Carrie. For everything." Then he let her go.

She squatted down beside Louie, grabbing his rope collar and holding it so he couldn't follow Ty to the buggy. A pink half-moon hung low, rising behind horizontal cloud wisps, but the shadows Ty's long body cast in the dark yard were bluish. She watched him untie the horse and climb into the buggy, and back it till he was facing down the mountain. Turning around in the seat, he lifted his arm. She forced a smile and waved back. The dratted tears were falling down her face like rain. But she was in luck; it was dark, and he was too far away now. He never knew.

When the sound of wheels and harness finally faded into silence, she sat on the ground to comfort Lou, because he was confused. "Good dog, what a good boy," she told him, while he licked the salty tears off her chin. Presently they both felt a little better; she even stopped crying. She started a game with a stick, and lured him inside the cabin with it before he could remember he didn't like it in there. Lighting the lamp, starting the stove, straightening the table — everything she did sounded too loud; it hurt her ears, but the silence was worse. She kept busy, kept moving.

What should she feed Louie? Her larder was low, and there was no meat in the house. She'd get him something in town tomorrow, but tonight he'd have to settle for table scraps.

She ate dinner too fast. The cabin was immaculate; after she washed her plate, there was nothing to do. She could draw the bat. She could do some mending. She could look at her Audubon book. No — she couldn't do that. Couldn't even touch it, she realized. In a few days, but not yet. Not now.

Louie sat in front of the rickety screen door, staring out. She thought he looked lost. The half-moon had climbed higher, white as a bone over the treetops. She'd have gone for a walk, but she didn't want to leave the dog alone, and she was afraid he'd run away if she took him with her.

In the end she sketched her bat, by lantern light, sitting at the table. His wings were translucent — she could see his bones right through them. He was in the order of Chiroptera, which was Greek for hand, "Cheiros," and wing, "Pteros." It felt funny to be drawing inside the house. Wherever he was, she hoped Artemis knew she wasn't gloating.

At nine o'clock she took Lou outside, using a piece of rope for a leash. At nine-thirty, she was washed and ready for bed. She blew out the lantern and lay down in her alcove, pulling back the curtain over the window so she could see the sky. The smell of wet pine was fragrant and fresh, the sound of crickets a comfort. Lou whined in his sleep. She dropped her arm over the side of the bench and stroked his soft head, soothing him. She said a prayer for Ty and his family. It took a long time to fall asleep, but finally she did. And that was how she passed her first night without him.

20

Columbia Barracks
Quemados, Cuba
September 8, 1900
Dear Carrie,

I'm sitting on the barracks veranda as I write this. We have a Chinese cook in charge of our mess, which is regularly first-rate. My quarters are typically sparse for military digs, but altogether adequate. Palatial, in fact, compared to my lodgings here two years ago, which consisted of a mackintosh on the steaming jungle floor. If I had time for them, I'd entertain a hundred memories of that long-ago farce of a war, but from my new vantage it only seems like a violent dream. We "liberated" the Cubans, but the real winners were typhoid and malaria and yellow jack. Did you know that disease killed thirteen times as many men as bullets did? I pray it's not arrogance, or not *only* that, that makes me believe I'm fighting for the right cause for the first time in my life.

I had intended to write to you sooner

than this, but Camp Columbia was a hornet's nest when I arrived a little over a week ago, and until this moment, quite literally, there's been no opportunity. A terrible yellow-fever epidemic has been raging through the town since June, in spite of the army's best efforts to scrub it, fumigate it, and even close down its bordellos. (There's a doctor here named Stark who theorizes that the fever only visits people of reprehensible character, and if he can keep the soldiers out of the whorehouses, the incidence of disease will go down.) All of Quemados is in quarantine now, off-limits to Americans. The locals watch the loco Norte Americanos' incessant cleaning and disinfecting with great amusement — while the death toll climbs. As a doctor whose job it is to try to discover this plague's cause, I find myself in the awkward position of viewing each new casualty as a chance to move a step closer to the goal.

There are five of us on the commission here. Major Walter Reed is our leader, and the only one I haven't met — he left for the States on business a few weeks before my arrival and isn't expected to return until October. The man he left in charge is a doctor named James Carroll, who's competent, I'm told, if not a particularly agreeable fellow. I'd make up my own mind on that score, but I can't — he's been near death with the yellow jack since I got here!

Yesterday, thank God, he started to improve, but he's not out of danger yet. The other team members, Jesse Lazear and Dr. Agramonte, have been beside themselves — Lazear in particular because he feels responsible. Agramonte had a mild case of the fever when he was a child, so he and I are the "immunes." But Lazear and Carroll agreed early on that they would subject themselves to the same risks they'd ask of anyone else during the course of the experiments. What's ironic is that until now, no one seriously believed the culprit is a mosquito, not even Reed, not for certain, and it was only one of the theories that the commission planned to test. So Carroll let himself be bitten, and two days later he came down with the disease.

Now that it appears he's going to recover, you'd think the mood among us would be jubilant, but it's just the opposite. Carroll was so sick and went down so fast, we're convinced the mosquito was the agent. But we can't prove it! Before he grew too delirious to speak, he admitted that he went into the yellow-fever wards of the hospital, the autopsy rooms, and even into Havana during the crucial interval, so all chance of control has been lost. If he'd died, his death would've proven absolutely nothing.

The need for controlled human experiments is obvious now, a thought that gives none of us any pleasure. The soldiers in the military hospital take all of this as a joke, and volunteer constantly. A trooper named William Dean from the Seventh Cavalry says he's ready and willing to let one of Lazear's "birds" bite him. God help us, and him, for we're set to do it. Everyone is of two minds, as you can imagine. Having once suffered the full course of the disease myself, I can honestly say I wouldn't wish it on Satan himself. But if Trooper Dean comes down with it on schedule, it would be the first case ever induced deliberately by the bite of an infected mosquito, and the implications would be enormous.

Forgive me, Carrie — can this be of any interest to you at all? I'm consumed by it, day and night. I'd thought to write you a pleasant letter about the camp — clean and comfortable; the weather — balmy and beautiful; the company — interesting to say the least. But I see I've jumped right into the storm that rages around us all the time, and dragged you into it with me without a thought. It's the enormity of what we've undertaken that confounds and humbles me, and the risks we can't help taking with each other's lives. If we succeed, people will say we were heroes, but if we fail, our hopes and our memories will be consigned to hell — and who's to say they don't belong there?

8:30 P.M. — Jesse Lazear dragged me away to the officers' mess, telling me I work too hard. I never told him that I wasn't studying pathology culture results, but writing a frivolous letter to a dear friend! Jesse is an awfully good fellow, by the way. I knew him slightly at Hopkins, where he was an assistant in clinical microscopy. His wife and son were here in Cuba until recently, but he sent them back home because of the epidemic. He and I spend our free time (such as it is) together, two homesick bachelors comforting each other.

It's an odd existence we lead here, Carrie. Already I miss the conversation of women, the sounds of children playing, the song of a plain, ordinary bird I recognize! I think of you in your cabin on High Dreamer Mountain, and wonder what you're doing. What wildlings have you found to doctor these days? How does your hospital look in September? Has Louie driven you completely insane? If so, that

426

would explain why you haven't written me a letter yet. Memories of the times we shared this summer warm me, and help me through some of the horrors here. You gave me a promise that you would tell me if you ever needed my help. I believed it or I wouldn't have left you. And now I'll simply remind you of it again. Ever, Carrie — for anything.

It's late, and the days are long and exhausting. Give my best to Frank and Eppy, and Broom, and Doc Stoneman if you write to him. Most of all, take good care of yourself.

Good night,
Tyler

Columbia Barracks
Quemados, Cuba
September 20, 1900
Dear Carrie,

Everything is chaos here. Jesse Lazear felt out of sorts two days ago, and now he's so frantic with delirium they've had to restrain him. High albumin, high fever — his chances look very poor to me. Still, he's young, only 32, and strong and fit; he may pull through. But time is the enemy now.

The hell of it is, it was another *accident!* He was securing mosquito samples in the hospital, holding a test-tube bug on a patient's stomach while it fed. Another mosquito lighted on his hand — he told us this before he became completely incoherent — and thinking it was the culex malarial variety that's common in the hospital, he let it bite, meaning to capture it in a minute and add it to his specimen collection. But he was busy, and it flew off before he could catch it. He made no note of the incident and never thought of it again — until five days later when he fell gravely ill.

Dr. Carroll, thank God, is getting stronger all the time. Did I tell you about Trooper Dean in my last letter? He was our first volunteer. He was bitten, contracted the disease, and is now recovering. If Lazear dies, it will be for nothing, and Dean's will be the only case that conclusively proves anything at all. I can't describe to you the guilt and anguish and desperation among us all. The irony is demoralizing — two of the members of the very board sent here to put an end to unscientific conjecture about the disease have become its random victims. And anyone who disagrees with the mosquito theory can use Carroll's or Lazear's cases as examples to prove almost any method of infestation he likes!

Walter Reed is still away; Dr. Carroll talks of going home soon for a rest. Agramonte and I keep working, but Jesse's agony makes it impossible to concentrate in any constructive way. And yet everyone feels we're on the brink of something important, one of the great discoveries of the century. If I didn't believe that, I would despair.

My family writes to me of all the news in Philadelphia. I keep my letters to them light and brief — because those two women in my life are volatile, and worry altogether too much about me. I hope that no word from you means that you are well, and happy on your mountain. I try to picture you there in autumn, but I find I can never see you in my mind's eye without flowers. Do you remember your first gift to me? A tiny bouquet of wildflowers, light as a feather. You wrote that the sweet everlasting smelled like "perfume," and so it did.

Be happy. Think of me sometimes.

Tyler

Columbia Barracks
Quemados, Cuba
October 13, 1900
Dear Carrie,
    Jesse Lazear is dead. We buried him two

weeks ago in the post cemetery with full military honors. He left a wife and son, and the unborn child his wife carries. They say he had no insurance, no pension, and they'll be left with nothing. I miss his tall, lanky shape hanging in my doorway at dinnertime, and drawling, "You planning to eat anytime this week, Dr. Wilkes?" He had an old-fashioned Southern courtliness that made him easy to know, easy to love. His passing has diminished us all, and the mood here is grim.

Dr. Reed arrived a week ago and is working feverishly on the preliminary report he plans to deliver to the American Public Health Association on the 23rd. But for all his activity, he's got precious little to go on, and we all dread the consequences when his colleagues realize his mosquito theory is based on three cases, two of which were uncontrolled. But death is all around us. September was the worst month for the fever in Havana in two years. Reed has no choice but to go forward with all speed.

I've been thinking of that night you met me on the bridge over South Creek, Carrie, after one of my patients had died — do you remember the old man with the brain lesion? I'd stayed with him all day, and he was lucid almost to the end. It hit me hard when he died, no doubt because he'd reminded me of my father. You didn't say much to me that night. But you leaned against me while we stared down at the water rushing under our feet. I can close my eyes now and feel the weight of you against my arm, and it comforts me. That warmth and that pressure. There must be a hundred things I've never thanked you for. Are you well, Carrie? Are you happy? I pray that you are, and that you'll keep your promise to tell me if you should ever need me.

Yours,
Tyler

Columbia Barracks
Quemados, Cuba
November 20, 1900
Dear Carrie,

There's time for only a note, in case you've been wondering how we fare. There was a storm here five days ago, a strong one that uprooted trees and — much worse, from our admittedly peculiar viewpoint — blew most of the mosquitos out to sea. Since then, Dr. Reed has had us scouring the island with cyanide bottles in a most undignified manner, hunting for eggs and larvae so that our experiments can go on.

His report to the APHA was greeted with

a great shrug of indifference by the attendees, and with open scorn by the newspapers afterward. The *Washington Post* called the mosquito hypothesis "the silliest beyond compare," and referred to the members of the team — yours truly included — as "whoever they may be." Reed was glad to come back, and now he's supervising work on a new observation camp being built about two miles from here. It's to be called Camp Lazear.

Since an animal has never contracted yellow fever in any known experiment, we find ourselves in the ethically questionable position of needing to recruit more human volunteers. We have eight so far, including an American army private and an American civilian clerk from General Lee's headquarters. The others are all Cubans, desperately poor men, overjoyed at the idea of earning $100 in American gold for doing what they consider nothing at all. I'm happy to say that the American volunteers have declined payment. Kissinger, the private, was bitten today by a carefully infected "ladybird." If he doesn't contract the disease, everything we've done is for nothing. If he does — he may die. It's a bleak, practically winless situation, and the pressure's beginning to tell on all of us. Dr. Carroll is back from his sick leave, but he seems bitter and remote. He and Reed were friends for years, but there's a strain between them now. Some say it's jealousy, that Carroll resents the professional advancement in store for Reed once — if — his theories are accepted. Even so —

Forgive me. This can't possibly be of any interest to you. I'm surrounded by these petty intrigues 24 hours a day and have lost my perspective. Well, what shall I say to you, then? Shall I describe the weather? The cold mango I ate for breakfast? Shall I tell you that I miss you, that I think of you more often than I have a right to? I might have once, but your continued silence tells me those words would not be welcome anymore. Might even cause you pain. I've hurt you enough in the past, Carrie, and would never knowingly do it again.

Yours ever,
Tyler

Camp Lazear
Quemados, Cuba
December 10, 1900
Dear Carrie,

This will be my last letter to you from Cuba. I'm going home in three days, assuming all goes well here in the mean-time. I plan to spend the week preceding Christmas with my family in Philadelphia, then report immediately to the Pathology Laboratory at the Army Medical College in Washington, D.C. I'll be a civilian bacteriologist there, working, at least initially, on identifying the specific agent of the disease carried by the *C. fasciatus* mosquito, and after that, we hope, on an immunizing agent. There's a great deal we don't know — but what we now *do* know, definitely and unequivocally, can't be underestimated. I don't think it's too much to say that our mission here has changed medical history. If it weren't for the loss of Lazear, we could claim absolute victory. But that's a loss we can never forget, and it tempers everything. The truth is, it's a bloody *miracle* that no one died besides Jesse. Even though so much is still a mystery, all of us are repelled by the thought of infecting more volunteers, and we're agreed that it has to stop.

Still — it's hard at times not to feel euphoric. Reed says that except for the diphtheria antitoxin and Koch's discovery of the tubercle bacillus, this is the most important scientific finding of the nineteenth century. His friends joke that he'll be the next surgeon general. He smiles his charming smile, modest as always. And yet, I think I see a twinkle of excitement in his eyes at the prospect — which is not far-fetched to me in the least. I count myself the luckiest of men to have served under him on this commission. Whatever reward is in store for Walter Reed is a thousand times deserved.

So. It's over. In hindsight, as with all successful detective cases, I suppose, what seemed mysterious now appears almost ridiculously obvious, and the real mystery is how the truth could have been overlooked for so long. What we didn't understand was the *time* — the crucial secret that the mosquito can only contract the virus from a victim in the first *two or three days* of the disease, and that *12 to 14 days* have to pass before the virus can multiply enough within the bug to enable it to infect another victim. That's why the sudden outbreak of yellow jack on a ship two weeks at sea confounded us, why —

But I'm doing it again. I apologize; these details must bore you to distraction. I wonder if you ever read my letters anymore. If you do, they must seem like jottings from the planet Saturn, by some creature you knew vaguely in another life. I have no excuse, unless it's —

"Shit."

Tyler threw his pen down in disgust, and a blotch of black ink marred the paragraph he'd just written. Good. He'd been about to write the word "loneliness." So it had come to this: trying to get Carrie to write back by making her feel sorry for him. The plaintive tone of the ink-blotted paragraph embarrassed him. He snarled at it, grabbed his warm glass of brandy and soda, and carried it to the doorway, hoping for a fresh perspective.

Another perfect day. How profoundly sick he was of perfect days. Carrie, he recalled, professed to like all days, all weathers. She had a particular fondness for the brown, dreary, truly ugly ones because, she said, they were temporary, they were friendless and pathetic, and they made good days seem even more beautiful by comparison. But surely the gorgeous sameness of the Cuban skies would daunt even Carrie's boundless enthusiasm eventually. Then again . . . probably not.

His memories of her were vivid and relentless, and lately they had all been of the last time he'd seen her — on Dreamy Mountain that final, wrenching night. He'd come to her in her hospital at dusk, and she'd been pottering around in her old blue dress, her beautiful

436

hair awry as usual, smiling to herself. *Smiling.* Later, she'd held his hand and told him, "I'll be fine. I'm happy now, I swear it." And when he'd kissed her and gone away, she hadn't cried. *He'd* wanted to cry, but Carrie hadn't shed a tear.

Recognizing the petulance, the discomfitingly churlish tenor of his thoughts, he set his glass down and rubbed his tired eyes with his knuckles. His mind slid effortlessly — from habit — to the night she'd given herself to him. Another woman contemplating such a choice might have waited for the magic words, the sedative, talismanic "I love you" from her intended lover before she risked everything. Carrie hadn't. She'd said them to *him.* "Did you think I thought you would marry me?" he could hear her asking. "Oh, Ty, I just love you. I just love you."

She had loved him, and the gift was absolutely free, absolutely without conditions. Because no one had ever loved him in that way before, he hadn't known quite what to do with Carrie's gift. It hadn't pleased him; it had made him guilty and uneasy. Not guilty enough to *refuse* what she was offering, of course; oh no, he'd been glad enough to accept that. He'd enjoyed her as long as he could, and squared it with his conscience by making sure he gave her as much pleasure as he received. As if that made them even.

And how lovely it had been. He shut his eyes tight, lost in a familiar blur of sensual recollection. Being with Carrie had made his liaisons with previous women seem practically sordid in comparsion. No — that was an exaggeration, "sordid." Barren, then. Yes, barren. The very word.

And now she wouldn't even write to him. Was this to be his punishment? To realize too late that the only woman he would ever love in quite this way, certainly the only woman who would ever love *him* with such an open, unselfish heart, had given him up and gone on with her life without him? If so, harsh as it was, it was a fitting punishment, because his reason for not recognizing what he'd had when he'd had it filled him with shame.

The truth was, as much as he enjoyed casting fond, superior, supercilious aspersions on his mother's high-minded hopes for him — the *truth* was that he shared them. Oh, not her *specific* hopes: he wanted no political career; his goal in life wasn't to be famous. At least not for the same things Carolivia wanted him to be famous for. His hopes for himself were nobler — perhaps — but were they any less self-gratifying? He wanted to cure diseases and reduce human suffering; he truly wanted that, genuinely and unambivalently, and he was fully prepared to devote his life to accomplishing it. Ah, but if he were *recognized* for it — if respected medical men admired him, wrote papers and dissertations based on his brilliant theories — if, God help him, they gave him *prizes* and *accolades* for his accomplishments — would he turn his back on the rewards? Far from it.

He had a picture of the rest of his life in his mind's eye, and whether he cared to admit it or not, Carolivia had helped draw it for him. Because he wanted to accomplish so much, he'd always seen himself, in the successful future, as a man who lived and thrived in the rarefied world of science. When he'd bothered to envision a partner in that life at all, he'd seen someone like Adele, someone familiar and comfortable, and eminently suitable. Suitable for what? Enhancing his esteem. Fulfilling his barely conscious dream of *himself*. But although he'd grown up with her, he hardly knew Adele. It didn't matter: from childhood everyone had assumed that they would marry. If, one day, he'd decided *not* to marry her, the reason — how demoralizing it was to admit this — would've been to thwart his mother, and not because he'd ever looked honestly at Adele and realized they didn't suit. And it was no consolation to know that her disappointment would've been as skin-deep as her happiness had he married her.

But never, not in a wild, maverick dream, had he ever seen himself linked for life — in the picture in his mind's eye — with someone like Carrie Wiggins. She was a foreigner; she might as well be from another country, another world. She didn't fit any niche or type he or anyone else in his set had ever known, ever even imagined. She was impossible. Eventually — how democratic of him! — he'd brought himself around to sleeping with her. But marry her? Good God. Out of the question. Not done, old man, simply not done.

His hypocrisy mortified him. He delighted in tweaking his mother and her sort for their hidebound social and political philosophies. Prosperous and potbellied, he called them. There was nothing he enjoyed more than reminding his own contented, conservative, conformist Philadelphia cronies of how enlightened he was compared to them. But he dearly loved a mountain girl named Carrie Wiggins, and her preposterous *unsuitability* to his comfort, his complacency, and above all his ambitions had prevented him from knowing it until it was too late. Too late. She wouldn't even write him a letter.

The perfect sunset depressed him. He went back into his room and sat down at the oak mess table he used for a desk, blinking down like an owl at the ink-stained last page of his letter to Carrie. Had he been too restrained? Yes, but he'd done it on purpose, written her brief, factual accounts of his time, leaving out anything that would remind her too strongly of the past they'd shared. That was the *kind* thing to do, he'd convinced himself. But, of course, fear had had at least as much to do with it as kindness.

Later, though, as the weeks and months passed, he'd found himself wanting more and more to write her long, personal letters full of his fears and dreams. He'd wanted to send her photographs of the camp, and silly pictures of his friends and himself, cutting up like soldiers away from home. He'd wanted to send her gifts, and jokes, and articles clipped from magazines that might interest or amuse her. In short — he'd wanted to act like a lover.

Too late. Obviously she was finished with him, and she had been since the night he'd ridden down the mountain and out of her life. Rightly so. She'd been too kind or too gentle to tell him then, but she'd known. He remembered her silence when he'd said he would write to her. She'd known *then* she would never write back. Why should she? Carrie was strong; it ought not to surprise him that her very strength kept her from hanging onto a memory that must bring her nothing but pain. Why should she?

Oh, but Carrie, Carrie, he thought, picking up his discarded pen, twisting it in his fingers. *Bear with me, my love. Be gentle again, forgive me one more time. I'm slow, but I'm rock steady, and now that I know the truth, I'm ready to claim you. Could you call this a grace period, this time I've needed to know myself?*

"My dearest Carrie," he wrote on a new page, and laughed out loud at how right it looked. He hadn't even finished his brandy; otherwise he'd have thought he was drunk. "My dearest Carrie. What an idiot I've been. Let's get married." He laughed again, and crumpled the paper into a ball. No point in scaring her to death.

"My dear Carrie. I'll be home in a week. May I come and see you?"

Too abrupt.

Dear Carrie,

I've been remembering the last time I saw you — the last moment. You were kneeling beside Louie, holding him so he wouldn't run after me, and your face in the twilight was full of sadness. You waved back to me, and the last I saw of you was the lacy white cuff of your blue dress. Even in sorrow, you looked strong to me, and natural; you fit, in my mind, in front of your cabin in the trees, with your mountain rising up dark and heavy behind you. And that night you told me you were happy. For a long time, those words and that picture gave me comfort. But they don't any longer. Forgive me, Carrie, I don't want you to be happy any-more, not without me. I want —

"Dr. Wilkes? Afternoon post, sir."

The trooper from the Seventh Cavalry who delivered mail to the barracks stood at semi-attention on the dusty steps outside the door, sweating in his khakis. Tyler got up and went to retrieve the short stack of envelopes the sol-dier held out to him. They gave each other lackadaisical salutes, and the trooper drifted away.

Before he was halfway back to his desk, Ty saw Carrie's letter.

He carried it to his bunk in both hands. One of his most abiding fantasies in the past few weeks was that she'd written to him often, but somehow her letters had gotten lost. *Here they were.* How very odd; a minute ago he'd been castigating himself for being a selfish im-becile, for throwing a rare treasure away out of ignorance and arrogance. Was this any way to reinforce the lesson — to receive, to hold in his hands, his very heart's desire? He must not have gotten the whole message anyway, because Carrie's letter — so thick, so heavy, her loopy handwriting so heartbreakingly dear — felt like a reward he deserved after a long period of suffering. He was going to have to work on that "deserved" part, he supposed.

Later, though. Not now. He felt the stupid grin stretching wider and wider between his ears. In a matter of seconds, his life had righted itself. He sat down on his cot and opened Carrie's letter.

He saw the money first. Uncomprehending, he took out the single sheet of paper folded around it. Dried leaf-pieces and a tiny twig floated down to his lap; he brushed them away with an absent hand while he scanned the page, dismayed to see that Carrie's message was only a paragraph long. The second sentence stopped his heart.

Dear Tyler,

You told me once it takes 5 days to get to Cuba. If a letter takes the same, then I guess in 5 days after you read this I'll be married to Eugene.

21

"And this time don't come back," Carrie commanded in a whisper. "Hear me? I don't want to see you again, or any members of your immediate family. This is good-bye."

With a flourish, she opened her cardboard trap and stood back so the big-eared, long-tailed mouse inside wouldn't panic as much when he scampered away toward the stone wall and freedom. Of course, there was no way to tell if he was the same mouse she'd caught and deported about six times by now during the annual autumn-long game, but she liked to think he was. She'd never taken him this far away before, halfway up the ridge behind her house to the crumbling stone fence, where he'd have plenty of natural food and protection. She wished there was some way she could mark him, for if he followed her home from this distance — well, for heaven's sake, she'd just have to let him stay. Even if he did keep her awake at night, hunting for crumbs in her kitchen.

The air smelled like snow. Through the black pine branches, the stony December sky looked glutted and overweight. If it did snow, it would be the first fall of the season. Three nights ago there had been an ice storm, but it melted early and by nine in the morning everything went back to looking smoke-gray and somber.

Back in the cabin, Carrie apologized to Lou for leaving him locked in. "But we know whose fault that is, don't we?" she reminded him. He was getting better about chasing things, but an escaping mouse still would've been too much for him. Sometimes she despaired of Louie. One day she might just have to face it: he was no Shadow, and chances were he was never going to be.

While she was taking off her coat, the mantel clock struck three. She'd never disliked a particular time of the day before, but lately the short, dark, dreary afternoons had been making her feel blue and mopey. With a sigh, she sat down at the table and pulled the half-empty bowl of black walnuts toward her. Tedious, delicate, time-consuming task, shelling black walnuts. She did it every winter with scarcely a thought, but this year she found the job almost intolerable. She felt restless and melancholy, keyed up and depressed, and today was the worst day yet. No need to ask herself why. It was the tenth of December, and by now Ty had surely gotten her letter.

She'd filled the morning with chores in town on purpose so she couldn't think about it. She'd even met Eugene for lunch at the drugstore, and gone over to Eppy's afterward to mind the new baby — Mary Ann, six weeks old and already a handful — for an hour while Eppy tried to take a nap. "I'm so sick of children," she'd grumbled to Carrie in a harsh whisper over the baby's head, as if Mary Ann might understand her if she said it any louder. "I hope I never see another infant after this one for as long as I live, and that's the truth."

It wasn't; she'd said the same thing after Fanny was born, Carrie remembered it clearly. But to cheer up her friend, she'd put aside her shyness and mentioned what Ty had told her about a woman's "cycles," and how some times of the month were safer for marital relations than others.

"Oh, for the Lord's sake," Eppy had snapped, impatient and irritable. "That only works if you're regular." Carrie had been thinking about that, off and on, ever since.

When she wasn't thinking of that, she was thinking about Ty's reaction to her letter. Now, with no distractions except a pricked thumb on a walnut shell from time to time, she couldn't get him out of her mind at all. He'd be relieved, of course, when he read her news. And that hurt — fool that she was. She might've gotten over him a little by now, started to at least, if he hadn't kept on writing to her. Just when she'd begin to think he'd quit, here would come a new letter, and everything would start up again. She knew every one of them by heart. "Shall I tell you I miss you?" he'd written in the last one. Oh God, oh God. She'd read it so many times, it was a wonder the paper hadn't disintegrated. He *missed* her. Just his handwriting gave her a jolt, a physical thrill. Just the sight of it.

"Stop it!" she said out loud — jarring poor Louie out of his sleep. "Sorry," she told him, in a softer tone. "I have to stop thinking about Ty." The dog's eyelids dropped closed again. "I have to now, because it's wrong. It's a sin. I belong to another." She stared into the log fire, listening to the words and trying to believe them — until Lou startled *her* by jumping up and dashing for the door. She couldn't hear a thing over his wild barking. Was somebody coming? Sometimes he barked at absolutely nothing. She snatched up her shawl and opened the door.

"Dr. Stoneman!" she cried, and rushed out into the yard to meet him. He was stiff from the cold, and he moved slowly as he climbed out of the buggy, bundled from his knees to his shoulders in a wool blanket. She touched his icy hands in a greeting. "Hello, I'm happy to see you! Are you all right? Is anything wrong?" He'd been back in Wayne's Crossing for two weeks. She'd been to visit him twice already, but he'd never come to see her before, never set foot in her house in all the years she'd known him. She could hardly believe he was here.

"A lot of things are wrong," he griped, his breath billowing out in a puffy white cloud. "Right now, the main one is that I'm freezing my behind off."

"Should I unhitch your mule? Will you stay to supper?"

"Leave 'im be, I'll only be here for the time it takes me to say my piece." She was used to his cantankerousness, of course; she wasn't even fazed when he shook her hand off his arm. "I'm not crippled, either," he grumbled, heading toward the house, Lou dancing around his legs.

"No, but you sure are cranky," she retorted.

He sent her a sideways glare. "I liked you better before you could talk." That just made her laugh. "Thunderation," he said to Louie, pretending to kick at him. "That's the stupidest animal I ever saw."

"Last week you said you liked him."

"That was before I found out how stupid his mother is."

Sighing, Carrie followed Dr. Stoneman inside the cabin.

"Hah. So this is where you live. Fusty, isn't it? Looks like a damn museum."

She followed his gaze around the room. He hadn't meant that as a compliment, she knew, but she took it as one. Besides her notebooks and journals, she'd moved all her natural specimens inside for the winter, and some of them were out in the open so she could look at them whenever she liked — her insect and moss collections, the tent caterpillar egg cases, the little dead shrew she hadn't gotten around to sketching yet. If he thought it was "fusty" in here, he ought to see Artemis's bedroom, she thought wryly, which was now her natural history storeroom. "Sit down by the fire," she urged, and he obeyed that order, at least, while she went to put more wood on.

"Anything hot to drink around here?"

"Sassafras tea?"

He made a disgusted sound. He wasn't drinking alcohol anymore, or not as much anyway, which just made him all the more irritable. But he wasn't dying anymore either, and that was about the best, most miraculous thing that had happened to anyone Carrie knew in a long, long time.

The kettle was already on. She made him a cup of tea with plenty of sugar, the way he liked it. Handing it to him, she noticed his color was better, and not just from having been out in the cold. He wasn't so scrawny anymore, and sometimes, when he turned his head a certain way, she could tell that once he'd been a very handsome man.

"What the hell's wrong with your hands, Carrie?"

"Oh," she laughed, looking down at her black fingers. "Walnuts. I should've worn gloves, but it's too late now. The stain won't come out for days." She went to get the chair she'd been sitting in at the table and pulled it up next to his by the fire.

"Well, I heard," he said after a pause.

"What did you hear?" But she knew, of course.

"I heard you're going to ruin your life by marrying that — that —" He stopped, and she realized the look she was sending him was a warning one. "That Eugene Starkey," he finished, frustrated. "I couldn't believe my ears when Eppy told me."

"Well, it's true," she said softly, plucking at her skirts over her knees.

He slurped his tea noisily. "Ty know about this?"

Carrie went stiff. Even Eppy hadn't had the nerve to mention Tyler to her since he'd gone away. Sometimes Dr. Stoneman took too

451

much on himself; if she didn't love him so much, she could be very, very angry with him. "I wrote him," she said, with no tone in her voice at all. "He knows."

"Hmpf. And what does he have to say about it?"

She worked up her courage to say, "Nothing that would concern you, I don't think." He made another "hmpf" noise, but this one sounded almost like a laugh. She thought his shrewd old eyes twinkled a little, and it bolstered her nerve. "Until you came back," she said boldly, "Eugene Starkey's been the only friend I've had in all of Wayne's Crossing. Except for the Odells, of course," she amended out of fairness. And Broom — but that went without saying. "Nobody else would have the least thing to do with me."

"That right? You must've been mighty lonely."

"No, that's not it," she denied, seeing where he was going with that. "I haven't been lonely at all. At least —"

"No? What is it, then? You're in love with him? Can't keep your hands off him?"

She looked at the fire and didn't answer. Angry and embarrassed.

"Sorry," he said finally, sounding tired. "Shouldn't have said that."

She heaved a sigh. "It makes sense for me

to marry him, Dr. Stoneman."

"How so?" he asked, in a voice that told her that maybe now they could really talk.

"Because . . . he wants me to, for one thing. That's the main thing. That's a lot. And even though — even if —" She started again. "I'm fond of him. He's been nice to me, and more patient than you'd think."

"Patient?"

"He's been asking me to marry him since —" Since Ty left. "For months. I always said no because I couldn't even imagine it, being married to *anybody*. But now . . ."

"Now?"

She sat up straighter. "Now," she said with dignity — but then she lapsed into a short, helpless laugh. "Now I need a husband."

He sent her a look of alarm she didn't understand. Then she did.

"Oh — no! No, I didn't mean that! No, I meant I can't support myself any longer. I thought I could, but I can't. Now I have to be practical. And Eugene loves me." She hoped. Lord knew, he felt something for her, and it was so stubborn it had finally worn her down. "He really does, I'm almost sure, and —"

"Explain that," Dr. Stoneman cut in. "Why can't you support yourself? Maybe not in much style, but what the hell do you want? You own this house, don't you? You sold that book, didn't you?"

"No, I don't own this house. I have to be gone by January first."

"What?"

"Mr. Mueller explained it to me. Since my stepfather never adopted me, I've got no legal claim on his estate." She gestured with one hand. "This is his estate. Now it belongs to some distant cousin of Artemis's in West Virginia, and she says she wants to sell it."

"Well, that's too bad, but what about your book? You could buy this place with that money, couldn't you? Or rent a place if it wasn't enough?"

"I couldn't afford to buy the cabin because the cousin won't sell it without the land, and there's quite a lot. My book —" She swallowed; this had been a bitter pill when she'd first received the news, and it still was. "The publishers Mr. Odell found will only pay twenty dollars for it, and they'll only print a hundred copies. Twenty dollars — it's a lot, but even if I was careful I couldn't stretch it past a few months, especially with rent to pay. Then what? Eppy's been trying to pay me when I help her out with the children, but money's tight for them too, and I know they can't afford it, not really. I'm charity to them, and I can't stand that." She hit her fist softly against her kneecap for emphasis.

Dr. Stoneman didn't say anything, just sat there rubbing his chin, and after a few minutes Carrie got up to stir the fire. "Shall I get you some more tea?" she asked.

"No." He put his cup down on the arm of his chair. "Listen to me and don't interrupt. I've got a lot of money saved up and not one damn thing to do with it —"

She interrupted. By yanking his cup away and standing over him with it in her hands. "Thank you very much, Dr. Stoneman. I'll never forget that you said that. You'll make me sorry I told you all this if you argue with me about it, though. I know you mean to be kind and generous, but I'm just not going to take somebody else's money for my own life. I'm sorry — I know I sound ungrateful, and I'm *not*. But I have to tell you this now, straight out, or else I can see you and me arguing about it till one of us dies of old age! Since I'm not going to accept your offer, I think it's better to get it over with fast, the arguing. But — thank you. Thank you very much."

She shut her mouth, took his cup to the sink, came back, and sat down. "Are you mad at me now?" He didn't answer. "You're thinking it's funny I won't take money from you, but if I'm marrying Eugene —"

"No, I wasn't thinking that," he barked.

"Stop telling me what I'm thinking."

"But if I'm marrying Eugene it's pretty much the same thing," she concluded stubbornly. "Well, it's not. I'm nineteen years old, a full-grown woman. My mother had me by the time she was my age. As long as I can remember I've wanted children, but I never thought anybody'd marry me because I was mute. Do you know what Eugene told me? He said he'd've married me even if I *still* couldn't talk." She looked at him for a reaction, but he just grunted, watching the fire, resting his veiny hands on his knees.

She turned to face the fire, too. "And I could do a lot worse," she said lightly, trying to keep defensiveness out of her voice. "Eugene's building a house. It's outside of town on the Antietam Road, near the tool and die factory. He's building it all by himself, so it probably won't be ready till next summer, but when it's done it'll really be — it'll really be —"

"Something."

"Something." She nodded. "And he's been promoted to foreman. People have a lot of respect for him where he works. You might not like him, but that's because you don't know him. He's a *man on the rise*," she summed up, using Eugene's own words a trifle self-consciously.

The fire popped and snapped. Lou growled in his sleep. Carrie stole a glance at Dr. Stoneman; he was thinking, but his pointy profile didn't give anything away. She thought back to the raw, foggy day when Eugene had proposed to her for the last time. He'd taken her to look at his new house, which was only a muddy hole and some scaffolding then, but he was so proud of it. While they stood in the bumpy dirt, he'd given her all his reasons again for why she should marry him. She needed somebody to take care of her now that she was being evicted; they'd known each other a long time; he was a man on the rise. And she'd hemmed and hawed, shivering in her shawl and wishing she was anywhere else but there. "Damn it, Carrie, I'm getting a brand new wringer washing machine!" he'd finally burst out, like that ought to clinch the deal. "We'll put it over there, right on the back porch." He pointed to four sticks with string tied around them to make a big square. "Well? Come on, enough's enough, and besides, what the hell else are you going to do?"

Because she didn't know the answer, she couldn't get mad at the question. So she'd just hemmed and hawed some more, until he'd tried to kiss her. She wouldn't let him; she'd craned away, pressing against his hard chest. "You let the *doctor* do it," he taunted, shoving at her shoulders and knocking her back a step. She'd run away then, angry and confused.

In a way it was fitting that he'd caught up to her at the South Creek bridge, since that was the place where, in her mind, he'd first changed from a bully to a person all those years ago. He'd never apologized to her in words for anything in his life, but he did then — in his way, which she had to admit was surly and ungracious. Still, it was more than she'd expected. Much more. "I'll be good to you," he'd promised. His solid body had blocked out the sky. A little later she'd let him kiss her, and he did it softly, even with tenderness. She told him she needed the night to think it over, and he didn't argue. The next day, she said yes.

Dr. Stoneman smacked his hands on his knees and teetered to his feet.

"Oh no," Carrie wailed, "do you have to go? Stay to supper, can't you?"

"No, I've got to go." Unexpectedly, he reached for her hands. "You sure you know what you're doing, Carrie?"

"Yes," she answered immediately, meeting his serious eyes full-on. "I've thought and thought, and this is the best thing."

"Then I'm for it. Shouldn't have come

tearing up here, I guess. I've got nothing against Starkey anyway, except that he's not good enough for you. All I know about you and Tyler Wilkes is what I hear from gossip, and I don't suppose you'd care to enlighten me any further on that score."

"There's nothing to tell. If there was," she added earnestly, "you'd be the one I'd tell it to."

His big hands surrounding hers were knobby and rough-skinned, but amazingly gentle. "Now, listen. I wouldn't want to *argue* with you till I die of old age, but that offer I made stands, for as long as I do. For good, in other words."

"I do thank you," Carrie whispered, squeezing his fingers. She followed him to the door. She hated to see him go; the thought of being alone tonight sank her down low. "Want to see a baby skunk?"

"No." He wound his muffler around his stringy neck and reached for the door handle.

"Wait, I forgot to tell you something. No, this is *good*," she laughed when he made a face. "Mr. Mueller just told me yesterday. Guess what?"

"What."

"My name isn't Carrie Wiggins."

"How's that again?"

"Artemis never adopted me, so I'm no legal

kin! I'm still Carrie Hamilton — that was my father's name." She blushed. "Catherine Hamilton," she said, bashful and proud. "That's my real name."

"Well, now." His eyes crinkled at the corners. "That's a fine name, a very fine name, indeed." Carrie couldn't have been more surprised when he took her hand again, raised it to his lips, and put a dry kiss on her stained knuckles. "I wish you every happiness, Miss Catherine Hamilton."

She wanted to hug him, but she was too shy. Then he started to turn away and she did it anyway, throwing both arms around his shoulders and holding on tight. He went stiff for a second, taken off his guard, then hugged her back quick and hard. "Getting late," he muttered, fumbling with the knob.

"Good night," she called to him across the frozen yard. "Be careful, it's getting dark — watch the ruts!" He said something irritable back; she couldn't hear what it was, but it made her smile.

"You come on back in here, Louie, right now and I mean it." Somewhat to her amazement, he obeyed. She praised him extravagantly. He flapped his ears and plopped down on the rag rug in front of the fire, groaning.

She followed more slowly, taking the chair Dr. Stoneman had sat in before. It was still warm. How could she be lonely with friends like him? After she was married, she'd live closer to him, be able to see him more often. She'd miss her cabin, though. She'd never discussed her wildling hospital with Eugene, so she didn't know if he'd want her to give it up or not. If he did, she would: she wouldn't have a secret one in the woods again, the way she had with Artemis. Marriage was different. There ought not be any secrets — not that big, anyway — between a husband and wife.

She clasped her knees and rocked a little, listening to the creak of the chair in the stillness. She wasn't nearly as positive of her decision to marry Eugene as she'd tried to make Doc Stoneman think. Sometimes she was full of doubts, and sometimes she wondered if this was how her mother had felt before she'd made up her mind to marry Artemis.

Oh no, that wasn't fair — Eugene wasn't like Artemis at all. And she did have feelings for him. Not love; to be honest, sometimes she didn't even like him. But gratitude, surely, for his kindness to her lately, and always for that other thing that had happened between them years ago. And then there was this strange . . . fascination she felt for him, simply because he wanted her so much. Why did he? What did he see in her? She'd thought and thought, and it always came back to that day when he and his friends had been ready to hurt and shame her; and all the time, underneath that ugliness in Eugene, there must've been a boy who liked her, or at least pitied her, and that was the part of him that had won a battle over his lower, baser self. So maybe she was like a triumph to him now, the triumph of his hopes for his own goodness.

Sometimes, though, because she was human, she couldn't help thinking what it would be like right now if she'd said yes to Ty when he'd asked her to marry him. She knew very well what had prompted him to ask — his conscience, his sense of honor, and the natural goodness inside him that would have put her happiness ahead of his if she'd let him. But what if she'd said yes anyway? What if she'd ignored her own conscience for once and taken what she wanted?

She would have him now. Her heart's desire. He would belong to her.

She felt a giddy fluttering in her chest — but only for a second, before the fantasy bubble burst. She might have bound Ty to her, but she could never have found happiness unless he was happy, too. *Forgive me, Carrie,* he'd said on the last day. *For everything.* She'd known then, as she knew now, that he meant for not loving her.

He must've read her letter by now, she

thought for the hundredth time, reaching down to pet the dog. Did her news surprise him? Probably; she was sure he thought nobody in Wayne's Crossing would want to marry her. That was partly why he'd felt so guilty about her. Did he care that it was Eugene?

She shut her eyes and put both hands on her throat, to press against the ache that came there so quickly out of nowhere. But she mustn't think of Ty missing her. "My life's taken a new turn," she'd written to him in her letter, and it was time to start believing that herself. "Please don't write to me anymore. It wouldn't be right, now that I'm promised to another. Thank you for your wonderful kindness to me, which I will never forget. I wish you luck and happiness and great success in your important work." Not knowing how to end it, she'd finally signed, "Sincerely yours, Carrie Wiggins," feeling quite idiotic. She'd enclosed the money he'd given her, and a little sprig of dried rosemary. For remembrance.

She sniffed, brushing tears from her cheeks, but for once she didn't chastise herself for them. Because they were the last. She'd mourned long enough. After tonight, she would only look forward, not backward, because anything else would be disloyal to her betrothed.

She felt so heavy, it was hard to get up and start fixing supper. She was tired every day these days, but it was worse today than usual. She dragged herself to the stove and put on a pot of water to boil. Potato soup sounded kind of soothing. Looking down at her walnut-blackened fingers, she chided herself again for not having worn gloves. Would the stains be gone by next Saturday? She hoped so, because that was the day she was getting married.

22

The man in the information booth at Broad Street Station had told Carrie the Makepeace Hotel was seventeen blocks away. That didn't sound like much, and she'd set off without a thought, clutching her cloth satchel to her bosom so nobody could steal it. ("Don't let go of it for a second," Eppy had warned her, "or they'll have it off you before you can turn around.") But the concrete sidewalks of Philadelphia were a far cry from the mossy, ferny trails of High Dreamer Mountain, and by the time she reached the Makepeace, her feet in the thin-soled half boots Eppy had lent her felt as tender as if she'd been walking barefoot.

The lobby was almost empty, which gave her the courage to go straight up to the desk and say to the man behind it, "I wrote ahead for a room."

"Yes, and your name?"

"Catherine Hamilton."

She knew she was imagining the skepticism in the clerk's eyes when she said her brand-new name to him; but knowing it didn't keep her from half expecting him to holler across the lobby at the people sitting around in big chairs, "This woman's a liar! Somebody call the police!" Of course, nothing of the sort happened. She signed her name in the register slowly and carefully, with the result that her signature looked like a child's. But otherwise it was perfectly convincing; it appeared to be a real person's real name. In fact, seeing it written there made her feel a little better about things in general than she had for days.

Her room on the third floor had an electric light in the ceiling, which was a good thing because when she pulled the curtains back to let in some light, she found that the window wouldn't open and all that could be seen from it anyway was a flat brick wall across a dark, dirty alley. She was sorry she'd looked; now she felt suffocated. She unpacked her belongings in two minutes, then sat on the bed and wondered what to do next.

It was the twenty-first of December. Ty was at home now, spending time with his family. The fact that it was still early, only four or so, and that if she wanted to she could go and see him now, not wait until tomorrow as she'd planned, filled her with a shaky, freezing-cold dread. *No, I'll stick to the plan,* she decided hurriedly, not caring if that was cowardly or not. She'd tried many times to write to him in the last nine days, and once she'd almost asked Frank Odell if she could use the telephone in his newspaper office to call him. But what she had to tell Ty was going to be awkward enough without trying to say it through a machine. Why in the world she'd thought seeing him face-to-face would make it any easier, she couldn't remember anymore. She must've been out of her mind.

She thought of the stiff note he'd written back after she'd told him about her engagement. "To Carrie and Eugene, Congratulations and best wishes for your happiness. Cordially, Tyler Wilkes." Oh, she should've written him, she should've written him! A letter would've been a far better way to say what she had to say. And even though she'd thought of nothing but seeing him for days, she still hadn't figured out exactly what she was going to say to him when she did. She'd think of his face, the way he smiled, and immediately her mind would go flying off on a girlish fantasy of happily ever after which got her nowhere. All she knew was that it would surely kill her if her news, that she was four months pregnant with his child, horrified Ty as much as it had horrified Eugene.

"You damn whore," he'd called her, three days before their wedding, shaking his head over and over as if he had a bug in his ear and it wouldn't come out. "I can't believe it. I can't believe it." He'd said that several more times before he'd gone back to "You damn whore." He'd never raised his voice, though, and he'd stayed more flabbergasted than angry — but then, she hadn't stuck around long to hear any more. She'd gone away as soon as he'd started to curse Ty. That she wouldn't tolerate.

When she'd caught sight of Eugene coming toward her this morning at the train station, she'd been positive he only meant to revile her some more. But he hadn't. He'd stood there on the platform and told her he'd still marry her if she wouldn't go to Philadelphia. She'd been surprised, to say the least. And moved. It wasn't till she told him she *had* to go that he'd started abusing her again. "Go on then! Run to him like the whore you are, but it won't do you any good. What do you think he's going to do, Carrie, marry you?" He had an ugly laugh; she'd always hated it. "He's as much of a bastard as you are a whore. He won't even look at you! And don't come crying and crawling to me when he leaves you flat, because I don't want you anymore. I gave you a chance, an honorable offer, but it's over now because you're a goddamn whore."

She lay back on the narrow, too-soft mattress and stared up at the electric light. She thought she could hear it humming, but that was probably just her nerves. "I have to go," she'd told Eugene this morning, "can't you see? It's his baby, I have to at least tell him about it. He deserves to know it exists. That's all I'm going for, just to tell him." Eugene hadn't believed that, and now, tracing a thin, spidery crack in the ceiling with her eyes, she had to admit that that wasn't really all she was going for. The shameful truth of the matter was, she had hopes. She couldn't think them out loud to herself, though; they were too embarrassing.

But sometimes, just before she fell asleep at night and her defenses were down, she saw pictures in her head that stood for the wishes she couldn't completely give up. She couldn't hear the words, but she saw herself talking to Ty, telling him the secret of the baby. His beautiful smile filled the picture. He put his arms around her and held her. "I love you, Carrie," he said.

She turned on her side and drew her legs up, shutting her eyes against the vision because it was preposterous and it might bring bad luck. By this time tomorrow, she'd know everything. All she could do in the meantime was wait, and try hard not to hope.

When she woke up, she had no idea where she was. After it came to her, she had a desperate need to know the time. But she had no clock, and her only clue was that the brick wall across the alley was black now — but that could mean anything. She had to force herself to calm down. She'd never taken a nap in her life until a few weeks ago — one of the many signs that, in her ridiculous ignorance, she'd missed before Eppy finally put two and two together and Dr. Stoneman had confirmed it — and even now the naps she took never lasted more than an hour or so. At worst, it was five o'clock. She was starving, as usual. Was it too early for supper? Dinner, she corrected herself; only country people called the third meal supper.

She had the new suit she was wearing, and one other dress, the visiting gown she would wear for Ty tomorrow. She went to the tiny closet in the corner to look at it, something she never got tired of doing. It was of clinging dark-blue merino, soft as cashmere, the simplest dress she'd ever seen; it didn't have anything to it except gracefulness. She'd loved it on first sight, but she'd never have bought it, or any other dress that cost so much, if Eppy hadn't insisted and insisted, until the dignified saleslady in the Chambersburg store had finally raised her eyebrows at them — the way Miss Fuller did with noisy children in the library. So Carrie gave in.

After all, she was temporarily rich. Even though it had almost killed her, she'd sold Ty's beautiful Audubon book to finance this trip, and she still wasn't over the shock of discovering that he'd paid much, much more for it than the publishing company was going to pay her for the book she'd written! If she had known, she couldn't have accepted the gift, though, and then she couldn't have come to Philadelphia. What was the moral? Sometimes ignorance had a few compensations? She sighed, and decided to wear the maroon to supper — *dinner* — even though she'd stupidly fallen asleep in it and gotten it even more wrinkled than the train had.

Eppy said the Makepeace was a "modest" hotel, but the restaurant down a long hall from the lobby made Pennicle's, which Carrie had always considered the height of elegant dining, seem like a feed store by comparison. Seated at one of the glossy tables, she had a moment of panic when a man in a white jacket bent close to her ear and seemed to be listening. She looked up at him in bewilderment. Just then, across the room, she saw a man in the same white jacket taking food off a tray and putting it in front of another diner. "I would like dinner, please," she said softly.

"Yes, ma'am. What would you like?"

She looked blank.

"Did you see the menu?"

The menu! She saw it now, a long, stiff card across from her on the table. She glanced at it without seeing any of the words: her eyes simply wouldn't focus while the man in the white jacket was standing over her.

"The pepper pot soup's always good," he said helpfully. "And tonight there's stewed snapper, very nice."

"I'll have that," she told him, overcome with gratitude.

The bill for dinner froze her in her chair for a full minute. She hadn't the courage to argue, but how could it be two dollars, how *could* it be? And a tip on top of that. She signed her name to the check wearily, aware that nearly a quarter of her Audubon windfall was already gone, and in ten days she'd have to vacate her house on the mountain and find another place to live. If Ty didn't want her, how was she going to get through the winter? How could she keep her baby with no money?

The panic had never gotten this far before; she'd always beaten it down before it could surface and take over everything. She did it again now, but it was harder.

She drifted out of the restaurant, at a loss as to how to occupy herself until bedtime. She had a horror of looking as if she didn't know what she was doing in front of the people sitting around the lobby in chairs. A walk would've soothed her, but she suspected such a thing wouldn't be proper here, alone and at night. For all she knew, it might not even be safe.

She took a seat apart from the three other people who were sitting in the Reading Room, an alcove off the lobby with desks and chairs and a table covered with magazines and newspapers. One of the newspaper headlines caught her eye — "Roosevelt Says Pact Premature." She felt a familiar shiver of pride, but this time it was mixed with anxiety. She, Carrie/Catherine Wiggins/Hamilton, had come to pay a call on a man who was personally acquainted with the vice president of the United States. She thrust the thought aside, because it would only make her crazy if she dwelled on it, and chose a *Lippincott's* from among the *Saturday Evening Post*s and *Ladies' Home Journal*s.

She'd never read a *Lippincott's* magazine but she'd seen them at Ty's house often enough. Tonight the words ran together on the pages almost as bad as they had on the menu in the restaurant, as if they weren't even in English, but some foreign language with different characters. When she forced herself to focus, she found an article on cats; here was one on women who had written novels in the eighteenth century; here was one on tea. *Tea.* She understood almost all the individual words in the essays; it was the tone that confounded her. Witty and bright, naturally, and book-learned clever. But underneath the wit and brilliance ran something she could barely put her finger on, some quality that wasn't too far from nastiness. No, that was too strong. "Superior," maybe that was it. Whatever it was, it lurked just under the smart, polished, tasteful phrases, and it implied to her, the reader, that having any other opinion on these odd subjects than the writer wanted her to meant not only that she was wrong but also that she was . . . lacking. And . . . pitiful.

Sophisticated — that was the word. Was this the way people in Ty's family talked to each other? She thought it must be. So foreign, so exclusive. So hopeless. Depression weighed her down like a wet sheet.

On the way back to her room, she stopped at the desk and asked the clerk — a different one from the man this afternoon — if he could give her directions to Ty's house, which was on Walnut Street. If he thought anything was funny about her asking, he didn't show it in his face; he was very kind, and even drew her a map. His kindness provoked her to ask another question.

"I'm a stranger here, so I don't know. Can

you tell me the proper time to pay a call on people?"

"A social call, that would be?"

"Yes."

"Ladies make what they call their morning visits between lunchtime and tea. That's to say, between two and four o'clock."

"They make their morning calls in the afternoon?"

"Yes, ma'am."

He looked like he was telling the truth. "Well," she said faintly. "Thank you very much."

"You're welcome."

Upstairs in her bright box of a room, she put on her nightgown and got in bed. She'd taken to rubbing her stomach when she was alone, even though it wasn't big yet, just as a way to be close to the baby. Eppy said it was a girl because Carrie was still so small. Sometimes when she thought about it, that she was going to have a child of her own that she could take care of and love for the rest of her life, nothing else seemed to matter or be of any importance whatsoever. Even if she lost Ty — and she had, she really *had* reconciled herself to that; it was only in crazy, unguarded moments that she let herself imagine something else — she thought she could still be happy. She'd always have his child, his little son or daughter. Whichever it was, they'd be friends, she and her baby, and neither of them would ever be lonely. She fell asleep dreaming about a beautiful child, with dark brown hair and eyes the violet-blue of gentians.

Ty's house was made out of marble. The word "villa" came to Carrie's mind as she stood on the far corner and gazed across Nineteenth Street at the three-story mansion behind the spiked iron fence. Through the posts she could see a neat tangle of wisteria and grapevines, roses, honeysuckle, and clematis. All dormant now, but how beautiful the garden would be in the spring. In any but this cold winter light the marble would glow almost gold, like honey, and look warm and hospitable even with its mighty columns and stately front porch — which even she knew enough to call a portico. And, Lord God in heaven, in a minute she had to go up and knock at the front door.

Christmas was in three days. A little while ago some men had driven a cart up to the curb and carried in the tallest balsam tree she'd ever seen that wasn't still growing in the ground. And just now a man with a black case had knocked on the door and been let inside. A doctor? She didn't think he looked like one, despite the case. A repairman, maybe. Was some affair going on in the house? Most of the fine arched windows were lit up. But it was a dreary day; maybe the Wilkeses just liked lots of light.

Ty's in there right now. In a few minutes you'll see him. He'll see you.

That was not the way to work her courage up. If she did everything one minute at a time and didn't look ahead farther than the one minute she was in, maybe she could get through this. She noticed her feet weren't moving, though. It was starting to snow; she was freezing. The feather on her smart new hat would be ruined if she didn't get moving. She stepped off the curb and went toward Ty's house.

She could hardly hear her first knock herself; her second sounded much too loud. She was expecting a servant, but when the wide door swung open, a young woman about her own age stood beside it. She said "Hello" with a friendly smile, and she was about to say more when an older woman's voice called out from behind her, "Is it the piano tuner?"

"No, Mother, he's already here. I think it's —" She turned back, the smile widened, and Carrie knew it was Ty's sister. "Are you from the caterer's?" she asked.

She felt her face go slack. What was a "caterer"? "No, I'm . . . no."

"No," Abbey echoed, kind brown eyes taking a closer look. "I beg your pardon." She opened the door wider in invitation. "Will you come in? You must be freezing."

The house was even more beautiful than the outside had prepared her for. She couldn't take it all in at a glance, she'd need a long time to really see the curving shape of the entrance hall, the gigantic fireplace burning on the wood-paneled wall in front of her, the chandelier, big as the crown of a dogwood tree, shining directly over her head. Everywhere there was scurrying and bustle, maids trotting this way and that, somebody winding fresh pine boughs around the banister rails, the sound of piano scales from another room.

She'd come at a bad time.

Abbey was watching her with friendly interest. Carrie wet her lips and said in a low voice, "I've come to see Dr. Wilkes."

"Oh, I'm sorry, he's not here."

"Will he be coming back soon?"

"He hasn't come home yet, he won't be here until the day after tomorrow. We expected him last week, but he's been delayed."

"The day after tomorrow. I see." She felt the way she had that time Petey accidentally butted her in the chest and knocked her on her back.

A woman appeared in the great arch of a

doorway off to the left. Abbey turned toward the woman and said, "Mother, this lady's come to see Ty."

"Has she?" Mrs. Wilkes glided forward, smiling cordially, holding out her hand. "How do you do, I'm Tyler's mother."

"How do you do?" Had she shaken too hard? Should she have taken her glove off first? "I'm Car— I'm Catherine Hamilton." She felt glad with all her heart to have such a fine-sounding name to give to this stately, dignified lady. *Formidable* — the perfect word. She was tall, with wide shoulders and a deep bosom, and she carried herself like an old-fashioned ship's figurehead. Carrie could see Ty in her strong-featured face, especially in the chin and around the mouth. She had hair the color of new pewter, dressed to perfection in a style Carrie had seen in pictures but never before on a real person.

"You've missed my son by two days, Miss Hamilton," she said with her queen's smile. "That's what all this madness is about, incidentally — Tyler's welcome-home party."

"I thought he would be here by now," Carrie murmured.

Mrs. Wilkes's perfect eyebrows went up ever so slightly. "Yes, so did we all; we only had the cable a few days ago that he'd been delayed in Havana, some business about a final report. But let's not stand in the hall — come into the drawing room, Miss Hamilton, won't you? We were just having an early tea. Will you join us?"

"Yes, do come in. I'm Abbey, by the way, Ty's sister. Are you a friend of his?"

Not quite knowing what else to do, Carrie let herself be gently towed through the high doorway and into another awesome room, the drawing room, she supposed, this one lined with crimson satin panels on all four walls, with a glittering mirror that went from the mantel all the way up to the ceiling. Abbey made her take off her coat and sit in a soft, high-backed chair near the fire. She brought her a cup of tea herself, took a seat nearby, and repeated her question.

"I knew Dr. Wilkes in Wayne's Crossing," she answered carefully.

"Really?" Her lovely, animated face lit up. "Ty wrote to us about some of the people he knew there. There was the girl who couldn't speak — remember, Mother? What was her name?"

"I can't recall," said Mrs. Wilkes, tapping her cheek with her finger. Mother and daughter looked at Carrie expectantly. She couldn't open her mouth.

"And a doctor, the one he replaced," Abbey went on after a curious pause. "He sounded like quite a character."

"Dr. Stoneman," Carrie said faintly. "He's back from the sanatorium in Harrisburg now, and almost all well. Dr. Wilkes insisted he go, so it's really his doing that Dr. Stoneman's so much better."

"I'll be sure to tell him so," Mrs. Wilkes said graciously. "And there was another gentleman he spoke fondly of, a journalist, I believe."

"Mr. Odell. Yes, they were friends." She set her untouched cup down, afraid her shaking hands would give her away if she held onto it another second. These kind ladies were trying so hard to put her at ease, she wanted to weep. She ought to leave, but they'd taken her coat and she didn't know what to say to get it back.

"Excuse me." A maid poked her head in the door. "Telephone call for you, Miss Abbey."

"Who is it, Irene?"

"It's Miss Adele."

Abbey shot her mother an apologetic glance and stood up. She had on a rose-colored gown cut in a style that hadn't hit Wayne's Crossing yet. Carrie thought she looked exactly like a fashionable clothes model in a magazine, only friendlier. "I'm sorry, Mother, Miss Hamilton — would you excuse me, please?" She continued in a wry, private voice to her mother, "Del's lost her mind, I think, she's so excited about the party. I'm sure this is another call with regard to the suitability of her sapphire crepe de chine versus her cream silk moire. I promise I'll only be a moment." She danced out.

It didn't last long, but to Carrie the silence between her and Mrs. Wilkes was dreadful. She broke it in a panic by blurting out, "You have a beautiful house."

"Thank you. I've lived here since my marriage — over half my life. It's been a happy house, by and large. I look forward to seeing my grandchildren in it one day soon."

Carrie hummed something, staring straight ahead.

"That was my grandfather."

She started, and realized she'd been staring at a dark oil painting on the opposite wall, a portrait of a distinguished-looking gentleman in a gray wig.

"Eustice Morrell," Mrs. Wilkes said fondly. "He was a Princeton man, although he read law right here in Philadelphia. People seemed to mature at a younger age in those days, don't you think, Miss Hamilton? My grandfather was secretary to the American minister in Paris by the time he was twenty-two. He attended Napoleon's coronation — can you imagine? President Monroe appointed him a director of the Bank of the United States, where he had a brilliant career."

Carrie murmured politely.

"But duty called, and eventually he allowed his friends to persuade him to take a seat in the United States Senate." She smiled slightly. "No doubt it sounds vainglorious, but I think of my grandfather as the last true representative of the Enlightenment."

Carrie gazed back at her. She understood the sense if not the reference, and could think of nothing to say in response.

Mrs. Wilkes waved her hand in a graceful little circle and laughed gently at herself. "I beg your pardon, what foolishness I'm talking. It's Tyler's homecoming that's brought on all this nostalgia, I believe. You'll forgive a mother's boastfulness, but we have hopes for Tyler that would make his great-grandfather proud of him." She leaned forward a little in her chair. "He's coming home a hero, you know. We think it's the perfect time to launch his career."

"His career?"

"In politics," she said lightly.

"And does T— does Dr. Wilkes want a career in politics?"

Mrs. Wilkes sat back. "I was referring to friends, people who can advise him. My son can become anything to which he sets his mind. One day he'll be a great man."

"Yes. Yes, I believe it, too." Carrie looked back at the portrait of Eustice Morrell, and this time she fancied she could see a resemblance to Ty in his ancestor's high forehead and the bones behind his clever blue eyes. The silence between her and Mrs. Wilkes rushed back, but this time it didn't sound dreadful; just hopeless. A log in the fireplace broke apart, sending up a flurry of sparks. Carrie stood up. "I have to go," she said quietly. "Thank you for receiving me."

Abbey came into the room and stopped. "Oh, are you leaving already? I'd have hung up sooner if I'd known you couldn't stay."

Carrie's coat appeared; soon she found herself in the hall by the door, with Abbey reaching impulsively for her hands.

"Excuse me — but you're quite all right, aren't you? Not ill?" Her fine eyes looked troubled.

An awful, humiliating urge to cry came over Carrie in a wave, but she beat it back. "Thank you," she murmured, "I'm just fine."

"Will you come to our party on Friday?"

She gave Abbey's soft, girlish hands a farewell squeeze and stepped back. "I'm going home tonight."

"Oh." She looked truly disappointed.

"Have you a message for Ty?"

There was a pause, and even to Carrie it sounded queer and forlorn. She was aware that the two ladies were looking at her strangely. "No," she finally managed to say. "There isn't any message."

"I'll just tell him Miss Hamilton called, then, shall I?" asked Mrs. Wilkes.

"Yes, tell him Miss Hamilton called." She did her best to smile then, to hide her sorrow because she'd never meet these women again. "Tell him — I was passing through and wanted to express to him the gratitude of the town for all he did for us. And say . . . no, that's all." She turned away hurriedly, and passed through the door and down the flagstone walk.

23

Eustice Morrell looked more pompous than usual, and that was saying something.

Through the half-closed library door, Tyler contemplated his great-grandfather's florid, smug-faced portrait, lording it over the heads of half a hundred party guests milling around in the high-ceilinged drawing room. *Don't look too satisfied,* he warned his ancestor gloomily. *You've got me now, but in two days I'll be gone, and not a damn thing either one of you can do about it.*

Either one of you meant Eustice and Ty's mother; he always thought of them as in cahoots, partners in the life-long struggle to turn him into something he didn't want to be. After almost thirty years, though, he could see the battle winding down. This ill-conceived welcome-home party was his mother's last stand, the final, formal skirmish in a long war. Sensing victory, Tyler could afford to be gracious.

Carolivia might not call hiding out by himself in the library the behavior of a gracious winner. He could see her point. He needed a minute, though, and Main Line Philadelphia could survive without him for that long. His mother's guest list was long on influential political connections, but it was even longer on youthful, unattached females. He eyed without interest the ladies drifting past the door to his sanctuary, sumptuous-looking in their bright gowns and elegant hairstyles. They all looked the same to him, indistinguishable versions of eligibility. He couldn't keep his eyes focused on them. Was it a good thing or a bad thing that he had no picture of Carrie? Good, if it kept him from thinking about her. But it didn't.

One of the bright, bejeweled figures materialized in the doorway and stood still, and Ty's mechanical smile of welcome turned genuine.

"Aha!" Abbey crossed to where he was standing on the hearth rug before the marble fireplace. But by the time she reached him, her laughing face had sobered. "Ty?" She put her hand on his sleeve. "Oh, dear. I can see that this wasn't quite as delightful a surprise as we'd hoped."

Instead of commenting on that one way or the other, he said, "You've grown so beautiful, Abbey." Not to distract her, but because it was true.

Her lovely brown eyes warmed with affection. "And you've gotten even handsomer. I'd been terrified you'd come home looking the way you did the last time, but instead you're tan and robust — in fact, I've never seen you looking so well. And Del," she added meaningfully, "agrees with me."

He glanced behind her toward the crowded drawing room. If Adele was out there, he couldn't see her. He shrugged and took a sip of his drink.

Abbey's hand on his arm squeezed softly. "Ty?"

"Hm?"

"How are you, really?"

Her low voice claimed his full attention. He stared at her for a long, telling moment, debating how to answer.

"If I'm wrong, just ignore me, but I can't help feeling something's not quite right with you. Something's making you sad."

"You just told me how well I look," he protested lightly.

"Under that." She didn't return his poor excuse for a smile. "I can't think what it could be. I know it makes you cringe, but Mother's right when she says you've come home a hero. What you accomplished in Havana must make you feel so proud."

"Satisfied, yes."

"And you're glad about your new job in Washington?"

"Very glad. I can't wait to get started." He ought to say more, keep nattering about anything; this was his chance to divert her. But with Abbey, he didn't have the will to pretend.

So she asked straight out, "Then what is it?" She ducked her head. "I'm sorry, you needn't tell me, of course. But if you ever want —"

"I've lost something, Ab," he blurted out in a murmur. "A part of myself I'd just found. It was the best part, and I'm grieving for it." That sounded lugubrious to him. He made a face at his drink and set it on the mantel.

Without a word, she took his elbow and turned with him to face the fire, their backs to the room, shoulders touching. He felt a mixture of relief and surprise at himself, for in the past he'd rarely confided anything truly important to his sister. To any woman, for that matter. Except one.

Abbey whispered, "How can I help you?"

"You can't," he said gently. "I've let something slip away. It's finished; it can't be retrieved."

"What, Ty? What is it?"

He shook his head, glad that he'd told her this much, but unable to go on with it. Fire fingers curled around the small, decorous logs behind the brass screen; his eyes blurred, and he saw the color of Carrie's hair in the flames. "Do you remember when you set the chimney on fire, Ab?"

"Vividly."

"How old were you?"

"Five or six. I thought I was helping."

"By burning all the newspapers at once."

"It seemed so sensible."

She slipped her arm through his; she was preparing some sweet, tenderhearted speech. He loved her for it, but he couldn't listen to it right now. "You're all grown up, aren't you?" he said quickly. "While my back was turned, you stopped being that pesky little girl and turned into this beautiful woman."

"Did I?"

"How many men are in love with you?" He grinned, bent on lightening the mood.

"Oh, dozens." She understood, and answered in the same airy tone. "Hundreds by now. I've lost count."

"I don't doubt it. Do you love any of them back?"

"Not one. I'm quite a ruthless heart-breaker."

"But you wish you did," he guessed. "You wish one of those depressingly eligible young men would break from the pack and sweep you off your feet."

"Wouldn't it be lovely?" She was smiling,

but she sounded a trifle wistful. "I'm really not that hard to please; all he'd have to have is a few qualities Mother doesn't approve of."

"Well, don't give up. There's bound to be a complete rotter out there somewhere."

They shared a good-humored pause.

Then she said, "Ty? If you ever need to talk about . . . anything, I hope you'll feel comfortable talking to me. I've always known I could say anything to you, and it would be nice to think you felt the same about me."

"I do."

"Because there's nothing you could say, nothing in the world you could do that could make me stop loving you."

"Well, I haven't killed anyone, you know." This new Abbey fascinated him. When her gaze on his stayed steady and sincere, he put his arm around her shoulders. "Thank you," he said from his heart. "I won't forget that."

They stood for a few more quiet minutes. He'd have stayed that way all afternoon, peering into the fire and exchanging desultory confidences with his sister. But Abbey knew her duty.

"You-know-who's going to catch us," she warned presently, glancing over her shoulder. "I'm afraid it's time to be sociable, like it or not. You're the guest of honor, after all. Have you spoken to Adele yet?"

"Yes, I spoke to her."

"Not much, I bet. Not nearly enough, considering all the trouble she went to to look pretty for you." She gave him another arch look, but he didn't rise to the bait. "Speaking of pretty girls, did Mother tell you about the lady from Wayne's Crossing?"

"What lady?"

"She came to see you."

"Came here?"

"Yes, the day before yesterday. A Miss Hamilton."

He frowned. "I don't remember anyone by that name. What did she want?"

"Well, I'm not quite sure. She said she was passing through, and wanted to thank you for everything you'd done for the town."

"Hamilton," he repeated, mystified. "What did she look like?"

"She was lovely. She had on a handsome blue merino wool gown, very stunning — even Mother thought so. But I think she was sad, Ty. Her eyes . . . I don't know, I couldn't shake the sense that something —"

"Tyler, for heaven's sake, there you are. I thought you'd left the house. Shame on you, and you, too, Abigail, for encouraging him." Carolivia sailed into the room under a full head of steam, amethysts glittering on her stately bosom like running lights on a frigate.

"What did I tell you?" Abbey said out of the side of her mouth. She wasn't so grown up that she couldn't still giggle. "I'm going, Mother; I'm gone." Winking at Ty, she glided away, abandoning him without a qualm.

But, against all the odds, his mother didn't scold him. She put her arms around him and gave him a quick, impulsive hug.

"What's this?" he said, laughing to cover his surprise.

"I'm so proud of you." Her strong voice quivered with telltale emotion. "And I'm so glad you're home. I've missed you a great deal, you know."

"I've missed you."

"I think there's only one more thing I could wish for on this very special day."

"And what's that?"

"That your father were here to see the man his son has grown into."

He kissed her smooth, perfumed cheek, noticing with a pang that she looked older than when he'd last seen her. She was still handsome, but she appeared to have softened. She was not quite so formidable as she had been.

In other ways, though, she hadn't changed at all. She blinked the uncharacteristic moisture from her eyes and asked casually, "I don't suppose you and Senator Lloyd had anything substantive to say to each other before he got away?"

"Substantive? I wished him a very merry Christmas."

"Nothing else?"

"Oh — and a happy New Year."

She clucked her tongue; but she said no more, and he took that for a hopeful sign.

"You know I'm going to Washington in two days," he reminded her. "I'm starting a new job that fills me with hope for doing something valuable with my life. With my real talents." She glanced away; he touched the side of her face to make her look at him. "Your only son's a scientist, Mother. Not a statesman, not even a politician. I'm a doctor." He saw something shift in her eyes, and entertained the hope that it was the beginning of acceptance. "There's only one thing," he said gently, "that I could wish for on this very special day."

She raised her aristocratic eyebrows somewhat fatalistically.

"That you'd celebrate with me because I've finally figured out what I ought to be doing with myself. And I can't wait to start doing it."

She sighed. "All I want for you is happiness, Tyler, whether you believe it or not. It's all I've ever wanted."

"If that's true, then you've got your wish."

"Have I?" Her eyes narrowed on him in a too-shrewd appraisal, and he was afraid she would see the same shadows that Abbey had.

"Absolutely," he said with conviction, taking her arm and moving her toward the door.

"Then I'll say no more. Except . . ."

"What?"

"Oh, just that it wouldn't do any harm to go and speak to Colonel Symington and his wife; they were in the dining room a moment ago. Well, you needn't look at me that way. They're guests, after all, it's a matter of common —"

"I spoke to them already."

"But not to much purpose, I expect." She had the grace to blush. "Well, heavens, Ty, it isn't only me — everyone's talking about who's going to replace Sternberg as surgeon general, and I see no reason in the world why it shouldn't be you. I'm serious!"

"I know you are." He gave her a noisy kiss, partly out of affection and partly to deflate her dignity a little further. "You're incorrigible, aren't you?"

"I just want you to be happy."

"And I keep telling you that I am."

"Very well, then." She set her lips.

"Very well, then? You'll say no more?"

"Not a word."

"So it's nothing to you whether I go over and charm Colonel Symington or not?"

"Perfectly immaterial."

"Oh hell, Mother," he laughed. "Now I suppose I'll have to go talk to the old gasbag."

"Don't swear, Tyler. And don't be vulgar."

"I hate this new tactic, by the way."

"I have no idea what you mean."

He chuckled and turned away — then back, remembering. "Abbey said a girl came to see me a few days ago. A Miss Hamilton?"

"That's right. Catherine Hamilton, I think she said. Who is she?"

"Well, that's it — I don't remember anyone by that name in Wayne's Crossing."

"How odd."

"What do you think she wanted?"

"To see you, she said. But she wouldn't leave a message. She was a pretty thing; I assumed she was one of your conquests."

He returned her playful smile automatically. But the mystery nagged him. He'd only made one "conquest" in Wayne's Crossing, and she wasn't Catherine Hamilton. And he was the last person Carrie would look up if she happened to be "passing through." Who had his visitor been, then?

The Symingtons were agreeable people, not gasbags at all; it was no hardship to exchange pleasant conversation with them

496

while nibbling on smoked ham and salmon tarts. The subject of the surgeon general's successor never came up. Ty moved easily from the Symingtons to the Dunaways to old Mrs. Waterton, lingered with his Uncle Andrew and Aunt Sally, and flirted for a few mechanical minutes with Adele. His cousin Teddy joined them, eager to tell stories about his first semester at Princeton. Adele wandered away. Tyler sipped from a cup of punch, smiling and nodding at the appropriate moments while Teddy detailed his strategy for making freshman crew coxswain.

Then he remembered.

The memory came to him on the sound of Carrie's voice, husky from disuse and soft from shyness. That first night. While they sipped iced tea with mint vinegar, and she blurted out her life story.

My father was John Hamilton, my mother was Rachel.

He shoved his punch cup into his startled cousin's hand and bolted from the room.

His mother's genteel laughter sounded from somewhere at the back of the drawing room. He started for her, then changed course when he caught sight of Abbey's lavender dress at the end of the foyer. She was moving toward him, arm in arm with Helen DeWitt, her best friend. Both women stopped when they saw his face. Abbey started to speak, but he seized her by her forearms, silencing her.

"What did she look like?"

"Who?"

"Catherine Hamilton — how did she look?"

Helen murmured politely and sidled away. Abbey looked flustered. "She — I told you, Ty, she was pretty, she had on a Lady Randolph hat, the rain had wilted the feather —"

He came very close to shaking her. *What did she look like?*"

"Well — I think her hair was brown —"

"Brown!"

"No, red, maybe. Light; there was blonde in it, too. She had blue eyes, I think — oh, Ty, I can't remember!"

He gentled his grip on her and spoke as calmly as he could. "Was she tall and slender, Ab?"

"Yes. She was, yes, taller than I —"

"And she had reddish-gold hair. Slippery hair, shiny, a lock or two of it falling around her face."

Abbey nodded dumbly.

"And her eyes were gray-blue, and cloudy because she was sad."

"Yes," she whispered.

He closed his own eyes and let go of Abbey's hands. "It was Carrie. My God, it was Carrie."

"Who is she?" Abbey asked fearfully.

"She's — Carrie. Carrie Wiggins. Hamilton, now." Empty-headed, he pivoted and started for the stairs. Abbey followed. When he halted and wheeled back, they almost collided. "What did she want?" he demanded. "Tell me again, everything she said."

"She didn't say much at all. Mother spoke to her more than I did. She only stayed a few minutes. When I told her you weren't here, she looked — more than disappointed, she looked . . ."

She didn't want to say it. "Tell me," he commanded.

"She looked . . . defeated."

He stared at his sister's troubled face, picturing Carrie's, straining to understand why she'd come. Two weeks ago she'd told him she was marrying Eugene.

"I invited her to your party," Abbey remembered.

He almost laughed. He brought the heels of his hands to his eye sockets and pressed.

"She said she couldn't come, she was going home that night."

"She was going home?"

Abbey nodded.

He backed up a step. "I'll go," he muttered.

"No — I'll call. Who?" He took another step backward. "Stoneman's still in Harrisburg. At least I think he is. Frank — would he be in his office on Christmas Eve? What time is it?" Abbey was gaping at him. "What time is it?" he repeated, then remembered he had a watch of his own. He yanked it out of his waistcoat and flipped it open. "Almost three. He might be there."

"Ty, what can I do to help?"

"Nothing. No — tell Priest to call a hansom. No, wait. Never mind, it'll be faster walking."

"Where are you going?"

"Broad Street Station, I hope. But first — Abbey, I don't have time to talk!" He backed into Uncle Andrew in the foyer. "Excuse me," he mumbled, whirled, and raced away to the telephone.

Pennicle's was surprisingly crowded, considering it was Christmas Eve, but Carrie didn't know anybody else in the restaurant. Anybody but Eugene, of course, who sat across from her at their table in the corner. She'd been struggling since they got here not to make comparisons between this evening and the only other time she'd ever eaten at Pennicle's, and so far she'd succeeded middling well. But when Eugene lifted his beer mug and touched it to her glass of milk in a toast — "To us, Carrie" — there was no stopping the rush of memories of that night when Ty had done the same thing. Only he hadn't toasted him and her, he'd toasted the start of her "new career." "What are you two celebrating?" Mrs. Stambaugh had wanted to know, and Carrie had felt light and airy as a balloon when Ty explained about the "imminent purchase and publication of Carrie's new book."

Tonight Mrs. Stambaugh wouldn't speak to her except to ask her what she wanted to eat. Respectable women like her and Mrs. Quick wouldn't even look at her. Since she'd found out about the baby, Eugene's mother could barely say two words in a row to her, and Mrs. Starkey wasn't exactly a leading light in Wayne's Crossing society. Eugene had had to bully her into attending her own son's wedding.

Carrie crumbled a piece of bread on her plate and looked across the table at the man she was going to marry at ten o'clock tomorrow morning in the Odells' parlor. He was wearing his second-best suit, which had black and white checks and a gray vest, and he'd put on a cheery red tie for the occasion of their pre-wedding dinner on the town. He'd recently acquired side-whiskers, and the oiled mustache he was so proud of met them at the tops of his ruddy cheeks. He looked healthy and prosperous and well fed. So well fed, in fact, that a disinterested corner of her mind wondered if he was going to get fat in a few years. It wasn't hard to imagine. Not hard at all.

He blotted his lips with his napkin and caught her eye. "So," he said, which was how he started most of his sentences. "You're not saying much. What're you thinking about? You nervous about tomorrow?"

"Yes, a little." She smiled. "Aren't you?"

"Nah," he scoffed, "nothing to it. Stoneman still giving you away?"

"I think so."

"You think so?"

"He wasn't sure he was feeling up to it," she said tactfully. Well, that might not be the whole truth, but it wasn't a lie. Dr. Stoneman was furious with her because she'd said yes to Eugene. She hadn't seen him since the night before last, when she'd returned from Philadelphia and he'd kept asking if Ty knew about the baby. She'd kept dancing and sidestepping and never answering the question head-on. She'd told Eugene what really happened in Philadelphia, but no one else. She felt she owed him the truth, but couldn't it be her private business from the rest of the world? As much as she loved her friends, sometimes the fact that everybody knew everything about everybody else in Wayne's Crossing got her down.

"Anyway," she went on, "Mr. Odell said he'd give me away if Dr. Stoneman wo— can't."

Eugene made his disgusted face, which involved looking like he wanted to spit. She never spoke to him about Dr. Stoneman, but Eugene was too smart not to know that the old doctor disliked and disapproved of him. It was disheartening to see the years stretching out ahead of her, and to know that her husband and one of her favorite friends weren't going to get along with each other.

But Eugene had asked her what she was thinking, and it wasn't really about Dr. Stoneman or the ceremony or her pre-wedding jitters. She put her hand out and touched the sleeve of his coat with one finger. "What I was thinking," she began softly.

He was immediately alert. "What?"

"I wanted to ask you something."

"What?"

She smiled — to let him know everything was fine, she hadn't changed her mind. "Maybe it's not the time."

"No, go ahead and ask."

"All right, then. What I'd like to know is

why you want to marry me. You've never said, and I — I'd just like to know."

He smirked and lowered his voice in a tone that was part affectionate, part mocking. "What do you want, love words?"

It wouldn't hurt, she couldn't help thinking. But she said, "No, just the truth."

His smart-aleck smile faded; he shifted in his chair. "Does there have to be a reason?"

What a strange question! Carrie couldn't think how to answer.

"Oh, hell," he said gruffly. He picked up his beer glass, but set it down when he saw it was empty. "I always liked you," he said in a funny, embarrassed voice. "You know."

"No," she admitted, equally shy. "Tell me."

"You're good. You make me feel . . ." He paused for so long, she thought he'd given up. "Easier in my mind. About things. More like a man." He laughed uneasily, as if he wished already he hadn't said that.

She sat still, thinking it over, feeling sorry for Eugene and realizing that words probably weren't going to be the best way for him to communicate serious thoughts to her during their life together. But maybe they'd find other ways. So what he said next floored her.

"There's something nobody knows. Nobody outside my family." She had to lean forward to hear his near-whisper over the clatter of cutlery and the drone of voices around them. "When I was a kid, my old man used to whale the bejesus out of me every chance he got. I'm not talking about a normal licking — any kid needs that once in a while. I'm talking about near to killing me."

"Oh, Eugene —"

His hand cutting sharp through the air told her she'd better not offer any sympathy. "The best day of my life was the day the sonofabitch dropped dead. I was only ten, didn't have my growth yet. I only had one regret then and I've still got it, got it right now this minute — that he died before I got a chance to beat the living shit out of him."

She recoiled, appalled by his violence, and even more by the raw hate burning bright as a bonfire in his eyes.

Then he grinned at her, and the hate went back into hiding. He pushed his plate away and crossed his arms on the table. "I was a pretty mean cuss from then on. I could lick anybody, any age, from the time I was fourteen. I enjoyed it. Sometimes I still do." The cocky smile loosened and he fell silent, twirling his empty beer glass around the wet rings on the table. "I can't say it in words exactly. You know, what you asked me. It started a long time ago. Remember that day on the bridge, Carrie?" He said it without looking up, twirling the glass in slow circles.

"I remember." He had never mentioned that day to her, nor she to him, not in five years. She swallowed and held her breath, knowing something important was coming.

Finally he looked up at her. She'd never heard his voice so gentle. "You were perfect for torturing, Carrie. You couldn't do anything back. You couldn't fight, you couldn't even talk. And I thought you were so pretty. Even then. I wanted to see you. You know — naked. But I also wanted to hurt you as bad as I could."

She whispered past the tightness in her throat, "Why, Eugene?"

"I don't know. I don't know, I just did." He looked baffled.

"Then why didn't you? Why did you stop them? Why, Eugene?" she persisted when he just shook his head.

He stared off past her shoulder for a long time, then went back to twisting his glass. She thought that if they were anyplace but in a crowded restaurant, neither one of them could've found the courage to have this conversation. He glanced up at her, then quickly away again. "I think —" He cleared his throat. "Maybe because when you looked at me, I could see myself. 'Make him stop,' you

506

kept saying with your eyes." He dropped his chin and stared down at his big hands, lying loose and open now. "Make him stop, Mama," she thought he said.

She leaned forward and slid both her hands into his. He squeezed her fingers so hard they hurt, then dropped them and shoved back in his chair. "Come on, let's get out of here, it's late. I told all the boys I'd be over at the Blue Duck by ten."

Carrie stood with him. "Your last night of freedom?" she teased him lightly.

"Hell, yes. Gotta get in my licks before they clamp the ball and chain on me, don't I?"

They walked home without saying much. The sky was cold and clear; there was no moon, but a million stars. As usual, Eugene nibbled on a toothpick, rolling it from one side of his lips to the other with his tongue. At Truitt Avenue, he popped a clove in his mouth. He was always particular about his breath, but she knew he was chewing the clove now because he was planning to kiss her.

On the Odells' front porch, she invited him to come in for a few minutes.

"Into that crazy house? No thanks, not on your life."

She had to smile, because even out here she could plainly hear the sounds of crying babies and screaming children. "Eppy told Charlotte she could stay up a little later because it's Christmas Eve, and now Emily's fit to be tied. Of course, Charlotte won't last past nine-thirty." She could tell Eugene wasn't listening. "Well. I guess I better go in."

"Why don't you invite me into the little house you're staying in, Carrie?"

"Frank's office?" Rather than squeeze her into their small, overflowing house tonight, the Odells had offered her the quiet and privacy of the old stables behind the house that Mr. Odell had turned into a study for himself last summer. "Oh," she said vaguely, "it's so small, and with no fire in the stove it'll be too cold."

"I'd warm you up."

"I don't think it would be right," she said primly.

He smirked and gave a harsh laugh, but he didn't argue. "Come over here, then." He took her hand and pulled her toward the rusty divan in the corner, where the light wasn't so bright. Even in her wool coat, his long arms went around her waist with ease. He squeezed her against him and kissed her on the mouth, long and hard. Since she'd come back from Philadelphia and they'd made their peace with each other, he'd been very bold with her body. He kissed her whenever he liked, but she still fought him when his hands tried to wander. Tonight there was something different in his kisses, though, something rough and not as easy to control. "Eugene," she gasped, trying to push him away without making him angry.

He brought his huge hands up to hold her head still. "I don't want you to ever say his name again, Carrie," he said in a fierce whisper. "Hear me? Swear you'll never say his name. *Swear.*"

She considered that choice, and agreed to it. "I swear."

"You're mine. Say that."

"I am."

"Say you're my wife."

"I will be."

But even that didn't satisfy him. "Swear you won't even think of him again."

"Eugene —"

"Swear!"

She finally pried his hurtful fingers away. "I can't. Not yet. But I'll *try*. That's what I promise." She rushed on before he could get mad. "And I swear I'll be a good and faithful wife to you for the rest of our lives. I'll never give you cause to regret marrying me, Eugene. I'll be your helper and your partner, and we'll have a good life together." His head came down, but she stopped him before he could kiss her again. "But you have to give me a promise, too."

"What?"

"That you'll try hard to love the baby. And that you'll never, ever treat it unkindly because it isn't yours." He didn't answer, and she just waited. He'd implied all of that already or she wouldn't be marrying him, but tonight she wanted to hear his promise in words. "Well?" she prompted. "Will you swear?"

"Okay," he said finally, "I swear. I'll treat it like it's mine. Try to." His fingers in her hair tightened, and he covered her mouth in a bruising kiss that left her feeling drained and shaky. The porch light gleamed in his eyes, two white triangles against inky black. "Tomorrow night you'll be with me in my bed, Carrie, in my house. Then you'll forget all about him. That's something else I swear."

He left her standing on the porch. She could hear him whistling in the street for another minute, but the jaunty sound couldn't block out the echo of his last words. For all the world, they sounded to Carrie like a threat.

She rubbed her arms with her mittened hands, shivering from the cold. She wasn't ready to go inside, though, where she'd have to join in all the gay, noisy Christmas Eve fun with the family. But she couldn't bring herself to retire to her own cold little room yet, either. So she stood still, watching the white clouds of her breath condense in the chilly air. It was a quiet night; no wind stirred the bare branches of the maple tree by the porch or the stalky privet hedges lining the sidewalk. She pretended the street lamp was the moon and made a wish. *I wish I could keep my promise to Eugene.* When she opened her eyes, she saw a man walking toward her in the middle of the street. Before he moved out of the light from the street lamp in front of the Conklings' house, she thought he looked exactly like Ty.

She bowed her head in despair. She hadn't even been able to keep her promise for one minute.

The sound of his footsteps changed, and when she looked up she saw the man had crossed the curb to the sidewalk. Sighing, Carrie resigned herself to it: he looked like Ty and he walked like Ty, he even swung his arms from his strong, handsome shoulders like Ty. And his hair, and his . . . he . . .

Her hands on the porch rail tightened like talons, and her eyes got big as an owl's. Her lips made the shape of his name, but all that came out of her mouth was a breathless puff of white air. She put her hand on top of her head, to keep it on, and watched Ty come up the flagstone path, stop at the bottom of the porch steps, and look up at her.

Such a flood of emotion swamped her then, she had no words to greet him, no gesture of welcome, not even a smile. Jubilation danced over her skin and bubbled in her veins. Her heart sang a giddy song of thanks for the gift of Ty, the miracle of him.

But under the song thrummed a warning in a somber voice, reminding her of her promise.

24

The porch light behind her shadowed her cheeks and made dark hollows of her eyes. Tyler couldn't read her expression. She wouldn't speak, and the tense clenching of her gloved hands could mean anything. "Hello," he said, to break the queer stillness, abandoning the fantasy he'd entertained for hours on the train — that they would hurl themselves into each other's arms, and all would be well without a word spoken.

She might have smiled; her voice was the barest whisper. "Ty," he thought she said.

Out of patience, he took the steps two at a time. When he was level with her, she reached out — to touch his face, he thought — but she pulled back jerkily, thinking better of it, and started to step away. He took her wrist. Inside the thick mitten, her hand was as rigid as a bird's claw. Before she could move, he whipped the glove off and brought her fingers to his lips. Dear, icy-cold fingers; they smelled like damp wool. He spread them across his cheek, murmuring her name. She stiffened in resistance, but only for a moment. He didn't know who moved first but slowly, little by little, they came into each other's arms, flowing into the embrace as effortlessly as currents merging in a stream.

They held each other with infinite gentleness, without speaking, without kissing. He felt her soft breath on his throat, the cupping of her two hands at the back of his head. And he could feel himself healing, jagged halves of himself merging, realigning; the painful ends of a fractured bone finally mending. When he could speak, he murmured, "My darling," and saying the words aloud called back the memory of the last night they'd spent together, when he'd been free to call her that. The night they'd made the child she carried. Unbearable tenderness gripped him in a gentle vise. He closed his eyes and held onto her.

Much too soon, she slipped out of his arms.

"Where can we go?" he asked hurriedly, streaking a hand through his hair. The world rushed back with rude energy; it was very cold, and the glaring yellow porch light stung his eyes.

She hesitated, then gestured behind her at the front door. "The parlor? It's empty, no one would come in."

"No, Carrie, not in that madhouse." Her fleeting smile mellowed his irritation at the

514

very thought of the Odells' parlor, which was empty because it was all set up for her damn wedding tomorrow morning. "Frank's office," he said firmly. "We can be alone there."

Her ungloved hand fluttered nervously to her hair, which she was wearing in a rather elegant bun on top of her head. "But . . . that's where I'm staying."

How could he have forgotten how husky her voice was? He said, "Yes, I know. Eppy told me."

"You've been here? You've already seen them?"

"I came straight here from the train station. They told me you were out, so I went for a walk. They said you were having dinner with your betrothed." He tried, he really tried not to sneer the word; but she looked pained, and he guessed he hadn't succeeded. "Come on," he urged her softly. "I have a lot to tell you."

"Eppy won't like it," she stalled. "It's not proper, Ty. I don't know if we should."

"Carrie." He sent her a look that brought some much-needed color to her cheeks.

"All right," she agreed after a few awkward seconds, and went down the steps at his side.

Frank's refurbished old barn was so obviously a hideout, not an office, that Ty had to chuckle when he saw it, by the glow of the oil lamp Carrie lit and set on a small table by the door. The only concession to work was a scarred oak desk; but it was littered with books and magazines, not articles in progress, and there was no typewriter in sight. The painted walls were bare except for a photograph of Eppy with all five children and, somewhat unexpectedly, a calendar whose sepia engraving for December featured a coy miss wearing drawers and a corset. An ancient swivel chair looked comfortable — he pictured Frank slumped in it with his feet on the desk, reading — and so did a worn leather sofa that took up most of the opposite wall. The sheets, blankets, and pillow piled on one arm told him it was to be Carrie's bed tonight.

He watched her as she went to the cold black stove in the corner, knelt, and struck a match to the wood and kindling already stacked inside. She was skittish, but under the nerves he sensed a patient, simmering excitement. She took off her coat for something to do, although the fire hadn't had time to warm anything yet. He'd never seen the maroon dress she wore with a jaunty jacket, a citified dress whose simple lines suited her perfectly. But he didn't want Carrie looking suitable. He wanted her in the faded blue gown she'd worn all summer. He wanted her to look like his Carrie.

"You look beautiful," he said from across the room.

She colored again and made a face at the compliment, clearly not believing it. He looked forward to a long, long life together during which, among other things, he would convince her of it. She looked healthy, thank God; "blooming" was the standard cliche, and despite her present agitation, it fit her. She wasn't showing yet, but her face had lost a little of its angularity, and her long, lithe body had a new womanliness that fascinated him.

The queer silence was back. She stopped fiddling with her coat, which she'd folded over the top of a small suitcase resting on the floor, and faced him. "Did you know . . ." she tried. "Did Frank tell you . . ."

"Tell me what?"

"That the wedding is tomorrow?"

"Yes, he did mention that detail." She looked down, embarrassed by his not-very-subtle mockery. He thought of telling her it was himself he was mocking. He moved toward her, tired of the artificial distance between them; but the closer he came, the harder she pressed back against the shuttered window. He stopped two feet shy of her, dismayed, making an effort to keep his hands to himself. Her reticence cut deep, but he couldn't blame her for it.

"Catherine Hamilton," he said slowly, relishing the syllables. "I love your beautiful new name, Carrie."

"Thank you." Her sweet, wary smile went straight to his heart. "You look wonderful," she said next, returning the compliment. "Tan and healthy and — strong. I was worried about you."

"You should've seen me when I had my beard." He grinned determinedly, rubbing his clean-shaven chin.

"Was it handsome?"

"Extremely. Dashing, too. I wanted to send you a photograph of it."

"Why . . ." She stopped.

"Why didn't I? Because eventually I got the message that you weren't interested." She dropped her eyes. "Why didn't you write to me, Carrie?" he asked softly.

"I wanted to," she said in a small voice. "When you lost your friend, Dr. Lazear, I wanted so much to tell you I was sorry. But I couldn't. It wouldn't have been right."

"Why not?"

"Because I was trying to let you go."

The truth of that washed over him in a hot wave of regret. It was because of him they were standing apart in this cold, ridiculous room, speaking in stilted half thoughts like strangers.

To save herself, Carrie had let him go, and it was his own ignoble doing that she didn't have a clue her abandonment had hurt him.

"Well," she said, head up, eyes level again. "You have a new job in Washington, D.C., I heard. Are you excited? When does it start?"

"I'm to report to the surgeon general in two days. I expect the job will start as soon after that as I can get settled."

"That'll be wonderful. I'm so proud of you and everything you did, Ty, all the —"

"I did very little."

"That's not true," she said, without a second's hesitation.

He smiled wryly. "You're not much better than my mother in this particular area."

"What area?"

"The foolish pride area."

She tried to smile back. But she was too distracted for small talk. "Why did you come here?" she asked straight out, brave as always.

"Don't you really know?"

"I think you must tell me."

Despite the gravity of the circumstances, her formal manner tickled him. "Can I kiss you first?" he teased.

Her luminous eyes went wide. *"No."*

"Can I hold you while I tell you?"

"No!"

He heaved an exaggerated sigh. "All right,

then, but you make it hard on a man." His jesting smile faded slowly. So much for lightening the mood. "I didn't hear until this afternoon about the lady who came to see me two days ago. Abbey said a Miss Hamilton was passing through, and she wanted to express the gratitude of the people of Wayne's Crossing for all I'd done for them. I was mystified; I thought it must be a joke. I asked Abbey what she looked like. She had on a handsome blue merino wool, and a hat with a feather. She was very stunning."

He paused, charmed by Carrie's robust blush and the unmistakable look of gratification that unclouded her eyes for a second. It was consoling to know that a small shred of vanity dwelled in her feminine heart. "I admit that I should've known, but the 'handsome blue merino wool' threw me off."

"Eppy picked it out," she said faintly. "We went all the way to Chambersburg."

He couldn't help himself; he reached out and took her hand, which she'd been clenching at her side. He opened it, forcing her fingers to relax. "Your pulse is racing," he murmured, his middle finger monitoring the little vein in her wrist.

"Ty, I'm so happy to see you," she said in a rush.

He kissed her knuckles. "Oh, Carrie —"

"But you shouldn't have come because it's too late — and you shouldn't be here with me because it's wrong — and you shouldn't hold my hand — because —" That reason eluded her.

He held on when she tried to yank away. "No, it's not too late. Sweet Carrie, I love you. I've come to ask you to marry me."

Her eyes went liquid with emotion. "Thank you, Ty," she got out in a tight-throated whisper.

"Don't thank me. Just say yes." He moved his hand to the back of her neck and tugged gently until he had her temple resting against his jaw. "I've missed you so much. I never stopped thinking about you, not for a minute. Lord, Carrie, I was an idiot to leave you." Her airy sigh tickled his ear. He touched his lips to hers, and rejoiced when he felt her soften, first her mouth and then her strong hands on his shoulders. "Marry me, Carrie," he murmured against her lips. "Marry me and let's be a family."

Her posture changed, but so subtly he might not have noticed if he hadn't been watching her eyes. In time with the slow stiffening of her body, they went from dreamy to stormy. When she drew away this time, he knew there would be no coaxing her back.

"What is it?"

She didn't answer; she crossed the room to the stove, and hunched over it as if she were freezing.

"Carrie, what's wrong?"

She finally raised her head. "Who told you?" she asked in a dead monotone.

"Who told me what?"

"Eppy. I should've known she'd tell."

"Tell me what?"

"I thought you were asking me just because you wanted me." She put the flat of her hand on her chest. "I thought it was just me. And even though I was still going to say no, it made me so glad, Ty, another memory I could keep forever. And now . . ." She couldn't go on because she was crying.

He couldn't stay away from her. But when he got close, she sidestepped nimbly and put the clanking, hissing stove between them. Holding onto his patience, he said calmly, "Explain that. I don't understand what you're saying."

She fumbled a handkerchief out of her jacket pocket and wiped her eyes. "I believe that you care for me. I couldn't have given myself to you if I hadn't thought you liked me. You're an —"

"Liked you?"

"You're an honorable man, and I understand why you've come. Oh, if only you hadn't known about the baby, Ty, maybe then — but, no, I still couldn't have said yes, but it would've been even harder."

"You've got this completely wrong."

She took a deep breath, gathering herself. "I know that you think it's your duty to offer for me now because of the baby. But I free you of your obligation to me, with all my heart. I want you to be happy, and to be everything you can be. Your mother's right — there's greatness in you, and you'll do good for the benefit of mankind. Your great-grandfather was the last representative of the Enlightenment."

"He was what? Damnation, Carrie, don't spout that nonsense to me! She told you all about the great Eustice Morrell, didn't she? She's —"

"Don't make fun of your family, Ty," she said severely. "You've been blessed."

He scowled, chastened. "All right, I've been blessed."

"But not if you're stuck with a backward country girl for a wife, and a baby that comes five months after the wedding."

"Sweetheart, that's something for me to decide, don't you think?"

"I don't even know what you're thinking of," she went on, gathering steam. "For one thing, and it's not even the main thing, your mother would never forgive you."

"What's my mother got to do with it? Besides, she'll love you."

She spread her arms wide; her expression said that for once she'd caught him in a lie. "Ty — I've *met* her."

"Poor Carrie," he sympathized, imagining what that must have been like. "Was it awful?"

"No, oh no, she was very kind, and your sister was wonderful. I'm not talking —"

"Isn't she? She'll love you, too."

She made a very impatient gesture with her hand. "Listen. It doesn't matter here about me, I didn't have any friends to lose anyway, or any reputation. I know you don't like him, but Eugene's been —"

"I don't want to hear about Eugene," he snapped.

"Ty, please, I have to say this!"

He shoved his hands in his pockets and glared.

"Eugene's been good to me from the beginning," she started again, speaking quietly so as not to antagonize him. "Even when he found out about the baby, he didn't stay mad, not for long. He knows how it'll be, what some people will think of me and the child for the rest of our lives, and he's willing to take us anyway. I've given him my promise, and I can't go back on my word."

He was nonplussed. He'd foreseen the need for some gentle persuasion to override Carrie's too-nice scruples, but he'd never seriously considered the possibility that she would refuse him.

"Are you in love with Starkey?" he asked after a pause. He didn't expect an answer, and she didn't give one; she just blinked at him. "Tell me you're in love with him, Carrie. Say that to my face, and I'll walk out. You can keep the baby and I won't interfere again in your life, if you can honestly say you love Eugene and you don't love me."

She folded her arms and frowned at him. "There's something you don't know, Ty, for all your smartness and your education."

"What's that?"

"Sometimes we can't have what we want just because we want it. I learned that lesson early, but you were lucky and you never had to. That's a good thing, and I don't hold it against you; I'm just saying it so you'll understand why I have to marry Eugene."

"Sorry, I didn't follow that. But you're avoiding the question. Answer me straight out — do you love Eugene?"

Her eyes flashed; she smacked the bottom of one fist against the top of the other. "And I

tell you the answer doesn't make any difference."

"How could it not make any difference?
Listen to yourself."

"You've set it up wrong," she insisted,
"you're trying to get me to say something that
you think makes you win the argument, but it
doesn't."

"How could it not matter if you love me?
How?"

"Eugene loves me, too."

"You're not carrying Eugene's child!"

She covered her cheeks with her hands.
"You can see it whenever you want," she said
hoarsely, fingers half-covering her mouth.
"I'd never try to stop you. Eugene says he'll
treat it right — if I didn't believe that, I would
never have consented to marry him. I thought
of giving it up —"

"Giving it up?" He skirted the stove and
closed the distance between them in one
stride. She quailed; he had to force himself
not to put his hands on her.

"I meant — to your mother to raise!"

He let his pent-up breath out. "Ah,
Carrie." He felt full of remorse for what he'd
thought she meant.

New tears were welling in her eyes. "Forgive me, Ty. I know it's selfish of me because
she'd give the baby a better home than I can,

but I just can't do it. Unless you want me to. I'd do it if you said I must. But I'm begging you," she whispered, "don't take the baby from me."

"I'd never take it from you." A premonition of failure flared at the edges of his mind, but he beat it back. "My God, Carrie, how did we come to this?"

"I'll raise it right, I swear. It'll have all the love there is in me, always. And it won't want." She looked at him beseechingly. "Eugene has a good job and — he's a man on the rise. He's the head of his whole department now, and he's building a house. It's got two floors, with a bathroom on the second floor just like yours, and the tub has a mixer faucet, which means one spigot for the hot *and* the cold. And a wringer washing machine — he's buying me one, he's putting it out on the porch . . ." She ran down. She looked exhausted.

He stared at her, allowing the lengthening silence to embarrass her as much as he thought she deserved. "I can't tell you how relieved I am to hear you're going to have a wringer washing machine, Carrie. That really sets my mind at ease." When she flinched at his sarcasm, he covered her cheek with his palm, feeling the coolness of her skin heat quickly.

Her dark lashes fluttered, and her breath trembled across his hand. "Don't touch me, Ty," she begged. "I shouldn't have let you before. You can't anymore, you just can't."

"No?" His fingers slid into her hair, sleek as cool water, the color of autumn sun on a maple leaf. He caressed the thin white ridge of her ear with one finger while the rose color in her cheeks warmed and deepened. "No?"

"No, I belong to —"

"Me." His kiss made her close her mouth and open her eyes — the opposite of his intent. She pushed him away, but she was shaking.

"That — won't — do anything," she got out in a rusty falsetto.

"It'll do something for me." He pulled her back, wrapped her up in his arms, and kissed her again. He felt her press against him, but only for a second, and then she twisted away and turned her back on him. Immediately he seized her shoulders to hold her still. "Why are you being so stubborn?" he asked behind her ear. Strands of her hair, which smelled like lilacs tonight, tickled his nose.

"Not stubborn," she said, stubbornly. "I'm doing what's right."

She wore a thin silver chain around her neck — a gift from her intended, no doubt. He fingered the fragile links, more to touch her throat than to examine them. "What's this?" A silver pendant, heart-shaped. The cheap metal repelled and infuriated him. He wrapped his fist around it, pulling it taut.

"Don't!"

"Did he give it to you?"

"Yes!"

"Take it off."

"Ty —"

"Marry me, Carrie."

"No, no, no —"

He made her stop shaking her head by putting his lips in the hot hollow behind her ear. He tasted her skin; she moaned and tried to strain away, but he'd pulled her little maroon jacket off her shoulders, and her efforts were hampered and uncoordinated. "Tell Eugene you made a mistake. I'll tell him for you." He moved his hands to her hips, holding her steady, then slowly up to circle her waist. She plucked at the air with her fingers, head tilted sideways because he had his mouth pressed to the underside of her jaw. "You have lovely costal cartilage," he noticed, stroking her sides.

"Don't, Ty. Stop." He slipped his hands under her arms, lifting her gently against him. "Don't shame me," she pleaded.

"There's nothing shameful in loving you." Her hair was coming down, falling out of the bun on top of her head, caressing his fingers as he pulled her jacket all the way off and let it fall on the floor at her feet. She was too riled up to notice.

"But you don't love me," she protested, stuck between bitterness and giving in.

"I do. I do love you."

"You don't, I know it. You didn't before — why would you now? You only offered for me before because we got caught, and now you're asking because of the baby. Don't touch me anymore, Ty. I told you, I've set you free."

"I don't want to be free." He had his hands on her stomach, and it was a moment before the truth sank in: that this was where he'd wanted them all along. "Carrie, my dearest, dearest love — no, listen, I figured it out on the train — our baby is seventeen weeks and either five or six days old." He heard the wonder in his voice and smiled at himself. After a few more seconds, Carrie stopped straining away from him. "Last week you felt him move for the first time, didn't you?" he whispered. "Just a fluttering sensation down here, deep inside you. That's called quickening. You thought it was pleasant, but it's probably going to drive you crazy in another month or two when he starts butting you at odd hours with his elbows and his knees."

Carrie's eyes were closed; she stayed tense,

but she was leaning back in his arms, resting her head on his collarbone.

"He — or she, excuse me — is about this long now." He widened the distance between his thumb and forefinger to three inches or so, bringing his hand up so she could see. "He's got all his parts already, although the proportions are a little strange; he's got a big head but his arms and legs are short, and his hands — he's even got fingernails, Carrie, no bigger than the petals of a tiny flower. He hasn't opened his eyes yet, but he can hear things. If you and I started yelling at each other, he'd hear that."

She sighed, and he bent his head to kiss her. When his cheek brushed hers, he discovered she was weeping. "Darling," he murmured, chasing a slow tear with his lips. "Say you love me. Marry me. You're mine, Carrie, no one else's."

Her throat worked; she could barely whisper. "Oh God, Ty. This isn't fair, and it's wrong."

Her energy and will were returning. He reached for her fidgeting hands and held them still between her breasts. "Nothing's felt this right since I went away. I'll never leave you again."

"You don't under—"

He turned her around and cut off whatever

it was he didn't understand with a long, passionate, ruthless kiss. She wilted, and he took the opportunity to back her up toward the couch. Her knees buckled when her calves struck the edge. He lowered her down, still kissing her, congratulating himself on the smoothness of the move.

"Ty, you're not —"

"No, I just want to hold you." He sat beside her quickly and put his arms around her. "Even if you win this argument, Carrie, you have to let me hold you."

"But —"

"And kiss the bride." This time her only protest was a pitiful catch in the back of her throat, and then a low, wailing noise with an utterly tragic quality that heartened him immensely. He expected resistance now, but when he pushed her back flat against the leather cushion, she went as easily as an anesthetized patient. Using the pads of his thumbs, he brushed the tears from the sides of her eyes into her hair. "Such letters I wrote to you in my head. I wanted to tell you everything. Why didn't I? If I'd written them, you'd be mine now." He put his lips on the worry line between her eyebrows, trying to press it away. "No, what I should've done was marry you in August. Should never have listened to you. Kiss me, Carrie, you know you want to.

And I want to feel your lips move."

She got one hand free and used it to turn his marauding mouth away. "Stop it, I mean it." But her voice was low and husky, and there was little force in the hand she had on his jaw. "How could I have married you? Where would we have lived, in Washington — Boston — New York?" She blinked her own tears away this time. "Can't you just see me there?"

"I see you everywhere." He sucked a tear off her cheekbone and kissed her again.

"No — you can't marry me!" He let her twist her head from side to side, stealing kisses each time her lips flew past. "It's Adele you have to marry. She had a new dress for you — her cream silk something or other —"

"Her what?"

"She couldn't decide, that or the something crepe de chine — Abbey said —"

He laughed, and started on the crystal buttons running down the bodice of Carrie's blouse. "I like yours better."

"No! Ty! I mean it!"

She did seem to mean it, so he settled for covering her left breast with his hand and her right with his mouth, and he could feel her hard nipples right through the thin silk and whatever she was wearing under it — not a corset, praise God. Her hopeless moan was music to his ears; he sucked on her and nibbled at her until she arched up and yelled. "Shh," he admonished lovingly. "Somebody might hear, and they'll think we're fighting."

"We are! Stop, I'm not doing this! Oh God, Ty, this is wrong, don't shame me. Ah! It won't matter, it won't matter." She said it like a mantra, but he'd gone back to the crystal buttons, and she wasn't lifting a finger to stop him. When he uncovered her breasts at last, she shuddered and let him touch her.

But she couldn't stop fighting him with her tongue. "I know what you're doing," she claimed, teeth clamped, eyes shut. "Let me go, set me free. I did it for you — be fair, let *me* go —"

He lifted his mouth from her breast to say, "Sweet Carrie, what you did was an unnatural act, and I'm correcting it. I'm righting a terrible wrong." He used his knee first, subtly, then his hand, less so, to push her skirt up. He got his fingers on her thigh; it was trembling, and clamped to its mate like a jealous lover. "New drawers?" he wondered, fingering an unseen lacy edge, but his real attention was on finding the opening in them between her legs. She was tense and straining, tight as a drum, resolutely against this seduction. Without a qualm of conscience, he stroked his palm across her plump little pubis, deliberately making her tremble. He'd never lost his mind in a sexual situation before, not even with Carrie, but right now joining with her was his sole goal; even saving her from Eugene Starkey came in a pale, distant, barely remembered second.

He shifted onto his side beside her. "Touch me," he suggested into the wild tangle of her hair, pressing his swollen sex harder against her hip. "Please."

She made another helpless sound and threw one arm over her forehead. "If I do, will you stop?"

"Yes," he lied unhesitatingly.

"I don't believe you."

"Do it anyway."

He didn't care anymore about her scruples, her convoluted honor, what reasons she'd decided to use to explain away giving herself to the wrong man. She reached out a blind hand and he seized it, pressing her palm where he needed it the most. No relief; he only ached worse, wanted her more. But at least her shaky legs had come unglued, and now he knew two places where she was wet — her face, from the tears that wouldn't stop their slow trickling no matter how high he took her, and this sweet, tight, throbbing furnace between her thighs.

"Let me come inside you," he whispered,

urging her with a slick-fingered, slow-moving bribe. "Unbutton my pants. Touch me, Carrie."

She tried to — after a whole minute she even got one button undone — but in the end the whole thing was beyond her. She let out a high, frustrated wail. "You'd make a terrible surgeon," he consoled her tenderly, and brushed her clumsy fingers aside.

That was the moment he heard the knock, and realized sickly that it wasn't the first one.

Carrie had the identical realization at the same instant.

Now there was scuffling and commotion — that too had a familiar sound — and then a sharp rap on the door, as if the knuckles administering it were fed up.

Fed up — then they might go away! Tyler seized on a conscious choice to make motionlessness his first line of defense. Carrie ruined it by rolling out from under him and jumping to her feet. At almost the same moment Eppy's voice, simultaneously alarmed and exasperated, came through the still-closed door, along with another rap. "Carrie? Carrie, open this — Stop it, now, I mean it, get ahold of yourself." The last part was muffled, as if spoken to someone other than Carrie.

Tyler sat up and put his feet on the floor.

He raised jaundiced eyes to his beloved, who was trying to button her dress. Pity was far from his mind, even when he saw she was no better at it than she'd been with his trousers. Her pleading look left him cold.

"Please!" she finally begged, in a heartrending croak.

He snarled. But he got to his feet. His blood still pounded; he felt like the unwilling survivor of a brutal drowning. The door burst open while he was still tying his tie.

He'd expected Eppy, naturally, or one of the children, but it was Broom who barreled inside on a rush of cold air, elbows churning, chin twitching.

"I couldn't keep him out to save me," Eppy explained from the doorway. "He —" Her mouth snapped shut as her eyes took it all in: the rumpled sofa, Ty's dishevelment. And Carrie. Poor Carrie. Everything about her was a dead giveaway.

"Hi, Doc," Broom said mechanically, without a flicker of surprise at Ty's presence; it was Carrie he'd come to see. He made a beeline for her and threw his jerking arms around her. "Don't do it!" he begged in a pitiful, braying voice.

"Broom, don't do this again," Carrie started, patting his shoulders to soothe him.

"Don't marry Eugene!" he cried, and

promptly burst into tears.

Eppy had gone beet-faced with righteous ire. "Dr. Wilkes," she said in a high, vibrating contralto, "I'm going to have to ask you to leave!"

He didn't move. "Carrie and I haven't finished." The sentence struck him as the ultimate in tragicomic ambivalence.

"I beg to differ."

"Carrie?" he tried, desperate.

She lifted her head and looked straight at him over Broom's shoulder. Chagrin, sadness, and determination mingled in her flushed face, but she said, "My answer's the same," in deadly, cold-blooded earnest. "Go away, Ty. I can't talk, can't —" She started to cry, too.

"This is a goddamn circus!" he shouted.

Humor unexpectedly leavened the indignation on Eppy's face. "That's exactly what I say, every day of my life." She widened the door. "Doctor?"

He ground out a few more swear words, damning everything indiscriminately. Carrie wouldn't look at him at all now. Short of kidnapping her, he couldn't think of anything else to do. Grabbing his coat, he stalked past Eppy, who evidently intended to escort him out to the street. Before she could slam the door shut behind them, he threw a last glance back. For his pains, he got to see Carrie and Broom sobbing in each other's arms, holding on like children in a thunderstorm.

25

"You pulled your hair loose again, didn't you? After I just got done fixing it." Eppy quit biting her nails long enough to smack her hands against her hips in frustration. "Now you look just like you do every day, and here I was trying to do something special."

"It's all right, though, isn't it?" Carrie asked anxiously. "I'm sorry, but you had it so tight my head hurt."

"Well, why didn't you say so?" She made a face. "Sorry — I don't know which of us is more nervous, Carrie, you or me. You look beautiful, you *really* do. You should start getting into your dress soon, though; it's almost nine-thirty and people are going to be coming any minute now."

Start getting into her dress? How long could it take? But Carrie said not a word, just stood up to take off her old flannel robe, because contradicting Eppy in any way this morning only made her crazier. She waited in chemise, drawers, shoes, and stockings while Eppy went over to the closet in Charlotte and

Emily's tiny bedroom and fetched Carrie's wedding dress — the blue merino she'd worn for Ty in Philadelphia. The mirror over the child-size dressing table was so low, she had to bend her knees to see herself above the waist. Did her stomach look thicker today? Maybe — maybe not. But it wasn't her imagination that her chemise fit tighter across the bosom than it ever had before. Oh Lord, what if her wedding gown didn't fit?

It fit, although maybe not with quite the same youthful *swing* as it had a week ago. "Lovely," Eppy declared, buttoning her up in back, smoothing the soft wool over her shoulders. "Are you going to wear that silver heart Eugene gave you?"

"Yes, I thought so." In the mirror, she saw Eppy looking doubtful. "Don't you think I should?"

"Oh no, wear it, by all means. I just . . ."

"What?" Carrie turned around.

"Nothing. I got married in this" — she drew something out of the pocket of her own best dress, a lime-green taffeta with ivory lace collar and cuffs — "but that pretty dress of yours probably doesn't need another thing."

"What is it? Oh, Eppy, it's beautiful. I've never seen it before." It was a cameo brooch carved on a pale pink shell, surrounded by a dainty silver filigree.

"It was my mother's. I was saving it for Charlotte's wedding — first, then the other girls', one by one: But if you'd like to wear it, Carrie, I'd be very glad and proud."

Tears were never far away these days; hugging Eppy, Carrie had to squeeze her eyes shut and scrunch up her face to keep them back now. "I'm very glad and proud to wear it. Thank you. Thank you for everything!"

Eppy hugged her back and took a secret swipe at her own cheeks. "You don't think it's too much?"

"No, it's perfect." She pinned the brooch to her breast and bent low to inspect the results in the mirror. "It's truly perfect. Now if only I didn't look like a day-old corpse," she added wanly.

"You look like no such thing. You look positively —"

"Eugene's here!" Charlotte swung the door open so hard, it struck the side of the bureau with a bang that made Carrie jump. "He's got on a striped suit that's sort of brown, and a high collar, and a bow tie, and a vest! The vest's sort of tan, with all this gold stuff —"

"Go out and sit down, Charlotte, you're supposed to be minding Fanny. That's your job, I told —"

"Okay, and Eugene's mother's got a cane and she takes up two chairs, one for herself

542

and one for her foot because her leg's got gauze or something wrapped all around it, and she has to keep it up in the air because the fleas bite it."

"She's got phlebitis," Eppy corrected, "and don't you say one word to her about it, hear me? What's your father doing?"

"Talking to Eugene. Eugene's got his hair all —"

"All right. Go out now, I told you."

"Okay, and Eugene's sister's name is Ethel, and she looks like him only her hair's lighter and she's fatter, and she asked Daddy if we got the piano tuned yet, and he said —"

"Charlotte! Go find Fanny *right now*."

On her way out, Charlotte slammed the door.

Eppy rolled her eyes. "I'd better go and greet them, plus I've still got some things to do in the kitchen. Are you all right?"

"I'm fine. I should be helping you, I feel silly just sitting in here not doing anything, while you —"

"Don't be ridiculous, you're the bride. Besides, everything's under control because this is going to be the simplest wedding breakfast anybody ever sat down to. I hope it'll be nice, though."

"I know it will be."

"Are you sure you're all right?"

"Fine!"

Eppy looked skeptical, but she was too harried to argue. "I'll be back in ten minutes."

Sinking down on the tiny stool in front of the dressing table, Carrie saw in the mirror what Eppy was worried about. "Day-old corpse" was no exaggeration at all in Carrie's opinion. She looked pale and dazed, as if she'd been locked in a closet for years and somebody had just yanked her out into the daylight. Brides ought to look excited, not tense and wire-tight and anxious. Her mouth had a strange, unnatural set, and the dark circles looked like bruises under her worried gray eyes from the sleepless night she'd spent wondering what was right to do. Last night Ty had said he loved her. If she could believe him, her way would be clear. But she knew what his sense of honor and duty was capable of, and she was afraid to put faith in his words. The dreary truth was, nothing had really changed. Maybe if Eppy and Broom hadn't come when they did and she'd given in and let Ty have his way with her, maybe then something would've changed.

No, that wasn't right either. The yardstick to measure her decision by ought not to be whether or not she and Ty had been lovers; it ought to be *love*. So she was back to that again: not believing him when he claimed to love her, because he was courtly and gentlemanly enough to pretend to in order to protect his child and her honor.

How could she know, how could she be sure? Her awful *unsuitability* always got in the way. She could never get over her horror of dragging him down, of holding him back. If she could just see a picture in her mind of the two of them married, if she *could* imagine them as a family in some setting other than in the cabin on High Dreamer — but she was cursed with knowing a fantasy from reality. She could see him in her life, but never herself in his. Certainly not at the Camp in Scarborough or the Schuylkill Regatta, and not at the Cape May cottage. Marry Ty? The son of the woman who wanted him to become president? He said he wasn't interested in politics, but what if he changed his mind? Too late. If she married him, she'd already have become a great, heavy stone around his neck.

The sound of the wedding march being played on the Odells' old upright broke in on her circling thoughts. She jumped up and started pacing. Did Ethel have to practice the dratted song *now?* And Louie was tied up in the backyard, barking and barking and barking. Eppy wouldn't let him in the house, and Carrie couldn't blame her; but he wasn't used to solitude, and his incessant howls and yelps were driving her wild. Between Louie and the wedding march, her nerves were shot.

Last night, after Carrie had sent Ty away and then Broom, Eppy had come back and tried to advise her. *Don't do anything rash,* was her main recommendation. Pregnant women go a little mad, she'd counseled from experience, so don't trust your emotions. Carrie hadn't wanted to hear that, since every emotion she had was screaming at her to go off with the man she loved and damn the consequences. But Eppy thought she should marry Eugene. "I'm sure he's a decent man under all the swagger," she'd said hopefully. "And you'll be happier in the long run with someone who's your own kind."

Oh, it was true, it was true, she knew it but she hated it! And Eugene needed her — Ty didn't. She'd also cried last night for the little boy whose father had beaten and abused him so cruelly. Was it any wonder Eugene had turned into a bully? No, the wonder was that he'd *reformed.* And anyway, she'd given him her promise. That meant something. She'd never deliberately broken a promise in her life. Eugene would be devastated if she went back on her word now, and he didn't deserve that. Ty . . . Ty would forget her if he didn't see her. She thought. Wouldn't he? But how could she know? And now there was the baby to consider.

Oh God, the baby. She wrapped her arms around herself, remembering Ty's arms around her last night, the way he'd stroked her stomach and the things he'd said. How she'd needed that! She hadn't known, hadn't known. He might not truly love her but he wanted the baby, that she couldn't doubt. Maybe they could make an arrangement. He could have it half the year, or less if that didn't suit him, and she — she — she could . . .

She found the edge of the bed and collapsed on it just before she broke down in a spasm of bitter, wracking sobs.

Eppy caught her that way before she had time to pull herself together. "Oh, baby," she comforted, holding Carrie in her arms, rocking her like she'd have rocked Fanny or Mary Ann. "Is it that bad?"

"No, I'm all right," Carrie snuffled, her face buried in Eppy's handkerchief. "I'm just . . . oh Lord, you know."

"I know. I brought my rouge pot, but it looks like you won't need it."

Carrie laughed wetly and blew her nose. "Who's here?" she asked, to keep from having to talk herself."

"Reverend Coughan. Eugene and his

mother. Ethel — but you've heard her. And Broom — my Lord, I've never seen him this bad before! I can't even get him to take his coat off."

"Is Dr. Stoneman here?"

"No, not yet." Eppy patted Carrie's sagging shoulder. "But there's still time, he might still come."

She nodded without much hope.

"But Eugene did say . . ."

"What?"

"He said it's getting late, and he doesn't want to wait past ten. He says Frank should give you away."

"Oh." Dr. Stoneman wouldn't stand up for her, wouldn't even come to her wedding. She wanted to lie down on the bed and sob.

"Mom!"

This time even Eppy jumped, Charlotte's shrill little voice was so piercing. "What!"

"Daddy says come out now."

"Why?"

"He says he wants to tell you something!"

Eppy got up from the bed, sighing. For the first time, Carrie saw the full extent of her fatigue. "Well, you've about pulled your hair apart completely, I see," Eppy said with a grin. "Do I dare trust you to get your own veil on by yourself?"

"I'll manage," she whispered, smiling back

broadly, because otherwise she was afraid she'd cry again.

Eppy widened her eyes and made a mad-woman sound, pretending to tear out her own hair. She followed Charlotte out and closed the door behind her.

Carrie's veil was a decorous length of maline the same blue as her dress. She repinned her hair as neatly as she could and fastened the veil to the top of her head. She felt like turning the veil the other way around so it would cover her face instead of trailing down in back, but Eppy said that style wasn't fashionable nowadays, and what's more, it was pretentious. Well, people would just have to look at her face, then. No need for rouge, that was for sure; she didn't even have to pinch her cheeks. And her eyes, which had only been tired and puffy before, were red-rimmed and bloodshot now. Oh, what a beautiful bride! What a lucky man Eugene was!

What in God's name was she doing?

Eppy thrust the door open, sidled inside, and closed it with a slam. Her face was as white as Carrie's was flushed. She had her arms out and her hands pressed flat against the door behind her, as if something terrible was after her and she had to keep it out. "Carrie," she said, breast heaving.

"What? What is it?" She went toward her fearfully, feeling her own heart start to pound.

"Dr. Stoneman's here."

"Yes?" She spread her palms in confusion. "But what's wrong?" A burst of angry male voices came through the closed door all at once. "Oh, no," she guessed. "He's drunk!"

"No — maybe, I don't know!"

"Then what —"

"Tyler Wilkes came with him."

Carrie's hairbrush slipped out of her fingers and hit the floor with a clatter.

"Frank told him to leave, but he won't. He and Eugene are swearing at each other. Tyler and Eugene, I mean, not Frank. No, don't go out there," she cried, aghast, when Carrie tried to push past her. "Stay here till it gets sorted out. Frank's talking to them." A loud shout jolted her onto her toes. "Trying to," she amended, wringing her hands. "No! Carrie, don't —"

But she had to go, she couldn't cower in here for one more second. "Sorry," she muttered to Eppy, and forcibly moved her out of the way.

There were twelve people in the parlor, and four of them were yelling at each other. Mrs. Starkey and Ethel were the only ones still sitting down, Ethel on the piano stool, her mother on two chairs in the middle of the room, wrapped leg stretched out like a long, thin mummy. Silent and gaping, Charlotte, Emily, and Jane huddled in the corner by a bank of poinsettias Eppy had artfully arranged on tiers, while Fanny sat on the floor at their feet and bawled. Broom was everywhere, in constant motion, looking like the ragman in his long, dirty duster. Reverend Coughan was almost as animated, and he too was dancing around the four shouting men in the bay window alcove, trying to get their attention.

Carrie got their attention. All the hollering stopped the second they saw her. Even Fanny quit crying — but that was because Eppy snatched her up off the floor. Carrie moved into the room by fits and starts, taking in random details like the telltale redness of Dr. Stoneman's nose, Eugene's new patent leather shoes, the white carnation in Frank's buttonhole. And the black glower on Ty's unshaven face. The glad, unspeakable tenderness it changed to when his eyes met hers. It pierced her heart like an arrow.

"Please," she said, holding out both hands, palms up and beseeching.

Eugene whirled on her. His eyes had gone white around the edges, like a horse in a panic. "You gave your word!" he shouted at her, furious, already sensing disaster. "You belong to me, Carrie, and you tell him. Tell him to get out of here and leave us alone!"

Nobody moved, nobody made a sound. Everybody looked at her, waiting for her answer. Cold, blinding, lemon-yellow sunshine streamed through the window and lit up a million dust motes around the faces and shoulders of the men in the alcove.

"Well?" Eugene prodded. "Tell him to go back where he came from because it's me you want."

Carrie watched the muscles in Ty's jaw flex and relax, flex and relax, whitening the fine, taut skin over the bone. His voice when he spoke felt like a deep caress. "Marry the one you love, Carrie." She opened her mouth to tell him it wasn't that simple. He smiled. "The one who loves you. What else matters?"

And finally she saw it in his face and in his beautiful eyes: all the love she'd been afraid to hope for. What his mother thought, where they went to live — none of it mattered. Her heart opened like a flower.

She reached out a compassionate hand to her betrothed. The muscles jumping in his arm frightened her, but she said in a quiet voice, desperate not to hurt him, "Eugene —"

"No!" Broom jumped between them, accidentally cuffing Carrie in the breast with a flying elbow. "Don't marry Eugene,

Carrie, marry me!"

In a rage, snarling and snapping like a dog, Eugene came at Broom and shoved him against the window. "Lunatic! All of you —" He started to turn around, but stopped dead when he saw Broom jerk a shotgun up and out of the folds of his long coat. "Jesus!" he bellowed. Broom pointed the gun at his heart.

Carrie felt Ty's hand on her shoulder, pulling her out of the way. Every female in the room but her was screaming, and all the men were talking at once.

"I'll shoot him, I will," Broom chattered. "I'm not afraid to because I done it before." When he looked at Carrie, he unwittingly turned the gun on her. Ty swore. Eugene started to bolt, but Broom saw it and spun back to face him. The heavy shotgun wobbled, and Eugene turned bright-red, then paper-white.

"I done it before," Broom said again, only this time he kept the gun on his target. "I shot Artemis after he hurt you, Carrie, and I ain't sorry. I didn't set out to do it, but he was still drunk and he was gonna hit me too after I yelled at him. So I picked up this gun and blew him clean away!"

Carrie flinched, but kept her voice as steady and calm as she could. "But you don't want to shoot anybody now, do you, Broom? Put the gun down or somebody might get hurt."

His eyes watered. "I love you, Carrie. I want to take care of you."

"I love you, too, and we'll always —" She gasped when his teeth clenched and he slid the hammer back to cock the gun. He was really going to do it. Eugene's bloodless lips moved, but no sound came out. Broom put the stock against his twitching shoulder and sighted down the barrel. Without thinking about it, Carrie slipped out of Ty's grip and stepped in front of the shotgun.

"Broom," she pleaded, "you know you can't shoot Eugene. Now, put —"

Ty's voice sliced across hers, "Damn it, Carrie, get out of the way!"

She felt an arm snake around her waist and jerk her backward. Eugene's whole body shook; she could feel the sweat that soaked his shirt through the back of her wedding gown. "You'll have to shoot her first, you damn maniac. Shit, would somebody *get him?*"

"Let her go!" Broom yelled. "Let her go!"

"Starkey, you let her go or I'll kill you myself," Dr. Stoneman said in a deadly quiet voice.

Eugene's breath smelled like cloves. He kept backing up, backing up, trying to make Broom follow so somebody could get behind him and grab the gun. "Look here, Fireman, see this?" He spread one hand across Carrie's stomach. "There's a baby in here right now. You don't want to shoot Carrie's baby, do you?"

"Carrie's baby?" Confused, Broom took a slow step toward them, then another. When he took his left hand off the gun so he could wipe the tears out of his eyes with his coat sleeve, Ty tackled him. They fell back against the bay window and broke it. But before the glass shattered, Carrie heard the trigger click. On an empty chamber.

Eugene's hands fell away from her. She ran to Ty, who was gently untangling himself from all Broom's skinny arms and legs and trying to pull him out of the glass under them before Broom could cut himself. Carrie knelt down between them and put her arms around Broom. "Shh, don't cry, it's all right now," she soothed him. "Everything's all right."

"Don't marry Eugene, Carrie, please, please, don't do it," he hiccuped, shuddering and holding her tight.

She looked up over his shoulder at Eugene, who hadn't moved. He held up his hand, the index finger extended as if he had something to point out. But he couldn't seem to say it, and presently his arm dropped back to his side.

"No," Carrie told Broom softly. "No, I won't."

She saw Eugene's face go a mottled red. The muscles in his neck looked like thick cables ready to snap; his fists clenched and unclenched under the cuffs of his spiffy white shirt. She wanted to say something to him, too. Something gentle — or was it something bitter? It didn't matter; he was leaving, walking out of the parlor without looking at anybody. His mother limped out after him, then his sister. They didn't look at anybody either.

Ty's big hand opened on the nape of her neck, and she tilted her head back a little, letting him support it. She felt his cheek against hers and heard him murmur, "Are you all right?" She nodded. She wanted his arms around her, she wanted to kiss his lips. But she stayed still. Broom stopped crying after a minute and let go of her to look at her. Ty's hand came around to stroke her cheek. She sighed, and couldn't keep from turning her head to press a slow, deep kiss into his palm. When she looked back at Broom, his mouth was gaping open, and he was blinking at her as if she'd flashed a blinding light in his eyes.

"I love you, Broom," she whispered. One of his wrists shot up; she captured it in her hands and brought it to her lap, stroking the tension out of it.

"I love you, Carrie." Silent tears coursed down his cheeks. "You gonna marry the doc?"

She nodded, and put her lips on his knuckles.

His bony chest heaved. He wiped his face on the sleeve of his coat and tried to smile. "Okay," he said.

26

Could it be this hot on Dreamy Mountain today? Not likely, thought Carrie, unfastening her navy-blue shirtwaist and white cambric chemise to uncover her left breast. "Indian summer" they called these lovely, surprise-present days in the middle of October; but she was pretty sure the gift was more extreme in Washington — the real summer had been, hadn't it? — than it was on High Dreamer.

"There, sweet, beautiful heart," she murmured to Rachel, settling her more comfortably to nurse. "Were you hungry? Mama's baby wanted her dinner, didn't she?" Carrie rested her head on the white latticework side of the summerhouse and blinked sleepily up at the domed ceiling. The phoebes had gone, flown south, but she could see their tidy little nest up there in the rafters. Would they come back and use it again next year? On the whole, she rather hoped not; they were a noisy bunch and their shrill *fee-bees* had interrupted more than one of her and Rachel's naps this summer. A nice family of wood thrushes, now, that would be ideal. They sang a beautiful song, she never tired of it, and a fat mother thrush brooding on a nest of eggs was so much more peaceful than a phoebe's hectic comings and goings.

"But what will be will be," she told Rachel philosophically, stroking her pert little nose with one fingertip. She was five months old today, and for nearly five months everybody had been saying she looked exactly like Carrie. "Oh no, she's got Ty's chin, look," she'd always object. But just lately she was starting to see what they meant. Rachel *did* have Ty's chin — truth to tell, she had Carolivia's chin even more than Ty's, which was probably even better considering she was a girl — but she definitely had Carrie's gray eyes, too, and her light-red hair, and especially her long, long, skinny body. "Slender," Ty called it, which had a nicer ring. And he was always quick to assure her that Rachel was in perfect health even if she wasn't fat and chubby and roly-poly like most babies. But Carrie already knew she was perfect. "Aren't you, pudding?" she cooed, wiping a tiny dribble of milk from her silky cheek.

Through half-closed lids, she watched the afternoon sun glimmer behind the hemlock branches between her and her beautiful house, a hundred yards away in the mellow distance. She lived in a stone house in Rock

559

Creek Park. It had four chimneys, a slate roof, a porch that looked right out over the creek, and best of all, a new addition on the southwest corner that she couldn't even see from here because it was hidden by a curtain of laurel, willow, and holly trees.

The addition was a bedroom, a late wedding gift from Ty to Carrie. They'd occupied it for only a month because it had taken the workmen all summer to build it. Carrie hadn't been allowed to go near it during June, July, and August, and toward the end the workmen had even put up a big yellow tarpaulin on the north side so she couldn't see it from the summerhouse. Now it was her favorite room in a house full of beautiful rooms, and not just because it was Ty's present to her or because he'd designed it himself. It was her favorite room because it was magic.

She lifted her head to see Louie loping up the leafy path and over the step into the summerhouse, tongue lolling and tail spinning, thrilled to see her. "Who let you out?" she wondered, putting a hand down to rub his nose. Rachel eyed him with interest but kept nursing. Louie was a sober, responsible one-year-old dog now; he'd all but stopped chasing birds, although chipmunks and squirrels still defeated him. Fortunately, he never caught anything. He was a good dog, and Carrie never doubted he was going to get even better. Ty said there must be retriever in him, and probably spaniel too because of the way he liked to lie with his chin on your foot, trapping you in your chair, out of charity, for an average of ten minutes a day longer than you'd otherwise sit in it. Ty said —

"I knew I'd find you two out here."

Carrie started grinning before she looked up and saw him. "You're early!" she called softly, so she wouldn't disturb Rachel. He came up the step with that long, athletic stride of his that made it hard to remember a time when he'd ever limped or looked gaunt or been sickly. He had on his brown tweed suit with a light blue shirt, and he'd loosened his tie and taken off his stiff white collar. Even when he had his reading glasses on, he didn't look much like Carrie's idea of an assistant professor of bacteriology and clinical microscopy. He was just too handsome and dashing and . . . well, beautiful. She didn't know any other word for it. She only knew one person who was more beautiful than he was, and that was his daughter.

"How are my two ladies today?" he asked, settling himself on the bench beside them. He gave Rachel's forehead a soft kiss, which pleased but didn't distract her from her purpose, and then he kissed Carrie on the mouth. Sometimes their welcome-home kisses were short, busy little pecks, and sometimes they weren't. This one wasn't. The sensation of Rachel's lips pulling on Carrie's breast became pleasurable in a slightly different way. Still kissing her, Ty slipped his hand inside her clothes and fondled her other breast until the nipple stiffened. She closed her eyes and sighed against his mouth, thinking this much contentment inside one woman must surely be a terrible, terrible sin.

"You're home early," she finally got up enough energy to say.

"Mmm."

She remembered he'd had to give a speech today to the Medical Society of the District of Columbia. "How did your talk go?"

He put his arm on the bench behind her, resting his hand on her far shoulder. "Very well. Nobody threw any fruit at me."

"Were you brilliant?"

"Naturally. They wanted to argue, they were *itching* to show me up, but they couldn't get past that one little hurdle."

"What hurdle?"

"That since the army began fumigating for mosquitoes in Havana in the spring, the city's been free of yellow fever for the first time in a hundred and fifty years. *That* little hurdle. Dr.

James Addison finally stood up and said the Reed commission's findings were more important than anything since the discovery of anesthesia."

She put her hand on his hard thigh and squeezed. The satisfaction and rightful pride in his voice filled her with pride, too. He never took credit, always claimed he hadn't done anything but follow orders and try to be a careful scientific observer. But Carrie knew better, and nothing would ever shake her certain knowledge that her husband was a genius.

"Mail came," he mentioned. He drew some letters out of his breast pocket, thumbed through them, and put one back.

"What's that?" she asked, curious about the one he'd stuck back in his pocket.

"That's for later," he said mysteriously. "Look, here's one from Stoneman."

"Oh, what does it say?" She wrote to Dr. Stoneman about twice a month, but letters in return were much rarer.

Ty opened the envelope and scanned the letter inside. He chuckled.

"What?"

"Oh, it's just the usual curmudgeonly carping. Poor Dr. Perry is 'an egomaniac with a roomful of shiny, utterly useless equipment that would put Dr. Frankenstein to shame.' I guess that means he doesn't use leeches."

Carrie giggled.

"Uh oh."

"What?"

"He's writing a book."

"A book!"

"*Forty Years of Country Doctoring*, he's calling it. 'Tell Carrie to enjoy her moment of glory while she can because it's almost over. Wayne's Crossing is about to boast *two* famous native authors.' He's got 'two' underlined about four times."

" 'Famous,' " she snorted, giving Rachel a kiss to keep her awake and sucking. Carrie's bird book had been wonderfully well received by the handful of people who'd bought it, but it had definitely not set the world on fire.

"Well, well," said Ty, reading again. "Guess who's getting married."

"Who?"

"Eugene Starkey."

She looked up at that.

"To Teenie Yingling. Stoneman says they deserve each other."

"Teenie's nice," Carrie protested automatically. Ty never had a kind word to say about Eugene, and she'd finally stopped trying to defend him. He'd loved her as much as he could, and she truly believed he'd have tried his best to make a good life for her and the baby. What he'd done at their wedding had shamed him very badly, she knew. He didn't deserve to be miserable forever, no matter what Ty said, and if he was marrying Teenie, it must mean he was feeling better about things. How could she be anything but glad?

"You're happy for him, aren't you? Admit it."

His accusing look made her smile. "I can't help it," she shrugged.

He shook his head and made a pretend-exasperated noise, then went back to the letter. "Stoneman went to see Broom at Brockhurst on Sunday."

"How was he?"

" 'I could almost envy the little bugger,' " he read. " 'He talks about missing Carrie, but except for that he seems genuinely, obliviously happy. He looks good; he's put on weight from the starchy institution diet, and the nurses are fond of him and keep him clean and combed. Personally, I think he could live out his life there in perfect contentment.' "

"I wonder if he will," Carrie mused, a little sadly. "Live out his life there, I mean." She watched Ty fold Dr. Stoneman's letter and put it away. "I told Broom I'd bring Rachel the next time I came to see him. I think she's old enough now, don't you, Ty? I'll go soon. Maybe tomorrow." He leaned over and gave her a soft kiss on the temple. She smiled and asked, "What's the other letter?"

"It's from my mother." He opened it while Carrie shifted Rachel to her shoulder and gently patted her between her shoulder blades. Ty passed her his handkerchief absently while he read. "Good Lord, she's coming again."

"Is she really? So soon?"

"Do you mind, Carrie? She can't seem to stay away. I'll ask her to put it off, if you like."

"Oh no, I don't mind at all, not at all." It was the truth. "I know it's Rachel she's in love with," she added slowly, "but do you know, Ty, I think she's starting to like me, too?"

"Well, finally. Isn't that what I've been telling you for about eight months? You know, for a bright girl, my love, you're kind of slow."

"Well, but you must admit, it's a bit of a miracle."

"Nothing of the sort," he scoffed. "My mother's not stupid. Why wouldn't she love you? You're supremely, egregiously lovable."

She never got anywhere with him when they had this discussion, partly because it was more fun to let him win. But she knew a miracle when she saw one, and Mrs. Wilkes's acceptance of her, once she'd gotten over the shock, was and always would be one of the main wonders of Carrie's existence.

"Abbey's coming with her," Ty mentioned, his nose in the letter again.

"Oh, good." Abbey was the first woman friend her own age she'd ever had, and the quick closeness they'd formed, founded on their mutual love of Ty, qualified as one more miracle in Carrie's opinion. "Maybe she'd like to go with me to that Rock Creek Garden Club meeting."

"What's this? You're not afraid to go by yourself, are you?" He raised his eyebrows at her humorously. Seeing her expression, he leaned in for a closer look. "Are you?" he guessed, turning serious. "But you already know a thousand times more than any of those ladies do, Carrie, about everything."

"Not everything. Just some things."

"Just the things their club is supposed to be about," he pointed out.

"But that's *not* what their club is about, Ty. It's about being ladylike and sociable, knowing how to dress and what to say. And being smart."

He gathered her up, Rachel between them, and heaved a great sigh. He was going to give her one of his bracing speeches, she could feel it coming. She liked his arms around her so she didn't pull away, but she forestalled the speech by saying, "I've already decided to go to the meeting, whether Abbey comes with me or not. I'm going to wear something mod-est and becoming — maybe that plum-colored suit with the Eton jacket if it's not too warm a day" — she digressed thoughtfully — "and I'll behave like a quiet young matron."

"A quiet young matron, eh?"

She could tell from the movement of his cheek against hers that he was smiling. "Yes. Quiet so they won't know how ignorant I am."

"Carrie —"

"At first. I'll go a few times, and I'll pay at-tention and study everything and figure out what's what. After a while people will quit paying me any mind, they'll get so used to seeing me, and then I'll make my move." She settled the baby on her lap and smiled down at her, although Rachel was getting so sleepy she could barely focus her eyes.

"Your move?"

"I'll talk to somebody."

"Aha."

"I'll have her all picked out beforehand. She'll be the nicest one there, the most ap-proachable."

"Good idea." He stopped stroking Rachel's cheek to pull Carrie's hair back behind her ear and kiss her.

"I'll just say something casual at first, to see how she takes it. If she wants to be friends, I'll know right away. Maybe she'll have children, and we can talk about babies and things. And maybe she'll have a friend, and I'll like her, too — or there might be two women in the garden club I can start talking to. Pretty soon . . ." She forgot the rest because Ty's open mouth on her throat was so hot, and he'd put his hand inside her dress again to caress her milky breasts.

"Pretty soon the house will be crawling with your sociable lady friends, and you'll have no time for me. Let's go inside and take a little nap before dinner, Carrie."

"All right," she agreed breathlessly. She loved their little naps before dinner — or lunch, or anything else they could think of to say to Mrs. Jordan, the housekeeper, to excuse their frequent withdrawals to the bedroom. "Kiss me first, though." He did, until her legs started to quiver from the delicious tension and she was afraid her shaky knees would wake up Rachel.

"I'll take her." Gentle-handed, Ty picked up the baby and rocked her while Carrie got her dress rebuttoned. Holding hands, they started walking toward the house — slowly, to prolong the anticipation; and also to throw Mrs. Jordan, if she happened to be watching, off the scent.

Rachel's nursery was across the hall from

their bedroom. Ty tucked her into her crib and then they stood over it to look at her for a while, marveling, whispering to each other about how pretty she was, how lucky they were. At length they gave her last kisses and tiptoed into their own room.

It was a magic room, and the most magic time of the day for it was now, when the setting sun twinkled and glimmered behind the trees that were clearly visible through the glass wall and the skylight in the ceiling. A glass wall! Carrie had had a month to get used to it, but every time she came into her new room, she had to stop, stare, and shake her head in disbelief. They could cover the glass wall just by drawing the heavy drapes, and maybe they would if it got too bright for sleeping once the trees were bare and the sun dropped lower in the winter sky. But for the rest of the year they would keep it open, they'd decided, even at night with the lights on, for the ground sloped away so steeply on the southwest corner that nobody could see in unless they stood on a ladder.

Was there ever such a room? "I didn't want you to be homesick," Ty had said on the day he'd finally unveiled the surprise. "I thought it might remind you of your mountain, Carrie." And when they lay in bed together, looking up through their skylight at sunshine or moonshine or misty rain falling on the waving branches of spruce and oak and maple trees, she did think of her mountain. But never, not once since he'd taken her away from High Dreamer and made her his wife, had Carrie been homesick. She had a new home and it was here. With Ty.

She hurried out of her clothes, leaving on only chemise and pantaloons and the ribbon in her hair — Ty liked her to keep something on for him to take off — and got under the quilt on top of their big bed. Their "sinfully" big bed, she'd called it on first sight; it took up half the room and could've slept about four grown-up people side by side. She'd gotten used to it pretty quickly, though, and she couldn't deny that at one time or another she and Ty had used every inch of it.

"Mmm, I really could go to sleep," she purred, burrowing deeper into the fresh muslin sheets, stretching her arms and legs into the four corners of the bed. She opened one eye to see how Ty had taken that. He was down to his pants, and the hot, I-dare-you look he sent her while he slowly unbuttoned them wiped away her teasing grin and every thought of sleeping.

Watching her in the wardrobe mirror, Tyler thought his wife looked like some dream an adolescent boy had conjured up in a sexual fantasy. He shucked off his trousers and threw them over the back of a chair, already randy as a jackrabbit — as Carrie would say. But he remembered the envelope in his jacket pocket at the last second, got it, and crossed to the bed, smiling to himself.

He sat on the edge of the mattress and pulled the quilt back so he could look at Carrie. She still blushed; he guessed she always would. But she wasn't shy in bed anymore. To prove it, she began to ruffle the hair on his bare thigh, gazing up at him with winsome self-confidence. "You look like a sleek, happy cat," he told her, untying the wide navy ribbon at the back of her neck and drawing it away so her hair could fall down over her shoulders.

She trailed her fingernails over his kneecap, ran them down his calf as far as she could reach, then back up to his thigh. "I am a happy cat," she said in her smoky voice, deliberately seducing him. Ever observant, she spied the envelope beside him. "You're not going to read me another letter *now*, are you?"

"This? No, it's to you, I thought you could read it yourself."

"It's to me?" She sat up against the pillows, intrigued in spite of herself. She could never resist a surprise. "Who's it from? Eppy?"

"No, not Eppy."

She read the return address and laughed. "Oh, this is a mistake. This is from the White House." She tried to hand it back.

"It's to you, isn't it?"

She looked down, then up again. "It says my name," she agreed, blank-faced.

"Well, then." He raised bland brows.

She opened it slowly, afraid to tear the envelope, and carefully unfolded the typed, one-page letter inside. Tyler went around to his side of the bed and got in while she read. Her body had gone taut as a bowstring. Every few seconds she said, "Oh, Ty. Oh, Ty." She finished the letter and gawked at him.

"What does it say?"

She didn't hear the question; she went back to the letter and read it all over again.

He leaned over and skimmed it with her this time. "Dear Mrs. Wilkes," the brand-new president began. "Your husband was kind enough to give me a copy of your book, *The Summer Birds of the Appalachians in Franklin County, Pa.*, and I wanted to let you know how much I enjoyed it. It's one of the best of the recent lists I've seen, and I must congratulate you on avoiding the sort of language in your text that drives the nonscientist away from most ornithologies faster than an angry hornet. You will scarcely credit it, but I recently opened a pamphlet by one of the more exalted bird blokes and found this sentence: 'The terrestrial progression of the Columbidae is gradient but never saltatorial.' By which, after careful study, I took it to mean that pigeons walk and don't hop!"

The same shameless charmer, Tyler smiled to himself. McKinley's assassination had been a terrible, shocking tragedy; politically speaking, though, it had only speeded up the inevitable, and in Ty's opinion Teddy Roosevelt was merely occupying the White House a little earlier than he would have anyway.

"Tyler tells me that you and I share an interest in land and wildlife conservation," the president went on. "It's shocking that in this great country we only have five national parks, and I assure you that part of my agenda for the balance of my term will be the expansion of," etc., etc. Tyler skipped ahead.

"Community participation at every level is what we need now to bring to the average citizen's attention the crying need for respect and conservation of our scarce resources. In that spirit, it occurred to me that you might be interested in either or both of two local projects I've been considering. One would be to write and illustrate a definitive catalogue, much on the order of the list you compiled for your fine book, of the birds of Rock Creek Park; the other would be to join a citizens' committee charged with lobbying members of the Congress to introduce a national Arbor Day."

Carrie couldn't stop shaking her head or saying, "Oh, Ty." He chuckled and ducked lower in the bed, sliding his lips down the cool skin of her arm to her elbow. "You talked to him about me," she breathed, facing him. "Imagine that. My husband and the president of the United States, having a conversation about *me*." She couldn't get over it.

He pulled her down so their heads were level. One-handed, he started to open the eyelet fasteners down the front of her chemise. "Which will you do," he wondered, "the birds or the —"

"Both," she answered immediately. "I can do it, I'm sure I can. Rachel can come with me when I'm in the park, and it'll be all right to leave her with the nanny when I meet with my" — she retrieved the letter from the rumpled quilt and glanced at it again — "my *committee*." He grunted, untying the ribbons at her waist and nudging her drawers over her hips. Her gray eyes searched his seriously. "Do you think I can be a good mother and still help President Roosevelt?"

"I'm sure of it," he said, sitting up to push the sleeves of her shift over her shoulders. As soon as her arms were free, she flung them around his neck and bore him back to the pillow, with her on top.

"Oh, Ty," she exclaimed, nose to nose. "Before I had everything, but now I have even *more*. How can it be?"

Impatient, he started to kiss her; that would end the conversation. But Carrie's ingenuous bafflement struck a complementary emotion he couldn't ignore. He moved his hands to her face and held it softly between his palms. "I don't know. I think about it all the time, and I can't explain it either. It's extravagant, it's — implausible. Exorbitant."

She frowned. "What is?"

"How happy you make me."

"Oh. That." She slid a long, smooth leg over his hips and straddled him. While he watched, the wonder on her face turned to smug delight. "That's just because you love me," she said huskily, gloating. She took his hands from her face and moved them slowly down her neck and finally to her full breasts. "I'm talking about the other. All these *new* miracles."

Her lacy pantaloons were at half mast. "Lie down flat," he suggested; she did, and he pushed her drawers down past her knees. "What new miracles?" he wanted to know, stroking her belly and her wide-open thighs until she threw her head back. He lifted her hips and held her poised above him on her knees. "What new miracles?"

"President Roosevelt's committee," she gasped. "Your mother — liking me. All that," she finished vaguely and impatiently. "Ty, come inside me right now, right now!"

"No, I want to hear more about the miracles. My mother, and — Ho!"

Carrie took matters into her own hands.

"There," she said on a quivering sigh, settling herself. She brought her head down and kissed him, at the same time she gave a clever little swivel with her hips that had him groaning against her open mouth. "This isn't a new one," she murmured, "but it's still a miracle. To me, anyway."

"Me, too," he assured her fervently.

"What I don't understand is what I ever did to deserve everything that's happened."

"I think you should stop talking now."

"I wasn't happy before I met you, but then again, I wasn't *miserable*. But now, Ty, *now* —"

"Now?" he asked hopefully, gathered her up, and rolled over on top of her.

Her breath whooshed out in a gusty, euphoric laugh. "That's not what I meant." She dodged his lips and tried one last time to explain it. "I thought it was already perfect, don't you see? It's *indecent*, how lovely my life is. And now —"

"Now," he cut her off firmly, snaring her hands and anchoring them to either side of the pillow. "Now it's about to get even better."

Much later, the moon crept up and hung for a while in a corner of the skylight, silvering the magic room before it dropped behind maple and oak leaves, and sank out of sight. Wisps of cloud drifted by, and once in a while a handful of raindrops struck the glass; they dried fast in the warm wind, but while they lingered the stars behind them looked like violet crystals.

"Are you sleeping?" Ty whispered. He had Carrie's foot between both of his, and she hadn't moved it in a long time.

But she whispered back, "No."

"It's late."

"I know." She took a full, deep breath of the damp air breezing in through the window. No crickets or night birds sang; there was just the sigh of the wind and occasionally the patter of the rain on the glass. And the soft, baby-quick breathing of Rachel, who lay fast asleep between them, because Carrie had been too lazy to get up and put her in the crib after her last feeding.

"Go to sleep," Ty murmured. He slid his fingers into Carrie's hair and began a soft, slow massage.

But she had one more thing to say. "I've figured it out. It's part of a grand scheme."

A pause, while he tried to connect that to anything they'd said or done recently. "A grand scheme?" he hazarded on a yawn, giving up.

"You did a good deed when you saved thousands of lives, Ty. God's decided to let me share in your reward. That's why I'm so happy. That's the explanation."

"Ah."

"I don't know why He did it, but He works in mysterious ways."

"He certainly does." He yawned again. "I'm too sleepy to argue, but you've got it backward. It's you He's rewarding if it's either of us." It was a burden sometimes, this pedestal she'd put him on. He'd set her straight, but she was bound to find out the mundane truth about him eventually. Why rush the inevitable?

She snuggled closer, capturing one of his hairy legs between her calves. "This is nice," she whispered with her eyes closed, "arguing about which one of us God is blessing." She was glad Ty thought it was her, but he'd find out the truth sooner or later, she expected.

The stars wheeled; the moon set. Carrie and Ty fell asleep in sympathy, savoring their mutual esteem and happiness. Between them the fruit of their love, the real blessing, slept on, oblivious.